Everyone is talking about Kari Lynn Dell

"When it comes to sexy rodeo cowboys, look no further than talented author Kari Lynn Dell."

—**B. J. Daniels**, *New York Times* bestselling author

"An extraordinarily gifted writer."

—**Karen Templeton**, three-time RITA Award-winning author for *Reckless in Texas*

"Real ranchers. Real rodeo. Real romance."

—**Laura Drake**, RITA Award-winning author for *Reckless in Texas*

"Look out, world! There's a new cowboy in town."

—**Carolyn Brown**, *New York Times* bestselling author for *Tangled in Texas*

"Great characters, great story, and authentic right down to the bone."

—**Joanne Kennedy** for *Reckless in Texas*

"Dell's writing is notable, and her rodeo setting is fascinating, with characters that leap off the page and an intriguing series of actions, conflicts, and backstory elements that keep the plot moving… A sexy, engaging romance set in the captivating world of rodeo."

—*Kirkus Reviews* for *Reckless in Texas*

"A standout in western romance."

—*Publishers Weekly* for *Reckless in Texas*

"Dell's ability to immerse her readers in the world of rodeo, coupled with her stellar writing, makes this a contemporary western not to miss."

—*Kirkus Reviews* for *Tangled in Texas*

"A wonderful HEA ending that is hard-earned and never predictable. This book has impressed me."

—*USA Today Happy Ever After* for *Tangled in Texas*

"Complex and genuine, this one grabbed me until I finished the final page."

—Omnivoracious for *Tangled in Texas*

"Rings with authenticity and vibrant color."

—*BookPage* for *Tougher in Texas*

"Dell's latest is not to be missed."

—*Publishers Weekly* Starred Review for *Fearless in Texas*

Also by Kari Lynn Dell

Texas Rodeo

Reckless in Texas

Tangled in Texas

Tougher in Texas

Fearless in Texas

Mistletoe in Texas

Relentless in Texas

Last Chance Rodeo

RELENTLESS *in* TEXAS

KARI LYNN DELL

Published by Sourcebooks Casablanca, an imprint of Sourcebooks
P.O. Box 4410, Naperville, Illinois 60567-4410
(630) 961-3900
sourcebooks.com

Printed and bound in the United States of America.
OPM 10 9 8 7 6 5 4 3 2 1

To everyone who has waited so long for me to finish this book, from the management of Sourcebooks to my editor, from my agent to my wonderful readers, and from my parents and son to my husband: thanks for sticking with me. Especially my husband. I really like being married to you.

Chapter 1

Early November, northern Montana

The first time Gil Sanchez drove west into Glacier County and came upon the Rockies, he had the distinct impression that the earth was baring her teeth at him. Over a year and a dozen visits later, standing at their feet still made him twitchy. As a native Texan he'd seen nature turn homicidal often enough—tornadoes, wildfires, blizzards—but in the Panhandle the land itself wasn't designed to rip a man to pieces and feed the scraps to the nearest grizzly bear.

He scowled up at the impassive peaks and cliffs, but the mountains didn't give a single damn about how he felt. Their attitude, at least, he could appreciate.

If all went as planned, this would be the last time they loomed over him. The lost boy he'd come here to help had found his way through the worst of his so-called dark night of the soul. Most of Hank's recovery was thanks to the woman called Bing, who'd hauled Hank out of a Yakima, Washington, hospital and brought him here to heal, body and soul. Now Bing had decided it was time for him to go home—and Gil was here to make sure it happened.

Gil wriggled on the sleeper bunk of his eighteen-wheeler, too restless for the confined space. Back home he would've hit the weight room to work off the jittery tension. Here he couldn't even go for a nighttime jog without the risk of being wolf bait. And he would not have parked across the road from the Stockman's Bar if he'd had any idea it would be this lively on a night long after nearly everything else around Glacier National Park had buttoned up for the winter.

Across the road, the rumble of vehicles pulling into the parking lot and the swelling cacophony of voices and laughter drew his attention away from the mobile app that allowed him to monitor the progress of other Sanchez trucks across the nation. The noise stirred up his already-too-alert senses and made him...want. Finally, he set the phone aside with a hiss of impatience.

Of course he wanted to join the party. It was his default setting, especially if there was alcohol involved. But he no longer craved the company of any random human who'd drink with him. For the most part he didn't crave the company of humans at all, with a few notable exceptions. And he'd learned there was no loneliness worse than being unknown in a crowd.

So why was he so compelled to cross this road, join this crowd? Distraction? That was safe enough in the form of people-watching and random conversation with a few of the locals. Escape? That was dicier if it meant putting himself in a place where over a dozen years of sobriety could end with a wave at the bartender.

No. It wasn't the company. And his fingers weren't itching to curl around a cold beer bottle. Tonight the music tugged at him...the unmistakable sound of a live band. But it wouldn't be the first time his addiction had tried to pull a bait and switch, so he stewed for a full hour before cursing roundly and yanking on his boots.

A neon-pink poster on the door declared that the festivities were meant to raise money to help offset medical expenses for a woman who'd undergone heart valve replacement, requiring an extended stay in Seattle. The silent auction promised work by local artists, so if nothing else, Gil might be able to pick up a couple of interesting Christmas presents.

Still, he hesitated, until the door opened and a couple stepped out, shooting him a curious glance as they angled past.

The familiar wall of noise hit him—the soundtrack of every western bar in the country. These voices had the distinctive, blunt accent of the Northern Plains tribes, and most of the faces were at least as dark as his own. To an outsider he could pass as one of them but this wasn't his clan. Then again, as his maternal grandfather had regularly pointed out, he wasn't much of a Navajo either.

But he was known. Recognition sparked in many of the eyes that swiveled in his direction. A person didn't come and go in an eighteen wheeler with *Sanchez Trucking* painted on the doors without being noticed, especially if their brother was a two-time world-champion bareback rider. If Gil had still been a drinking man, he could've milked Delon's fame for a few free rounds...or more, judging by some of the appraising glances the women shot him.

Definitely not going there.

He made his way to the bar, ordered a Coke, and dropped a fifty-dollar bill into a donation can before sidling over to lean against one of the peeled pine columns at the edge of the dance floor. Curious gazes followed him, but no one worked up the nerve to speak to him...yet. Gil avoided eye contact and dialed up what his brother called his resting prick face, hoping to keep it that way.

Nope. Not here for the company. Just the noise, the music, and something to drag him outside of his own head.

The song ended, followed by a drumroll and a crash of cymbals. The lead singer leaned into the mic. "And now a rare treat! Tonight only, here is the lovely Carmelita!"

The crowd cheered as a woman—somewhere around thirty, Gil estimated—stepped onto the floor wearing a short fringed-and-beaded buckskin jacket and matching midcalf moccasins over a body-hugging black dress and black leggings. Her ebony hair was pulled into a thick, straight tail that reached the middle of her back, her face nearly round, but her brows and mouth sketched in bold lines. Murmurs rustled through the crowd, and Gil caught the distinct aroma of ripe gossip.

Her chin came up and she flashed a smile, wide and bright, that was the equivalent of a stiff middle finger. Well, now. This was getting interesting. Gil took a sip of his Coke and settled more comfortably against the column, prepared to enjoy the show.

She dropped two ropes near her feet and built a small loop in the shortest. A trick roper. Nice. There weren't as many as there used to be, although the art seemed to be making a comeback. The band struck up a decent version of "Boot Scootin' Boogie" and with a flick of her wrist, she set the small loop dancing around her in a series of pirouettes and launched into a fairly standard routine. Well executed, but nothing Gil hadn't seen before.

On the opposite side of Gil's leaning post, a man drawled, "First time I've seen her out and about since Jayden dumped her. S'pose she's ready to give someone else a shot?"

"Like you?" A second man snorted his skepticism.

"She might be a little less particular after supportin' his ass all those years, then gettin' swapped for a hot little blond soon as he made the Finals."

"Don't mean she'll look twice at anybody else around here."

The first man grunted, half in annoyance, half in agreement.

Jayden. The name would've been familiar if the guy had qualified for the upcoming National Finals Rodeo in any of the roughstock events, but Gil didn't pay much attention to the ropers. Like a whole lot of cowboys who got a taste of success, though, this Jayden must've decided he could do better than the girl back home.

Watching Carmelita perform with that diamond-bright smile firmly in place, Gil felt a twinge of sympathy…until her gaze snapped to his, dark and fierce. *Don't you dare feel sorry for me.*

What the hell? Gil glanced over his shoulder to see if she might be glaring at someone else. No. It was definitely him. He could swear his expression hadn't changed, but she had singled him out as if she knew what he was thinking.

What the hell?

She abruptly spun around and tossed the short rope in the corner, plucking the longest one from where she'd left it on the floor. The band segued into "Ring of Fire"—and Carmelita began to dance.

Just a sway of the hips at first. Then shoulders. Subtle shifts of her body that in any other woman would have been a harmless sway to the music. No one but Gil seemed to interpret it as more than a graceful dance, fit for a family audience.

He saw an intense awareness of her own body, a pleasure in the way it moved that went beyond just dancing. She raised her arms to start the big loop spinning around her, and when her jacket hiked up, Gil's eyes were drawn to the curve of her hip and thigh. Hunger punched through him—instant, hot, and inexplicable. Geezus, what was wrong with him? Yes, she was attractive, and yes, he'd come looking for a distraction, but this was *not* what he'd had in mind.

Her gaze met his again. Her eyes widened...and once again there was no doubt she knew exactly what he was thinking.

The woman hadn't made a single overtly sexual move, and still Gil could barely blink, let alone tear his eyes off her. There was something elemental about the way she inhabited her body that filled his head with visions of dust devils chased ahead of a freshening rainstorm, cloud shadows undulating across the prairie, the snap and crack of a campfire sending a flurry of embers spiraling into a velvet sky.

Most performers projected their energy onto the audience. Carmelita was magnetic, pulling the static out of Gil's mind. His entire consciousness was consumed by the sight of her. And then, with the final *ba-ba-bum* of the song, she whipped around and stopped, feet spread, head and arms flung back, eyes locked on him.

He should have looked away. Backed down. Walked out.

Instead he smiled—a taut, challenging curl of his mouth. *How far are you willing to go, sweetheart?* She held his gaze while the applause compounded the roar of blood in his ears, nearly drowning out the little voice asking if he'd lost his fucking mind. She faced him, eyes narrowing, as if she was debating how to react. Slap him with a cold stare? Ignore him? He saw her come to a decision an instant before she tossed an equally carnal smile right back at him.

Then she pivoted and walked to the corner, where she shrugged out of her jacket and unclipped her silver barrette so her hair fell loose.

She said something to the lead singer that made him laugh, then say into the microphone, "And now we're in for the real treat."

All around Gil, heads turned and whispers hissed. Now every eye angled his direction, gleaming with speculation. The music started and for the first throbbing notes of "Tennessee Whiskey," Carmelita stood utterly still, every generous curve of her body outlined by the tight dress and leggings. Then she lifted her arms and the loop became her lover, dancing away, then back, turning and twisting, floating into the air and dropping over her head to embrace her. Her expression went dreamy as she arched her back and the loop rolled over the long bow of her body from shoulder to breast, belly, and thighs.

Gil was insanely jealous of that rope.

The light seemed to dim and the already close confines of the dance floor to draw in around her—around him—a private bubble that was theirs alone. She pulled him into the music with her, where every thrum of the guitar and thud of drums vibrated through both of them, their bodies tuned to the same intimate beat.

And with each turn, her gaze skimmed over him, and his body reacted as if she'd dragged a fingernail across his bare chest, skin pebbling and lungs tightening. His breathing went shallow, perilously close to panting. She pirouetted around the edge of the floor, so close that her rope brushed his thighs, sending twin bolts of lightning to his core.

Before he could clear the haze from his vision, the song moaned to a climax and she once again spun to a stop in front of him, her loop floating up and over his head, settling light as fallen leaves onto his shoulders.

Captured.

For the space of a dozen heartbeats they stood, two wildland creatures frozen in a single, blinding beam of desire. Then he caught the rope with his free hand and she let him draw her closer, until he could feel the heat rising off her glowing bronze skin, smell her sweet cherry-almond scent, and see the gold that shot through her brown eyes.

For a moment the bar went quiet. Then the audience broke into an uncertain smattering of applause.

Carmelita let her eyelashes drift down as she inhaled—drawing Gil in molecule by molecule. Her mouth curved, a deeply knowing smile that nudged his thermostat up another few degrees. She didn't say hello. She didn't ask his name.

She just gave the rope a tug and said, "Let's get out of here."

If following Carmelita was a bad idea, it was going to be one the more interesting mistakes Gil had made. He didn't just want her. He *craved* her…and that rarely boded well for him. But just this one time…

"Well, that was subtle," a tight voice said.

Carmelita's gaze broke from Gil's with a nearly palpable snap. The woman who'd spoken could have been her younger, thinner sister. Her painstakingly sketched eyebrows arched. "I hope you don't mind being used for payback," she told Gil.

Before he could express his opinion, Carmelita cut in, her voice flat and cold. "What are you doing here, Jolene?"

Jolene angled her chin in defiance. "Bryson is feeling fine now."

"He was running a hundred-and-three fever a few hours ago. How much better can he be?"

"Good enough to stay with Grandma and Gramps while I get out for a change."

Gil could all but hear the curse Carmelita ground between her teeth. "It's been two weeks since Grandma got out of the hospital, and you're exposing her to this crud? What the hell were you thinking?"

"I assumed you'd do your thing, then sashay out of here with your nose in the air, so he'd only be alone with them for an hour or so." Jolene slid an insolent smile toward Gil. "I didn't realize you had a special show planned for tonight."

Carmelita didn't flinch. "Well, now you do, so you can go fetch him."

"I barely got here." Jolene waggled her cell phone. "They can call if they need me."

For an instant, Gil was afraid Carmelita might try to throttle her, and he'd have to do something. Nothing good ever came of a man stepping between two furious women. Then Jolene spun on her heel and flounced into the crowd. Carmelita swore under her breath and stalked away in the opposite direction. The band decided the show was over and swung into a new song, drowning out the buzz that accompanied the sly looks aimed at where Gil stood holding her rope.

A smart man would turn around and run.

Gil went after Carmelita, weaving through the couples filtering onto the dance floor. She paused beside the bandstand to kick off her moccasins, stomp into insulated boots, and shove her arms into a hooded Pendleton blanket coat. He handed her the rope, and she stuffed it into a bag with the discarded pieces of her costume while he zipped his own insulated jacket. November was more like winter than fall up here in the north country.

When the back door of the bar thumped shut behind them, Carmelita stopped and dragged in a long, deep breath. Her words came out in puffs of vapor. "God, that was suffocating."

The closeness of the overcrowded bar? The argument with Jolene? The attention? "Why did you come?"

"My grandmother volunteered my services. Fund-raisers are the worst, though. Everyone is so…" Her hands fluttered in a broad circle, encompassing the tearful outpourings of gratitude that marked benefits.

"You're used to being in the spotlight."

"I prefer an audience to a crowd," she said flatly.

And the difference was in the separation. She could walk off a stage without interacting with the masses. But she didn't seem to mind connecting with him, and despite what the charming Jolene had implied, the attraction between them was undeniably real. He could feel it even now, in the frigid air, with their bodies separated by layers of canvas and wool.

She tipped her head back to gaze into the heavens and her body language slowly shifted, as if she was drawing in the stillness. When she started off through the parking lot, she once again moved with fluid grace. Gil matched her stride, closing the space between them so his coat sleeve swished against hers.

"Bing told me about you, and introduced me to your… friend," she said.

With that slight hesitation, she summed up Gil's uncertainty about his relationship with Hank, past and future. "I'm his sponsor," he corrected stiffly.

"Mmm." A sound that translated to *if that's what you want to tell yourself.* "We lack many things up here on the rez, but we do not have a shortage of recovering addicts."

Unfortunately true, but none of them would be in Texas when Hank was sucker punched by what Gil knew was waiting for him…and hadn't been able to tell him. "I watched Hank grow up. I understand him."

She angled a searching glance beneath lowered lashes. "I see."

Yes, she did. There was something in the way she looked at him—*through* him—that made him want to both hide and move closer. He did neither. The breeze caught her hair, sending a strand fluttering and carrying the scent of pine needles and snow down from the mountains. Their shoulders bumped as they squeezed between parked cars, toward the gleaming red hulk of his truck, the white box trailer a bright billboard in the far reaches of the bar's security lights.

He swung around to face her as they stopped beside the door to his cab, and when he looked into her eyes, he felt as if he was losing his balance, falling into one of the bottomless mountain lakes—only much warmer. He could just keep sinking and sinking…

She caught him, pressing her hands flat against his chest, but her smile was tinged with regret. "I wish I could stay. You and I would be very good together, I think."

The image of Carmelita naked and lush under his hands sent heat shuddering through him. Then he registered what she was saying.

"You're leaving?" Gil frowned at her in disbelief.

The hitch of her shoulder set the moonlight shimmering through her hair. "I can't leave my grandparents with a sick baby."

"His mother didn't seem overly concerned." Gil's voice was harsh, along with his judgment. Even when he'd been regularly popping Vicodin like breath mints, he'd managed to stay clean on the weekends he'd had his son.

Her gaze slid away from his. "She knows I'll take care of them all."

"Instead of yourself?" And Gil, dammit.

Carmelita smoothed her palms over the front of his jacket. "Next time?"

"I won't be back."

She angled her head to give him another searching look, then nodded. "You're taking Hank home. That explains it."

"What?"

"This." Her hand moved down, pressing with unerring accuracy over the clutch in his gut. She reached up with the other to brush cool fingers over the knot of tension in his forehead. "And this."

He wanted to lean into that touch—into *her*—and let her wipe his mind clean for a few hours.

"I'm sorry I can't do more." She stroked a blissful circle on his temple. "But I can give you something for that headache."

"A fistful of ibuprofen?"

"A promise." Her eyes were steady, her tone certain. "Hank will be fine. He's stronger than you think, and whatever you're keeping from him, he'll understand it was for the best. So will the others."

Gil jerked his head back. "I never said anything to Bing about that."

Her hands fell away and she angled her gaze upward, eyes going distant. In the Panhandle the stars were painted on the sky. Here it seemed as if they were standing among them.

"I don't *know*," she said. "I just feel it. But I'm almost always right."

Without warning, she tipped onto her toes and pressed her mouth to his. Her lips were cool, but at the touch of her tongue the glowing embers they'd been gathering between them burst into flame, whooshing through him like a prairie fire. His thoughts, the last of his reservations, the ability to think at all were consumed by a wall of heat. He gripped the lapels of her coat to drag her hard against him, and she fisted her hands in the sides of his jacket, pressing even closer. Her tongue slid over his, the friction setting off more sparks.

Too many clothes, coats, infinite layers separating them. He growled in sheer frustration, pushing his hands inside the collar of her coat to find the only accessible skin, curling his fingers around the nape of her neck and feeling her pulse hammer against his thumb. Her hair flowed cool over the backs of his hands, an almost painful contrast to the fire raging between them.

Her fingers skimmed through his hair, nails digging into his scalp and creating another layer of exquisite pain that intensified the sharp, nearly unbearable stab of need. He took a step, pulling her with him as he fumbled for the door of the truck.

A palpable shudder ran through her. She braced her hands on his shoulders, slowly, inexorably separating her mouth from his.

"Well, that got out of control in a hurry." Her unsteady laugh was a puff of steam in the space she'd created.

His hands tightened in the thick folds of her coat, and it was all he could do not to drag her close again. The desperation leaked into his voice. "Don't go yet. Give me an hour, at least."

She blinked her gaze into focus and shook her head. "I don't like to rush good things, and it's gonna take a lot more than an hour to do this justice."

Geezus. Was she trying to kill him?

"I know. The timing sucks." She smiled, a copper-skinned Madonna with fathomless eyes, and pressed a palm over his thundering heart. "You should get some rest, Gil Sanchez. You've got a long drive tomorrow."

He stared at her in disbelief. How could she admit the power of their attraction in one breath, and shrug him off in the next? "That's all? We're just...done?"

"Maybe. Maybe not." Her gaze tracked across the sky before coming back to meet his. "We'll see what the stars have in mind."

"I don't believe in Fate."

Her laugh was a low, husky rasp that played across every hypersensitive nerve in his body. "Well then, you should've steered clear of a woman called Carma."

She touched his cheek one last time, then turned and walked away. Watching the taillights of her car disappear into the darkness, Gil jammed his empty hands into the pockets of his coat, threw his head back, and swore at the twinkling Milky Way. She was really gone. Just like that.

But she'd left what felt like a permanent impression.

Why was he even surprised? This was just about his luck. The fact was, he'd lied about not believing in Fate. He was on close personal terms with that stone-cold bitch, and recognized the distant, spiteful echo of her laughter.

Chapter 2

Earnest, Texas—Christmas Day

Six weeks later, the memory of that kiss still burned whenever Gil let it slip past his defenses—and today they were worn down by an overdose of holiday cheer, cinnamon-spiced candles, and public displays of affection.

Fucking Christmas. It was practically designed to string bright, blinking lights around every empty space in his life, especially when his son was three hours away in Oklahoma City. Even Gil wasn't selfish enough to drag the kid away from his sisters on the big day.

Tomorrow Gil would drive over to bring Quint back to Earnest for the rest of the holiday break. *Today* he was the only unattached adult in the room, unless he counted his dad snoozing in a worn recliner—and Gil did not. Single was Merle's happy place. If he hadn't been saddled with the care and feeding of two young boys, Gil wasn't sure he would've even noticed when their mother left.

A lot of years and twelve steps later, Gil had figured out that Merle's indifference was a big part of why she'd never come back. Might've been nice to know that when he was six. Or he might've just resented both parents.

Grown-up Gil understood why his mother had to leave. There had been no one else to care for her ailing parents, and no persuading her father to leave their remote hogan, and Rochelle Yazzie Sanchez hadn't been wrong when she'd insisted it was better for Gil and Delon to stay in Earnest, where they had friends, sports, a good school, and their father—when he wasn't on the road. And gaining Steve and Iris Jacobs as surrogate parents had been one helluva consolation prize. Some of the best hours of Gil's life had been spent in this big old frame house...even when he felt like the one mismatched sock.

He paused in the archway between kitchen and living room, too fidgety to sit. Once the table had been cleared, Miz Iris had shooed them away from the cleanup. Now she and Steve stood shoulder to shoulder, washing and drying pots and pans with the wordless efficiency of decades of marriage. Their oldest daughter, Lily, was a round ball of joy eight months into a long-awaited pregnancy, tipped back in a recliner while her husband hovered protectively.

Violet Jacobs Cassidy staggered down the stairs and collapsed onto a couch next to her own husband with a gusty sigh. "Rosie's down for the count."

"Thank God. A couple hours of peace on earth." Joe rubbed a hand over his well-fed but still-flat belly. "I believe I'll follow her example and sneak over to our house for a nap."

"I'm in," Violet said.

"Hah. Nap. So that's what they're calling it these days," Gil's sister-in-law, Tori, said, from where she was tucked under his little brother Delon's arm on the love seat.

Violet flapped a limp hand toward the den turned game room. "Shhh. Child present."

Twelve-year-old Beni—son of Violet and Delon from a time long before either had found their happy endings elsewhere—was sprawled on his stomach in the den, waging low-volume carnage in his new video game.

Behind him, the world's most unlikely couple had lapsed into a post-turkey coma on the massive sectional sofa. Cole Jacobs had one big hand buried in Shawnee's mop of curls, cradling her head against his chest. She looked almost...okay, *sweet* might be pushing it. But not her usual salty self.

Gil deliberately looked away from all that wedded bliss, only to be blinded by Hank's grin. The lovesick moron hadn't moved two feet from Grace's side all day. All the Brookmans were gathered around the kitchen table playing pitch, although in Gil's experience they might as well just hand over their chips to Hank's older sister, Melanie. Or her husband, Wyatt, who was a shark at a whole lot more than cards. Grace had been a sheltered child, lacking the killer instinct, and Hank sucked at strategy even when he wasn't goggle-eyed. Hank's dad wasn't much better, mooning just as obviously over Bing.

Geezus. Now there was a shock. Who would've guessed that she'd come rampaging down here from Montana to protect Hank from Johnny, and end up falling for the man instead?

Even Carma hadn't seen that coming.

Carma. Carmelita. Her name melted in Gil's thoughts like homemade fudge with bits of cool peppermint. Her prediction had been right on the nose. Hank was more than fine, and he *had* forgiven Gil...eventually. It was still driving Gil nuts, though, wondering how Carma had known. She couldn't actually see the future.

Could she?

Bing lifted an eyebrow, and Gil realized he was staring. He looked away, but there was no escape from the suffocating *coupleness* on all sides. His mouth twisted as he realized he was the nineteenth wheel. Seemed about right for a glorified truck driver…and this spare tire was ready to hit the road.

He turned abruptly and went to clap Steve on the shoulder, dropping a kiss on the top of Miz Iris's head. "Thanks. Dinner was awesome as always."

"Leaving already?" Steve asked.

Gil shrugged. "The trucks keep on rolling, even today."

"I suppose you're going to hole up in that office of yours." Miz Iris turned to study his eyes, concern creasing her forehead. *Alone. On a holiday. Is that a good idea?*

"I'm going to call Quint," he promised her. "He can tell me about his loot, and we'll decide what we want to do for New Year's."

"Tell Quint to call me soon as he gets here!" Beni called out as Gil zipped his jacket. Everyone else called their goodbyes as he left. No one tried to stop him. They were used to Gil being the last to arrive and the first to leave.

Outside, the air was damp with the remnants of the previous night's freezing fog, but the ice and hoarfrost had melted under today's clear blue sky. Purple dusk was gathering when Gil parked his Charger in front of the shop at Sanchez Trucking. Unlike at his cold, dark house, someone always left a light on in the office. The comforting aromas of grease and stale coffee greeted him, but his computer monitors didn't offer up the usual heaping helping of distractions. The trucks might still roll on Christmas but most warehouses and businesses were shut down, so there was only a handful of loads to pick up or drop off and very little traffic to snarl their schedule.

Nothing in his email but tidings of comfort and joy… dammit.

Gil cradled his cell phone, checking the time. He hadn't lied to Miz Iris about talking to Quint, but he knew better than to call in the middle of the Barron family's formal evening meal. Quint's grandfather had never hidden how he felt about Gil, but he treated Quint as well as any of his other kin. Rather than stir up trouble for his son, Gil would find something to occupy the time—and his mind—as Christmas Day drifted into evening.

He should call his mother. In the past few years, she had made a real effort to reconnect, especially with her grandsons. She and Quint got along great, and she never turned down an invitation to a championship game or one of his choir concerts. Gil reluctantly pulled up her number in his contacts. If all else failed—as it generally did—they could always talk about how things were going with the business.

The phone buzzed in his hand, and he jerked as if he'd been stung. His heart thudded when he saw that the unfamiliar number started with 406. Montana. The only state with a single telephone prefix.

His finger wasn't quite steady when he tapped the screen. The first GIF was Simon Cowell at his most know-it-all smug. What did I tell you? The second was a cheesy fortune-teller waving her hands dramatically over a crystal ball. Never doubt the power of Carma.

Gil stared at the texts, almost convinced it was a prank. He didn't have to ask how she'd gotten his cell number. It was listed on the Sanchez Trucking website for all their clients to see. He started to punch out How did you know about Hank and Grace?

Then he stopped. Duh. Bing, of course. And firing a question like that back at Carma made it sound like he wasn't happy to hear from her. He was *way* too happy for his pride or his peace of mind. But how was he supposed to play this?

Hey! What's up?

Because they were both still in junior high, apparently. Delete, delete, delete.

Wanna meet me in Wyoming some weekend so I can take that rain check you promised?

Probably not a good choice, either. Since words were failing him, he found a GIF of Hermione from the Harry Potter movies rolling her eyes and slow-clapping in mocking approval. His thumb wavered—God, was he actually nervous?—before he hit Send.

The wait was interminable. Finally, his phone pinged with a GIF of an owl-eyed old Englishwoman looking down her snooty nose. Sarcasm is the lowest form of wit.

The hell she said.

He texted her back a meme of a Katharine Hepburn type playing the classy broad, complete with cigarette holder. Sarcasm is an art, darling. If it was a science, I'd have a PhD.

Her reply was a smirking dude bro flashing a peace sign. Just messin' with you, man.

And he'd chomped on the bait. He grinned, but before he could figure out what to say next, another image popped up, silver stars in a midnight-blue sky.

Happy everything. Sweet dreams.

Damn. That was it? Disappointment dragged the smile off his face as he signed off with a winking Santa emoji. Bleh. So weak. He set the phone on the desk, face up. With one fingertip he scrolled to the top of the exchange, then back down again.

And sitting there in the mostly dark office without another soul around, he felt less alone than he had all day.

Chapter 3

Glacier County—mid-January

Carma wasn't the only one in her family with special talents. There were legends stretching back for generations before the Blackfeet had been corralled on the reservation, stories of those in the White Elk line who could supposedly read minds...and the future.

Unfortunately, the gift didn't extend to automobiles.

"Are you sure this thing isn't going to leave me stranded on the side of the road?" Carma asked, casting a dubious look at the vehicle parked in front of her parents' house.

"Never has before." Her uncle Tony gave the buckskin-colored hood of his eighties-era van a fond pat. "Unless you get caught in a blizzard. It isn't worth a shit in snow."

Which didn't matter to Tony since the powwows where he was a drum singer were held mostly in the summer. And with her intentionally flexible itinerary, Carma wouldn't have to push on if the roads got bad. At the moment, they stood basking in the sunny side of Montana's disposition, with temperatures in the sixties. It would inevitably turn bitter, though, probably just in time for calving season to start.

"I still think I should wait until at least the middle of April," Carma told her mother.

"We'll be fine." Her mom gave one of Tony's braids a tug. "This one's a real-good night man, 'cuz he likes to sleep all day."

He grinned. "Long as I got my ol' gray mare. She can sniff out a newborn calf in the pitch-dark."

"And you promised your grandmother," Carma's mother pointed out—again. "December might seem like a long way off, but your brother's enlistment will be up before we know it."

The best any of them had been able to do was make him promise to wait until the last possible moment to sign away another four years of his life to the U.S. Army. Give them a chance to find a better option. Eddie insisted that he had two families—this one and the military—and he didn't want to be separated from both. Since he had no interest in being a rancher and there were no other jobs around home to suit him, the army kept winning.

While Eddie lost. More of the sparkle in his eyes. More of the laughter. Each time he came home from a deployment—and there had been so many Carma had lost count—she could feel the added weight of death and disillusion on his soul.

They all feared that eventually it would drag him under.

After his too-short, too-quiet visit while on leave over the holidays, Grandma White Elk had decided to take charge, sitting Carma down and shoving a check into her hand. "You take that and go find what it will take to keep Eddie safe."

Forty thousand dollars? Carma gaped at her. "And I'm supposed to use this to do what?"

"I've been looking into programs for veterans who're disabled or having mental issues. Lord knows with so many of our people serving, we need something for them right here. Plus, Bing sent me this."

She dropped a copy of *Amarillo Country* magazine into

Carma's lap. The glossy cover was a photo of two soldiers in jeans and camo T-shirts, smiling on horseback. The woman was missing an arm from just above the elbow. The man had no visible injuries, but that didn't mean he wasn't deeply wounded.

Beside them, a handsome sixtysomething man had an arm thrown over a younger woman's shoulders. The headline read *Patterson Foundation's Equine-Based Therapy Program Provides Much-Needed Therapy to Recovering Soldiers.*

Everyone in the country who'd watched the news in the past decade knew former U.S. Senator and Texas billionaire Richard Patterson. Before abruptly leaving politics, he'd been the most likely conservative candidate for the next presidential election. He was also CEO of the family's business empire, including one of the oldest and largest ranches in Texas where he kept an eye on their legendary Quarter Horse breeding program.

His daughter was not a public figure. Tori Patterson had chosen to keep a low profile, working as a physical therapist at a respected but hardly famous clinic in Amarillo. In fact, there was only one reason Carma recognized her on sight.

She was now Tori Patterson-Sanchez. Delon Sanchez's wife. Gil's sister-in-law.

Carma flipped to the feature article, intensely aware of her grandmother's all-too-knowing scrutiny. Of course she'd heard that Carma had left the Stockman's Bar with Gil back in November. Half a dozen friends and relatives had called to tattle before Carma crawled out of bed the next morning.

Grandma had not been pleased to hear why Carma

had cut the encounter short. "You finally meet a man with potential, and you let Jolene ruin it?"

Carma could have argued that the *potential* was limited to an hour in a truck sleeper. Or she could have admitted that there was a good chance she would have chickened out anyway, after that kiss. It was like opening a box of what she thought were firecrackers and finding dynamite. This was not a man to play around with. Gil Sanchez had the power to rock her world.

But after Bing called on Christmas morning to share all their joyous news, Carma hadn't been able to resist making contact. Just a text. A joke. He probably wouldn't even answer.

Then he did, and it had started…something. The texts were random, infrequent, and never more than GIFs, memes, and emojis, as if they'd established the rules with that first exchange. She certainly couldn't call them conversations. Maybe that was the point. Connection, but from a safe distance.

For Carma at least, it was easier to let the pictures speak for her.

She smoothed the pages of the magazine. Wow. The arena alone was stunning—two hundred feet wide, three hundred feet long, fully handicapped accessible. A state-of-the-art physical therapy clinic built right in; a mental health program in development. All provided without cost to anyone whose insurance didn't cover their treatment.

"This is amazing," Carma said. "But I still don't understand…"

Her grandmother tapped a photo of a soldier grinning as he sent his horse over a small jump. "This is what we need. If you went there and learned what they do, you could persuade Eddie to stay home and help start our own program."

Carma gave a stupefied laugh. "We couldn't do a fraction of this. The equipment alone..."

"I bet Eddie could build even better stuff. Maybe sell his designs to bring in more money."

And immerse himself in the challenge, using his engineering skills that were not otherwise in high demand in ranch country. Oh yeah. This woman knew her grandson well. But Carma...

"I can't just walk in there and demand to be hired."

"Who better?" Grandma leaned back and folded her bony arms. "You've got schooling in counseling. You can handle horses, and these patients can't be any harder than the idiot actors you've had to work with. Plus you can teach them trick roping. That'd be great therapy. And that's not even counting the other."

The *other*. Even Grandma had never found a name for what Carma was...and did. She'd failed miserably at fitting the mold of a traditional holy woman. Even the more progressive sects of the Blackfeet religion felt restrictive. Like having someone tell her how to breathe.

Carma never had been good with rules and rituals. She'd flunked out of Sunday school when the teachers got tired of her asking, "But why do you have to tell us how to talk to God? Can't we just go outside and listen instead?"

Religion didn't exactly agree with her version of spirituality.

A place like the Patterson Clinic would have a lot of rules. And the kind of people who weren't likely to be open to her particular style of therapy.

"What about you and Grandpa?" she asked.

"His youngest sister is moving home from Missoula, now that she lost her husband. She needs family and all." Her eyes softened as she squeezed Carma's knee. "You've done your part for us. Lord knows you've wasted enough of your life on Jayden. And if the man of your dreams was anywhere around here, you would've met him by now."

Carma's eyes filled as she laid her hand over her grandmother's papery fingers. "What if people like me don't get to live happily ever after?"

"I won't lie, Carmelita. This gift has never made life easier for those who bear it." Her expression hardened. "But you will *not* go sour like Norma. You have to find your own happiness. Look at Bing. She barely hit Texas before she landed herself a good-lookin' cowboy who thinks she painted the stars."

Yay for Bing. After all she'd been through, she deserved it. But considering the age difference between the two cousins, if Carma followed Bing's example she'd find her own soul mate in a couple of decades, give or take.

Grandma took both of her hands and forced Carma to meet her piercing gaze. "Promise me you'll do this. For Eddie. And for yourself."

There was no denying Grandma White Elk once her mind was set, something else that tended to run in the family. Carma smiled reluctantly. "Okay. I swear."

"I'll make sure you don't dawdle."

She was true to her word, damn her stubborn, congestive heart. A week later, in the middle of a rerun of *Murder, She Wrote,* she'd slumped over on the couch, as if she'd simply gone to sleep. Grandpa's sister had moved in right after the funeral—and Carma was left with no choice but to get on with keeping her promise.

The purpose of her trip was twofold. Tony had connected her with his friends—healers and shamans across Montana and the Dakotas who were willing to share their knowledge and hopefully help Carma understand and develop her own unusual skills. She'd also made a list of equine-based therapy programs to visit along the way, learning everything she could before she reached the end of her winding trail—Bing's new home in Earnest, Texas.

A thought that made Carma's belly clutch every time. How would Gil react to her showing up out of the blue?

But she wouldn't stay away for fear of what Gil would think. Besides being one of her favorite cousins, Bing was her connection to Tori and the Patterson Clinic. Carma had considered texting Gil about her visit, but advance notice felt like an expectation.

Get ready, Big Boy, here I come.

Besides, she didn't know exactly when she'd arrive. The lack of a set schedule chafed at the part of her that insisted on straightening out every tangle—from a necklace chain to Jolene's latest squabble with their mutual aunt Agnes—but the freedom to follow wherever the wind pushed and the sky beckoned made her heart swoop and dance like a starling on the breeze.

She caressed the wide strip of intricately painted beadwork that ran along the van's hood and down the sides. She certainly wasn't going to sneak across the country. And she wouldn't lack in comfort. Behind the red-velour bucket seats, Tony had installed a fridge, gas stove, closet, drawers, and a queen-sized bed.

Everything Carma needed for her own personal voyage of discovery. Almost. She pulled the last piece out of her coat pocket and stashed it in the cubbyhole beside the radio. Then she tipped her head back and drank in her sky and her clouds. Let the breeze finger through her hair and caress her face as she sent up a silent goodbye.

And the wind whispered *Be safe, friend,* in a voice that only Carma could hear.

Chapter 4

Oklahoma City—late January

Like every second Sunday evening for the past fourteen years, Gil drove into the plushest section of Oklahoma City and parked in front of Krista's house, delivering Quint back to his mother. He didn't care what anybody said about modern architecture, he still thought the place looked like a two-million-dollar dentist's office. An opinion he probably should have kept to himself, but it had gotten a rise out of Krista, which Gil enjoyed far too much.

Then he'd gone home and made his house a place for running and wrestling, scattering Legos, and scribbling on walls. God knew that and getting caked with grease and ranch dirt were the only things Gil could give the kid that Krista didn't.

The door swung open, and Krista Barron-Tate stood framed in the entrance, a splash of bright poppy in her silky pantsuit and excruciatingly pointy shoes. A pantsuit, for God's sake. The renegade who'd blown Gil's college-boy mind would've sneered at the picture she made now, with her blond hair set in sleek, bulletproof waves. Maybe that was why Gil could never resist agitating her until the shell cracked and he caught a glimpse of the girl who'd run wild on the rodeo circuit with him for most of his rookie year.

Now she waved a perfectly manicured hand at him. "Come on in, Gil!" she called. "We need to talk."

Not good. Since the day she'd told him she was pregnant

and God no, she wouldn't marry him, those words from Krista had never boded well.

What did she want this time? Spring break in Tuscany? A two-month summer music program in New York City? Then Gil would have to argue that the horizon in the Texas Panhandle was wide enough for any kid, and the boy could get plenty of culture from his grandmother, the same way she'd tried to ingrain some sense of their Navajo heritage into her sons.

Efforts Gil had resisted with every fiber of his being, starting with screaming at the top of his three-month-old lungs through the entire length of a ceremony intended to celebrate his first laugh.

Gil thumped the steering wheel once, muttered a curse, then climbed out of his midnight-blue Charger and followed Quint up the walk. Krista stood aside to let them in. "Quint, go change out of your good clothes while I talk to your father."

Quint regarded the pair of them with the *Are you sure you can handle this?* pucker between his brows that had been making Gil feel inadequate since—equal parts awed and terrified—he'd stared into a hospital bassinet at what was unmistakably his child.

He'd been playing catch-up for most of the fourteen years since.

With one last doubtful glance, Quint disappeared into the sterile depths of the house. Gil tucked his hands in his pockets and strolled past Krista into what they called a living room—as if anyone could survive in there for more than an hour. He declined a seat on a couch that appeared to be made of upholstered concrete slabs and said no thanks to the glass of sweet tea sweating politely onto a stone coaster, choosing to lean against a mantel made of gray slate. The obligatory family photos were so flawless they looked like they'd come with the frames, except that unlike his two younger sisters, dark-haired, dark-skinned Quint was obviously not the child of Krista's pale, sandy-haired husband. And speaking of Douglas...

Gil glanced toward the nearest archway. "Are you sure you don't want to have your attorney present?"

Of course she'd married a lawyer. A Harvard graduate. The son of a family whose social and business dealings were so interconnected with her father's that their union was borderline incestuous. And to top it off, he was a decent human being who adored Krista and Quint and showed Gil nothing but respect...the son of a bitch.

Krista sank onto a chair that matched the concrete couch. The cushions didn't give under her weight. "Can we just have a civil conversation?"

"Depends on what you want to talk about." Gil held up a hand. "No, wait. Let me guess—you want to take the kids to South Korea while Douglas helps negotiate some new trade agreement?"

Krista took a sip of her tea, then set it down with a sharp click. "Close. He has been offered a position as a commercial attaché at the U.S. Embassy in Namibia."

"That's an actual country?"

She smiled faintly. "It's in the southwest part of Africa. Douglas has always been interested in foreign service, and this is an excellent opportunity to get his foot in the door."

"Wait a minute." The gist of what she was saying slapped Gil in the face. "You're talking about a job."

Krista ran her fingers down her thigh, pleating the thin fabric of her pantsuit. "The posting could be up to five years."

Five. Years. Gil bunched his fists, panic coiling in his chest as he scrambled for some angle of attack. There must be a clause in their custody agreement that barred her from taking his son to the opposite side of the planet. "No goddamn way."

"That's also what Quint said…minus the obscenity."

Cold sweat sprang up between Gil's shoulder blades. "You can't make him go."

"I don't intend to try." Krista continued to worry the fabric of her pantsuit. "The girls are young enough to adapt, but Quint starts high school this fall, and he's not willing to give up football and basketball."

"But if you're going with Douglas—" Oh *shit*. Her father and stepmother. She was gonna leave Quint with the man who'd thrown all his money and influence at erasing Gil from Quint's life.

A corner of her mouth quirked. "Give me some credit. I am painfully aware that if you and Daddy had to deal with each other, someone would end up in a shallow grave."

And Gil had proven to be remarkably hard to kill. Otherwise high speed, a motorcycle, and a sharp curve would have done the job shortly after Krista had gutted him on her way out of Texas. Instead, he'd destroyed the rodeo career he'd loved even more than the woman who was still not looking him in the eye.

"If you're not staying and he's not going…"

Her gaze lifted, and behind the shadows in her eyes he saw a glint of mockery as she repeated almost the same words she'd said to him once before. "Congratulations, Gil. You're gonna be a *full-time* daddy."

He…*what*?

For the first time in all the times he'd been in her house, he had to sit down.

It was after nine when Gil got home, still in shock from Krista's bombshell. He parked in the driveway of his house, conveniently located only steps from the back door of the Sanchez Trucking shop, slammed the car door, and headed for the shop. Even at this time on a Sunday one of the drivers must have a problem that would give him an excuse to yell at someone.

But when he stomped into his office, Analise, the night dispatcher, shooed him out again. "Everything's under control. Go annoy someone else."

Who? His brother was in Houston for most of the week, and their dad was off on one of his monthly fishing trips. Hank would be cuddled up with Grace. All the Jacobs crew were on the road with their bucking bulls and horses, so he couldn't drop by Miz Iris's kitchen tomorrow morning to let her promise him that yes, he could handle living with his own child.

Geezus. He had to go meet with the school principal this week about getting Quint enrolled for spring term, like a real fucking parent.

He couldn't even text Carma because it was her turn. And yes, that was as juvenile as it sounded, but those were the rules that kept him from sending every meme and GIF that made him think of her—which would be at least once a day.

He paced through the reception area and into the manager's office to snatch up a pile of envelopes from the desk his dad and Delon shared. Their latest receptionist showed no sign of grasping the software program that integrated every facet of the business, but he'd figured she could at least sort the damn mail.

Gil did it now, dropping payments into his stack to be reviewed, signed, then taken to the accounting firm downtown that did their bookkeeping. He wished yet again that they could outsource the receptionist, too. The position had turned into an ongoing headache since their old battle-ax, Mrs. Nordquist, had had the nerve to retire. And the company might have doubled in size over the last eight years, but the office had not. The fewer bodies that occupied the cramped space the better, especially when one of them was Gil's.

He tried to warn the new hires, but they never seemed to grasp that keeping fifty drivers both busy and on schedule was the equivalent of having a dozen balls in the air at all times, any one of which was likely to burst into flames without warning—and Gil with it.

He tossed a fistful of junk mail into the trash and set a stack of others aside. His dad could deal with whatever the Chamber of Commerce wanted now, and the Rotary Club, and the Booster Club. Catalogs and sales flyers for tools and parts went into the in-box marked *Shop* for the foreman, Max. Gil started to flip a brochure that direction, then paused when he saw it was addressed to Delon. Six years after his brother had moved out of the apartment above the office, his personal mail still showed up here.

Gil's hands went still when he turned it over and saw the bareback rider on the front, chaps flying as he spurred a horse that all but leapt off the page. The old longing crashed through him, as powerful as ever. Three years after the surgery that had finally set his hip right, his body felt as good as he had at twenty-one. Better, since he wasn't fighting a hangover more often than not.

He ran his thumb over the bold, black font on the

brochure. *Diamond Cowboy Classic! Find your nearest qualifying event!*

Always a glutton for punishment, Gil broke the seal and spread the flyer on the desk. Delon didn't need it. As the reigning world champion, he was one of the five who'd gotten an engraved invitation directly into the Classic.

But it was the open-to-the-world qualifying events that made the Diamond Cowboy a huge draw for spectators and cowboys alike. Old and young, wannabes and current contenders—all they had to do was pony up a five-hundred-dollar entry fee for their shot at glory. The top four contestants from each of the regional elimination-style competitions would all meet in Amarillo for the nationally televised showdown.

David versus Goliath, rodeo-style.

When the dust settled, only one challenger and one headliner would remain. Two competitors. One ride. Winner takes home fifty grand and a diamond-studded horseshoe ring.

Who wasn't a sucker for an underdog story? A chance to cheer on a steer-wrestling insurance agent from Oregon or a barrel-racing teenager from North Carolina?

But not this trucker from good old Earnest, Texas. Gil's fingers creased the edges of the brochure as he fought off a stab of longing. Nowadays, he could slap the entry money down without blinking an eye. What he couldn't afford was to screw up the near-miraculous work of an entire team of surgeons, or risk a return of the grinding pain that had kick-started his opioid addiction. The doctors might let him run and jump and bang around in the occasional pickup basketball game with his kid, but no one knew exactly how much abuse his reconstructed hip could take.

He could still play pretend, though.

He stuffed the brochure into his back pocket and strode back through the reception area and down a hall that led past a restroom and break room, into what had once constituted the entire shop area. The space was barely big enough to accommodate one semi tractor, minus a trailer. After they'd built on the first full-length truck bay, Gil and Delon had stripped out everything except the workbench along one wall, installed a kick-ass stereo system, and converted this to their gym.

Gil locked the door and set his phone on the narrow metal stairs that led up to an apartment that had been his father's bachelor pad, Gil's jumping-off spot for three breakneck years after high school, then Delon's home for over a decade until he'd taken up residence at Tori's place in Dumas.

In four years, *Quint* would be old enough to have his own place. Geezus.

Gil rubbed at another heart spasm as he walked over to push Play on the ancient boom box and cranked up one of Delon's heavy-metal mix CDs. The cardboard box he pulled from under the workbench had once held fuel filters but was now the final resting place of rodeo gear that had reached the end of its competitive life. Gil grabbed a rigging whose stiff rawhide handle had been mashed by a horse that had reared up and crushed it against the back of the steel chute. The bronc would have done the same to Delon if a buddy hadn't yanked him out of harm's way. Gil had pounded it back into good enough shape for his purposes. He cinched it onto the spur board—an ugly plywood contraption built to mimic the shape of a horse's back and shoulders—all too aware of the irony of now being the brother on the receiving end of hand-me-downs.

As Gil pulled on one of the old gloves from the box, he

glanced in the direction of the office. Normally he wouldn't do this when there was anyone around to pity the poor has-been reliving his glory days, but Analise was busy, and the thumping of his feet would blend into the music.

He fetched an MP3 player from a drawer and plugged in the earbuds. When he'd worked his hand into the rigging, he cued up an audio clip he'd recorded from a televised rodeo performance. The announcers' voices filled his head as they launched into the play-by-play for a section of bareback riding from last year's Fiesta de los Vaqueros pro rodeo in Tucson.

As they rambled on about the first cowboy and the horse he was about to ride, Gil tucked his chin, lifted his free arm, and rocked onto his hip pockets to tuck his knees against the imaginary horse's shoulders. The fluorescent lights faded and he was *in* Tucson again, his nostrils filled with the smell of horse, dust, and rosin, and his heart with fire. At the shouts that signaled the gate had opened, his heels snapped into the neck of the spur board, then rolled up, his knees jerking wide as his boots clicked the front edge of the rigging.

Again, and again, and again, his feet lashed out and dragged back, and he could practically feel the horse exploding beneath him, yanking on his arm and slamming his shoulders into its rump. Then the recorded eight-second whistle blew, the crowd roared, and Gil let his feet fall, breathing hard as he spiraled back to reality.

It was a pathetic substitute. A fantasy that inflicted as much pain as pleasure. But unlike so many of the things he'd had to give up, indulging in a taste of this one wouldn't kill him.

It just felt like it sometimes.

Chapter 5

Near Amarillo—late March

In the spirit of what she'd christened *The Quest*, Carma had sworn off malls and soulless chain restaurants, but there was a world of difference between weathered charm and downright dingy. If she'd possessed a lick of sense—sixth or otherwise—she would have turned around and walked out of the café when she was greeted by a waitress with dirty cuticles and so much suppressed *I hate my life* rage that Carma felt obliged to offer her a smile and a sizeable tip instead.

Big mistake.

She'd felt the first pangs of nausea as she crossed the border from New Mexico to Texas. By the time she spotted the first exit to Amarillo, there was no denying the truth.

She was gonna puke.

Her stomach lurched and spit pooled in her mouth as she wheeled into a space in the parking lot of a sprawling truck stop. Another spasm racked her gut as she slid out of the driver's seat, fumbling for the toggle switch to lock the doors before staggering into the bathroom and the first open stall, where she fell to her knees and was violently sick.

Some interminable amount of time later, a tentative voice asked, "Um, are you okay?"

Seriously? She was hugging a toilet in a public restroom. Hell no, she wasn't okay. She raised a hand in a feeble *just give me a minute* gesture, then reached up to flush away the stench. When the next wave of nausea failed to materialize, she cautiously pushed back onto her butt, head flopping against the metal side of the stall.

A college-age girl in an employee uniform shirt watched, one hand clamped over her mouth and nose, as Carma pulled a length of toilet paper off the roll to wipe her face.

"Food poisoning," Carma croaked.

The girl relaxed slightly. Not the bubonic plague, or a drunk who'd bottomed out in her restroom. "Do you need an ambulance or something?"

Wow. She must look as bad as she felt. Carma rolled her tongue around her mouth and grimaced. "Water."

The girl scurried away and Carma closed her eyes, letting her thoughts swirl down a metaphorical drain. At the sound of footsteps scuffing on the tile, she hoisted her eyelids to accept a bottle of water. Carma didn't try to drink, just rinsed and spat, rinsed and spat, until she'd gotten rid of the worst of the taste.

"Paper towels?" she asked.

The girl gave her a fistful. Carma wet them with what was left of the water and pressed them to her face, neck, and chest as the earth beneath her slowly solidified. Finally, her head cleared enough to attempt standing.

Whoa. Her vision swam and the empty water bottle went skidding across the floor as she threw out both hands to catch herself in the narrow stall. After several deep breaths, her thighs stopped feeling like she'd been Tasered, and she shuffled over to the sink with the truck-stop attendant hovering out of range of possible projectile vomit. So far Carma was just dizzy. Maybe she'd get lucky and this would be a one-time, purge-the-tainted-hamburger episode.

Several other women came and went, giving Carma a

wide berth...with good reason. With her stringy, sweat-soaked hair and grotesquely smeared makeup, she looked more like a zombie than the time she'd actually played a decomposing extra in a horror movie.

She wasn't showing up on Bing's doorstep like this.

"Where's the nearest motel?" she asked the attendant.

"Right down the street."

Bed. Air-conditioning. Please God, yes. Carma dug a crumpled five-dollar bill out of her jeans to pay for the water. "Thank you for everything."

The girl waved it off. "Customer courtesy."

Outside, brilliant sunlight stabbed through Carma's pupils and into her brain as she paused to orient herself. There. Her van. Sunglasses. She crawled behind the wheel, cranked the engine and the AC and reached for the purse she'd left on the passenger's seat. Her hand encountered nothing but red velour. For several uncomprehending beats, she stared at the empty space. Then the impact of what she wasn't seeing slammed into her.

Her wallet. Her phone. Her... Geezus, *everything* was in her purse.

She scrambled out of the van, panic momentarily overriding any lingering nausea. She jerked open the passenger's door and didn't find the purse wedged alongside the seat. Or under the seat. Or behind the seat. Shit. *Shit.* It was gone. But how? Then she recalled jabbing blindly at the electric button until she heard a click. She must've hit *unlock* instead of *lock*—and some asshole had taken immediate advantage.

Son of a bitch. She'd been *robbed.*

Oh God. What if... She hauled herself up and across the seat, sagging in relief when she saw the familiar flash of blue inside the cubbyhole on the dash. The hollow, crystal-lined stone wasn't valuable to anyone but her, but it looked like it could be. Ditto for the feather dangling from the rearview mirror, her uncle Tony's version of a Saint Christopher's medal. Maybe even crooks knew better than to touch something blessed by tribal elders.

But her purse…

Her muzzy brain tried to wrap itself around what that meant. She could kiss close to a hundred dollars in cash goodbye. No credit cards. No checkbook. She would have to report this to the cops, for all the good it would do. The thief was probably miles away already. She had to notify her bank and her credit card company. Replace her driver's license and her tribal ID.

She shuddered at the thought of a stranger pawing through her wallet, knowing her birthday, her height and weight and home address. If she hadn't been sick before, she would be now. And her phone. At least it was password protected so they couldn't go thumbing through her pictures, her emails, her contacts.

All the texts she'd exchanged with Gil.

A whole different kind of nausea punched her in the gut. She had to contact the company to lock and deactivate the phone ASAP. How much of the data, if anything, could they recover? And seriously, was a bunch of lost texts really her main concern right now?

Carma fished out the bedraggled five-dollar bill that, along with half a tank of gas, was now the sum total of her resources. So much for the motel. Looked like she was headed straight to Earnest after all.

Gil had had full custody of his child for slightly less than a month, and he still didn't have a clue what was going on inside the kid's head. Quint lounged in the extra chair in the dispatcher's office while Gil stared at a slip of paper informing him that his son was academically ineligible to participate in the upcoming track meet.

"How can you be failing PE?" he asked.

"Only for the week. I was tardy last Thursday and Friday, and I forgot my gym clothes on Monday so I got a zero." Quint shrugged, supremely unconcerned by his grade or his father's potential displeasure. "I'm still getting used to not having Mom to get me up and make sure I have all my stuff."

Quint's nonchalance only ratcheted up Gil's anxiety. Could this be a subconscious cry for attention? God knows Gil didn't micromanage the boy like his mother had, but Krista hadn't been trying to keep dozens of trucks moving despite Mother Nature's far-flung wrath. Wildfires in California, an offshore tropical storm pushing torrential rain and flooding into the Gulf States, and a freaking snowstorm all the way across the upper half of the country, turning highways to skating rinks and closing mountain passes in Washington, Idaho...and Montana.

After lunch he'd paused to text Carma a meme of a cowboy riding through snow so deep his horse was completely buried, titled *Spring in Montana*. She still hadn't answered. She *always* answered. Was she tired of their game? Moving on with some other...

Gil dragged his attention back to the boy who wouldn't get to show off for his new, intensely curious hometown crowd. A string of private clinics and a constant whirl of school and regional leagues had developed Quint's natural athletic ability to the point Gil had argued that he was a kid, for Christ's sake, not an Olympic hopeful.

To which Krista had replied, "You never know."

Only if it was what Quint wanted, and at the moment his give-a-shit level seemed pretty damn low. Was the competition here so soft he didn't consider it worth his time? But he'd cared enough to beat Sam Carruthers in the runoff for who got the coveted anchor leg on the 1600-meter relay. According to thirdhand reports, Sam hadn't taken the loss well. No one had heard whatever he'd said before storming off. Quint had declined to comment. Even Beni was being cagey, and Delon's son had not inherited his father's tact.

What could some teenaged brat have said that they didn't want Gil to hear? When pressed, all Quint would say was that Sam was fried because he was used to being the best athlete in his class, but he'd have to get over it.

Quint did not lack confidence.

Gil tossed the note onto his desk. How was he supposed to deal with this? Sympathy? Tough love? Ignore it and let the boys work it out, the way Merle Sanchez had always done? The hell if Gil knew. He was the dad who'd been there every other weekend and a month in the summer. Who let his kid stay up too late and play too many video games. He'd never had to worry about gym clothes or homework or juvenile feuds, and none of the drama seemed to bother Quint much.

Or, as the son of parents who'd never been able to resist a chance to take a swipe at each other, Quint was just really good at playing it cool.

Gil closed his eyes and pinched the bridge of his nose. The realization that he now had full responsibility for a half-grown boy stopped his heart about eight times a day.

"If you're having trouble getting up and off to school on your own, I can come back to the house to check on you." And walk away from the multiple fires Gil was generally trying to stomp out at that time of the morning.

"It'll be fine," Quint said. "I just need to turn my alarm up."

Gil hesitated. Was he was supposed to prove he cared by putting Quint ahead of work, or give his almost-a-man child another chance to show he could handle the responsibility? And why wasn't there an app for this shit? Gil sighed as his computer beeped with an urgent notification from yet another driver whose route was either on fire, underwater, or buried in snow.

"Okay. But I'm calling the school to make sure they tell me the next time you're tardy." His cell phone rang, adding to the chorus of electronic nagging. "Go on out and sweep the truck bays for Max."

"Can I grab a snack first?"

Pita chips. Hummus. Those green peapod things. What self-respecting teenager called that a snack? "Yeah. But no video games for the rest of the week," he added, belatedly realizing there should be some kind of consequences.

"Fine." Instead of slamming out of the office like Gil would've done back in the day, Quint shut the door behind him with a sedate click.

Fuck.

Tonight Gil would knock off at six, go home, and stay there. Analise could handle whatever shitstorm was brewing here—and Gil had to make himself let her. He'd always known his insane work hours and the need to have his hands on every aspect of the business were alternative forms of dependency. Hell, he wasn't even special. Half the recovered addicts he knew were workaholics, control freaks, or both. Shuffling paperwork until two in the morning had been a damn sight better than closing down the bars—and until now there'd been no one at home to care.

Unfortunately, he'd constructed an entire trucking company around his compulsions. The business couldn't change overnight because he had suddenly acquired a family life, and to top it off they'd lost another receptionist. Apparently even the graveyard shift at the all-night diner in Dumas was better than working with Gil.

He swore yet again when the main phone rang and no one picked it up. Delon was on another call in their dad's office, and Analise wouldn't be in for another five minutes. *She* was worth her weight in gold…and the ass-chewing Gil had gotten when he'd lured her away from Jacobs Livestock with a hefty raise and the promise that she could wear whatever she wanted.

If only he could clone her. And himself.

Letting the phone go to voicemail, he shot to his feet, strode through the reception area and into the manager's office just as Delon hung up the phone.

"Do you have anyone lined up to interview?" Gil demanded.

"Have you seen the applications?" Delon waved a weary hand at a folder on the corner of his desk. "No one knows the difference between a cattle hauler and a reefer, and two of them can't spell 'references'…or provide any."

The main line started to ring again. Gil ground out another curse. "Grab that damn thing before I smash it with the nearest wrench. I'm going to the weight room."

Maybe in the process of banging some weights around he'd figure out what to do about the empty receptionist's desk. Or how to give Quint more of his time when the work was piling up faster than he and Analise could get it done, and Delon was due to take off to California for a two-week rodeo trip.

He didn't bother to change into workout gear, just grabbed a set of kettlebells to warm up, their weight nothing compared to the constant pressure bearing down on him. There were fifty drivers counting on him for their livelihood, a shitpile of clients who'd put their freight in his hands, and a son who deserved more than what Gil had left over when the rest were done with him.

And a sneaky, sympathetic voice that insisted he'd earned a stiff drink.

Gil dropped the kettlebells onto the rack, his arms burning. When he was done here, he'd call his sponsor. They just had their regular coffee date after the Tuesday night meeting in Dumas, but since Quint's arrival they chatted a lot more often. As a single parent herself, Tamela could relate. Gil had watched her maintain her sobriety while seeing her two sons through junior high and high school—proof that it could be done.

But unfortunately, he'd also seen that it never got much easier.

Chapter 6

The cops had barely contained their eye rolls when Carma admitted that yes, she had probably left the door unlocked and her purse in plain sight. Easy pickings. They'd taken down her information and promised to call if anything turned up, but no one pretended she had a prayer of getting her stuff back. Whoever had her phone was at least smart enough to turn it off, thwarting a signal trace.

The helpful truck-stop clerk had offered her use of their phone—but Carma had decided against calling Bing's office. The mental health clinic was another half hour north of Earnest in Bluegrass, and knowing Bing, she'd cancel the rest of her patients and rush to the rescue, which was not necessary. If Carma left immediately, she'd be at the Brookman ranch before her cousin had time to worry, so she crawled in her van and started driving while her head was clear and her stomach reasonably quiet.

It was almost five o'clock when she broke free of the Amarillo suburbs and onto open highway. Around forty-five miles north to Dumas, then fifteen east to Earnest, then a dozen north to the ranch. At Dumas her stomach started to knot. She gritted her teeth and tried to bargain with her uncooperative body. *Just hang with me for another half an hour. Then we can keel over, and I swear I will never be this stupid again.*

The prairie crept by in slow motion, until finally she crawled past a massive, low-slung wooden building with a huge neon longhorn head mounted above the doors. *The*

Lone Steer Saloon. Bing had mentioned that the honky-tonk was only a few miles outside of town. Carma drew in a relieved breath—and her gut spasmed at the scent of grilled beef.

Oh God. She wasn't going to make it.

She searched desperately for a spot to pull over along the narrow, shoulderless highway. Nothing, nothing, nothing... and then she crested a small rise and came upon a large steel-sided building, pale yellow with red and black trim, surrounded by a gravel parking lot, chain-link fence, and gleaming semis, all sporting the same unmistakable logo.

Of course the first place she came to would be Sanchez Trucking.

The next spasm twisted her stomach so hard, she nearly swerved off the road. Hell. She turned into the wide gates and pulled to a stop by a door marked *Office,* slumping over the steering wheel as she put the van in park. It had to be around six o'clock Texas time, but a flashy red car and a couple of service pickups were still parked outside.

Double hell. If they'd all been gone for the day, she could have retched behind their neatly pruned bushes, then collapsed on her bed with the air-conditioning cranked until she was fit to drive on. Now she'd have to go inside.

The instant her feet hit the ground, her vision went gray around the edges. She lurched to the shop door and all but fell inside. A dizzying jumble of racks and tools and partially disassembled trucks filled the space to her left. Her stomach lurched again, and she blinked hard, trying to focus. There had to be a bathroom. Maybe through that door on the right. She braced one hand on the wall as she wobbled toward it.

"Can I help you?"

Her head jerked around, almost tilting her off-balance.

It took a moment to locate the boy who had stepped from behind the nearest truck, packing a long-handled broom.

"Gil?" she croaked.

"In the office." The kid pointed toward the door.

"Thanks." Her vision fuzzed again, so she got only a vague impression of a cramped reception area and rows of filing cabinets before a movement caught her attention. Past another door on her right, a man rose from a desk, a blurred shape against a window filled with sunlight so blinding Carma had to close her eyes.

"Hello. Is there something… Whoa, are you sick?" The familiar voice held surprise, concern…and no hint of recognition.

Seriously? After that kiss, and all those texts, he didn't even recognize her? As if this wasn't humiliating enough. Thank God she had decided not to let him know she was coming, as if she expected him to want to see her. She clutched the doorframe, trying to force her brain to make words come out of her mouth. "I… We…"

Her legs buckled. As her hands and knees hit the floor, a trash can was shoved under her nose and she retched up what had to be her intestinal lining. There was nothing else left.

When she paused to gasp for air, another, almost identical, voice came from behind her. "What the hell?"

"I was hoping you knew," the man in front of her drawled. "Otherwise, my wife will not be amused."

Wait. Now that she heard him speak again, that voice wasn't quite right. Relief cascaded through her as she realized she had staggered in on the wrong Sanchez brother.

"She asked for Gil," the teenager from the shop said. "She looked pretty desperate. Geez, Dad. Did you knock up another one?"

Carma jerked upright. "I am not—"

Then everything went white as she fainted.

Carma was finally in Gil's bed, but these were not the circumstances he'd imagined in such frequent, vivid detail. She wasn't supposed to be in the vacant apartment above the office. His fantasies had all involved a truck sleeper. Parked somewhere far from this place where he worked. And lived.

Gil paused at the door to the bedroom, trying not to stare outright. God, it was so *weird*. This woman seemed even more like a stranger than when he'd met her in Montana, and it wasn't just because she looked like Death's daughter. He'd been communicating with her for months and didn't have a clue what to say now.

Maybe he could leave his phone on her pillow with a *Text me* note and Analise's number.

He tucked the sheet up to her chin. The apartment was musty, but clean. The nurse on call at the clinic in Dumas had agreed that it did sound like food poisoning, instructing him to try to get some fluids in her and to bring her in if she couldn't keep anything down by morning.

He laid the back of his hand on her forehead. She wasn't running a fever, but she shifted restlessly under his touch.

"Feeling any better?" he asked softly.

She didn't open her eyes. "As long as I don't move."

"I'll be right outside. Yell if you need me."

She winced, as if the idea of raising her voice was physically painful. "You'll call Bing?"

"Right now. Try to sleep."

He edged a plastic bucket closer to the bed, then paced through the apartment and outside, leaving the door open a crack. The evening sun was warm on his back as he leaned on the railing of the exposed second-floor landing, where the conversation wouldn't disturb Carma but he was within earshot if she needed him.

When Bing picked up, she said, "Hey, Gil. I'm heading into a group session so I've only got a minute. What's up?"

"I have someone here you might be looking for."

There was a puzzled beat of silence, then, "Carma? What's she doing with you?"

So Carma hadn't intended to pop in the minute she arrived in Earnest. He'd figured. "Funny you've never mentioned her."

"Neither have you."

Point taken. And he refused to ask if they had discussed him. "Are the two of you close?"

"Reasonably, given the age difference. We're first cousins. My mother is the oldest and her dad is the youngest of five."

He should have guessed. They had a certain look, not to mention attitude. "I can't believe you haven't given me shit about this. It's not like you to butt out."

She laughed her low, throaty laugh. "Carma is the exception."

"To what rule?"

"All of them." Bing's voice sharpened with concern. "Why *am* I talking to you instead of her?"

Gil sketched out what he'd been able to gather about Carma's situation, including the stolen purse.

Bing swore. "As soon as I'm done here, I'll come by and pick her up."

"Don't. I put her in the apartment. She's comfortable and not throwing up…for now."

"Then I'll have Johnny bring me some clothes so I can stay with her."

"If you want, but I already sent Quint home with Delon. I can crash here on the couch." Lord knew he'd mopped up plenty of vomit, between looking out for Delon when they were kids and Quint's motion sickness—not to mention the times Gil had woken up in a puddle of his own puke. At least Carma hadn't upchucked on the shag carpet of that van, which appeared to also be her current home. "How long has she been on the road?"

"About six weeks."

"Doing what?"

"Talking to people and seeing places."

Which told him absolutely nothing. "Is she on some kind of pilgrimage?"

"I'd call it more of an expedition."

"To where?"

"It's more of a what. And you'll have to ask her if you want to know more."

Gil tried another angle. "How long is she planning to stay with you?"

"As long as it takes."

She was toying with him. Gil clenched his teeth, refusing to let her hear his frustration.

"Doesn't she have a job back home?" he asked.

"Whenever she wants one. Substitute teacher, backup receptionist at Indian Health Service, ranch hand, dealer at the casino… Carma can do about anything."

And Bing hadn't even mentioned the trick roping, or the list of movie credits, which Gil had found when he'd typed her name into an Internet search engine, as either an extra or a stunt rider. If she'd had dreams of being a headliner, they hadn't panned out. Along with any of her other careers.

"She's not flighty or irresponsible or any of those things you're thinking," Bing said.

"What is she?"

Bing made a sound that was half laugh, half sigh. "It's not my place to explain Carma, even if I could. And I've got to go to my meeting. I'll see you later."

When Bing arrived, Carma was asleep. The older woman peeked in at her, nodded in satisfaction, and ordered Gil to call if she was needed. He followed her down to her car.

"You could have warned me she was coming," he said, then immediately regretted it when her eyebrows soared.

"I didn't realize it was an issue."

Shit. Now he'd made her think it bothered him. "It was just awkward," he said stiffly. "I have to think of Quint now."

Her eyes gleamed with merciless humor. "And what did you tell him?"

"Nothing. I mean, there was nothing to tell. Carma and I just..." He cut an annoyed hand through the air. "Never mind. Go home and torture Johnny. I'll give her a phone so she can call if she wakes up and wants to talk to you."

Bing laughed, gave a cheeky wave, and left Gil with no more of a clue about Carma's intentions than when the conversation started.

Damned maddening woman.

Chapter 7

When Carma woke up, Gil was lounging on the couch directly outside the open bedroom door. Her entire body ached, her mouth tasted like sewage, every individual hair on her head hurt—and still the man gave her a jolt. She'd told herself that she'd exaggerated his raw sexuality, that it was a figment of her own desperation that night at the bar.

If anything, her memory hadn't done him justice.

She kept still, studying him from beneath her lashes as she tried to get a reading on his mood. Some people were easy, their emotions glowing like bright, primary reds, blues, and yellows. Others were like the chaotic smears and swirls of a child's finger-painting, the colors going muddy where they mixed.

And some, like Gil, were a kaleidoscope of the thousand subtle shades between. No sooner would she make out a certain shape or tint than it would shift.

Tonight she got the impression that even he wasn't sure how he was feeling. His head was tipped back against the couch cushion, his face shadowed by his thoughts and late-day scruff as his agile fingers picked out the sensuous notes of "Tennessee Whiskey" on his guitar.

She wasn't the only one remembering.

"You're gonna have to wait a day or two if you want to see me dance," she said.

Gil jerked, then squinted at her, annoyed at being caught off guard. "Are you going to be sick again?"

"I don't think so." She blinked a few times, her eyelids gummy. "It doesn't hurt to look at you anymore."

He folded his arms on top of the guitar. "I didn't know my face could inflict pain."

"No, I just swoon at the sound of your voice." She gingerly pushed onto her elbow. When the change in altitude didn't wreak havoc, she said, "Did you catch the stray dog that crapped in my mouth?"

"'Fraid not, but there's breath mints, a bottle of ibuprofen, and a glass of water on the nightstand."

She glanced over, then back at him, eyebrows sketching a question.

"I've had a lot of practice at waking up feeling like shit," he said.

She let that pass without comment, levering herself upright by degrees, then shook a mint out of the plastic box and set it on her tongue. When her stomach didn't immediately revolt, she rolled it around her mouth. At least her breath would be fresh. The rest of her...*ugh*. Her peach-colored shirt and khaki shorts were grubby and creased, and lank strands from her braid straggled into her eyes.

So much for that killer turquoise sundress she'd bought for the express purpose of knocking his socks off the next time they met.

He slung an arm along the back of the couch, body relaxed, dark eyes cool and appraising. "Bing stopped by, but she didn't want to wake you. We thought you'd rather stay put."

"Thanks." She had a woozy memory of him hauling her down a hallway and up a set of stairs. Was anyone else still hanging around downstairs? Carma pulled the elastic off and began working her hair out of the braid. "So...that's your son."

"Yeah." Gil made a pained face. "I'm sorry. His sense of humor is a little…unpredictable."

She shrugged. "I did make quite an entrance."

"He's gonna apologize to you." *And make it good*, Gil's expression implied.

"If you insist." She'd rather hear the story behind that specific joke, but Bing could tell her. Carma twisted her head to the side, sniffed, and wrinkled her nose. "God, I reek."

And Gil had had ample opportunity to appreciate her stench. Wow. Could she get any sexier?

"I brought your suitcase in so you could change," he said.

She grimaced. "I need a shower first."

"Not tonight. You can barely sit, let alone stand."

"You could prop me up." She was kidding, of course, but then she got caught up in the thought of warm water streaming over her head and sticky, sweat-coated skin…

Gil stared at her. "Are you serious?"

"As a heart attack. Or food poisoning, as the case may be." She could not sleep like this. If she took a deep breath, her own body odor was going to make her start gagging again.

She stood, inch by inch, with one hand on the bed for balance. Yikes. The ol' legs were definitely wobbly. No doubt her judgment was also impaired. Salmonella and Gil Sanchez both appeared to have that effect on her, but she would deal with the consequences in the morning. Right now, she had to have that shower. "I am willing to sacrifice what modesty I have to feel human."

It never had been one of her virtues. As a kid, she'd snuck away every chance she got to skinny-dip in Badger Creek, or bask naked in the tall summer grass, reveling in the total contact between her skin and the sun, the sky, and the earth.

She waved a hand in front of her torso. "Anyone who watches R-rated westerns has seen all this anyway—minus the fifteen pounds I've put on since the last time I worked as a body double."

Gil blinked, and she could see him searching his mind for roles he might have seen her in. "How did you get into the movie business?"

"My dad. If it was filmed in the U.S. in the past twenty years and had horses, he probably provided them. He's the best wrangler in the business." She swayed slightly, then caught herself. "Now, if you don't mind..."

She took a tentative step. Gil dumped the guitar and sprang off the couch to loop an arm around her waist. She let him guide her into the bathroom and steady her while she brushed her teeth. Then, without giving herself time to chicken out, she pushed her shorts and underwear down to her ankles. Shirt and bra followed, leaving her buck-ass naked in front of a man who looked like he wasn't quite sure how his night had come to this.

And not necessarily in a good way.

Don't stare. Don't stare.

Gil jerked his gaze away, straight into the too-convenient mirror, and every thought in his head morphed into *Boobs!* Lush and full to match her hips, with nipples several shades darker than her smooth bronze skin. Whatever weight she'd gained had distributed itself very nicely.

"How are you feeling?" he asked, fighting the temptation to reach out and see for himself.

Bracing one hand on his arm and the other on the vanity, she lowered herself to sit on the toilet lid. "A little weak in the knees, but I don't think I'm going to upchuck again." She tipped her head back and smiled. "Your turn."

Gil swallowed. Shit. He was not shy, but he'd never had a woman he barely knew strip down and expect him to do the same. At least not without a little foreplay.

He gritted his teeth. *Not sex. This is not about sex.*

When he hesitated, she said, "I can just sit on the floor in the shower while you operate the taps."

And let her think he didn't have the guts to join her? No damn way. He yanked his T-shirt over his head and tossed it aside as he toed off his running shoes, then had to fight the urge to turn away when he peeled off his jeans and boxers.

Her gaze locked on his torso, forehead pleating as she reached out to skim her fingers over the mottled, roughened skin that extended down his left side—ribs, hip, and thigh. "Burns?"

"Road rash. I laid a motorcycle down on the highway doing seventy miles an hour." He could still feel the asphalt tearing his flesh, eclipsed by the blinding agony when the bike slammed into an embankment, dislocating his hip and shattering his pelvis. Remembered wishing he hadn't been wearing a helmet, so he could've been knocked senseless.

Then he'd realized opiates were almost as good as a coma, especially if you washed them down with a slug of Jack Daniel's.

Carma touched the newest of the surgical scars, pink and raised compared to the thin white lines of the old ones. "It's better since this?"

"A hundred percent." Thanks to his sister-in-law's connections in the highest echelons of medicine. He was one of the first to undergo the experimental procedure that had reconstructed his shattered hip socket using computer imaging, robotic assistance, and a form of bone grafting akin to 3-D printing, allowing for the insertion of the hip prosthesis.

Every pain-free step he'd taken since was a testament to the wonders of science.

He cranked the taps, adjusted the temperature, then reached down and latched his hands under her armpits to hoist her onto her feet. "In we go."

He kept his back to the spray, shielding her as she leaned against the wall. With his palms planted on either side, she was bracketed between his arms, unable to slip down or sideways, but he was careful to keep his body canted away from hers so their only contact was the press of the sides of her breasts against his forearms.

Soft, wet breasts.

She closed her eyes and began running the bar of soap over her neck, arms, chest, and lower. The sight was enough to set his body throbbing, but he couldn't close his eyes.

Finished, she handed him the soap. "Shampoo?"

He grabbed the bottle he'd brought from her suitcase and squeezed a dollop into her palm. The shower filled with a sweet cherry-almond scent that transported him back to Montana. She bowed her head and began working the lather into her scalp, and Gil had to bite back a groan as the trailing ends of her hair feathered over his hard-on. He didn't know whether to sigh in relief or groan in disappointment when she twisted her hair into a sleek rope and looped it over her shoulder as she straightened.

She glanced down, then up, then leaned in to plant a soft, openmouthed kiss below his ear. "I guess I owe you a double rain check."

He gave a pained laugh. "Is that like the double coupons at the grocery store?"

"You clip coupons?"

"I have insomnia and a teenage son. Who lives with me." He still couldn't say it without a slight, disbelieving shake of his head.

"I take it that's recent." Carma narrowed her eyes, doing some kind of calculation. "About…three weeks?"

He shoved out to arm's length, as if she'd poked him in the gut. Was this another of her…whatever they were?

She shook her head as if in answer. "That's about the time you sent the GIF of the guy getting buried by a dump truck full of chocolate kisses. *Be careful what you wish for.*"

"Oh. Right. That was the day he volunteered me to help run his home track meets."

At the mention of the text, there was an almost audible click in his mind, as if the real, physical Carma and his electronic pen pal had finally snapped together into one person. Why was he even surprised to find himself standing in a shower with her? This was the woman who—when Gil had memed that late-night television was designed to torture insomniacs—had presented the entire plot of *Fifty Shades of Grey* in emojis, leaving him laughing his ass off.

And weirdly turned on.

The water started to go cold, so he reached back to turn off the faucets. "Bing didn't tell you about Quint?"

"We don't call each other every Sunday to giggle over boys. Actually, we haven't really talked since she moved down here, except when she was home for Grandma's funeral."

"I'm sorry. I didn't realize her grandmother and yours were the same person." Or what? He would have sent her a *So sorry for your loss* meme? "I know she meant a lot to you."

"Yes. She did."

And they were still standing in the shower, but at least the conversation had put a damper on his arousal. He grabbed a towel to wrap around his waist, bundled Carma into another, then set her on the toilet. There. Much better. He was having enough trouble with her stepping out of his dreams and into his life without the nakedness.

He handed her a third towel for her hair. "You knew about me before we met."

"Duh." Her smile was only about half-strength, but still packed a punch. "The mysterious Gil Sanchez who popped in every month or so to visit the nearly as mysterious Hank who was squatting in the woods with Aunt Norma? *Everyone* asked Bing about you."

He gawked at her. "*Aunt* Norma? The hermit? With the shotgun?"

"Yep. My personal worst-case scenario."

Gil frowned. "How's that?"

Carma ducked her head, letting the towel fall over her face and muffle her words. "Oh, you know. One of those things that runs in families. Speaking of... Will this be a problem for your son? Me, I mean."

She was blatantly changing the subject, but Gil had been trying to figure out how to bring this one up since he'd gotten over the shock of seeing her pass out. "I'm not sure," he admitted. "I...um...wasn't expecting the two of you to meet."

She dropped the towel and flipped her damp, tangled

hair over her shoulder to meet his gaze. "I'm not expecting anything."

Oh. Well. That was…good? He tried for a wicked grin. "Not even a rain check?"

She smiled—the real deal—and his pulse stuttered. "Let me know when you're ready to cash it in."

Now would be good, his randy body whispered.

No chance. Even though she looked much better, her face was still chalky and her eyes were a little glassy, so he said, "Count on it."

He walked her to the bedroom, sat her on the edge of the bed, and did not offer to help her off with the towel. "Pajamas?"

"Sleep shirt and underwear in my suitcase."

He dug them out of the roller bag and set them in her lap. "I'll be right back."

After a quick pause in the bathroom to pull on boxers and jeans, he grabbed a couple of single-serving cups of lemon Jell-O and a ginger ale from the refrigerator. He found Carma dressed and half-heartedly tugging a wide-toothed comb through her hair.

"Let's see if you can keep this down." He plucked the comb from her hand and gave her a Jell-O cup and a spoon.

She scooped out a tiny bite, set it on her tongue, and sighed blissfully. "Ah. That's perfect."

She finished both Jell-O cups and a few sips of the ginger ale, then toppled sideways onto the pillow. "Okay. I'm done."

"What about your hair?"

She grimaced, raising a hand to her head. "I don't have the energy to dry it."

But she'd be chilled all night if she slept with it wet. He

fished out the blow-dryer he'd seen in her suitcase. "Roll over."

She did, and he gently scraped her hair back so it spilled off the mattress.

"What are you doing?" she mumbled, already fading.

"I can't let you catch pneumonia on top of everything else." Plugging the dryer into the outlet beside the nightstand, he sat cross-legged on the floor and began to work his fingers through the strands, scalp to tips, following with the dryer.

She angled him a drowsy, bemused look. "I didn't peg you as the nurturing kind."

"Only when it suits me."

And the feel and scent of her hair turning to warm silk as it dried was incredible. He was fascinated by the hundred shades of auburn, deep brown, and black caught in the glow of the lamp.

It was so mesmerizing he didn't realize she'd fallen asleep until he switched off the dryer. He should get dressed, go downstairs, and catch up on some of the administrative crap, but he was tired, and relaxed from the warmth and the rhythmic motion of his hands, and he could stand to rest for a while.

Besides, what if Carma got sick again?

He switched off the lamp, shucked his jeans, and eased into the bed. Careful not to wake her, he edged as close as he dared, then closed his eyes. He should be worrying about what he was going to do with her, and with Quint, and about a million other things that regularly kept him up at night, but his brain was oddly uninterested in anything but the soft whisper of Carma's breath.

He unconsciously matched the ebb and flow, and drifted off to sleep.

Chapter 8

Carma dreamed that Gil was irritated she was still in his apartment, but even though he was standing beside the bed, scowling down at her, his voice was distant and muffled. "Nice try, but you've probably heard that this isn't my first rodeo."

Sorry, she tried to mumble, but her mouth was tacky and her tongue thick. *I'll go. Just give me a few minutes...*

She struggled through layer after layer of the sludge that filled her head, and surfaced as he said, "Well, too bad for you that I read all the fine print. We're not signing any contract that has..."

The rest was an indistinct rumble, as if he'd turned away, but when she peeled her eyes open, she was alone. She hitched up on one elbow. He wasn't by the bed. Not in any part of the living room she could see. But suddenly his words were clear again. "Great. I'll keep an eye out for your email."

Then a phone rang, and he cursed, and she located the source of the sound—a floor vent along the wall. She sank back into her pillows, relieved. Whoever he was annoyed at, it wasn't her. Besides, he was the one who'd put her here.

And he had dried her hair.

She ran her fingers through the slippery strands, bemused. He'd been so patient with her. So gentle. Not words she would have associated with Gil Sanchez.

Maybe that was the dream.

Then she rolled over and found a cheap cell phone on

the nightstand with a sticky note that ordered her to *Call if you need anything* in bold, black letters. When she picked it up, there was a number already keyed in. If it had been her phone, she would've texted him some GIF about the dead rising.

Crap. Her phone. Her purse. All those texts.

She flopped back onto her pillow, taking stock. Well, they had finally seen each other naked, and the view had been even better than she'd imagined—and she had imagined plenty. She could handle a post-sex morning after, but she'd never had to face a man who'd watched her puke. Nursed her. Fed her. Bathed her and watched over her while she slept. The smoking-hot, sardonic Gil she'd met in Montana could melt a nun's chastity belt, but the adorably gruff man who'd fed her Jell-O...

Just the fact that she'd inserted Gil and *adorable* into the same thought was enough to send red flags flying in every direction.

Either way, she had to face him sometime, so she might as well make it now.

When she pushed aside the blankets and stood, she was relieved to find that her legs had lost the rubbery feeling and her head didn't spin as long as she took it slow. She swapped her sleep shirt for a deep-green waffle knit shirt and jeans, thankful to find her hands were steady enough to apply eyeliner and mascara.

Ah. Better. Less zombie, more sallow-faced apocalypse survivor.

Out in the kitchen she found a loaf of bread on the counter, along with a bunch of bananas. She cautiously nibbled a slice of toast and a banana, but her stomach showed no sign of revolt, and her strength grew with each bite.

The apartment had two doors—one in the kitchen that led to a set of metal stairs on the side of the building, and the other in the living room that opened into the shop. She took the second and paused on the landing above a well-equipped gym. So this was where Gil kept that body so exquisitely toned.

The scent of fresh coffee led her down the stairs and into the reception area. The door marked *Dispatcher* was closed. Someone had taped a sign on it that said *Danger! Explosion Hazard.*

From the sound of it, whoever Gil was talking to now had struck a match.

The phone on the reception desk rang. And rang. And rang. Carma started when Gil yelled, "I swear I am going to beat that thing to death!"

Since there was no one else around to save its life, Carma picked up the receiver. "Um, Sanchez Trucking. Can I help you?"

"Who's this?" the caller demanded. "You don't sound like that weird chick who usually answers the phone."

"I'm new here." Which was the God's honest truth.

"Well, good. Maybe *you'll* actually pass along a message. This is Billy Ray Tolliver. I been trying to make a lunch date with Delon, and I don't seem to have his cell phone number."

Asshole. Her impression was instant and unshakable. If this was a client, he was a constant annoyance. Carma spotted a large dry-erase calendar on the wall that had the dates of Delon's rodeos marked. He was leaving the next day for California.

"I'll let him know you called, but he's out of the office until a week from next Monday," she lied without a twinge.

"Then give me his number so we don't miss each other when he gets home," Billy Ray demanded.

"I'm so sorry," she said, ladling on the sugar. "I don't have permission to share that information. No, not even with friends."

She made vague, sympathetic noises until he realized he couldn't bully her into submission and hung up in a huff. Carma set the receiver down with a satisfied clunk.

Wow. The walls in this place must be made of Popsicle sticks and construction paper. Without Billy Ray's blathering she could hear every word as Gil verbally dismantled someone who was holding his truck hostage, unable to unload because they'd had a holdup in production and were short on warehouse space. If his driver was late to pick up her next load, he declared, they could expect any penalties to be tacked onto their invoice. Sanchez Trucking wasn't footing the bill for their problems.

"Fine," he said, in response to what must have been a threat. "Try to find another company that will deliver on time, every time, so you don't have to shut down for lack of stock." A pause, then a low growl of a laugh. "Sorry. My dad has gone fishing, so there is no one more reasonable for you to talk to. But if you've got any suggestions for how you can make this right, I'm listening."

The argument shifted into a negotiation, with Gil wringing every advantage out of an otherwise negative situation. Damn, he was good. And he was enjoying himself, a born warrior fully engaged in battle. He would be a movie director's dream in nothing but a few feathers, paint, and a loincloth, astride a horse honed to an equally lethal combination of sinew and muscle.

Carma dragged her mind out of the fantasy and into

the present, where the message light on the receptionist's phone blinked. And blinked. She couldn't stand it. Circling the desk, she settled into the chair, located a pad and pen, then pushed the playback button. She could at least do this much to earn her night's stay.

As she worked through the voicemails, she sorted the notes into piles for Gil, Delon, and Merle, who she assumed was their father. She had just scribbled down the last message when Delon walked in and did a double take.

"Good morning," she said. When he blinked in response to her smile, she added, "I'm Carma. The one who swan-dived onto your office floor?"

"Actually, it was more of a belly flop." He hung back as if he feared a repeat performance. "I take it you're feeling better."

"Much. These are your messages." She held out the stack of notes addressed to him.

Delon blinked again, then took the pink slips. While he leafed through them, the phone rang.

Carma picked up. "Sanchez Trucking. Can I help you?"

"Oh! Are you new?"

"Yes. What can I do for you?"

"Well, um..." The woman left a space for Carma to insert her name. She refrained. The caller couldn't find a reason to ask outright who she was and what she was doing there, so finally said, "I need a digital image of the company logo for the ad in the high school rodeo program."

"Not a problem. If you'll give me your email address, someone will get it to you as soon as possible," Carma promised.

She ended the call and looked up to find Delon gazing in awe at one of the slips. "You got rid of Billy Ray?"

"For now. I assume he'll be back."

Delon clutched the scrap of paper to the *Freightliner* logo on his black T-shirt, his smile so brilliant her breath caught. He was even prettier in person, built on a shorter, thicker frame than his brother. "You're hired."

Carma's jaw dropped. "What?"

"Our receptionist left...again. Need a job?"

She laughed. "I appreciate the offer, but I can't—"

"Why not?" Gil cut in.

She whipped around to find him lounging against the filing cabinet beside his door. "I've got, um..."

"What? From what Bing said, it sounds like you can set your own schedule." Like Delon, he wore jeans, running shoes, and a just-snug-enough T-shirt. If this was the company dress code, Carma was all for it. He folded his arms, doing even nicer things for the T-shirt. "Obviously, we need the help. I can make it worth your while."

The gleam in his eye said he wasn't just talking money, but his tone was all business.

She shook her head, fighting the tug of his considerable will. "You don't even know if I can operate a computer."

"But you got rid of Billy Ray," Delon repeated. "And you can't be any worse than the last one."

"Was she the *weird girl*?" Carma asked, echoing Billy Ray.

"No. That's Analise," Gil said. "She's not weird. She's a force."

Carma glanced at the overflowing inbox. "Then why..."

"She's also the only one who's allowed to touch Gil's precious dispatching system," Delon said. "She works the night shift. I'm PR, so I'm in and out when I'm not on the road. Gil generally works all the hours of all the days."

Carma tapped the stack of notes for Merle Sanchez. "What about your dad?"

"He schmoozes the clients after I get done pissing them off," Gil said. "And handles administrative odds and ends. Right now he's at his cabin over by Lake Texhoma."

When they were short-staffed and Delon was due to leave for ten days? The question must've reflected on her face because Gil hitched a shoulder. "He had the trip planned before What's Her Name quit."

"I see." But when did Gil have time to be a parent? "So I would mainly make the damn phone stop ringing and fend off the idiots you claim to attract by the dozens?"

His grin slashed at the reminder of the meme he'd sent…and her response. "You can have your very own Whac-A-Mole hammer."

"I'm missing something here." Delon's eyes narrowed a fraction, looking from one of them to the other. "Will you at least consider the job?"

And let him hit the road with a clear conscience? She could feel the guilt dragging at him. How could he leave Gil scrambling to cover everything while he took off rodeoing? Carma could make it much easier for him.

Which should play in her favor when she met his wife, Tori, who was the driving force behind the Patterson equine therapy program. But sleeping with his brother might not be such a great strategy, which was why Carma had intended to keep her distance from Gil until after she'd established a connection at the clinic.

So much for that plan. She and Gil had crossed too many lines the night before to step back again. If she was going to do this—and helping out for a while seemed like the straightest path to what she needed—they would just have to keep it from getting messy. She leaned back in her chair and waggled a finger between herself and Gil. "What about us?"

"*And* this is where I check out," Delon said.

Carma thrust up a hand to stop him. "No. We need a witness."

Gil's eyebrows slanted in amusement. "To avoid accusations of sexual harassment in the workplace?"

"By you...or me?"

That brought a flare of the now-familiar desire scorching along her nerves. His eyes sparked with challenge. "I'm good at separating business and pleasure."

"Which means...?" she asked.

Their gazes locked with a nearly audible *zap!* His mouth curled. "I will refrain from bending you over my desk...when you're on the clock."

He was being deliberately crude, testing her limits. If she blushed or stammered, he would withdraw one of his offers—and she'd bet it would be the sex. Gil's emotions might be a tough read but his priorities were very clear.

"I'll try not to hump your leg every time I catch you alone," she countered, matching his sarcasm edge for edge.

Delon made a choked sound and retreated a step. "I really think I should—"

"Stay," Carma and Gil commanded simultaneously. She raised her forefinger. "Rule number one: No molesting each other in the office. Number two: What happens outside the office stays outside. No sulking or sniping inside these walls."

"That would be a nice change," Delon drawled.

Gil ignored him. "Agreed."

"I can't commit to anything long term."

One corner of Gil's mouth quirked at how that declaration could be misinterpreted. "All we ask is two weeks' notice. Do we have a deal?"

"Not quite." This job—and this man—could easily consume her, and she couldn't let her mission be derailed. "I can only work four days a week."

Gil's brows slammed together. "Monday and Friday are when I need you the most."

"Pick any weekday. And I'll work ten hours on the others so I'm still putting in my forty."

"Fine," Gil said. "You can have Tuesdays."

She smiled, knowing he expected her to argue that Tuesdays were useless. "Okay."

"Okay." He stepped forward and they shook on it, the brisk clasp generating a hot pulse of lust from the skin-to-skin contact. "Now we have a deal?"

"Now we do."

Then the phone rang, a series of beeps sounded from Gil's office, and Delon's cell chimed. Before they all turned to answer their respective summons, Gil said, "Delon can give you the passwords and a quick intro to the software that runs everything. When Analise gets here at four, she'll start showing you the rest." His mouth pressed into an uncompromising line. "And you will go upstairs and rest if you start feeling puny."

She snapped off a salute that would have done her brother proud. "Yes, boss."

He rolled his eyes and disappeared into his office. Carma reached for the phone, passing the caller off to Delon before settling in to attempt to comprehend the inner workings of Sanchez Trucking.

And the man who appeared to make it all tick.

Chapter 9

At just before eleven, Delon rapped once on Gil's door and settled into the extra chair, meaning this was going to be an actual conversation. Gil muted his computer and tossed his Bluetooth earpiece on the desk.

"I sent Carma upstairs to rest—she was looking a little peaked." Delon folded his arms. "She's an interesting woman."

"I noticed. What's that look for?" Gil snapped, when Delon kept staring at him.

"Your love life has been nothing but a series of right swipes and out-of-town overnighters since they invented dating apps. Now you're planting your latest in our office? I'm trying to figure out what this means."

"That we needed a receptionist, and one dropped right in our laps. Bing told me that Carma works off and on at Indian Health Service. You know what Beth deals with at Tori's office, with all the insurance, juggling schedules, and crap from patients. If Carma can handle that, she can handle us."

Delon considered, then grinned. "Damn. You almost made me wonder if that's all there is to it."

Gil flipped him off.

Delon paid no attention. "I'm also curious. Yesterday you said you'd only met her once—and that got cut short."

"Yeah?"

"So how do you already have inside jokes?"

Gil flushed as if he'd been passing secret notes under his desk to the cute girl in science class.

"It must be karma." He leaned into the sarcasm to cover his reaction, then asked, "Has Beni said anything else about how Quint's getting along at school?"

Delon took a beat to decide whether to let him change the subject, then hitched a shoulder. "Not much. He says the kids are all kinda intimidated. They know Krista's family is a big deal in Oklahoma City, and *you* know how Quint can be."

Gil did. And he didn't. Krista had assured him the boy was what the therapist had labeled naturally reserved, which was not the same as shy. Quint was extremely well spoken when he chose, or the situation required. He was just... *discerning* was the word the shrink had used. Freakishly mature, in Gil's opinion, which was probably also a tad off-putting to the average small-town eighth grader.

Or Quint was learning that being Gil Sanchez's son was not a blessing when it came to making friends in Earnest.

The town owed a lot to Sanchez Trucking. Only the school district had more employees, and drivers boosted the economy by renting or buying homes here. But Little League sponsorships and donations to charitable causes couldn't erase memories, and Gil hadn't had the time or inclination to try to win their hearts or change their minds.

Until now. He sighed moodily. "I just hope they aren't holding my actions against him."

"There aren't near as many people who think you're an actual spawn of the devil these days." Delon laced his fingers over his belt buckle and studied the bridge he made of his thumbs. "Did you warn him about the other rumors?"

"All the money we supposedly rake in smuggling drugs? Yeah, as soon as it got back to me." By way of the oldest Jacobs daughter, Lily, who heard all the dirt thanks to being a local minister's wife.

Delon growled his contempt. "Our trucks never cross the border, and we have zero connections in Mexico."

Definitely not through their dad. The Sanchez name was courtesy of a great-grandfather who'd taken it from his foster parents and died soon after passing it along to a single son, who'd done a disappearing act before little Merle could eat solid food. Merle had left his unhappy childhood home immediately after high school and lost touch with his mother and her kin. Then he'd created two sons who were Native by blood, assumed Latino, and raised in a lily-white town. No confusion there.

Gil picked up a pen and spun it between his fingers. "You haven't heard the latest. Since the cartels are moving into the reservations, the word is we're working with our Navajo relations to pick up shipments there and deliver them all over the country. And of course I have my former dealers."

"Who all had medical licenses. I doubt any of them were peddling heroin out the back door of their offices."

"You didn't meet some of these people." Gil curled his lip, recalling how freely some of those doctors had dispensed narcotics. "They weren't exactly the cream of the health-care crop."

And they were in four different states. Handy, living in the Panhandle where he could pop over to Oklahoma, Colorado, or New Mexico, playing the part of the chronic-pain patient in search of relief—and making it less likely that a pharmacy or medical office would catch the multiple prescriptions.

Even when he was a complete disaster, he'd been too smart for his own good.

Delon made a rude gesture in the general direction of town. "Well, screw 'em if they can't give credit where it's due. Speaking of which...have you looked at that contract from Heartland Foods?"

"Just a glance. I'll dig into it this weekend."

"Great. I'll tell them to expect to hear from you next week." Delon clapped his hands together. "Damn. I can't believe we're gonna land that deal."

"*You* landed it."

Almost single-handedly. When they'd learned that the second-largest grocery supplier in the country was building a new distribution center in Amarillo and would need a dozen reefer trucks dedicated solely to their loads, Delon had used his world-champion clout to wrangle an introduction to the CEO, who was an avid rodeo fan. Then he'd flashed his charm and Sanchez Trucking's stellar track record to beat out dozens of other contenders.

Now it would be up to Gil to make good on all the promises Delon had made. And keep the rest of the fleet rolling. And figure out what was up with his kid.

And somehow find the time to get Carma all to himself.

At lunchtime, Carma sat down at the table in the apartment and took a can of 7UP from her cousin—their family's cure-all for anything that ailed a stomach. Carma was ambivalent about the chicken casserole and mashed potatoes, but fully expected that Bing would also be able to dish up plenty of information.

First, though, Carma had to explain how she'd somehow become a full-time employee of Sanchez Trucking.

"And the next thing I knew, I was saying yes," she said, as she accepted the plate Bing held out to her.

Bing rolled her eyes. "The Sanchez brothers tend to have that effect on women."

"You're telling me." But she'd been hard-pressed not to climb out of bed and plaster her ear to the floor vent when she'd heard the murmur of their voices after Delon had sent her upstairs. She didn't need ESP to know they were talking about her. "They also pay extremely well and offered me free use of this apartment."

Which would be cash she could set aside in case the Patterson ranch wasn't hiring. Their website welcomed volunteers, though, so she could probably hang out there as long as she could afford to be free labor.

She certainly couldn't advertise or monetize her special skills. There was no license for what she did, and even among Natives she wasn't a recognized medicine woman, shaman, or healer—titles bestowed upon those who studied the ancient customs and followed age-old traditions. Carma was just...well, Carma. She had always been odd, but as she'd matured, that oddity had manifested itself in ways she was still learning to accept—and apply.

"What's this mean for you and Gil?" Bing said. "As far as I can tell he doesn't even mix sex with his *life*, let alone his business."

"Well, it's a little late now. We've already seen each other naked."

Bing's elegant brows snapped together. "Since when?"

"Last night." Carma held up a hand when Bing's jaw dropped. "He wouldn't let me take a shower alone in case I keeled over again."

"So the two of you just..." Bing spread her hands in disbelief.

"Showered. Then he fed me Jell-O and tucked me into

bed." Carma sorted out a carrot, pushing it to the side of her plate. "And he dried my hair."

Bing stared at her. "Gil Sanchez. The man who—if I heard correctly through that vent—just told one of his drivers he didn't give a shit if he froze his dick off, he'd better get his ass out there and chain up his effing truck before he left Rapid City."

"That's the one."

"Huh. Well…I guess Gil does look after other people"—Bing winced at another volley of profanities—"in his own way. He practically raised himself and his brother. Merle was a very hands-off kind of parent."

"Still is if he's gone fishing when they're up to their necks and shorthanded."

Bing shrugged. "He turned sixty-five last month. Analise says he's been in the process of retiring for the last few years."

That would explain why Gil had only seemed mildly annoyed by his dad's absence. "What about their mother?"

"Rochelle. She's Navajo, from out in the back country south of Shiprock. Her dad had a major stroke and her mother couldn't take care of him alone. Gil was in the first grade, and if she'd taken the boys with her, they would have had to go to boarding school."

Both of them grimaced. The modern versions were a major improvement on the original, grim institutions designed to indoctrinate the students into white culture—by force if necessary. But they were still institutions, not homes.

"And Merle and Rochelle are still technically married." Bing pointed her fork for emphasis. "They were hitched by the justice of the peace here, but also had a traditional Navajo ceremony, and she only divorced him in tribal court."

"I never get why people do that." Carma sent another carrot off into no-man's-land. "I would want to be totally finished, no strings."

Bing shrugged. "Even do-it-yourself divorces cost money. And as long as neither of you wants to remarry..."

Or reconcile, which was apparently the case with Gil's parents. "Who took care of the boys while Merle was busy trucking?"

"Mostly Iris and Steve Jacobs. You know, Jacobs Livestock, the rodeo stock contractor? That's where Gil and Delon learned to ride bucking horses. Melanie and Hank pretty much lived there, too." Bing made a face at the mention of her newly acquired if as yet unofficial stepson and daughter. "Not something Johnny is real proud of, pawning his kids off on the neighbors, but he was trying to run a ranch single-handed, and that wife of his was more harm than help."

"With the ranch or the kids?"

"Both."

So the legendary Miz Iris had gathered them all under her wing...shades of Grandma White Elk. "No wonder you fit in here. They make up family out of strays and almost-relatives just like on the rez."

"Yep. They also raised Steve's nephew, Cole, from when he was sixteen." Sadness dug grooves around Bing's mouth. "His parents and brother were killed in a car accident."

God. A whole family destroyed in the blink of an eye... and Carma included the living among the casualties. No one truly survived that sort of loss. They would never be the person they'd been before.

Carma took a few more bites, then paused to let them

settle. "You know, my first roommate at college was Navajo, and she lived with relatives in Albuquerque almost all the way through school. She called them her foster parents. None of Rochelle's family would've thought twice about her leaving Gil and Delon here with their dad."

"Plus Rochelle's a full-blood from a very traditional clan. Her father was one of those who believed mixed marriage is the equivalent of genocide by degrees."

Carma winced, but had to say, "It's a valid issue."

Smaller tribes like the Blackfeet had had to choose between inbreeding and diluting their genetic identity. With an estimated three hundred thousand descendants, the Navajo—or more correctly, Diné—had more options.

"It's valid in theory, *if* you're hung up on blood quantum as a measure of Nativeness—and worth." Bing stabbed at a chunk of chicken. "For two little boys whose grandfather treated them like a disease their mother brought home? It's no wonder they didn't embrace their Native roots."

Duty. Motherhood. Harsh reality. The poor woman must've felt like she was being torn into tiny pieces. "Speaking of kids, Gil's son witnessed my grand entrance."

Bing grinned. "Ah. Quint. The boy Yoda."

"Huh?"

"A thousand-year-old soul in the body of a Disney heartthrob. Did he even blink?"

"I dunno. I was facedown in a trash can. But he asked if Gil had knocked me up."

Bing spewed 7UP down the front of her blouse.

"Gil said it was Quint's idea of a joke," Carma added.

"Oh God." Bing thumped herself on the chest, clearing the soda out of her pipes. "That is classic. The kid might not say a word for two hours, then he'll drop a zinger like that."

"His father was not amused."

"I don't imagine." Bing grabbed a napkin to mop up. "From what I understand, Gil and Krista have never pulled any punches with Quint. He knows they were only together for about eight months before she got pregnant, why they didn't get married, and all about Gil's addiction."

"How long has he been clean?"

"Since Quint was about a year old. He's never seen his dad wasted, but I assume he's heard a lot of cautionary tales from his mom's side." Bing mimicked a snooty, Southern tone. "You know how those Natives are with booze, and you've got his genes..."

Also a valid concern, and just as hard to stomach.

Bing gave a fatalistic shrug. It was what it was. "If anything fazes that kid, you'd never know." Then she laughed. "Well, *you* might. It'll be interesting to see how you read him."

Carma wished it was that simple, like X-ray vision she could turn on when she wanted. Or better, *off*. What would it be like to stand in a crowded room and feel only her own feelings?

Most people were just background noise, barely registering unless they were experiencing something strong. Fear, anger, pain, and all their permutations—the negative stuff was the easiest to pick up. Carma could barely set foot in a nursing home, where the air was thick with the anxiety and confusion of residents suffering from dementia.

She also enjoyed secondhand bursts of joy, pride, love and its more earthy cousin, lust, but they were always fleeting. What was it about humans that made happiness so hard to hold onto, while guilt and shame clung like tar?

Modern psychology had an explanation for her gift: extreme empathy resulting in subconscious recognition of nonverbal cues and patterns of behavior. Most of the time she could work backward and identify the clues that had led to her conclusion. Not magic. Just logic. Well, except for how she'd been able to sense Gil's secrets, but that was the extreme part of the empathy...wasn't it?

If all the psychologists in the world couldn't agree, Carma wasn't likely to figure it out. Most people preferred to slap her with their own labels anyway. She was a Chosen One. She was delusional. The spirits spoke to her. It was some stunt she did to get attention.

More creative profanity wafted up from Gil's office. Bing gave the floor vent a doubtful look. "Are you sure you can handle that all day long? You had to quit working in the resource room at the elementary school because of the ambient stress."

"Teachers are under a crapload of pressure. Besides, *that*"—she pointed down—"is recreational rage. Sort of like watching professional wrestling."

"All for show?"

"In a way. Gil runs naturally hot, but he can dial it back when he wants. Underneath, he's all about control." She sculpted a mountain of her mashed potatoes, then decapitated it. "Maybe I could learn from him."

Bing reached across and squeezed her hand. "Sweetie...I know you've been struggling, but I don't think Gil is the best example of healthy coping skills."

"Hey, at least I won't try to run his life. Can you imagine how he'd react if I started laying my *you should* lines on him?" Carma asked bitterly, echoing Jayden's favorite complaint, although he was generally fine with blaming her when things didn't go well. "Gil would crawl from here to Montana before he'd lean on anyone. He's just looking for good sex and someone to answer his phone."

Bing frowned. "You deserve a lot more than that."

Did she? She'd contributed a lot of the dysfunction to her relationship with Jayden by being his crutch, and taking too much of the responsibility. And to be brutally honest, at least some of the time they'd been together because neither of them had found anything better.

And still Carma had been caught completely off guard when he'd dumped her for the blond. Stupid, fickle, so-called gift. Why didn't it ever warn her about her own damn love life?

"It is so unfair. The instant I laid eyes on Johnny, I knew it was forever with him and you. Why can't I tell how a man really feels about *me*?"

Bing sighed. "Maybe the Creator figures it's something even you have to take on faith."

"Well, I'm fresh out." Carma forced down one last bite before pushing her plate away. "I'd rather have someone who'll tell it to me straight, no games, no promises."

Bing sighed again. "Then Gil Sanchez is definitely your man."

No, he wasn't. And as long as Carma didn't pretend he ever could be, she could enjoy him, and learn from him, and hopefully leave Earnest, Texas, smarter than she'd arrived.

And wasn't self-improvement most of the reason she was here?

Chapter 10

When Carma walked back into the office, a petite version of Lucille Ball was planted on the desk with her legs and arms wrapped around what could be another Sanchez brother.

Carma waited a full minute before she cleared her throat.

The guy broke the kiss to look at her. Nope, not a Sanchez, but vaguely familiar. The woman gave her a bright, scarlet smile without loosening her grip on him. "Oh hey! Carma, right?"

"Uh, yes."

"I'm Analise." She dropped her legs and twitched the skirt of her fifties-style day dress over her knees before grabbing a tissue from a box on the desk to dab a smear of lipstick from her lover's cheek. "Cruz is leaving for the California rodeos. I had to give him a suitable send-off."

Cruz? Carma took a better look. Yeah, that was him. Marcelino Miguel Ruiz de la Cruz, bullfighter extraordinaire, able to materialize in the exact right spot to save a cowboy from getting stomped by a ton of pissed-off bovine.

"I gotta go." He kissed Analise's brilliant red hair and gave Carma a bashful smile. "It was nice to meet you."

As he left, he held the door for an older man in grease-stained coveralls. "Hey, Max," Analise said. "Have you met Carma?"

"Not yet." He offered a weathered hand and a warm,

creased smile. "I'm the shop foreman. And you are the person who owns that van parked outside."

"Guilty," Carma admitted.

His smile widened. "You decide you want to get rid of it, let me know. I had one just like it when I was in my twenties. Some good memories in that van."

"I'll bet," Analise drawled. Her kitten heels clicked on the tile floor as she hopped off the desk to pluck the papers from his hand. "Come and sit down, Carma. I'll show you how to enter work orders and update the maintenance logs."

Max excused himself with a promise to see Carma in the morning. She took the desk chair while Analise leaned in, smelling of Estee Lauder Youth Dew and fresh-starched cotton.

"This is command central." Analise tapped a truck-shaped icon on the screen. "The GPS units in the trucks, electronic bills of lading, mandatory DOT reports, drivers' logs, payroll, accounting—everything feeds into this program."

She provided a running commentary as she flashed through screens and entered the information from Max's work orders into the mandatory maintenance records for each truck, and was showing Carma where to file the originals when Gil's door opened.

"Can I come out now, or are you still molesting Cruz?" he asked.

"He's gone, Grandpa."

The door opened wider, and Gil rolled into view in the black-leather Satan's throne version of a desk chair. "I suppose Carma got treated to the full show."

"Oh, please." Analise rolled her eyes. "She barely even blushed."

Gil tipped back and stretched out his legs. "Hard to top the entrance she made yesterday."

"I'm glad you all got a chuckle out of that," Carma said dryly.

Analise blanched, and a beat later Carma felt a ripple of nausea. But she swallowed and it was gone.

Not hers, she realized. "Whew! I thought I was gonna puke again for a second. What did I say? Was it ch—"

"Don't!" Analise plastered her hands over her ears.

Carma looked at Gil for a clue.

"Synesthesia," he said. "She tastes colors, hears numbers, and certain words literally make her sick."

Analise dropped her hands and gaped. "Wait. You *felt* that?"

"Um...yes?" Hell. How could she explain...

"Oh. My. God." Analise breathed it like a prayer. "You're an INFJ."

"A what?" Gil demanded.

"You know, Myers-Briggs?" When Gil remained blank, Analise huffed impatiently. "Seriously? You run a business, and you've never heard of personality typing?"

"I work with my father, my brother, and a shop foreman who's been here since I was six years old. What's the point?"

"Maybe you could keep a receptionist long enough for their butt to warm up the chair?" Analise sketched an oval around Carma, as if outlining her aura. "This is the magic unicorn of personality types. Introverted, intuitive, feeling, and judging. The super-empath."

Carma relaxed. *Bless you, Analise.* Here was an explanation Gil could accept. "How did you know?"

"My grandmother was INFJ. We're all special in my family." She bobbed a *thank you very much* curtsy, then shifted her attention to Gil. "It's like how dogs can hear sounds we can't. INFJs pick up mega-subtle nonverbal cues, and since humans are so predictable, sometimes seem to be able to tell the future."

Gil's mouth crooked in satisfaction. "So that's how you did it."

"Pretty much." Carma shut the filing cabinet drawer and returned to her desk. "Now that we've established my brand of freakishness, can we get back to work?"

One mocking eyebrow rose. "I dunno. How much of my business can you poke around in without my permission?"

"Don't be a dick," Analise said.

He grinned, quick and sharp. "But that's *my* superpower."

"As we all know." Analise mirrored his narrow-eyed scrutiny. "You're already plotting ways to use her."

"*Use* me?" Carma echoed, startled. "How?"

"The same way I use everyone—to my best advantage," he said, without a hint of apology.

She waved at the computer and phone. "We agreed that this is all you get from me."

"Not quite all." His smile went wolfish as his gaze tracked down her body, and Carma flushed.

"Whoa. Heat wave." Analise fanned herself.

"Get used to it," Gil said, then frowned, his gaze caught by something outside the front office window.

It was Quint, swinging a leg over his bike and pushing it toward the open truck bay, a backpack slung over what were framed to be impressive shoulders. Dang. Bing wasn't kidding when she said teen heartthrob. The boy could've stepped off any screen, large or small. They all waited as they heard him call out a greeting to Max, then push open the door from the shop. When he saw Carma seated at the desk, he didn't falter, only stopped to study her with a slight, curious pucker between his brows.

Then he smiled, a weapon of mass female destruction. "Hi, Analise. Love the pearls."

"Thank you!" Analise twined them around scarlet-tipped fingers. "It's the little things that really make a look come together."

"Well, you nailed it." He muted the smile to well mannered with a touch of remorse. "Hello, Miss White Elk. I'm Quint. I'm very sorry for being disrespectful to you yesterday."

She held his gaze for a few beats, searching for an undertone of sarcasm, but found none. "Thank you. And you can call me Carma."

He nodded in acknowledgment, his dark eyes level and measuring as they took in her computer screen, then the legal pad at her elbow, covered with notes. "Are you helping Analise catch up?"

"She's the new receptionist," Gil said. "For as long as she can stay."

Again, Quint showed no sign of surprise or disapproval. If Gil was a pile of glowing embers, prone to bursting into flames at the slightest breeze, his son was a cool, old-growth forest, undisturbed by anything short of a gale. Carma glanced at Gil and caught an identical pleat between his brows, only deeper. To him, Quint's nonreaction must seem unnatural—possibly unhealthy—but if the boy was repressing anything, it was buried so deep Carma couldn't get a whiff.

"Welcome to Sanchez Trucking." Quint stepped forward and extended a hand. "I hope you'll enjoy working here."

"I...um...thanks." Carma accepted the handshake—brisk, professional, his grip exactly the right amount of firm. He could have been wearing a three-piece suit instead of running shorts and an Oklahoma Sooners T-shirt. Dang. That took some guts when he'd only just moved onto rival turf in rabid football country. Either Quint Sanchez really didn't care about fitting in, or...

He saw her eyeing the logo and one corner of his mouth quirked, ever so slightly. It was all Carma could do not to laugh. Oh, yeah. This was Gil's son. He hadn't worn that shirt by accident, and he'd enjoyed every second of aggravation it had caused.

He turned to his dad. "Coach wants to know if you're still gonna help out at the track meet tomorrow."

"You're not eligible to compete," Gil said, frowning.

"I still have to show up and make myself useful, and they're expecting you, too."

Gil made a visible attempt to stifle a curse, then sighed. "What time do I have to be there?"

"Three o'clock. You're running the high jump."

"And of course I will be happy to come in early and cover for you," Analise chirped.

Gil's hands clenched on his armrests. "Fine."

"Awesome. It was a pleasure to meet you again, Carma." And even though there wasn't a hint of mockery to be heard or seen, Carma could feel him laughing on the inside as he left.

"Nice kid," she said.

"Yeah." Gil turned dark, turbulent eyes on Carma. "If you can tell me what's going on inside that head, I'll double your wages."

Uh-uh. She had sworn off jumping into the middle

of other people's problems. When she only shrugged, he grunted and gave his chair a shove, disappearing back into his lair.

"Good call," Analise said. Then she leaned in and whispered, "But if you want to tell me what either one of them really thinks, I am *dying* to know."

Chapter 11

At ten minutes to four on Thursday afternoon, the loudspeaker at the Earnest High School athletic field squawked to life, ordering athletes to report for the boys' high jump, girls' long jump, boys' discus, and girls' shot put.

Individual bodies emerged from the herds jogging, stretching, roughhousing, and lounging across the infield, and Gil was immediately surrounded by a mob of boys. Nearby, a posse of Earnest athletes settled onto the grass to cheer their teammates on.

One girl flashed a nervous smile in Quint's direction. "Hey, Quint."

"Hey, Kenzie." He didn't smile or make eye contact, just stood with his arms folded, looking more official than any of the coaches. None of the other kids attempted to make conversation. Was this how Quint always acted? Was he upset about being ineligible? Embarrassed by Gil's presence? Maybe he was wondering why he'd ever wanted to live here.

Or he could be plotting to overthrow the government of some small, unstable Eastern European country. Damned if Gil would know either way. He put his fingers to his mouth for an earsplitting whistle.

"Listen up!" He held the clipboard with one hand while flattening the sheets ruffled by the stiff breeze, reading off the instructions he'd been given, finishing with, "Don't forget to check out if you have to leave for a running event. You have five minutes to get back here after you're done or you'll be scratched. Now here's the order."

He barked out the names. Halfway down, he came to Sam Carruthers. So this was Quint's newfound rival. The kid who flicked a hand in response had hair so blond it was nearly white and not an ounce of fat to hide the wiry muscle in his legs. He didn't glance at Quint, who was posted on the other side of the huge foam landing pad, not glancing at anyone.

Gil finished roll call, grabbed one end of the bar, and signaled to Quint to hoist the other onto the stanchion. "Let's get this show on the road."

When the winners of both the boys' and girls' high jump were finally, blessedly declared, Gil walked a gauntlet of angry mutters and hostile glares to turn in his clipboard to the woman at the scorer's hut.

She blinked in surprise. "Wow. That may be the first time in history the high jumpers were the first field event to finish."

"I like to keep things moving."

"So I've heard." At Gil's flat stare, she stuttered, "I mean, isn't that what a trucking company does?"

"I guess so."

She fiddled with the top paper on the clipboard. "The Childress coach wasn't very happy about having his best jumper scratched."

"I was just following the rules. They said five minutes."

"Ah…well…most of our volunteers don't really keep track of that."

"I did." And Gil was not used to giving a flying shit who he annoyed—but until now he'd never had to worry about stirring up trouble for his son.

"I suppose they do have to learn." She offered a tentative smile. "You don't remember me. Sharla Turner? I was three grades ahead of you."

The name was familiar, but Gil drew a blank on the face. He recognized her as a townie, though, which explained why she'd made no impression on him. He'd preferred the girls he met at junior and high school rodeos, from towns far enough away that he didn't have to play boyfriend during the week. When he'd hit the pro rodeo circuit, he'd discovered an infinite supply of women ready to party all night long in a different town every weekend, and he'd gone hog wild...until he'd met Krista.

He'd fallen in love the way he'd done everything else—too fast and too hard. She'd been right there with him, one crazy high to the next, until she'd announced she was pregnant and the party came crashing to a halt—and his motorcycle with it.

In the months that followed his wreck he'd removed himself from his family, his friends, and as much of reality as the pills and booze could erase, but now that Quint was here, he'd have to make more of an effort to be part of the community. He still wouldn't have anything to do with women like Sharla Turner, though, who would forever be underfoot in a town this small.

And yet, there was Carma, making herself indispensable on only her second day in his office, and that seemed to suit him just fine.

Sharla's smile was wilting, so he said, "Glad I could help. If you're done with us, I'll grab Quint and get back to work."

"I hear he's some kind of athlete." She gave the smile one more boost. "Must take after his daddy."

God help him if he did. Gil settled for a nod and made his getaway.

He was leaning against the hood of the Charger when Quint and Beni strolled out to the parking lot, a dark smudge in the crowd of otherwise pale-skinned parents, kids, and coaches swarming from the stadium. At twelve, Beni was the same height as Quint, with a heaviness to his bones that suggested he might grow up to be as big as Steve and Cole Jacobs, both well over six feet and built like Mack trucks. Even his mother, Violet, could look Gil square in the eye and possibly take him in a wrestling match.

Beni said something, Quint gave him a shove, and Beni shoved back, grinning. Gil had to tighten his arms over a sudden ache in his chest. Roll back the clock a couple of decades and that could've been him and Delon. Where there was one Sanchez brother, you were damn near guaranteed to find the other, with Delon usually trailing along begging Gil to ease up. Don't spur so wild. Don't drive so fast. Don't tear through life like it was a race to see who could get to the end first.

And most of all, don't ever slow down enough to feel anything but the rush.

He shook off that cheerful thought as Beni flashed him a cheeky grin. "Hey, Uncle Gil. Looked like you were having a great time out there." Beni held up a smartphone. "I got videos in case Sam's dad actually took a swing at you when you scratched him in the high jumping."

"I'd already DQ'd the Childress kid for being late. I couldn't play favorites." Even knowing it would pile fuel on the fire. Quint hadn't blinked, smiled, nothing, even when some of his teammates shouted *boo.*

"Coach is furious," Quint said, seemingly more

perturbed by the mosquito he swatted off his arm than his coach's anger.

"I noticed." Gil couldn't help adding, "They never let that stuff slide at your meets in Oklahoma."

Beni rolled his eyes. "Those people acted like they were training a bunch of future Olympians."

"They were," Quint said. And his prep school had a wall of fame to prove it.

"Sam's usually not a jerk." Beni frowned at Quint. "It would help if you didn't stand there looking all superior and bored. They think you're judging them."

"I am." Gil and Beni stared at him, sure it must be one of his oddball jokes, but he just shrugged. "In a town this small, you're stuck with the same people forever. I want to find friends like Dad's, or Hank's buddy Korby, that I'll still want to hang out with when I'm old."

Jesus. Christ. What eighth grader thought that way? And then…

Wait a minute. Quint planned on staying in Earnest until he was as ancient as his dad? Gil wasn't sure whether to be thrilled or insulted.

"*Hank* isn't old," Beni said.

Okay. Insulted for the win. Gil glanced around but didn't see Violet's black Cadillac. Oh right. She was in Atlanta this week. Jacobs Livestock had decided to take on the pro bull-riding tour, so she and Joe and the best of their herd had been crisscrossing the country from New York City to Sacramento since January.

"You need a ride?" he asked Beni.

"Nah. I'm Tori's problem until Grandpa and Grandma get home from their vacation."

A trip to Brazil, where Iris was giddy over the tropical

foliage and Steve was making the Jacobs breeding program known to the contractors who provided stock for the country's growing rodeo craze. Beni had been lobbying to enroll in an online program so he could travel, too, but Delon and Violet insisted there was more to school than the classwork, which occasionally left Beni to bond with his stepmother for a few days.

"There she is," Beni said.

A silver SUV turned into the lot and rolled to a stop beside them. The window slid down and Delon's wife gave them all a nod of greeting, still wearing her *Panhandle Orthopedics and Sports Medicine* polo shirt. She pushed her sunglasses into her caramel-brown hair and studied Gil with cool gray eyes.

"I hear you have a new receptionist," she said, cutting straight to the point as usual.

"Temporarily." Something he seemed to stress every time the subject came up. Maybe that's why he wasn't freaking out about Carma's invasion of his little kingdom.

"Hank and Beni and I are gonna rope a few steers tonight, so I got burgers to grill," Tori said.

"Is Grace working?" As an athletic trainer at Bluegrass High School, Hank's girlfriend spent most of her evenings either at practices or sporting events.

Tori nodded. "Her junior varsity had a track meet in Canyon. Come to supper...and bring Carma."

It was not a request.

"If she's feeling up to socializing," Gil hedged.

"I don't think Carma's gonna want to even smell a burger for a while," Quint said.

"I'll grab something else on the way home," Tori said. "See you in about an hour?"

As if saying no was an option when she used that honey-dipped steel voice.

"I'm gonna go with them," Quint said, and climbed in Tori's car without waiting for a response.

Gil stayed put, watching Tori drive away.

God, he wanted a beer. The craving came out of nowhere, and instantly he could taste the cold, yeasty tingle across his tongue, feel it hitting his bloodstream in a river of golden bubbles. If he swung by the Kwicky Mart on the way home and grabbed a six-pack…

Christ. In the space of two thoughts he'd gone from a single drink to half a dozen. Even in his imagination, one was never enough. He slammed into the driver's seat and gunned the Charger out of the nearly empty lot, spitting gravel and turning heads.

One more parental fail to add to his growing list.

Carma watched Gil turn into the Sanchez Trucking gates from where she was lounging on the outside landing of the apartment, using cushions from the couch as a makeshift chaise. After a day of staring at software training videos and trying to memorize unfamiliar acronyms—BOL, IFTA, ELD—even the wind felt wonderful.

The Charger glided to a stop below her and Gil stepped out, instantly disrupting the atmosphere. Frustration. Worry. Desire. His raw emotions washed over her like scalding water before he reined them in.

"How are you feeling?" he asked.

Bombarded. And still, as always, turned on. She suspected she could get hot for this man in the middle of a blizzard. But what she said was, "Stranded. Turns out replacing a Montana driver's license when you're stuck in Texas is no small feat. By the time my mom gathers up all the stuff they want, it might be quicker to fly home and do it myself—if I could get on a plane without a photo ID."

"Are you in a big rush to get out of here?"

Was that a hint of a sulk, as if she'd offended him? She tossed her hair, smirking down at him. "I'm not that easy to get rid of."

"Most of my receptionists don't need much encouragement." But he was slightly more relaxed as he propped an elbow on the open car door, looking like every girl's bad-boy dream and dialing up Carma's internal thermostat another few degrees. "Did you get a new phone yet?"

"I called the place in Dumas, but I want the same model as my old one, which is not the latest, greatest, and most expensive, which is all they have in stock. I have to wait for them to order it." Almost the whole truth. The phone would actually be in tomorrow. She wasn't confessing that the only guy who knew how to retrieve her old texts wouldn't be back from vacation until next week. She tilted her head to verify that the car was unoccupied. "Did you forget someone at the track meet?"

More important, did this mean they had the rest of the evening to themselves?

"Quint went home with Beni. And unless you have an extremely good excuse to say no, the Princess has requested your presence."

His dry tone put a damper on her lustful thoughts. "The...who?"

"Delon's wife. I'm supposed to bring you to supper."

Carma glanced down at her scruffy jeans and sweatshirt

with a picture of the mountains and a *Get High in Babb, Montana* tagline. Not the outfit she would have chosen for her first encounter with Texas royalty.

And not an easy person to impress, by all accounts.

“Tori doesn’t give a shit what you’re wearing,” Gil said. “She just wants to get a look at the only woman who’s ever dared to follow me home.”

Carma’s face stung, but instead of flinching she gave him a hard stare. “Flying the asshole flag pretty high today.”

“Believe me, about two hundred people made that perfectly clear.” He pinched the bridge of his nose, a gesture she already knew meant he had a headache. “Consider it part of your job description to tell me so anytime you feel the need.”

“Count on it.”

He gave her a twisted smile that did foolish things to her pulse. “I could learn to count on you for a lot of things, Carmelita, but I don’t think that would end well for either one of us.”

And she should thank the stars that Gil knew it as well as she did.

“They’re gonna be roping after supper,” he said. “You’re dressed fine for hanging out in the arena. If you want to come.”

She was hardly going to turn down an opportunity to meet Tori. Plus there would be horses, ropes, and dirt. Where was the downside?

“Give me ten minutes,” she said.

“Whatever you need. I’ll be at the house when you’re ready.”

“The house?”

He gestured toward the back of the trucking yard. “Right back there.”

She got up, walked to the edge of the landing, and leaned out as far as she dared. It took a few seconds to register what she was seeing. Holy shit. That was Gil's house? Carma had to blink twice. Tucked against the back fence of the Sanchez Trucking lot, hidden from sight by the shop, it looked like a movie set, labeled on the script as *Respectable Suburban Home*. The fence was actual white pickets, the paint powder-blue with crisp white trim, the lawn neatly clipped, with shade trees, and a basketball hoop above the two-car garage. There were even flowers spilling out of pots that lined the steps.

Carma sensed that he was waiting for her reaction and, perversely, chose not to give him one. "So this is why you can't help wandering over to the office at all hours."

"It's not like I'd be sleeping anyway."

"Are you naturally an insomniac?"

"I've always been a night owl. After my wreck..." He shrugged. "There isn't a whole lot of difference between night and day when all you do is sleep, eat, and stare at screens. That's when my internal clock got really screwed up."

"And you can't take anything for it."

His head jerked in affirmation. "None of the good stuff. Melatonin doesn't do anything for me. Same for relaxation exercises, deep breathing, all that crap. So I figure as long as I'm awake..."

He could turn those empty hours and untapped energy into the force that drove Sanchez Trucking. All the competitive drive that had made him a champion. There was something intrinsically cowboy about the way he cocked his hip and squinted up at her. He must've been incredibly hot in chaps, pearl-snap shirt, and a cowboy hat.

She couldn't say for sure, since his career had ended before rodeo embraced the Internet. The search she'd done had turned up nothing but a mention of his Rookie of the Year title. All the action shots on the office walls were of Delon—by Gil's choice, she assumed. She had a vision of a pile of broken frames, shattered glass, and glossy paper, going up in flames. Truth, or the echo of a powerful impulse on his part?

She was tempted to ask, but that would kill the buzz that made every inch of her skin feel exquisitely oversensitized. It was a rare treat, this level of attraction, and made her want to stretch out the anticipation, savor these moments when her body quivered for his touch.

"I don't suppose I'm invited in for a quickie?" she asked.

His gaze practically smoked when it traveled over her. "There is nothing quick about what I want to do when I finally get my hands on you."

Everything inside her contracted, then released in a slow, hot *whoosh*. She let out an audible breath. "Well, let's not rush into it, then. You only get one first time, you know."

And this delicious torture would end when she actually touched and tasted. The desire might still be powerful, but it would never be quite the same again.

His eyes mirrored everything she was thinking. "It'll be worth the wait."

That was a promise…and Gil Sanchez was more than capable of making it come true.

Chapter 12

Supper at Tori's was everything Gil had imagined—and worse.

When he and Carma arrived, the boys had already grabbed their burgers and gone to watch the Astros-Dodgers game in Beni's room, since you could spit on the TV from the dining table shoved into one corner of Tori's cramped living room. The primary selling points for the property had been the indoor arena and a relatively easy commute into Amarillo. Other than a few pieces of original art and the most treasured of Delon's trophies, there was nothing impressive about their house.

It was definitely not designed for *entertaining*, as those house-hunting shows liked to say.

But Tori was a pro, playing the consummate hostess while conducting a ruthless interrogation. What the hell? She normally saved that routine for her father's unfortunate dates. Tonight she'd served up grilled snapper with a side of endless questions about Carma's family, their ranch, life in Montana, the trick roping, her work in the movies, and other jobs she'd held.

Gil kept waiting for Carma to shut her down—a skill she practiced regularly in the office when callers were too persistent, bless her unflappable heart. He'd forgotten what it was like to have the annoying, irrelevant, and just plain crazy screened out of his calls.

But now Carma was acting weird, smiling a little too

much and being careful with her answers. Was she trying to impress his sister-in-law for his benefit?

Tori swirled a carrot stick in ranch dressing. "It sounds like you've led a very interesting life."

"I've been lucky enough to have some unique opportunities," Carma agreed.

"You must enjoy new challenges."

A barely polite way of saying that Carma didn't seem to stick with anything for very long—which shouldn't annoy Gil so much when he'd asked Bing the same question only a day earlier.

"Yes." Carma pushed aside her plate, and Gil had the distinct impression that they'd come to the reason she'd tolerated Tori's inquisition. "The latest is something that might interest you."

Tori's carrot stick paused midcircle. "What's that?"

"We're starting an equine-assisted therapy program back home." Her mouth curled into a wry smile. "On a much smaller scale than yours, of course."

"There's a lot more to it than sticking someone in the saddle," Tori said.

If Carma took offense to her bluntness, it didn't show. "So I'm learning. I've visited half a dozen facilities in the last few weeks to observe the different methods."

Wait. This was what Bing had meant by an expedition?

Tori cocked her head, cautiously intrigued. "In your climate, an indoor facility will be a must."

Carma nodded. "David Parsons has offered us the use of the arena he's building a few miles west of Browning."

"The tie-down roper?" Gil asked. Even he'd been caught up in the drama at the National Finals two years back, when David came up just short of winning the world championship even though he'd arrived in Vegas well behind the season leaders. Gil vaguely recalled the announcers going on about David losing his good horse—missing, not injured—getting it back halfway through the season, then going on a tear.

"We've met." Understanding flashed in Tori's eyes. "His stepson has fetal alcohol syndrome."

Carma nodded. "That's Kylan. And David's wife, Mary, is in special education. They're part of our core planning group and will continue to be involved once we're up and running."

Tori dropped the carrot stick, all business. "Are you planning to provide any therapies other than riding?"

Carma's gaze veered away. "We're still working that out."

Gil caught Tori's frown. He gave a slight shrug. Why would that, of all the things Tori had asked, be a sensitive subject?

"I assume you'd like to visit our clinic, too," Tori said.

"If it's not a problem."

For an instant, suspicion reared its ugly head. Was this what she'd wanted from Gil all along? But no. Getting tangled up with him was a hindrance, not a help. Tori wouldn't be so suspicious if Carma was just Bing's cousin.

"We are more than happy to share our expertise and shamelessly promote our mission," Tori said. "Just call the clinic. They'll set up a day and time when there's someone available to show you around."

"Thanks. I'll do that," Carma said.

But there was still an odd tension in the air, as if Tori still had questions, and Carma hadn't gotten quite the answers she wanted, either.

Two hard raps sounded on the front door and Hank sauntered in, somehow looking like his perpetually boyish self but also infinitely more hardened than when he'd left the Panhandle. He gave Carma a guarded smile. "Hey. Nice to see you again. I was sorry to hear about your grandmother."

"Thanks. We miss her." Her smile was a little misty. "Your dad made a very good impression when they were home for the funeral."

Hank snorted in disbelief. "With his outstanding people skills?"

Carma laughed. "This is my family. If you never get tired of talking about horses, you're in."

"In that case, they probably want to adopt him."

Tori waved at the leftovers. "Did you eat yet?"

"Yeah, but I can clean up that potato salad for you." Hank could always use the calories, with his tendency toward skinny.

Gil pushed away from the table and told Tori, "You and the boys go saddle up while Hank licks the plates. I'll stick 'em in the dishwasher when he's done."

"I'll help," Carma chimed in.

Tori stood. "Thanks. We'll meet you at the arena."

She yelled for the boys, and when the door shut behind them, Carma let her breath out in a quiet *whoosh*. "I feel like the Secret Service will be running a background check on me before we get out of the driveway."

Hank swallowed a gigantic forkful of potato salad. "She did that an hour after Delon told her they hired you."

"Are you kidding me?" Carma shot a worried look at Gil, almost as if she had something to hide. Did she think Tori would disapprove of the naked movie roles?

Gil stacked plates and carried them over to the dishwasher. "She's just being weird because it's the first time she's gotten a look at anyone I've dated."

Her brows rose into intrigued arches. "We're dating?"

"Do you have a better word?" He sure as hell didn't, and he'd been searching high and low for a tactful way to explain their *arrangement* to Quint. The English language was sadly lacking in alternative labels for how two consenting adults could interact.

She pressed a finger to her bottom lip. "Well, you did bring me to dinner, so I guess that qualifies."

"Dinner with the family, no less. That'll really set the tongues to wagging." Hank flashed his patented troublemaker's grin, but his eyes were shrewd. "It's like he's not even the Gil we all know and tolerate."

Gil bared his teeth.

Hank laughed, then made an apologetic face at Carma. "You'd best prepare yourself. You're already the hottest gossip in town."

"You know where I come from. I'm used to it."

And Gil had seen and heard for himself how little she'd enjoyed the unwelcome attention. Having the entire population of Earnest discussing their every move wasn't gonna encourage her to stick around. Not that he expected her to stay forever. Or even long enough for anyone to start thinking they might be more than a spring fling.

Gil slapped the last dinner roll into Hank's hand and gave him a shove. "Go play outside, Junior."

Hank set the empty potato-salad bowl on the counter, grabbed a Dr Pepper out of the fridge, and did as he was told.

"He sure has lightened up since I saw him last," Carma said.

"Yeah." Gil scowled. "It's annoying as hell. He used to be scared of me."

She smiled, eyes soft and warm as the rest of her. When she touched her fingertips to his chest, his system jolted as if she'd pressed the live end of a set of jumper cables to his skin. "It's hard to be terrifying once you've let someone see your heart."

Which was why he didn't go around baring his soul. He wasn't sure he liked the idea of Carma being able to look right through him, but it was a little easier to accept since Analise had explained away the mystique.

She pressed her palm to his chest, the way she'd done that very first night, and Gil wondered if she could feel more than just the thud of his heart. Could she really see inside him, to all the ugliness and scars that didn't show up on any CT scan?

If so, what the hell was she doing here, and how could she still look at him that way?

"Almost no one is pretty all the way through," she said, a direct answer to what he'd only been thinking.

Nonverbal cues. Human predictability. What addict didn't hate themselves? She was reading him, not his mind.

"Don't worry. *You* are definitely not an open book." She gave him a reassuring pat on the chest. "Now let's head to the arena before we end up making out in your sister-in-law's kitchen."

~

Carma slouched in one of the cheap plastic patio chairs set near the roping box and tipped her head back. It was good to smell dirt and horse manure, but she couldn't see anything but black beyond the arena lights. Too bad. She could really use a massive dose of open range and stars.

It was stupid to get defensive because they'd mentioned a background check. They'd be looking for her credit and work history, a criminal record, not sending undercover agents out to ask questions about Carma's reputation as "that chick who thinks the clouds sing to her."

She brought her gaze back down to earth. The small, squat house, simple pole barn, and indoor arena were set close together to leave as much space for pasture as possible. Across the driveway, this outdoor arena was a brand-new addition. The steel rails were shiny and pristine, but immediately beyond the east fence, rusting hunks of deceased farm equipment slumped in acres of overgrown weeds.

"That's gonna be pasture eventually." Gil settled into another of the chairs while Tori, Beni, and Hank uncinched horses and packed away their gear. "They bought this old junkyard last fall, and we spent all winter dragging scrap metal out to make space for the arena. We had to take off the first foot of topsoil to clear out all the nails and glass and oil spills, then haul all this sand and clay in."

Carma dug her toe into the perfectly blended dirt. "It's beautiful ground."

"Should be. Fixing it up cost more than the property. We just got the sprinkler system installed a couple of weeks ago." He frowned at a puddle below one of the posts that had a sprinkler head mounted on top. "It still needs some adjusting."

"Did you ever compete?" Beni piped up.

"Just through high school. But I used to be a trick rider." And nothing made a person appreciate safe footing like hanging off the side of a galloping horse in a suicide drag, with your arms and head skimming the ground.

"Why did you quit?" Quint asked.

"It's like being a gymnast—you can't carry extra weight." She spread her arms to display a body that sported a lot more curves than when she was twenty. "The older I got, the harder it was to stay skinny. And I like to eat more than I loved trick riding."

"I saw you kick all the guys' butts in the cross-country race at Heart Butte." Hank strapped a protective boot onto his stirrup for safe-keeping. "I figured you'd take a run at the Indian relays too."

She laughed, flexing her feet. "I don't have the springs for it."

"Indian relays?" Tori glanced up from stowing ropes in a bag. "That's where they race around bareback and bail off one horse and onto another?"

"With no help from the guys holding the horses," Hank said. "The riders have to be able to jump on by themselves, while the horse is going bonkers because there's other teams flying all over the place. It's nuts."

"Since they've started putting up big money, it's hella competitive," Carma said. "Racetrack-bred horses, and the riders are state champion basketball players."

"Those Blackfeet boys can definitely jump." Hank made a face. "They schooled me in the open league up there."

Hardly. Hank was a former high school all-star himself. "I heard you held your own," she said.

He only shrugged, and Carma caught a whiff of guilt and pain, the residue of past failures still clinging to every reminder of the God-given talent he'd squandered. But he was only twenty-five. He had plenty of time to rebuild his bullfighting career, plus people in his life who would do everything in their power to help him succeed: his father, Grace, Bing, and of course, Gil.

They *were* friends, no matter how Gil tried to pretend Hank was just an obligation.

"I want to try." Beni shot a challenging look at Quint. "I'll race you around the arena."

Quint shook his head. "I'm not good at riding bareback."

Ironic coming from a Sanchez, but rodeo broncs were a whole different matter. Besides, living in Oklahoma City with his mother, Quint probably hadn't had the opportunity to ride all that much.

Damn, it would be good to jump on, feel the prickle of horsehide through her jeans, and absorb the coiled energy of muscle that could spring into explosive motion in a heartbeat.

She had told Tori that her prospective staff could handle horses. This was a prime opportunity to show that she included herself in that number.

"I'll do it." Before Beni could get too fired up, she added, "Just a demo, not a race. And only if these horses can be trusted."

"Ranger and Ruby will be fine." Hank put one hand on the saddle horn of a lanky brown gelding and rubbed behind the ear of his sorrel.

Gil hitched up his eyebrows. "Didn't that mare buck your dad off and break his shoulder?"

"Yeah, but I've put a lot of time on her since then, and quite a bit without a saddle 'cuz Grace likes to ride bareback."

"I'll bet," Beni muttered.

Tori elbowed him, but her mouth twitched. She patted her horse on the neck. "Fudge and Cadillac are both bulletproof."

"I call dibs on Fudge and Ruby," Carma said. They were the shortest, and she hadn't swung onto a horse without the aid of a stirrup since last summer. "Usually we'd have three horses each, but we can switch back to the first one on the second exchange."

She stood and waggled her butt experimentally. Thanks to hiking through forests and canyonlands every chance she'd had on her trip, she wasn't carrying the five pounds she usually gained over the long, cold winter.

Since it was conveniently at his eye level, Gil gave her butt a leisurely, appreciative inspection, then cupped his fingers to mimic the shape. "If you need a boost, I'm happy to lend a hand."

Her pulse tripped, and her laugh was embarrassingly breathy. "That's against the rules, remember?"

He smiled lazily. "Have I ever told you how I feel about rules?"

"Um…I can guess." She slid her hand across her back pockets, the skin tingling as his eyes tracked its path. Then she realized Hank was watching, too, and Tori. She cleared her throat. "Let's do it, then."

Gil smirked and she lost a couple of seconds of brain function.

While the others slung saddles and blankets onto the fence, Carma jogged halfway down the arena and back again, then did a few low lunges, intensely aware of Gil watching every move.

Hank led the mare over, stripped down to just a bridle, and wrinkled his nose at the dark patch on her back. "You're gonna get sweaty."

"Won't be the first time."

He opened his mouth, glanced toward Gil, then snapped it shut again.

Carma gave herself a mental head smack. She had to

stop handing Gil fuel for that fire in his eyes. "Hang on to this beast," she told Hank.

He did, and she grabbed two fistfuls of mane, took a breath, then half jumped, half swung aboard. Whew! That went better than expected. Then she watched Beni hop onto Cadillac as if the tall gelding was a kid's rocking horse.

Damn boys and their pogo-stick legs.

She gestured toward the closest end of the arena. "Gil, hold Fudge right there, and Quint, you get ready to catch this horse as I jump off."

Everyone except Quint moved into position. He stood, rocking indecisively on his feet, giving off a whiff of…not quite fear, but definitely *I'd really rather not.*

"Scratch that," Carma said. "Gil, you should be the mugger. It takes more experience."

"I can do it." Quint set his jaw, and Carma let the matter drop. He might get bumped around a little, but this experience could help him get more comfortable with horses.

"Great." She trotted the mare straight down the arena, grabbing the mane again as she swung off the left side, keeping her knees soft to absorb the impact and one hand on Ruby's neck for balance as she jogged alongside the horse.

She and Beni practiced a few dismounts, then Carma sketched out an area along the left fence. "This is will be our exchange zone, where we jump off one horse and onto the next." She pointed at Quint and then Hank. "You catch the incoming horse and get it out of the way. And you—" She pointed to Gil and Tori. "Hold the next one while we jump on."

Hank scratched a starting line across the front of the chute with the heel of his boot while Carma rode into the roping box on one side and Beni on the other. Gil, Quint, and Tori took up their positions in the exchange zone.

As they turned to face the starting line, Carma shot a warning look at Beni. "This is *not* a race."

"Sure." But his grin said otherwise.

"Ready?" Gil asked. At their assent, he held up one hand like a pistol and said, "Bang!"

They took off faster than Carma had intended, but still well under control, circling the edge of the arena as if it was a track. As Carma completed the first lap, she tugged on the reins and Fudge slowed, but her feet slammed into the dirt hard enough to make her stumble. While she scrambled toward Ruby, Beni hopped onto Ranger and was off down the arena before Carma got aboard.

When they took out after Beni, the mare pushed into the bit, eager to catch up. Carma eased her grip and Ruby stretched out, dirt scattering from beneath her feet as they rounded the far end of the arena. Carma's heart pounded along with the mare's hooves, both of them wishing they had the space to really stretch out and fly.

They were only a couple of lengths behind Beni as they approached the second exchange. The mare slowed at Carma's first tug on the reins, nearly at a stop when Quint grabbed for the bridle. Then suddenly, Ruby snorted and lunged, slamming into Quint. Carma clutched at her mane, nearly coming unseated. *What the…*

Her blood chilled as she caught a glimpse of what had spooked Ruby.

Snake.

Chapter 13

Gil's heart stopped as the mare plowed into Quint, flinging him on his back in the dirt directly in her path. Before Gil could react, Carma hauled on the reins and the horse reared, going almost vertical. For a frozen eternity her front hooves pawed the air above Quint's helpless body. Then Carma tilted sideways, the drag on the reins and her weight enough to tip the horse off-balance—and away from Quint. Ruby flopped on her side, taking Carma with her.

Gil leapt to grab Quint, hauling him out of range of flailing hooves.

Sprawled half on, half off the mare, Carma kept her grip on the reins, pinning the horse down while Gil dragged the boy clear. Then she let go and rolled free as Ruby scrambled to her feet and bolted to where Tori held her stablemate, Ranger. Carma came to her knees and jabbed a finger toward the base of a post only feet from where Gil was standing. "Snake!"

Everyone froze.

Gil rotated his head one degree at a time, searching the ground, while his hands dug into Quint's shoulders to keep the boy still. He saw nothing but dirt. "What color was it?"

"Brown, with dark blotches."

"Copperhead. Bastard probably came out of the junk-pile." Tori's eyes darted side to side as she turned a slow circle, but the snake had beat a hasty retreat.

"Attracted by the water." Gil glared at the puddle around the base of the post, where the sprinkler head had leaked. "I'll get someone out here to fix those tomorrow."

"Are you okay?" Beni asked, sliding down from Cadillac to inspect Carma.

She clambered to her feet, shaking dirt out of her hair. "Fine…thanks to this nice soft sand."

"It's lucky Ruby didn't land on you. Or Quint." Hank captured the mare and ran a calming hand down her neck.

"That wasn't luck." Tori's gaze was sharp. "You pulled her over on purpose."

Carma shrugged, impressively calm. "It's a reflex. I help my dad train his movie horses, and we have to teach them how to fall. Like in a battle scene, you know?"

"You're a stunt woman?" Beni blinked at her in awe. "In what movies?"

"Have you seen *The Trail of Blood and Tears*?"

His eyes went even wider. "Were you the one who stole the cavalry's horses and chased them down the side of the ravine?"

"Yes. In one take, thank God. There was no way I was gonna do that again."

Beni was practically bouncing in place. "What else?"

"Um, a few." She glanced at Gil, who realized his fingers were still digging into Quint's shoulders. Shit. His hands were shaking. He stuffed them into the pockets of his jeans. In mere seconds a little harmless fun could've turned into the unthinkable. Gil's voice was gruff with the effort to keep from letting his terror show.

"Are you hurt?" he asked Quint.

"Nah." He brushed dirt from his shoulder, as if that was the worst he'd suffered, but his hand wasn't quite steady, either.

Carma met Gil's gaze and her eyes reflected his fear, mingled with reassurance. *It's okay. We're all okay.* Then she turned to the others. "I think we should quit while we're all in one piece."

"Thanks to you." Quint offered her a rare, unguarded smile, then went to join Beni, whose excited chatter echoed across the yard as they walked to the barn.

Carma turned to Gil. "Are *you* okay?"

He just shook his head, his heart still banging like a bass drum. Carma stepped close and rubbed a slow circle over the painful thud. Gil felt a strange tug in his chest—as if she were a ground wire draining the electric sizzle of fear from his body—and wanted to lean into her touch until his nerves stopped jangling.

"My mother says it's less painful to be in a wreck than watch her kid take one," she said, her voice as soothing as the caress.

"No shit." In all the times he'd been bucked off and stomped on, Gil had never felt this gut-curdling terror. What if Quint had been seriously injured, with Krista half-way around the world? The full weight of the responsibility crashed down on him, nearly buckling his knees. This was only the beginning. There would be driving. And sex. Booze, and drugs, and God knew what else. And it would be up to him to help Quint make the best possible choices.

Gil Sanchez. The king of bad decisions.

"You'll do fine," Carma promised.

He barely noticed that she'd answered another question he hadn't asked. "Why would he listen to me, of all people?"

"You can tell him you've already been there, done that, and show him the scars to prove it."

Lord knew, he had one for every occasion. Carma's eyes

went sympathetic, echoing the thought back at him. His hand started to come up, reaching for her, then dropped when Tori called out to him.

"We're taking the horses to the barn. Hank's gonna bring back flashlights. Could you help him look around for our uninvited guest and any of his friends?"

Gil jerked his gaze away from Carma, grasping at an excuse to put some distance between them before he gave in to the urge to drag her into his arms and bury his face in her hair until the nightmares cleared from his vision. "I'll check under the rest of the sprinklers right now."

He paced off to do just that. Carma wandered over to grab a rope Tori had left hanging on a post and began idly twirling it. Her way of releasing tension? Gil could barely concentrate on his search, his eyes drawn to the hypnotic flicker and dance of the loop.

He was just finishing his circuit of the arena when Hank came back with three flashlights, offering one to Carma. "For the walk back to the house."

"I'll come with you." She coiled the rope and tucked it into the crook of her elbow before taking the light. "I know the drill. We get a few stray diamondbacks at home."

Hank raised his eyebrows. "Is there anything you won't do?"

"Oyster shooters." She gave an exaggerated shudder. "I got tricked into trying them one time…and I still gag every time I think about it."

Hank laughed, tossed a flashlight to Gil, then brandished the shovel that had been leaning on the fence. "How do you feel about deep-fried snake?"

"Like there's too much good food in the world to bother," Carma declared.

Hank laughed again, and Gil had an absurd urge to remind him that he was supposedly head over heels in love and shouldn't be flirting with another woman. Christ. That acid burn behind Gil's sternum wasn't…

No. He ground his fist into his chest. Just indigestion from too much horseradish sauce on his fish, curdled by a dose of sheer terror. Jealousy went hand in hand with possessiveness, and that was a very short, very dangerous step from the ultimate form of addiction.

Gil snatched the shovel from Hank and headed for the horse pasture, the beam of his flashlight sweeping wide over the ground as he walked. Hank and Carma moved toward the steer pasture, their words ringing clear in the cool night air.

"What's with the rope?" Hank asked. "Is that how you Montanans catch snakes?"

Carma's tone was solemn. "It's an old Blackfeet trick. If we find one, I'll spin my loop to hypnotize it while you sneak up with the shovel."

"Really?"

There was a long beat of silence. Then Carma broke out laughing, and something clenched in Gil's chest at the sound. No one laughed like Native women. Deep and throaty, as if it came from the very bottom of their hearts. His mother used to laugh that way when he was little. With him. Sometimes at him, when he'd do and say any silly thing just to hear her. But she hadn't taken the laughter with her when she left. When she came to Earnest, or he and Delon went to visit, her smiles had been muted, the laughter replaced by painfully fierce hugs.

He shoved the memory away to concentrate on the task at hand. The ground was dry and snake-free around the compact electric waterer the horses used.

"All clear over here," Hank said, from where he'd split off to search the fence line along the edge of the junkyard.

"Here too," Carma called out from near the oblong steel tank where the steers watered.

"He must've gone back into hiding." Hank trotted over and fell into step beside Gil, nudging him with an elbow as they walked toward where Carma waited. "I like her. And I think she actually likes you."

Gil's heart clutched, forcing him to inject more acid into his words. "Super cool. Lend me a Sharpie, and I'll write our initials on my arm and draw a heart around them."

"You might as well have hired a skywriter when you invited her to move into your apartment. And don't even try to tell me you just needed a secretary." Hank pivoted to skip backward, mimicking a playground singsong. "Gil's got a cru-ush. Gil's got a cru-ush."

Gil considered throttling him, then his gaze met Carma's. She held up the rope and angled a pointed glance from Hank to the open tank beside her. Gil stifled a grin as, with a flip of her wrist, she built a loop.

He scowled and advanced on Hank, who predictably danced away with a *Catch me if you can* laugh. Carma took one quick swing and dropped the loop over his head. Hank yelped as she pulled it tight to pin his arms to his sides. Then she gave a hard tug. He stumbled backward, collided with the knee-high side of the stock tank, and toppled into the chilly water with a satisfying splash.

"Nice," Gil said, holding up a hand.

She slapped his palm in a celebratory high five. "Thanks. Excellent teamwork."

They left Hank sputtering and swearing. As they strolled back to the house, Carma slipped her hand into

Gil's, startling him with the intimacy of her fingers sliding into spaces that no woman had occupied since Krista. His instinct was to jerk away, but his grip tightened instead, a reaction that felt as dangerous as anything that had happened in the past hour—snake included.

Hank sloshed out of the water tank, calling after them. "You know what? You two deserve each other."

Deserve?

Gil pulled his hand free. Any woman deserved more than what he had to offer. Especially one who would risk her neck to protect his son.

It was after midnight when Gil closed his laptop, pulled out his earbuds, and stood to stretch, vertebrae popping as he arched his back. He really should put a decent desk and chair in his bedroom for nights like this, when sleep was out of the question and he couldn't slip over to the office. He might be able to sneak past Quint, but he wasn't sure he could stop himself from going straight to Carma.

He knew better than to make big moves when he was off-balance, and after the night's raw terror had shredded his defenses, he needed time to make repairs.

He eased the bedroom door open and soft-footed out to the kitchen, intending to get a glass of milk. A soft murmur froze him in his tracks. Ears straining, he crept toward Quint's bedroom. When he held his breath, he could almost make out words. The urge to press his ear to the door was almost irresistible, but he refused to invade the boy's privacy. And, he had to admit, he was a little afraid of what he might hear about himself.

He did have to know who Quint was talking to at this hour, though.

With a sharp knock as a warning, he pushed the door open and took two swift steps, to where he could see over Quint's shoulder. His breath rushed out in relief at the sight of a lovely blond girl. "Gwen."

"Uh, hi, Mr. Sanchez," Quint's sister said, covering any guilt or surprise with a cheery smile while Quint hunched against the headboard, his entire body screaming, *Busted!*

"Just call me Gil."

"Um, okay." But probably not, considering he'd been telling Gwen that for most of her twelve years.

Gil leaned against the wall beside Quint's headboard and crossed his arms. "Looks like a beautiful day in Africa. Unlike here, where it's the middle of a school night."

Pink flared under her creamy skin. "Quint said he's getting plenty of sleep."

Quint made a noise like *I'm just going to crawl under my blankets now.*

"Yeah. Especially after his alarm goes off." Gil narrowed his eyes at Gwen. "Shouldn't *you* be in school?"

"Daddy hired a local tutor. He said we should learn the culture and language from a native of this country instead of being holed up in an embassy school." She primly smoothed the skirt of her sundress. "We're taking a break."

Which, knowing Gwen, meant bribing the tutor to get lost while she chatted with Quint. That poor soul was going to get an education of his own, trying to wrangle Krista's daughters.

"I'm glad you're keeping in touch," Gil drawled. Thrilled, in fact. At least Quint was talking to someone. "But your brother has a social studies test tomorrow."

Gwen's expression went fierce. "You're not going to punish him, are you?"

"Do I look mad?"

"Um…yes?"

Gil frowned, then tried to rearrange his face into something less intimidating. Oh, to hell with it. "I'm not mad. I just want Quint to hang up now. And we have to make rules about when you two can talk, so he's not collecting tardy slips and you're not skipping class."

"I'm not…" she began, then opted for an angelic smile. "You know, Mom said I should call Quint anytime I want."

Translated: *But she didn't mean at 1:00 a.m. Texas time, so please don't mention this to her.* "Uh-huh. Say good night, Gwennie."

She sighed. "G'night, Quint."

"Night." He managed a tense smile. "Tell Lizzie I'll talk to her this weekend when I call Mom."

Quint hit the disconnect button and folded the tablet into its protective case. The snap of the magnetic clasp echoed in the silent room.

"How often do you call her?" Gil asked.

Quint hunched his shoulders again, not looking at Gil. "A couple of times a week. But only when I can't sleep anyway."

An infliction inherited from his father? Damn. But Gil was dying to ask what they talked about. Did Quint tell his sister everything that happened at school? He'd bet she'd heard about today's track meet, the crap with Sam Carruthers, how Quint really felt about nearly being stomped by a horse…

"Did you tell her about the snake?" was what Gil asked.

"Yeah." Quint's shoulders relaxed a few degrees. "She

wasn't impressed. Their gardener caught something called a zebra spitting cobra last week and let them look at it before he took it out of town and turned it loose."

"Does it spit zebras or venom?"

Quint snorted. "Venom. It's striped like a zebra."

"Huh. Sounds like another good reason not to move to Namibia." He pushed off the wall and grabbed the tablet from Quint's lap. "Try to go to sleep, before I change my mind about tattling to your mom."

As if Gil would confess that this had been going on under his nose—while he was obsessing over a woman instead of paying attention to his kid. He paused by the door. "Listen, Quint, about Carma..."

"It's cool," Quint said.

Sure, he was saying that now, when he was possibly in trouble. "The timing isn't the greatest," Gil said.

Quint shrugged. "I figured she'd show up sooner or later. I mean, you've been texting with her for how long? And I assume you've been seeing her, too."

Gil's jaw sagged. "I... How do you know about the texts?"

"I snooped," Quint said matter-of-factly.

"When?"

"You always have me read and answer your texts while we're driving. Carma's name caught my eye 'cuz it's kinda odd. I only sneaked a peek, then quit when I realized it was personal, in case there were dick pics or something." He wrinkled his nose. "That would be gross."

"Yes, it would. And I didn't. *We* didn't. It was just..." Gil ran out of words. How had he ended up explaining himself?

"Anyway, it is cool," Quint said. "She's...different, and

I see why you like her, so don't go messing it up on my account."

Gil gave his head a shake. "Um...fine. Glad we have your blessing."

"You're welcome." Quint slid down and pulled the blanket to his chin. "I should probably get some sleep."

"Yeah. Me too."

Gil went out, shut the door, then stood staring into the dark and wondering if there would ever be a time when he felt like he was actually in charge.

Chapter 14

The cursing started at seven minutes after five. Carma groaned and pulled a pillow over her head. It was no use. Gil's voice was like a damn dog that would stop barking just long enough to let her doze off, then start yapping again and jolt her awake.

At ten to six she flung the pillow at the wall, tossed back the covers, and stomped into the bathroom, hoping it knocked dust off the ceiling and into his morning coffee. A long, hot shower would've soaked away some of the aches from the previous night's adventures in snake wrangling, but she wasn't in the mood to be soothed. When she'd washed, she slapped on some makeup and dressed in a denim skirt and a ribbed sweater the color of a new copper penny.

Then she stomped down the stairs and into the rear hallway, slamming every door behind her.

Gil stepped out of his office. "You're up early."

"Not by choice." He jerked back when she stabbed a finger into his sternum. "You absolutely had to tell someone their lumpers are a bunch of incompetent sloths before the sun was even up? And what the hell is a lumper, anyway?"

"How did you hear..." Then his eyes widened in comprehension. "Oh shit. I forgot about the vent."

He shoved his tanker-sized, insulated coffee mug into her hands and jerked open a drawer to pull out something puffy that had once been white, decorated with a picture of...was that Winnie the Pooh?

"A disposable diaper?"

"One of Quint's." He flashed a quick, electric grin. "They're also good for absorbing noise."

She took a sip of the coffee, surprised to find that he took it with sugar. Lots and lots of sugar. She took another, bigger sip, enjoying the view as he pushed aside papers and scrambled onto his desk. His hair was the usual rumpled mess of finger tracks and his jeans the right amount of snug across prime hindquarters as he reached up to pry off a vent cover.

"I usually keep this blocked so the noise doesn't travel up into the apartment, but I forgot to put it back after we had the ducts cleaned." He stuffed the diaper inside the vent, the loose hem of his T-shirt sliding up to expose the taut, bronze curve of his back.

Carma leaned against the doorframe and shamelessly gawked.

"There. That'll fix it." He shoved the vent back into place and hopped down, light as a cat.

Meanwhile, the secondhand aggravation still crawled along her nerves. This had always been the problem. She sucked up emotions like a sponge, but it was a helluva lot harder to wring them out again. The first step was getting rid of the source. "Thank you. Now go away."

He did an almost comical double take. "Excuse me?"

"Go. Away. I've had all of you I can take right this minute."

His eyes narrowed. "Maybe you should crawl back in bed and try getting out of the right side."

"Too late." She was amazed at how easy it was to fling his attitude back at him. This man brought out the worst in her. Or was it the best? She flicked her hand. "Go have breakfast with your son, and don't come back until he's gone to school."

He stared at her in disbelief. "I have things to do."

As if to verify, the cell phone on his desk rang. Carma reached over and snatched it. "Good morning, Sanchez Trucking. Gil's not available at the moment. Can you call back after eight?"

"He's not in yet?" The voice on the other end of the line sounded as stupefied as Gil looked.

"Not today." She thanked the caller and shoved the phone into his hand. "There. See how easy that was?"

He actually growled. She countered with a sunny smile and turned to stroll to her own desk, taking his coffee with her. After a few moments of simmering silence, he said, "Fine. Enjoy yourself."

Instead of the expected stomping followed by the slam of the hallway door, she heard his footsteps pause, then march back in her direction.

Uh-oh.

His face was hard and his eyes had an unholy gleam. He skirted her desk, spun her around, and stepped so close that his thighs pushed her skirt up and his jeans scuffed along the bare skin of her inner thighs—and about a million nerve endings wired directly to vital parts of her anatomy. Bracing a hand on either arm of her chair, he leaned in until they were eye to eye, nose to nose, his breath playing across her mouth and sending a whole new surge of *Oh God, yes please* racing through her body.

It was all she could do not to cower. Or pounce. "What?" she asked.

"This." And he kissed her, a demand that stirred an instant response low in her belly. She reached up to grab the nape of his neck, the clipped hair on his nape bristling against her palm as her system revved like the caffeine and sugar had been injected straight into an artery.

As abruptly as he'd started, he pulled away.

She blinked up at him. "What? Why?"

"I never thanked you for saving Quint's neck last night." He pivoted on his heel and retraced his steps down the hall, calling back over his shoulder, "And I've been craving another taste of you."

He did slam the door behind him, a sharp exclamation point on the end of the statement he'd so thoroughly made. Carma let her breath trickle out as she leaned back in her chair, crossed her legs, and let one bare ankle swing while she waited for the arousal zinging through her to settle. Damn, that man could kiss. She took a sip from the mug, rolling the coffee over her tongue. It tasted like Gil's intentions—black as sin and guaranteed to give a girl heart palpitations.

She had almost thirty seconds to savor it before his phone rang and his computer started beeping.

To his credit, Gil contented himself with lifting one I-told-you-so eyebrow when he collected his stack of messages.

Carma dug all ten knuckles into her jangling skull. "Would you please make your computer stop that god-awful racket?"

"If you give me back my coffee mug."

"It's probably cold anyway." Lord knew, she hadn't had a chance to drink it. She shoved the mug into the hand he held out.

"Thank you." He practically beamed at her, the jerk.

And then the stupid phone rang again and he took his coffee, his messages, and his fine ass into his office.

She barely had time to take a breath for the rest of the

morning, with drivers popping in and out, piling their paperwork on top of all the rest. At nine, Max stopped in to offer her a stack of packing slips for truck parts and her choice from a box of doughnuts en route to the break room. It was totally worth sprinkles in her keyboard. Gil came out of his office and stalked Max down the hall, talking on his wireless headset as he snagged a doughnut.

She didn't see him again until lunchtime.

Her stomach had started to send out *feed me now* signals when a soft-bellied, sandy-haired man arrived with a paper bag that oozed the aroma of warm french fries. He greeted her with a wide smile. "Hello, Carmelita. I'm Kevin, from the Corral Café. Welcome to Earnest."

She thanked him, not bothering to ask how he knew her by name when she hadn't set foot in the town proper. Gossip floated on the breeze in these places. Back home on the windy side of the Rockies, her dad liked to joke that smoke signals traveled faster than high-speed Internet.

"Do you need money?" She hadn't asked about petty cash.

"Nah. Gil runs a tab." Kevin handed her the bag and a photocopy of their menu. "Breakfast, lunch, or dinner. Part of your benefit package. Same goes for the Smoke Shack."

"Wow. That's a nice perk."

Kevin rolled his eyes. "It's the only chance you'll get to eat most days. Lunch breaks around here tend to be optional."

When she stuck her head in Gil's door, he held up a hand to indicate that she should wait while he listened to the latest person talking into his headset. She used the time to study his space. The dispatch office was like the cockpit of a spacecraft, crammed with monitors and electronics, including what she recognized as an old-school CB radio.

On his left, two screens displayed the real-time maps that showed the locations of each truck along with current traffic and weather conditions and forecasts. A third monitor sat directly in front of Gil's chair. His guitar was propped in a narrow gap between desk and table.

When did he have time to play? All morning she'd listened to him scheduling loads, routing trucks through or around unforeseen obstacles, and dealing with either driver or customer complaints. And there were a *lot* of complaints. Carma hadn't realized it was so difficult to drive to one place, load a pile of stuff, haul it to another place, and unload it. Now she was beginning to think pulling it off without a hitch was a minor miracle.

"It's not a problem." Her ears perked at how friendly he sounded. "We'll have a tractor down there by rodeo time tomorrow. The boys will love the road trip, and I could stand to get out of here for a couple of days."

Tomorrow? He was leaving for the weekend? A sharp jab of disappointment deflated her lust-filled bubble. So much for the designs she'd been making on him.

"Emergency road trip?" Carma asked, when he disconnected and swiveled to face her.

He slouched in his chair, looking relaxed and pleased. "Jacobs Livestock has their stock in Huntsville this weekend, the clutch is going out of one of their trucks, and they're supposed to leave for another rodeo in Arkansas first thing on Sunday. None of the shops down there can get them rolling before Tuesday—for almost twice what we charge."

Carma knew Huntsville. Her dad had worked on a documentary about the now-defunct prison rodeo there. "That's almost to Houston."

"Eight hours from here." Gil stood, pushing his clasped

hands above his head and arching into a full-body stretch that made her want to run a slow hand down the long, hard curve of him, from throat to thighs…and everywhere in between. "If we're on the road by six, we can slide right through Dallas-Fort Worth and stop for the night, then get into Huntsville in plenty of time for tomorrow afternoon's performance."

She blinked her attention back to their conversation. "We?"

"Me, the boys, and Tori's coming straight here after work. She'll drive the replacement tractor, and I'll bring the tow truck to haul theirs back." At Carma's obvious surprise, he added, "Tori has a commercial driver's license, and some weird kink about trucks. I don't even think about what she and Delon do in our sleepers. You wanna come?"

She blinked again. "To Huntsville, or the nearest sleeper?"

He flashed one of those deadly grins. "Huntsville…for now. You might as well see some of the countryside."

Excitement trilled at the idea of jumping into a truck, rumbling through the night, and waking up on the other side of the state. "How will we all get home? There's not room in the cab of one truck."

"We'll rent a car for the trip back."

"Isn't that kind of expensive just so I can ride along?"

"Consider it on-the-job training. You can learn how to operate the onboard computer, so you know how it works from the driver's end. And I'll give you a rolling seminar on the trucking industry." Gil laced his fingers behind his head and pushed his elbows back, biceps popping and his navy-blue T-shirt pulling snug over the fascinating ridges and valleys of his chest. "I don't suppose you have a CDL tucked in your bag of tricks."

"Only a school bus endorsement, not heavy commercial. And I have no license at all until my mother gathers up seven forms of legal documentation to prove to the State of Montana that I am really me and she is acting on my behalf." Carma scowled at the strip of taut stomach peeking from under the hem of his T-shirt. "Are you trying to show off?"

He grinned and flexed again. "Is it working?"

She curled her lip at him. He laughed but dropped his arms, rolling his shoulders. Carma had to bite her tongue to stop from offering to massage out the kinks. "Your lunch is here."

"Sweet. I'm starving." He stood and deliberately brushed against her as he passed, a quick imprint of male flesh and a scent that hinted at shadowy woods and a bed of pine needles. She inhaled, savoring the wash of heat at the thought of being naked with Gil, surrounded by trees, earth, and sky.

He would be magnificent in the moonlight.

She lingered on the image while he rummaged in the bag of food, pulling out a Styrofoam carton and offering it to her. "Fish and chips special."

"Thanks."

"You're welcome." He skimmed a knuckle under her chin, sending a shiver racing across her skin, but before he could do more, his infernal cell phone rang. He sighed and stepped away. "We're rolling out of here at six thirty."

"I'll be ready."

She stayed put until she regained the equilibrium he so effortlessly disrupted. Huntsville. The nearest truck sleeper. Up the stairs to the apartment. At this point, Gil Sanchez could take her pretty much anywhere he wanted.

Chapter 15

The prospect of getting out of town had improved Gil's mood exponentially. Spending those hours on the road with Carma only sweetened the pot. Mostly alone because Quint had opted to ride with Tori and Beni in the newer and much fancier Freightliner, with life-sized images of Delon in action plastered on both sides. If they were going to send a truck cross-country with Jacobs Livestock, it might as well be a rolling billboard for Sanchez Trucking.

Their tow truck was actually a *truck*—a semi tractor with a modified flat deck and low-roofed, cab-level sleeper, painted electric yellow with red and silver flames licking down the sides. Carma swung into the passenger's seat, carrying a small wool duffel printed in a southwestern pattern of black, teal, and orange.

"You pack light."

"It's only overnight." She tugged her denim skirt lower on firm, bronzed thighs. "And I don't have a purse, or my wallet, or my phone, or even my ChapStick. Basically, I'm screwed if you decide to dump me out alongside the road."

Son of a bitch. Bad enough to be robbed of very personal possessions. She also had to rely on others for her safety and sustenance.

Rather than dwell on the negative, he ran his tongue along his top lip. "Cherry ChapStick. Yum."

She gave a little shudder, then huffed out a breath. "It's gonna be a very long drive if you keep making me imagine you licking me like a Popsicle."

"I live to torture," he said, and put the truck in gear before he gave in to the temptation to drag her into the sleeper, start at her toes, and work his way up.

Normally Gil would have skirted the edge of town, but today he rolled straight down Main to give Carma a drive-by tour of Earnest—a bank, the Watering Hole bar, the Corral Café, and the Kwicky Mart with the Smoke Shack barbecue joint a block behind. He waved at the defunct drugstore, cleared out to make a place for meetings and such. "That's where Analise and Bing go for yoga."

"Cool. I'll have to join them."

At the intersection with the highway, he stopped to wait for a battered pickup and stock trailer to clatter past, headed north. "Johnny Brookman's ranch is up that way."

She nodded, because of course she'd know that if she'd come to see Bing. Gil turned south, showing her the school and the athletic fields, the feed store, and finally the worn but serviceable rodeo arena used mostly for youth events. And yes, he confessed, there was a *G.A.S.* somewhere in the scribble of initials on the water tower.

As they put Earnest behind them, he pointed out the ragged edges of the Canadian River breaks, just visible before the road dipped below a long line of chalky bluffs. A house, barn, and corrals were tucked at the base, the driveway marked by a black iron gate with a J inset in the overhead arch.

Carma twisted in her seat for a better look. "Is that the Jacobs ranch?"

"Part of it. That's Cole and Shawnee's place." A second, identical gate loomed ahead. The big, white frame house was set near the road and surrounded by towering trees, with a second, manufactured home across the driveway.

Beyond there were a bunkhouse, a shop, a barn, more corrals, and an arena with bucking chutes. "The big house is Miz Iris and Steve's. The other is Violet and Joe's."

"When are your aunt and uncle *inviting* me to dinner?"

"They're in Brazil until the end of next week." Gil shook his head. "And we're not related, other than Violet being Beni's mother."

"But your families have always been close."

"I guess. Before they got their own truck, Dad hauled their bucking horses to the rodeos and Delon and I tagged along whenever we could."

"And your mother?"

"Yes." His mind stumbled over a fuzzy, unexpectedly happy memory. The four of them crammed into the cab of the old white Peterbilt, his mother singing all the annoying kids' songs with them, parceling out snacks, telling them ancient stories sprinkled with Navajo names and words. For an instant time wobbled, then steadied. "After she left, we stayed with Miz Iris whenever Dad was on the road. And we always spent holidays and stuff there. The food was a lot better than at home."

The CB radio crackled to life, and Beni's voice filled the cab. "*Break one-nine. This is the Chaos Kid. You got your ears on, Big Brother?*"

Carma burst out laughing. "Oh my God. Those may be the best nicknames *ever*."

"They're called *handles*," Gil replied loftily. But yes, Beni's was dead-on, and the drivers at Sanchez Trucking had tagged Gil for his habit of electronically peeking over their shoulders. Delon had designated Tori the Panhandle Princess, much to her amusement.

They bantered back and forth for the next hundred

miles, with Gil and Beni tutoring Carma on proper CB etiquette and lingo. Carma's eyes sparkled as she clutched the mic. "This is so much more fun than talking on the phone."

"It's a grown-up version of a kids' clubhouse," Gil pointed out. "Secret code names, a made-up language—all we need is a *Keep Out, Losers* sign and it'd be perfect."

She grinned, fingering the knobs on the radio. "I'm surprised you still have CBs."

"Low tech for the win. Hackers can't mess with 'em, and they still work during tornadoes and hurricanes when every cell tower in the state is jammed."

A female voice crackled over the radio. "*Glory Girl here. Sounds like you're packing a spare, Big B. You bring a friend home from your last trip to the rez?*"

Carma barely stiffened, but it was enough, especially when magnified by the sudden, humming silence on the radio as they all waited for Gil's reaction. Shit. What could he say over the open airwaves that wouldn't make it worse?

"*You can call her Miss Karma,*" Tori cut in, with a chill that could slice through skin and bone. "*And you know what happens if you don't show her some respect.*"

"*Sorry,*" Glory Girl muttered.

Not really. But she would be the next time she rolled into the Sanchez shop. In the meantime, the fun had been sucked out of the moment. Gil frowned. "I wish I could say that wasn't one of our drivers."

Carma shrugged as she hung up the mic. "That's how I talk. I'm not ashamed of it."

No, but he'd heard her mute her Native accent when she was on the phone with customers, the same way he clipped his vowels when he was doing business with non-Texas clients. The thicker the drawl, the more they tended to downgrade his IQ. His real favorites, though, were the people who informed him that he didn't *sound* like a Sanchez.

And the assholes meant it as a compliment.

Personally, he had been disappointed when he'd learned he didn't have any Hispanic blood. He had harbored fantasies of relatives in haciendas who would teach him to speak rapid-fire Spanish and play mariachi music. Eventually he'd realized he wouldn't have belonged there any more than with his mother's Navajo family.

As the saying went, *Red on the outside, white on the inside*...and once an apple, always an apple.

"When Bing moved to Earnest, she joked that she increased the Native population by twenty-five percent," Carma said.

And Bing was still the only brown-skinned woman in town, as Rochelle had been before her. Gil had tallied all the reasons life here would've been difficult for his mother. *All her excuses,* a mean little voice whispered. He tried and, as always, didn't quite succeed in ignoring it.

But his mother had been only nineteen when she'd answered Merle Sanchez's ad for a receptionist and dispatcher. Like Gil, she'd been in a rush to get out and experience the world. It must've been scary, though, especially for someone who looked and sounded different. *Was* different, in ways far beyond appearance.

Gil had always thought he'd understood. But now, seeing the sparkle die in Carma's eyes at a single, ignorant jibe, he *felt* it in a way he never had. And his father would have been zero help, brushing it all off under the general heading of *They don't mean anything by it,* the same as he had with his sons.

"What was it like for you?" Carma asked.

"Not so bad. We were born here, so people were used to us, and we had a built-in gang. We *were* the arrogant bastards." From elementary school on, they'd been the star athletes, the homecoming kings and queens, the rodeo champs from Pee Wees on up. And he'd had Xander—his best friend, his confidant, his settling influence. Until, of course, Xander had died.

Once again in mental step with him, Carma said, "It must've been horrible when Cole's brother and his parents were killed."

"Yeah."

Even now, Gil had to force himself to believe it was true. For all of them, it had been a devastating loss, but while the others had huddled together, Gil had retreated. Into himself. Into a bottle. The night of Xander's funeral, he'd stolen a fifth of whiskey from his dad's cupboard and hid out in one of the trucks, the first time he'd drank himself unconscious.

One of many possibly inevitable steps down the path to addiction, given what he understood about himself now. But it was impossible not to wonder how different it all might have been if only…

It was also a waste of time.

Carma pulled a strand of hair forward over her shoulder and wove it through her fingers. "What about Quint's mother? Do you get along?"

"Well enough." He paused, debating how much to share. There wasn't much of the story that made him look good. "It was ugly when we broke up. I was crazy about her…and just plain crazy, going balls to the wall in Georgia overdrive."

"Georgia what?"

"When you turn off the truck and let it roll downhill. No brakes. No steering." And the farther down the slope, the more out of control he got. "When we found out she was pregnant, I wanted to marry her. She ran home to Mommy and Daddy instead, and I decided she thought she was too good for some half-breed trucker's son." His grip tightened around the gearshift knob. "It took me a long time to admit that she had to bail out to save herself…and Quint."

Carma laid her hand over his and let it rest there. His fingers relaxed of their own accord, and a steady warmth radiated up his arm, muscle by muscle, as if she was pushing it into him. For a few minutes he let the vibration of the gearshift accentuate the feeling.

Then he pulled free and touched her bare ring finger. "Have you ever been married?"

She yanked her hand back into her lap. "Not quite."

"Which means?"

The lines around her eyes and mouth tightened. "I've been falling in and out of love with the same man damn near my whole life. We dated in high school, broke up when I went to college. Got back together when I dropped out. Then Jayden went pro and moved to Arizona to be closer to his team-roping partner and we split up again. And so on, and so on…"

"Last year was his first trip to the National Finals?"

"Yeah. He has all the talent in the world, but…" She shrugged. "You know how it is—the season is long, and when the going got tough, Jayden would start fighting his head and fall apart. I was always there to put the pieces back together." She made a self-deprecating face. "I am very good at telling everyone else how they should fix their lives. And then last year he finally got it together."

Gil shot her a narrow look. "You make that sound like a bad thing."

"Not for him. For me?" She made a bitter sound. "Same old story. Hometown boy makes good, trades in hometown girl for a blonder, shinier version. I mean, that's how you know you've really made it, right? When even the whitest white girls want you?"

Gil winced. He'd done practically the same thing. And Delon too. They didn't get any shinier or blonder than Krista, or Tori in her early twenties when she and Delon first met. It was possible the Sanchez brothers' preferences had come at least partly from being the only two brown boys in Earnest, Texas. The realization didn't sit comfortably in his gut.

He accelerated around an RV, settling into his own lane before asking, "Were you already planning this program of yours when I met you?"

"No. My grandmother came up with the idea right before she died, because of my brother."

"He needs rehab?"

"Maybe. Eventually." She twined the strand of hair around her fingers. "Eddie has been in the Army for almost half his life, and this country has been at war the entire time. He's been deployed so many times..." Her face pinched with worry. "You can't do that to a human being and not expect them to have some kind of problems."

Anxiety. Depression. PTSD. Drugs. Alcohol.

Suicide. So many suicides.

"Your grandmother wanted him to have a place to go if he needed it," Gil guessed.

"More than that. Eddie is the guy the other soldiers

always come to with their problems and he does what he can to help. We're hoping if we give him a way to do that full time, he'll come home instead of reenlisting. Grandma gave us forty thousand dollars out of her settlement as seed money for the program."

Forty grand? Not exactly chump change. "Settlement?"

"You know, the Elouise Cobell lawsuit, for trust payments?"

Gil remained blank. She obviously didn't realize how far he was out of the Native loop. "Never heard of it."

"Oh. Well..." She took a minute to decide how to explain. "In the late 1800s the government tried to make farmers out of us by allotting each member an acreage, held in trust by the Department of the Interior. Then they found oil and gas and other good stuff on the land so they leased it out to developers and such, but not all of the money they collected made it back to the trustees. Elouise was working at the Blackfeet Bank and realized the payments didn't add up, and hadn't for about a hundred years. The class action lawsuit was settled for almost two billion dollars, payable to current owners of those allotments."

And Carma's grandmother had bet a big chunk of her windfall on being able to lure her grandson out of the military, for his own good and that of everyone else who would benefit from the program.

"You're supposed to make this happen?" Gil asked.

"Not by myself. There's people doing all the paperwork and planning. My job is to learn what other programs are doing and figure out what we can use." She hesitated, then admitted, "The Patterson program is hands down the best in the country. That's why I'm here. And to visit Bing, of course."

But not Gil. He had never been part of her plan, a realization that left an ugly gouge in his ego.

"We texted three or four times while you were on the road, and you didn't even tell me you were coming," he said, something that had been nagging at him.

"I couldn't find the right GIF." Carma ducked her head. "And I wasn't sure where we stood in real life, so I figured I'd just show up and see what happened."

And then Fate had intervened in the form of a bad hamburger. Maybe he shouldn't call it *that other four-letter f-word* after all.

Quint's voice cut through the low static on the CB. "*Break one-nine. Big Brother, you got your ears on?*"

Gil snagged the mic. "Loud and clear."

"*The Princess says she's ready for a pit stop, and she'd like a place that serves Dr Pepper floats with real ice cream.*"

Gil knew just the spot, for refreshments and a few other things he wanted to pick up. He flipped on his turn signal. "Follow me off the next exit."

The truck stop Gil had chosen had a fifties-style diner and soda fountain. The instant they rolled to a stop, the boys scrambled out of the Freightliner. When Gil held the door for Tori and Carma to walk in, they were already huddled over the old-fashioned jukebox in the corner.

Tori made a beeline for a large corner booth upholstered in turquoise pleather with red trim. Carma slid into one side and Tori the other, but instead of joining them, Gil said, "Order me coffee and a chocolate shake."

"With a cherry on top?" Carma guessed, a reference to his ChapStick comment.

He rewarded her with a sizzling smile. "Two. Extra whipped cream."

"And you make fun of Delon's sweet tooth," Tori drawled.

"I don't buy Hershey's Kisses in bulk."

"No. You just raid his stash in the god-awful hours of the night."

Gil held up his hands. "No witnesses. No foul."

The jukebox boomed out "Rock Around the Clock," and Carma's system buzzed with something akin to a sugar rush as she watched Gil push through the door into the adjacent convenience store.

Tori followed her line of sight. "I probably owe you an apology."

"But?" Carma asked, detecting zero remorse.

"I wouldn't really mean it." Tori's gaze was as direct as her words. "You have to admit, it's awfully convenient."

Carma blinked. "Excuse me?"

"Gil has been notoriously hard to pin down. Then all of the sudden, you show up when he's as vulnerable as he's ever been—getting custody of Quint, shorthanded at work. He wouldn't be the first man to jump into a relationship to solve his problems."

Carma gaped at her. "And you figured Bing and I plotted out how to nab him?"

"I am extremely suspicious, by nature and nurture." Tori rested her hands on the table, fingers laced, gray eyes steady. "I've seen a couple of receptionists at Sanchez Trucking who were looking to take home more than a paycheck. And they would've been happy with either brother."

Carma almost sputtered. "I have no interest in your husband."

"And they aren't that kind of men." Tori flicked dismissive fingers. "Like I said, I was wrong about you."

"What makes you so sure?" Carma blurted, caught between disbelief and outrage.

"I called David Parsons last night." Tori smiled when Carma goggled some more. "Didn't he tell you that he and my first husband knew each other pretty well? They grew up a couple of hours apart and went to all the same junior rodeos. David had very good things to say about you. I believe 'unique' was the word he used."

"Oh. Well. That's...nice," Carma said faintly.

"He's a very nice man. And I was kinda a bitch at dinner last night." Tori screwed up her face. "My husband tells me I can be a little...overwhelming. But it's bizarre, feeling like I need to protect Gil. I mean, come on. *Gil?*"

Carma actually laughed, just as the boys piled into the booth. Beni pulled his phone out and logged onto the free Wi-Fi to check the results from wherever his dad had ridden that night—Delon was sitting third with an eighty-seven score—plus highlights and scores to see how the Jacobs stock was performing at the bull-riding event in Atlanta. Quint leaned in to watch, adding a couple of dry comments that had Tori snorting into her water glass.

He knew rodeo and could talk the talk for his cousin's benefit, but he didn't share Beni's boundless enthusiasm. The only spark of real interest Carma observed was when Tori countered by pulling up a video of the top ten teams in a big all-girl roping from the previous weekend. While Beni waxed poetic about superhuman efforts of one of the Brazilian bull riders, Quint's gaze strayed to Tori's screen.

Interesting.

The waitress came to take their orders, and Carma was stirring cream and sugar into her coffee when Gil reappeared carrying a plastic shopping bag.

He slid into the booth beside Carma and dropped the bag in her lap. "That should get you by until you have a chance to go shopping."

She fished out a pink camo canvas purse with fake alligator trim and a blinding array of rhinestones and metal studs. Her jaw came unhinged. "I…um, thanks?"

Tori didn't bother to be diplomatic. "Did you *try* to find the most hideous thing in the store?"

"Yep." When they both blinked at him, Gil bared his teeth. "Too ugly to steal."

Carma's heart gave a lurch, like the combined thrill and terror of a carnival ride. No one—certainly not Jayden—had ever given her something that was so exactly what she didn't know she needed. Gil had replaced her stolen property in a way that made a smile tug at her mouth, diluting the sickening aftertaste of violation with the tart fizz of a shared joke.

He nudged the purse with one finger. "I grabbed a few necessities while I was at it."

The glint in his eyes had her tucking the purse close to her chest as she opened the clasp and peeked, aware that the boys and Tori were watching with intense curiosity. The main compartment held a travel-sized pack of tissues, a small vial of ibuprofen, a tin of breath mints, a pair of nail clippers still in the package and—her smile widened—a tube of cherry ChapStick. He'd tucked a couple of Sanchez Trucking pens in one of the side pockets, and in the other…

Hot color rushed to her face, and she slapped the purse shut on the pack of condoms.

Tori's eyebrows peaked. "Do I have to ask?"

"Uh..." Carma stammered.

"What?" Beni demanded.

Quint folded his arms, prepared to be amused by their explanation. Honestly. Nothing short of the threat of bodily harm rattled that kid.

Gil slung an arm along the booth behind Carma, his fingers brushing her shoulder, all loose-limbed arrogance. But this was no casual gesture. He had declared for all to see that outside the office, his relationship with Carma was not purely professional. "Just some personal things."

"Like...oh." Beni's eyes went wide, and his face reddened to match Carma's. "You mean girl stuff."

Tori smirked but said, "Geez, Beni. You wanna yell that any louder?"

Beni glanced around and realized they now had the attention of all the other diners. "Oops. Sorry."

Carma tucked the purse between her and Gil on the seat. "That was very, um...thoughtful."

"Wasn't it, though?" Tori drawled. "If I didn't know better, I might think I'd witnessed you performing an act of kindness."

Gil's smile sharpened. "There's always something in it for me, Princess."

Literally, in the case of the condoms. But Carma couldn't help thinking, self-serving as he might claim to be, Gil paid more attention to what she needed than the man who'd claimed to be in love with her ever had.

And from the way Tori was eyeing the two of them, Carma wasn't the only one who'd noticed.

Chapter 16

When Carma stepped out of the truck in Huntsville late the next morning, the increase in humidity was immediately noticeable, giving the air both softness and heft. The Jacobs crew was camped around back by the stock pens, consisting of a large fifth-wheel camper lined up beside a four-horse trailer with living quarters in the front.

A tarp was strung between the trailers to shade a patio area complete with all-weather carpet, gas grill, tables, and a dozen or so lawn chairs and loungers. A generator hummed, powering air-conditioners and the flat-screen TV, part of an entertainment center that folded out of the side of the camper. Several cowboys were sprawled in the shade watching a severely lopsided college football game, and a large man hunched over one of the tables, repairing a heavy leather bronc halter. Beyond the trailers, a woman tossed a rope around the horns of a plastic dummy steer.

They all turned to stare at the newcomers.

Beni bounded ahead, diving into a chorus of greetings and good-natured insults, while Quint hung back, his body relaxed but his eyes alert.

Cole Jacobs pushed aside the halter and rose to his full, impressive height and mass to clap Gil on the shoulder. "Glad you could make it. If you're up for it, I'll put you to work. There's a rookie crawling on Crazy Ex-Girlfriend today. He could use all the help he can get."

"Sure," Gil said.

"What about us?" Beni asked, tipping his head to include Quint.

"We can use an extra hand or two on the stripping chute."

Quint shrugged his consent, with no sign of lingering fear from the incident in Tori's arena, but also no hint of Beni's enthusiasm.

The woman who had to be Cole's wife coiled her rope and fisted a hand around it to prop on her ample hip. Shawnee was wearing flip-flops and denim shorts and had pulled her hair into a high ponytail, the long, unruly curls spilling across a racer-back tank that bared powerful arms. She was...well, *interesting* was too mild a word. *Compelling,* Carma thought instead. This was one of the best female ropers in the country, the only woman currently working as a pickup rider in professional rodeo, and her confidence shown like a lighthouse beacon.

She cocked her head and studied Carma with unabashed curiosity. "So you're the famous Carma."

Famous? Yikes. Just how much discussion had there been among Gil's friends?

He performed introductions, pointing out Cole, Shawnee, the two bullfighters, and the truck drivers—identical twins somewhere over the age of forty. Gil dismissed the remaining cowboys, saying, "And the rest of these guys are just here for the TV and free food."

The men grinned and nodded in greeting.

"Are you staying the night?" Shawnee asked.

"Yes!" Beni declared. "We're gonna help sort and load in the morning."

"Wouldn't want to miss it," Gil said dryly.

Beni definitely didn't. He talked to the men with authority and a sense of ownership. Analise had said he also knew Sanchez Trucking from top to bottom, having lived in the apartment above the shop off and on until Delon and Tori got married. In a way, it was almost criminal. Back home Carma saw so many bright kids who had almost no opportunities, born into families who came from nothing, had nothing, and could barely imagine the possibility of anything more. Meanwhile, here were Quint and Beni, who could choose between their fathers' and mothers' legacies, unless they pursued another of the nearly unlimited options their educations, money, and connections provided.

Shawnee shook out a new loop. "Come and play PIG with me," she ordered Tori.

"Hah! You know I hate losing. I'm grabbing a lounger and a cold Dr Pepper, thanks."

Shawnee looked at Carma. "What about you?"

"Me?" Carma's voice almost squeaked at being the sudden focus of all that competitive energy. "I…um, I'm not that kind of roper—"

"She's a rancher," Tori cut in, her gaze also speculative. "She ropes necks, not horns."

Her tone caught Gil's attention, and a calculating gleam came into his eyes. "What are the rules?"

"Just like basketball." Shawnee gestured at the roping dummy. "I take a shot. If I catch, the other person has to repeat exactly what I did, or I win a letter. If I miss, she gets to call the next shot. The first to spell *PIG* wins."

"I assume there's a trick to it," Gil said.

"*Trick* being the key word. The person calling the shot gets to throw in any twists they want, and the other has to match them exactly." To demonstrate she twirled her loop into a flat circle and sent it spinning once around her body before whipping it out and around the dummy's horns with a decisive *whack!*

"I don't think—" Carma began.

"Take the horns off so it has to be a neck catch and she'll do it," Tori said.

Shawnee's grin was downright malevolent. "The usual bet?"

Tori snorted. "We don't make guests polish your stinking boots."

"Then what—"

"I'll put a hundred bucks on Carma," Gil tossed out.

Carma gaped at him. Holy crap. She'd been about to agree, thinking it was a casual game. "I don't even have my own rope."

Shawnee ignored her, focused on Gil. "Cash?"

He pulled out his wallet and extracted five crisp twenties. Everyone under the awning swiveled to take in the proceedings, the football game forgotten in favor of some real drama.

"This is silly. We can just play for fun…" Carma's protest withered under Shawnee's glare.

"Where's the fun if there's nothing on the line?" She jerked a nod at Gil. "You've got a bet."

Oh hell. "I am not ponying up the cash if you lose," Cole said, frowning his disapproval. Not surprisingly, he was the conservative voice in their relationship.

"Are you implying that you don't have faith in my abilities?" Shawnee asked, eyes wide with mock hurt.

"Just so we're clear." The lawn chair groaned as Cole settled into a front-row seat.

Carma heaved a resigned sigh. "I have to find a rope and take some time to warm up—without an audience."

One of the men—tall, lanky, with a long face that shaded toward homely—popped out of his lawn chair. "I should have something you can use."

"Brady will set you up." Shawnee stood, loop in one hand, coils in the other, feet braced like a gunfighter. "Meet me back here in half an hour."

Carma had to stifle a nervous giggle. Geezus. It was like an old western movie—the stranger rides into town and is immediately challenged to a showdown at high noon.

And like all those idiots, her pride refused to let her walk away.

When they returned exactly thirty minutes later, her new friend flopped into one of the chairs that had been lined up for optimal viewing. "I hope you brought your A game, Pickett," Brady said.

"I always do." But beneath Shawnee's steely determination, there was a flicker of uncertainty. This was Carma's one advantage. Shawnee didn't know what to expect from her, while Carma had spent years watching Jayden and his friends play these games.

"You want in the side pot, Brady?" one of the truckers asked, clutching a fistful of cash. "Twenty bucks. Pick your winner."

"Carma." He dug out a pair of tens and passed them over.

Beni flipped a quarter to see who would go first. Shawnee won. She started out easy, with a repeat of the same trick she'd demonstrated earlier, the loop rippling around her in what was known as an ocean wave. Carma successfully mimicked the throw, although her loop didn't snap around the steer's neck with the same authority.

"Not bad." Shawnee gave her a long, measuring look before stepping up to take her turn.

She went with another basic trick, making the loop stand upright and dance side to side in a butterfly maneuver before swinging it around to settle neatly over the steer's head. Carma duplicated the trick. The half of the crowd who'd bet on her cheered.

Shawnee bared her teeth at them. "Apparently some of you have forgotten who does most of the cooking around here."

She changed it up on the next trick, spinning the loop in the opposite direction and roping the dummy backhanded. The spin was no problem, but Carma's rope sailed over the dummy at the end.

"*P* for me!" Shawnee crowed, to the applause of her supporters.

Carma's cheering section groaned. Crap. She'd shown a weakness that Shawnee wouldn't hesitate to exploit.

"Did we mention that you can't do the same trick twice?" Tori asked. "House rules."

Carma threw her a thankful look. Shawnee scowled, then walked up, did one reverse rotation of ocean wave, switched directions, then caught the loop in her right hand, took two swings and threw. Another clean catch. Again Carma cruised through the twirls, but her loop smacked the steer on the side of the head.

"*I*!" Shawnee pumped a fist.

Another chorus of groans and cheers from the audience.

Carma glanced at where Gil leaned against the side of the camper, hands tucked in pockets, totally relaxed. Well, it was his money. If he wasn't worried…

Shawnee gave her a smile packed with false sympathy. "I was hoping you'd at least give me a run for it. Let's see what you can do with this, Sunshine."

They went back and forth several times, with Carma duplicating Shawnee's moves while getting more comfortable with the catches. Neither of them missed, so Shawnee maintained control of the shots. On her next turn she did a wedding ring, dropping the big loop over her head, stepping out, in, then out before catching the loop in her hand to make the throw. It snapped tight around the empty sockets that usually held the interchangeable horns.

Shawnee swore. Tori smirked.

"That counts as a miss," she said. "Carma gets to call the next shot."

So this was why Tori insisted on neck catches—to level the playing field between Carma and a woman who was in the habit of literally roping steers and bulls by the horns.

Gil deliberately caught Carma's eye and lifted his phone, now plugged into the speaker system. He tapped one finger and the unmistakable riff of Guns N' Roses's "Sweet Child o' Mine" shredded the air.

"Finish it," he said.

Shawnee snorted in patent disbelief.

Oh yeah? Match this. Carma closed her eyes, letting the beat throb through her for a few bars before she launched into a reverse ocean wave, then a trio of pop-outs with first her right hand, then her left, a forward ocean wave, and a series of butterflies. Finally she squared up to take careful aim and set the loop precisely over the steer's head.

The crowd went wild.

Shawnee said a very bad word. "How am I supposed to remember all that?"

"Give it your best shot." Carma smiled sweetly. "Sunshine."

Cole groaned. Shawnee hissed, built a loop, and launched into the routine, catching the steer neatly at the end.

"You forgot the second ocean wave," Beni said.

"Are you sure?" Shawnee demanded.

Brady held up his phone. "I have the video replay if you want to throw a challenge flag."

"Fine." Shawnee yanked her rope off the dummy and stalked a few paces away to stand, arms folded, in front of a growing crowd of contestants and random passersby who'd gathered to watch the show. Carma picked up the rhythm of the song at the end of the second chorus, whipping her rope into another complicated series of tricks with some footwork thrown in for good measure, ending with a loop that sailed prettily through the air to capture the steer.

Halfway through her attempt to duplicate the routine, Shawnee bobbled and her rope wrapped around her head. She swore a blue streak while untangling it from her ponytail.

"*I*," Carma said.

Cole pointed an accusing finger at Tori. "This is your fault. And I'm stuck in the pickup with her all the way to Arkansas tomorrow."

"It's not over!" Shawnee snapped.

"My sympathies, big guy." Tori smiled back at Cole without a hint of apology.

Both combatants were winded, and Carma was

dripping sweat in the unaccustomed heat. Shawnee scraped damp curls from her forehead. "Go ahead. Do all your fancy shit. Just don't miss the steer."

Nice. Put a little negative imagery in your opponent's head. If that's the way she wanted to be…

Carma kicked off her sandals, the grass prickly under her feet as she built her loop into a huge wedding ring above her head, then let it settle to a bare inch above the beaten grass. As it skimmed around her, she sank into a full split, floating the loop up and out to land around the steer's neck just as the final notes of the song faded away.

The crowd went wild, sending lawn chairs tumbling as they leapt to their feet.

Shawnee threw her hands and the rope into the air. "Screw it. If I try that, I won't walk upright again for a week."

"Not to mention…" Cole began, then went beet-red as every eye turned on him. He lunged out of his chair. "I better finish fixing that halter."

Laughing, Carma checked for Gil's reaction. He was frowning at his phone. Oh. Well. She assumed he'd been paying some attention since it was his hundred bucks on the line. The glow of triumph dimmed slightly, and she coiled her rope as the applause died to a single, slow clap. She pivoted to find the source.

Flaming icicles speared her heart. *Oh shit. Jayden.*

The buzz of Gil's phone barely penetrated his cloud of lust. Geezus. Watching Carma, her rope, the way her body moved…

Then he read Analise's message about Asshole Ted

at Express Auto. He always called on the weekend and refused to talk to anyone but Gil, no matter how basic the question. Ted didn't deal with minions. Only the Man.

If car transport wasn't one of the most profitable segments of their business, Gil might've been less flexible, but Ted kept five or six Sanchez drivers very well employed, shuffling his rentals between airports all over the Southwest.

Unfortunately, Ted knew it, and milked his clout for all the special attention he could get.

Gil bit off a curse. He'd done this to himself, wooing clients with the promise of his full, personal attention, twenty-four seven. Not a problem back when he'd had the time to give to every whiny, self-important bastard in the country. He started to reply that Analise should say he was unavailable until Monday morning, then became aware of a shift in the atmosphere, the chatter and laughter dying.

Beni nudged him. "Uncle Gil."

He looked over to where a man stood in front of Carma—square-jawed, stocky, and Native. Every one of Gil's hackles snapped to attention when the guy smiled. "Hey, Carma. Lookin' good, as always."

She nodded, unnaturally stiff.

"I heard you were in Texas, but I didn't expect to run into you here." The guy took a step closer. "I tried to call. Your phone is out of service."

She nodded again, still silent, her shoulders rigid.

Shawnee stepped in, thrusting out a hand. "I don't think we've met. Jayden, right?"

Fuck. The name exploded in Gil's head. This was Carma's ex? No wonder she looked gobsmacked. Gil shoved his phone into his pocket and shouldered through the crowd toward them.

"Heard you've had a tough winter." Shawnee made a show of looking to Jayden's left, and then to his right. "Is that why the arm candy isn't still hangin' around?"

Jayden's face darkened, and he gave Shawnee a fuck-you glare before turning to Carma, who still hadn't moved. "I was hopin' to talk to you alone."

Oh, *hell* no. After what he'd done to her, and the shit people had been saying that night Gil had first seen her in the Stockman's Bar? This bastard was not gonna pretend it was all fine and dandy. It was about time Carma got a little payback instead.

Gil moved fast, catching her around the waist and tipping her back. She dropped her rope to clutch his shoulders as he kissed her, swift and hard.

When he lifted his head, she blinked up at him. "What was that?"

"Part of your reward for winning my bet," he drawled. "I also owe you dinner...and whatever you want for dessert."

She made a choked noise at the blatant implication, and when he set her back on her feet, she immediately stepped out of reach. Okay. Not quite the reaction he was expecting, but he had caught her by surprise. Gil turned to Jayden. "Gil Sanchez."

Their eyes locked, and Gil thought Jayden might slap away the hand he'd extended.

Jayden ignored it instead, jerking around to head for the rows of contestant horse trailers. "Never mind. I've gotta get saddled up."

Carma stared after him for nearly a count of ten, then turned dazed eyes on Shawnee. "She dumped him?"

"That's the word."

Brady chimed in. "Like Shawnee said, Jayden's been stone cold since the beginning of the year. He went into one of his poor-me funks, and she said 'adios.'"

Geezus. Gil had forgotten that pro rodeo was such a small world, and gossip traveled as far and fast as the cowboys who roped full time. Of course Shawnee and Brady would know all the gory details of Jayden's breakup.

Brady smirked at Shawnee. "Just guessin', but I think you just got crossed off his Christmas list."

She made a rude noise and turned to yell at her crew. "One hour to rodeo time. Get a move on, kiddies."

They all scattered—Shawnee to her trailer to change clothes, Cole toward where his pickup horses were stalled, and the rest to the stock pens…with Beni and Quint on their heels.

Hell. Gil had forgotten his kid was watching when he'd jumped to what he thought was Carma's rescue. Was he ever gonna get the hang of this dad thing? Gil's phone rang, vibrating across the stainless steel shelf where he'd left it. Double hell. Dickhead Ted had no doubt bypassed Analise and was calling Gil directly. He ignored the summons and stayed beside Carma.

She stared at the ground, hands clenched. Mad? Hurt? Longing for what might have been, even after everything Jayden had done? Gil's temper stirred—along with something that felt uncomfortably like jealousy.

"If you go after him, you could probably still get him back," he drawled.

Her head jerked up and her eyes blazed when she turned on him, biting off each word. "Don't be a prick."

"Why not? Apparently it's what I do best."

"No, it's not." She looked straight past his sneer, into a part of him that flinched away from her gaze. After a tense beat, she huffed out a breath, flicking a hand toward where Jayden had stood. "That isn't what you think."

"Then what is it?" As if he had the right to demand an explanation.

"It's just...I can't..." She gave a frustrated shake of her head. "It's hard to explain, and I need some time to process. Go answer your phone before we say something we'll have to pretend we didn't mean."

"Fine." Gil ground the word into dust and stalked over to grab the now-silent phone.

She wanted space? Great. He had his own shit to deal with. He didn't need to go on trying to play the hero for a woman who obviously didn't want to be rescued.

It wasn't like the role suited him, anyway.

Chapter 17

Carma yanked a comb through her hair hard enough to make her eyes water.

The fucking *nerve* of Jayden, looking at her like she should be thrilled to see him. Screw that bullshit. But had she told him so? No. She couldn't say a word while she was being gang-tackled by the ghosts of feelings past—hers and his.

But she'd managed to call Gil a prick for trying to salvage a few scraps of her pride.

She heaved a disgusted sigh and tossed the comb aside. The interior of Shawnee's trailer was dim, the shades pulled tight against the midday sun. It was tempting to hide out in there for the rest of the afternoon. Bad enough that she had to explain herself to Gil, but she also had to face Tori. And Shawnee. And…everyone.

God, why couldn't she just be normal for five stinking minutes? And had she mentioned—*damn* Jayden.

She pulled on a camisole constructed of layers of black lace and gauze to replace her sweaty tank top. God. It was like a bad dream, Jayden and Gil coming face-to-face.

But seeing—and feeling—the two men in close proximity had been a revelation. In contrast to Gil's diamond-hard sheen, Jayden wavered like a candle, vulnerable to every breeze and in need of a constant outside source of oxygen. No wonder she'd sometimes felt suffocated. He used up a lot of air.

She pushed her hair back over her shoulders and tied

on a beaded headband to hold it off her face. Then she made direct eye contact with herself in the mirror. *Suck it up, Sunshine.* Lord knew it wasn't the first time she'd looked stupid where Jayden was concerned.

But thanks to Gil, it might be the last.

When Carma pushed the door open, she found Tori sprawled in one of the loungers, also in shorts and sandals, a snug red tank layered under a matching crocheted tee, sunglasses pushed onto the top of her head.

Carma curled her fingers in a *Bring it on* gesture. "Go ahead. Hit me."

"If Gil hadn't been here, would you have gone with him?" Tori said promptly.

Carma sighed. "I don't know."

"Well, that's honest at least."

Carma slumped into a lawn chair, dropping her face into her hands so she wouldn't have to read the judgment in Tori's eyes. "I don't even know how to explain to a person like you."

"And that would be what kind, exactly?"

"Someone with too much self-respect to let that happen." Carma flung an arm toward where Jayden had last been seen.

"I haven't always been this cool," Tori said dryly. "You're looking at a woman who dragged some cowboy home from a New Year's Eve party, jumped his bones, then let him waltz in and out of her door for months—no calls, no flowers, not even a damn Valentine's card in between."

Carma hands dropped limp between her knees. "You?"

"Me." Tori shrugged. "I was nuts about him, and my self-esteem wasn't the best back then."

"Did you end it, or did he?"

"I moved to Cheyenne and didn't leave a forwarding address, because I knew if he called, I'd cave. Then I met my first husband and he taught me what it means to be in a real relationship." Her expression clouded, and Carma recalled that she'd been widowed in her twenties. Then Tori grinned. "For the record, Shawnee would've body-slammed you before she let you leave with that jerk."

Carma blinked. "She doesn't even know me."

"Like that'd stop her. And she knows enough. If you want to do a really thorough background check, just talk to a few team ropers. And what they didn't know, Analise told me."

Carma's stomach dropped. "So you also know..."

"About the semi mind-reader thing? Yeah." She made a wry face. "You have no idea how hard it's been not to ask you to guess what I'm thinking."

"It makes some people uncomfortable," Carma said carefully.

"So I imagine. But weirdly enough, Gil doesn't seem to be one of them, considering how much he hates sharing his feelings."

Carma stifled a grin at the hopeful note in her voice. "Sorry. He's good at projecting what he wants the world to see. Even I can't get past it most of the time."

"Well, that's disappointing, but I doubt you would've told us anyway."

"Why's that?"

Tori smiled. "Gil is also very good at knowing who to trust."

Possibly past tense. Carma blew out a defeated breath. "He's pretty pissed at me."

"He'll give you a chance to explain." Tori settled her sunglasses onto her nose as the rodeo announcer launched into his welcome spiel. "When you live by the twelve steps, you don't leave things to fester."

She could only hope. Carma let the sudden blare of music be an excuse to stop talking and follow Tori—not to the bleachers, but to the space behind the bucking chutes. They stepped around bronc saddles, dodging elbows and knees as cowboys flexed and kicked, warming up. Carma spotted Beni and Quint over at the stripping chute, even more striking in their cowboy hats, pretending they didn't notice a gaggle of girls ogling them from the stands. Lord, those two would be a hazard if they put their minds to it.

Or should she say *when*. Just give them a year or two...

Tori and Carma climbed up to a catwalk that led to the announcer's stand and commandeered a space along the rail. The grand entry was already in progress, with flag bearers galloping around the arena, sponsor banners snapping. Tori gestured down at the bucking chutes. "One of the perks of being tight with the rodeo contractor. We get the bird's-eye view."

"Nice."

Directly below, a cowboy squatted on the narrow platform that ran along the back of the chutes, knees splayed wide and head bowed either in concentration or prayer. His horse peered out between the bars of the gate as if picking the spot where it would like to head-plant him.

Tori nudged her with an elbow. Carma looked where she pointed, and whatever she'd been thinking dissolved at the sight of Gil in a white straw cowboy hat, his dark-purple western shirt tucked into starched jeans, a belt with a gleaming trophy buckle cinched around his hips. He bent to adjust the flank strap on a huge piebald sorrel and Carma whispered, "Oh my God."

Tori laughed. "And bless Him for his generosity, for He gave the world a rare treat when He created the Sanchez boys."

"Amen," Carma said fervently. She could brood later. For now, she intended to enjoy the scenery. Recalling their stroll through the mob of contestants, she asked, "Do you ever run into that cowboy you used to…um… date?"

"Constantly."

Oh. Well. "That must be awkward."

"It was when I first moved home from Cheyenne."

"And then?"

Tori grinned. "Since he was so determined to be underfoot, I went ahead and married him."

Once upon a time, Gil had thought he would get over the aching void that opened up inside him every time he heard a rodeo announcer and smelled rosin. He never had. And now, with no pain in his hip to remind him why he couldn't ride, it was actually worse.

As he stood watching the grand entry and the first couple of bareback riders, his muscles twitched in anticipation, expecting to hear, "Hey, Gil! We're coming your way next," from the chute boss, relaying orders Cole barked from out in the arena.

He glanced up to where Carma stood, her hair rippling in the wind, her brown skin glowing in the sun. Could she tell, just by looking at him?

He jerked his attention back to the pasty-faced rookie beside him. "You ready?"

"Yep." But his prominent Adam's apple bobbed as he gulped.

Gil didn't blame him. Crazy Ex-Girlfriend was a brute—her back nearly level with the top rail—and she had earned her name. Every trip out of the chute was an explosion of raw equine fury. Most rodeo broncs just loved to buck, and any injury to the cowboy was incidental. Gil was convinced this one enjoyed inflicting pain. As he double-checked the position of the rigging and flank strap, the mare's ear swiveled, tracking him like a radar dish.

And taking aim.

He tapped the second highest bar on the chute and told the kid, "Keep your feet up here and try not to touch her while you're getting set."

Crazy-Ex rolled her eyes back to watch the cowboy work his hand into the rigging. Gil latched onto the kid's vest, ready to haul him out of danger if the horse blew up inside the dangerous confines of the chute.

The mare shifted as noise welled from the crowd. Another horse bucked across the arena, half a jump ahead of a rider who couldn't get his feet moving fast enough to catch up. Gil winced at every yank and slam. He remembered how that felt, too. Mercifully, the whistle blew and Cole and Shawnee closed in. She tripped the flank strap so the horse would stop kicking. The rider threw an arm around Cole and swung across the pickup horse's rump to land on his feet on the other side, safely clear of flying hooves.

Gil paused a moment to admire their flawless teamwork as they escorted the horse out of the arena. Then the gateman and the judges moved into position in front of his chute.

Gil held his breath as the rookie eased down, knuckles white where he clutched the top bar of the chute. The mare's eyes rolled again, showing the whites. Her nostrils flared. Gil could feel her winding up to explode.

Hurry up, kid.

He did, his butt barely making contact with Crazy Ex's back before he gave a slight jerk of his head. His spurs lashed out, planting in the mare's neck…a full beat before the gate opened.

Oh, shit. The horse had nowhere to go but up.

There wasn't time or space to get clear as she reared and twisted, hooves lashing. Her foreleg caught Gil square across the chest and sent him flying. For an endless moment he was caught in the sickeningly familiar sensation of hanging in the air. He clearly heard every gasp and shout. Then he slammed into the hard-packed dirt—a one-point landing square on his so meticulously reconstructed right hip—and new agony exploded through him.

No. *No.*

Goddamn it, not again.

Chapter 18

Gil couldn't move. Couldn't breathe. Hands grabbed at him, but he couldn't respond to their shouted questions. If he stayed still long enough, kept his eyes shut, maybe it would turn out to be one more of the nightmares that had stalked him for so long.

Then a panicked voice cut through the pain. "Dad! Are you okay?"

Gil opened his eyes. Quint's terrified face peered at him through the fence between Gil and the stripping chute, his usual calm shattered. Then he was blocked by what seemed like a hundred bodies until another voice snapped out a command to give him some space. A pair of EMTs dropped to crouch beside Gil, with Tori right behind them.

"Don't move." Firm hands gripped his shoulder and thigh to immobilize him as he'd fallen, sprawled on his right side.

He hissed air between clenched teeth. "I know the drill."

"Where does it hurt?"

"Everywhere."

Fingers poked and prodded along his spine, his neck, and over his scalp. Gil automatically responded to their questions, wiggled his toes and fingers, told them his name, the date, where he was and what happened, but he was focused on measuring the depth and quality of the pain in his hip.

"No sign of spinal cord or head injury," the lead EMT declared. "Where does it hurt the most?"

"My right hip."

Tori swore softly, then introduced herself as his sister-in-law and his physical therapist. "He has had a pelvic reconstruction and a total arthroplasty of that joint. Since I'm familiar with his previous injuries and normal functional capacity, if you don't mind, I'd like to do the evaluation."

Up in the chutes, the next bareback rider was climbing onto his horse. The EMTs stood. "If it's okay with him, we'll get back to the action."

Gil nodded. They cleared out along with most of the onlookers, leaving Tori crouched beside him and Carma standing back a pace, eyes dark with worry. Beni tugged Quint away from the fence. "We gotta get back to work. Unless you want me to get someone else to help?"

Quint hesitated, shooting a fearful glance at Tori. "Is he..."

"I'm fine," Gil said, waving his arm to demonstrate. "Nothing life-threatening."

Carma moved over and squeezed Quint's hand where it gripped the fence. "I can help Beni if you want to stay with your dad."

"Dressed like that?" A measure of Quint's composure slid back into place, and he squared his shoulders. "There's only a couple more bareback riders. Then I'll come see what Tori has to say."

"Good call," Carma said, and squeezed his hand again.

Quint let her, then straightened and went back to work with only a single, worried glance over his shoulder.

Tori waited until he'd turned away, then asked, "Can you roll onto your back?"

"Yeah." Pain shot up to Gil's armpit and down to his knee when he moved, and the new position left him staring straight up into the midday sun. He squeezed his eyes shut against both forms of torture.

Tori laid her hand on his rigid thigh. "You're gonna have to relax."

"Hah." Not his strong point—which Tori knew well from the dozens of times she'd tried to get him to loosen up so she could test his joint integrity.

"Can I help?" Carma asked from somewhere above his head.

He opened his eyes, squinting against the glare that haloed her.

"How?" Tori asked.

"It's a relaxation technique, sort of like meditation."

"I've tried that," Gil said.

Carma bit her lip, but persisted. "This is different. It's hard to explain."

Yeah. That's what she'd said about Jayden. But he also remembered how good it had felt when she'd put her hands on him after Quint's near-wreck. "Can't hurt," he said gruffly.

Tori waved a hand. "Go ahead and give it a try."

Carma kneeled to cradle his head on her bare thighs, then leaned forward so her hair fell around his face, a thick, dark curtain against the heat and commotion. Her fingertips rested in a line along either side of his face, barely perceptible points of pressure from temple to jaw. "Close your eyes and try to focus on my voice and my touch."

He did, and she began to murmur something between a chant and a song. The cadence rose and fell, and his breathing shifted to match as he struggled to make out what seemed to be verses and a chorus. With each repetition his eyelids grew heavier. He felt the knot between his brows release, and the relaxation spread from his forehead to his jaw, down his neck and into his shoulders. Once again he had the impression that she was pulling the tension out of his body.

He lost track of the minutes that passed, until finally Tori said, "Are we ready?"

"I think so," Carma said softly.

Gil stiffened when Tori lifted his thigh, but relaxed again as Carma increased the pressure of her fingers, as if she'd pushed a series of buttons linked directly to the muscle fibers.

"Good," Tori said, with a hint of amazement. Ever so slowly, she moved his hip—flexing, straightening, rotating—as they both waited to feel the all-too-familiar grind of broken or dislocated bone.

It didn't come. There was pain, but not the sickening sense of *wrongness*. Hope trickled into his chest. Maybe—

Tori set his leg down, and he opened his eyes to meet her gaze as she rocked back on her heels. "There's no obvious fracture or displacement."

And now that the pain wasn't being magnified by panic, it had decreased by half.

"So that's good?" Quint was climbing over the fence with Beni right behind him, their job done for the moment.

"Looking okay so far," Tori said, always cautious. "We need X-rays to be sure."

Overhead, the announcer was bragging up the first steer wrestler due to compete. Sliding gates banged as saddle broncs were loaded into the chutes. Beni handed a bareback rigging to the rookie Gil had been helping, who appeared to be no worse for wear. Gil breathed a sigh of relief. The kid could've been seriously hurt if he'd been caught inside the chute, crushed by the mare's weight.

He peered down at Gil, worry and guilt etched on his face. "I'm so sorry. Cole chewed my ass for almost getting us both killed, jumping the gun like that."

"Rookie mistake." Gil pushed onto his elbows, then almost collapsed again as Carma sat back and all the noise and the heat rushed over him. "I'm guessing you won't get trigger-happy again."

The kid grinned. "No, sir. And they gave me a reride. Juniper Flats."

"Definitely a lot more user-friendly." Gil accepted the hand Tori offered to help him into a seated position and looked over the cowboy's shoulder. "You'd better go get your rigging set or you'll be hearing from Cole again."

The rookie shot a fearful glance over his shoulder. "Right. Thanks. Sorry again. Hope everything's okay."

You and me both, kid.

"I'll go get Cole's pickup and pull it around." Tori aimed a commanding look at Quint and Beni. "You two bring him out there and make sure he doesn't put any weight on that leg."

"Yes, ma'am," they chorused.

"I'll come along," Carma said. "If you don't mind."

Gil met her uncertain gaze, but their earlier spat seemed trivial now. "I'd appreciate it."

She smiled, and a dollop of that odd calm filtered into his system.

Beni handed him a slightly worse-for-wear cowboy hat. While Gil dusted it off and put it on, Quint shifted from one foot to the other. "I could come, too."

"If you want to," Gil said. "But I've visited my share of emergency rooms, and I'm betting the rodeo will be over by the time they take X-rays and get us the results."

And the waiting would be hard enough without having to put on a brave face for his son.

"We'll text you if we learn anything sooner," Carma said.

Quint considered, then nodded. "That'd be great. Thanks."

But only if it was good news. Gil did not intend to share anything else via a damn message.

He held out his hands to the boys. "Help me up."

As Gil had predicted, it was over an hour before he was checked in, another thirty minutes for the X-rays to be taken, and then he was parked in a curtained cubicle to rot. He refused to sit around in a hospital gown, so he changed back into his dusty jeans and shirt before stretching out on the bed. He'd been instructed not to eat or drink until the radiologist reviewed the films, but Tori brought him a Coke anyway.

"I would've noticed anything that might require emergency surgery," she declared, handing over the blessedly cold can and another for Carma before settling into a chair with her Dr Pepper. "And nothing against Huntsville, but if it does need fixing, we can have you back in Boston in a few hours on Daddy's jet."

The mention of surgery made his gut twist. Starting over with all the rehab, hobbling around for who knew how long. The potential that it might not ever be back to his current version of normal.

Carma scooted her chair closer and laid her hand over the fist he'd unconsciously made. His fingers relaxed, as if his body remembered whatever it was she'd done to him earlier.

"What is that?" Tori asked, her sharp eyes catching his reaction. "And why does it work on him, unlike everything else I've tried?"

Carma started to pull away, but Gil caught her fingers. "I'd like to know, too."

She shrugged, her gaze tracking to some random point in the corner. "You would probably call it chi, or prana if you're into yoga. It's about channeling energy by applying pressure over specific points or along certain lines."

"And the humming or singing or whatever?" Tori asked. "What was that?"

Carma looked even more uncomfortable. "It just gives the mind something to focus on, like the music in those meditation apps."

She was lying. Or not telling the whole truth. Gil could see from the way Tori's eyes narrowed that she knew it, too. Why? Was it some kind of tribal ritual? Gil considered what little he knew about Navajo healers and their complicated ceremonies. Weren't there taboos against discussing certain details with outsiders?

He slid a meaningful glance at Tori. "I don't need to know the specifics. It worked."

"Amazingly well." She smiled, and a fool might think she was letting it go. Then she said, "You're only working four days a week, right?"

Carma tensed, looking equal parts alarmed and hopeful. "I have Tuesdays off."

"Hmm." Tori pulled out her phone, thumbed quickly through a few screens, and frowned. "That doesn't work for me. What about Wednesday after next?"

Alarm won out. Carma looked hunted when she asked, "For what?"

"You wanted to come to the ranch clinic. I'd like to go with you the first time."

"I...um, maybe?" Carma cast a *Help me!* glance at Gil.

"That'll be great." He gave her back a *This is what you wanted* look. "Right?"

"Um...right." She gathered herself and nodded. "Thank you. I can't wait to see it."

The orthopedic surgeon pushed through the curtain, and the conversation was forgotten in the sudden swell of apprehension.

"Everything looks great," he said, and the tension *whooshed* out of the room in one collective exhale, leaving Gil as limp as a spent balloon.

The doctor flipped on the wall-mounted flat screen and pulled up a series of X-rays. The ceramic and titanium parts of Gil's hip glowed brilliant, opaque white, with the bones in varying shades of translucence. The doctor used a pen as a pointer. "It's incredible, actually. The prosthesis doesn't show any signs of damage or displacement. The pelvis looks remarkably normal other than some thickening of the ischium and pubis around here, where they buttressed it with bone grafts. Our radiologist doesn't see any microfracturing around the shaft of the prosthesis, but I recommend an MRI to be sure."

There was more, but Gil's ears were filled with the rush of relief. It was okay. *He* was okay. And geezus. He was shaking. He tightened his grip on Carma's hand, and she squeezed back.

A white slip of paper appeared in front of him. "This will make you more comfortable for the next day or so," the doctor said.

Hydrocodone. Gil's addict brain deciphered it instantly,

upside down and in a physician's scrawl, and his heart gave a single joyous thump before he forced a shake of his head. "No narcotics. I'll be fine with ibuprofen and ice."

The doctor hesitated, then nodded. "If you say so."

Gil's traitorous eyes tracked the paper all the way into the pocket of the man's scrubs.

"If you can take a fall like this and walk away, you're tougher than most—and so is your hip." The doctor gave him a broad wink. "Maybe you should be riding those bucking horses instead of working the chutes."

The jolt was instant and electric, a current that jerked Gil, Tori, and Carma all to attention. Was he suggesting...

Holy shit. Gil fists clenched, trying to maintain his grip in the tsunami of excitement.

Did the man just say he could ride again?

Chapter 19

By the time they finished dinner that night, Carma was desperate for space. Quiet. Solitude. The day had sucked her dry.

She had removed herself as far as she could from the center of attention—a.k.a. Gil. He was kicked back in one of the loungers with his right butt cheek packed in ice, rolling his eyes at the volley of sore-ass jokes. On the other side of the fairgrounds, the midway and the beer garden were going strong in the rapidly lengthening shadows, but with the rodeo wrapped up the Jacobs rigs were the only ones left in the contestant parking area.

Through all the questions and ribbing, Gil hadn't mentioned the doctor's last offhand comment, but Carma felt the knowledge simmering inside him. The tangle of shimmering possibilities and cold realities. Too much to share while he was still trying to sort it out.

Beni dumped his empty plate and silverware in a tub, then snagged a couple of cookies before offering the tin to Gil. "I guess I don't have to be so careful about throwing body blocks when we're playing basketball."

"Neither do I," Gil shot back. "The two of you better prepare to be schooled."

"In your dreams," Quint scoffed, back to his normal zen self.

Beni handed off the cookie tin and flopped into a chair. "You might be sound, but you're still old."

"Hey, Peyton Manning had a couple of years on me when

he won his last championship ring," Gil retorted, but it was clear behind the jokes he was considering his new limits. How much could his body take? How well could it perform?

What if the MRI and his Boston doctors confirmed that he could ride again?

Tori's phone chimed and she checked the message. "It's Delon. I assume *WTF?* means he heard about Gil's wreck."

She was dialing as she let herself into Shawnee's trailer. Would she tell him what the doctor had said? Gil was her patient, but technically she hadn't been on duty today, so she wasn't bound by confidentiality.

Carma guessed that Tori wouldn't hide behind a technicality. If Gil wanted Delon to know, it would be up to him to break the news.

As if on signal, the men rose and began gathering the remains of supper and dishes, hauling them into the crew trailer in what appeared to be a routine division of labor.

Beni and Quint moved to help, but Shawnee shooed them away. "Go out on the midway and waste all your money winning cheesy stuffed toys. You know how that impresses the girls."

The boys exchanged an eye roll, then looked to Gil for a nod of approval before sauntering off toward the twirling lights.

"I'll tell Tori you'll be back by ten to head to the motel," Gil called after them. Then he levered his chair into an upright position and tossed the half-melted ice packs toward a nearby cooler. "I'm going for a walk to loosen up."

His steps were slow, his body held in careful alignment as he moved off down the road that circled the rear of the arena. No doubt his back, neck, and shoulder were also feeling the effects of the fall. Carma started to say she'd go with him, then realized he had very specifically not invited her. Heat stung her face as she wondered if anyone else had taken note. Maybe they would chalk it up to Gil being Gil. Maybe he just wanted to be alone with his thoughts and was all too aware that Carma couldn't help intruding.

Or, like Carma, he was a little freaked out by how easily she could tap into his energy and direct it where she wanted. When it worked—and it often didn't—the sensation was always unnerving, like sticking her fingers into a human light socket. Or in Gil's case, a nuclear reactor. But she'd expected him to make her fight through layers of resistance, not meet her more than halfway.

And this energy had nothing to do with the sexual arousal on constant simmer between them. It ran far deeper, at a level that required implicit, almost unconscious trust from an extremely guarded man.

What did that say about him? And them? Her head reeled with the implications.

She massaged her aching temples. God, it had been a day. Days, actually. From the moment her purse had disappeared, she'd been on a nonstop roller coaster of drama and emotion. She could feel it all roiling inside her, pushing her system toward overload. She had to get away from these perfectly lovely people.

She excused herself on the pretense of heading over to the exhibitor showers in the livestock pavilion, which wasn't a complete lie. She'd end up there eventually. Grabbing her bag and a towel from the black Freightliner—her assigned quarters for the night—she set out in the opposite direction from Gil.

Given her druthers, Carma would've escaped to a patch of grass out on the edge of the rodeo grounds, far from the noise and lights. Unfortunately, the memory of that snake was all too fresh. When she was out of sight of the others, she cut through the bleachers, climbed the fence, and made her way to the darkest, quietest corner of the empty arena, where she changed into her already grubby tank top, kicked off her sandals, and stretched out on her back with her bag for a pillow.

Ah. That was better. The sandy dirt was cool against her bare legs and arms, in contrast to the still-sultry air. She dug her fingers into the earth and tipped her head back to gaze up at what stars shone bright enough to penetrate the haze of light from the midway.

Breathe in, the scent of earth and rodeo stock and the nearby trees. Breathe out, tension floating into the endless void above.

Slowly her system leveled, her mind cleared, and the man-made noises faded to the background in favor of the whirring cicadas. There were dozens of nuances, from chirrups to something like the sound of a squealing fan belt. She began to hum along, the rising, falling, repetitive notes flowing through and out of her, along with the day's accumulated stress.

Ten, twenty, maybe thirty minutes—she couldn't have guessed how long she'd been there when she became aware of someone watching her. She lifted her head and blinked her focus to the near distance, where Cole Jacobs leaned on the arena gate.

"Don't let me interrupt," he said, voice almost reverent. "When I saw you lyin' there, I figured someone had had too much beer. Then I heard…" He shook his head, as if he had no words. "I shouldn't have eavesdropped, but it made me feel good."

"Me too."

His curiosity was palpable, so she lifted a hand to

beckon him inside. He hesitated. "I don't want to interrupt your private time. We consider that precious around here."

"I'll bet." Bing had told her Cole was autistic, and no doubt he'd heard about her unique mental capacity. She sat up. "If I stay much longer I will pass out."

He pushed through the gate and joined her, lowering himself to sit with hands on bent knees, not beside her, but not facing her directly, so eye contact wasn't necessary. "I use music to control my anxiety," he said, "but I've never heard anything quite like that. As if you were singing along with the cicadas."

"Pretty much." Now that her concentration had widened, she could hear a whole chorus of night insects and birds. "For me it works better when the sounds come from nature."

"I thought it might be a prayer. Something, um, Native."

"No." At least not in the usual way. Uncle Tony said it was a connection she'd made before anyone had told her it wasn't that simple to talk to the spirits—if that's what she was doing. "It's just a thing I've done for as long as I can remember. When I was a little girl, I'd go lie out in the tall grass and sing along with the sounds it made in the breeze. Or sit in the door of the barn during thunderstorms and make up rain songs. If you know how to listen, everything has a rhythm."

She didn't add that on very special nights, she also heard music in the stars.

Cole went silent. After a few minutes he nodded. "I can hear it, but don't expect me to sing it."

"Hearing is enough. Touching." She scooped up a handful of dirt and let it trickle through her fingers. "It's easy to lose contact with nature when you're surrounded by concrete and metal."

"And humans." He heaved a powerful sigh. "Funny. I

have to work at reading people and you're the exact opposite, but we both ended up out here tonight."

Alone. But Cole had Shawnee. "How do you do it? You and Shawnee, I mean. The two of you are so different."

"Only on the surface. And we fill each other's gaps. Shawnee runs interference so I don't get overwhelmed by the people stuff, and I… Well, she'd been on her own for a long time and she needed someone solid."

He was definitely that. Carma wondered, with more than a touch of envy, what it would be like to be the one who flew free, instead of always being the anchor.

She considered her next words carefully. "Was your brother Gil's rock?"

Cole ducked his head, but couldn't hide a low pulse of grief.

"Gil mentioned him on the drive down," she added. "I got the sense that losing Xander was a big turning point in his life."

Cole thought for a moment, then nodded. "Gil was closer to him than he was to anyone, even Delon. Or maybe just in a different way. Gil didn't have to be the big brother with Xander."

And with Delon he'd had to act as both parent and brother, which would've also affected their relationship.

"He listened to Xander." Cole scuffed a divot into the dirt with his heel. "If Delon or Violet or anyone else tried to tell him to ease off, he'd get pissed. But Xander had a way of talking him down. Joking. Teasing. He was good at that. When he was gone…"

Cole left her to imagine the hole he'd left behind, in so many lives. And Gil had fallen into the abyss. They sat for a few more minutes, then Cole angled a bashful smile at her.

"I see what Analise meant. For whatever reason, a person wants to tell you things." He pushed to his feet, graceful for such a big man, and offered her a hand. When she was standing, he said, "Gil's more shook up than he's letting on. You can always tell when he goes off by himself."

"Maybe he needs private time, too."

Cole shook his head. "He's not like us. Leave him alone, and he'll just wind himself tighter and tighter."

The part of her that lived to be needed strained at the leash. *You could save him. Soothe him. Fix him.*

Send him running in the opposite direction, bruised ass and all.

Carma lifted her brows. "Are you suggesting I should loosen him up?"

"Ah…that wasn't exactly what I meant." Cole's wince was nearly audible.

She laughed. "I'm messing with you. He's not in any shape for extracurricular activities tonight."

"Don't be so sure." Cole's grin flashed in the darkness. "If he has the will, he'll find a way."

So she'd seen, but Cole didn't realize it wasn't today's fall that had knocked Gil sideways. It was the possibility of how far he could rise.

Carma knew, though, and after his response this afternoon, she was sure she could offer him relief, both mentally and physically. But it would require a demonstration of more of her special skill set, and she wasn't ready to have that also become general knowledge.

Gil had cut Tori off when she'd started pushing for explanations, though. And he had trusted Carma with his inner self.

The least she could do was return the favor, right?

Chapter 20

Gil was flat on his back in the tow-truck sleeper with the lights out, strumming his guitar and trying to slow his wildly spinning brain, when the soft knock came.

"Yeah?" he called.

The door opened a cautious crack. "I heard the music."

"Carma?" He squinted against the sudden brightness of the dome light.

Her mouth tilted into an uncertain smile. "Do you need anything before I go to bed?"

A handful of Xanax. A few beers. You. "I wouldn't mind some company."

Something to focus on besides his own thoughts. With a few offhand words, that doctor had turned all the old wild urges loose, thundering through Gil's veins. He wanted to run with them. To throw his head back and spur a bronc so high and wild that he saw stars.

As distractions went, Carma was as good as it got.

She climbed up to sit sideways in the seat, facing him, the scent of freshly showered woman wafting in with her. When she shut the door, the light went out and he could only make out her silhouette as she fiddled with the strap on her bag. "I brought something that might help with the sore muscles."

"What is it?"

"Nothing pharmaceutical. Just peppermint essence." She held up a small, dark bottle.

"Do I snort it, drink it, or rub it on?"

She hesitated, her face coming into soft focus as his eyes adjusted to the dimness. "It works best if I do it."

"You, me, and a massage?" He put a suggestive drawl in his voice. "That could definitely alter my state of consciousness."

Her dimple winked in the silvery glow from the security lights outside. "You must not be hurting too bad."

"If I couldn't get horny while I was in pain, I wouldn't have gotten laid for a very long time."

She made a noise that was part laugh, part sympathy, but she didn't move any closer. "I also wanted to talk to you about today. Before the rodeo."

Aw, hell. He'd known they'd have to hash that out, but he would've liked to wait until he'd had time to get a better grip on himself. He set the guitar aside. "You were right to be mad at me for interfering. I should have let you handle it."

"Well, that's the thing. I wasn't handling anything." She blew out a long breath. "When I get blindsided that way... it sort of paralyzes me. Especially when my emotions have been tangled up with his for so long."

Shit. He hadn't considered that she might literally feel Jayden's pain. "I'm sorry. I should've realized..."

"Why would you? And I appreciated the gesture, even if I did a crappy job of showing it. Thanks for letting me be the cool one for a change."

"You're welcome." Damned if she didn't make him feel almost noble, saving the damsel and all. "So we can forget about it now?"

She huffed a laugh. "That would be awesome."

"Done. Now come on into my lair." He patted the sleeper mattress. Like him, she'd changed into gym shorts and a T-shirt after her shower. As she eased into the space he'd made for her, he caught a strand of hair and brought it to his nose. "You smell like a maraschino cherry."

"It's my lotion and conditioner." Her hand came to rest at his waist, safely above the worst of the bruises. "Other than your hip, what hurts?"

"Back and neck, mostly."

"Can you lie on your stomach?" she asked.

"If I have a pillow under my hips. You want my shirt off?"

She gave another of those low, pulse-stirring laughs. "Always."

His groan wasn't entirely from pain as he rolled into position. God, this woman turned him on, in ways that went beyond physical. She challenged him, fascinated him, and somehow made him feel like a better man. He'd read that INFJs were called human chameleons, able to transform into whatever a person or situation demanded. It wasn't a comfortable thought, that she might just be mirroring his own desire back at him.

"What?" she asked.

"Nothing." Then he decided what the hell. "How do you keep other people's feelings separate from yours?"

She sighed. "I don't, especially if the feelings are about me. It's like pouring cream into coffee—harder to tell one from the other the more they get stirred up."

The idea that her crystal ball could get muddied was reassuring, if selfish. He rested his cheek on folded arms as she tipped liquid from the bottle into her palm. The scent of peppermint filled the sleeper and he was instantly transported back to Montana and hiking with Hank, their breath misting in the evening air—in freaking May—as they hiked up a boggy draw where the peppermint plants grew wild.

"Did you make that yourself?"

"Yes." She rubbed her hands together, intensifying the aroma. "It's a tea, not an oil. My dad's aunt taught me how to brew it."

"Not your grandmother?"

Her hair whispered along his arm as she leaned over him. "The healers are in Granddad's family. Breathe with me."

He closed his eyes and began to match the soft whisper of her breath. Her hands moved above him, not quite touching, creating an eddy that swirled peppermint into the still air.

Then she began to speak, her voice low, in a cadence as old as time. "Once there was a girl who loved the sky. Near her home there were mountains and lakes, rivers and forests, but she looked most often to the sky that stretched high and wide above it all, always changing, from the palest gray to deep, dark black, purples and pinks and every shade of blue in creation."

"Is there going to be a moral to this story?" he asked, but already the spell she was weaving had smoothed the mocking edges from his words.

"Shhh. It's just a quiet place for your mind to go while your body relaxes."

The way she'd taken him out of the gut-clenching panic that afternoon. If she could work that magic again...

She picked up the thread of the story. "The girl would stare and stare, trying to pull the sky colors inside her head to save them forever. And she loved the clouds—strands that flowed like her horse's mane, waves that rippled like whitecaps, fat beavers and herds of buffalo—even the wild wind clouds. At dawn, when the sun painted the sky, she would reach up to try and touch the brilliant red and gold.

And when the clouds piled thick and high, she would sit and watch Thunder as he roared and danced."

As she went on, Gil realized that even though she wasn't touching him, he knew exactly where her hands were by the warmth that radiated over his skin. His blood rose to the surface as if drawn by a magnet.

"Winter, spring, summer, fall—she greeted the sky, the birds, the clouds, always finding something precious to store in her heart. But one day, when she had become a woman, she walked far up into the mountains, her gaze cast downward, until she reached a small, hidden lake. As she watched, the water became still and a shadow passed over its surface. She looked up to see a massive eagle gliding down to land on a nearby branch.

"'*What makes your heart so heavy that you cannot lift your eyes to the sky?*' the eagle asked.

"'*My brother must go into battle, and I am afraid for him.*'

"'*As you should be,*' the eagle agreed. '*But because you have worshiped the sky and its creatures, I will bring you a piece of it, inside a special stone, for him to carry for protection.*'

"As the eagle took flight and disappeared, she settled upon the shore of the lake to wait. The sun sank behind the mountains and the moon appeared above her in the darkening sky. She had no food, no blanket, no defense against the bear or the wolf, but still she waited, shivering and frightened. As Morning Star faded and the sun painted the mountains in pink and gold, the eagle appeared far up in the sky, spiraling down and down until it once more perched on the branch above her, a plain, lumpy rock clutched in its talons. When she reached up for the stone, he dropped it onto a slab of rock beneath the tree, where it broke. She snatched up the halves and saw that inside its dull shell the stone held all the colors of the sky trapped in its glittering crystals.

"'*Give one half to your brother and keep the other for yourself. And when you sing to the spirits, they will fill your hands with the power of the sun.*'

"The eagle flew away. The woman returned home, where she gave her brother his half of the stone and taught him her favorite sky song. He took both song and stone with him and survived many battles with their protection. And from that time forward, the woman could sing to the sky and gather power to use as she needed."

Carma's touch was so light that Gil almost thought he imagined her fingers circling each sore spot and plucking softly, pulling the pain out of his body the way she'd released his tension that afternoon. Again, and again, and again her fingers circled and stroked, until he stopped anticipating the next touch and sank into the sensation.

"How does it feel now?" she whispered.

Gil blinked. Had he drifted off to sleep? He had no recollection of when she'd stopped touching him, or how long she'd been sitting motionless. He shifted, testing. There was still the sharp bite of the bruise on his hip, but the muscle spasms had been replaced by a liquid awareness, his body accepting the aftereffects of the trauma instead of fighting it.

"Better," he said.

"Good." Her fingers trailed the length of his back, from the nape of his neck to the base of his spine. "You should be able to sleep now."

She shifted as if to rise. He caught her wrist and held tight, gripped by something close to desperation at the prospect of being left alone to stew. "Don't go."

"You need to rest."

"I won't. As soon as you're gone, my brain will start up again." And what about her? She'd had emotions dumped on her from every direction today—Jayden, Gil, even Quint. She must need a release of her own.

And Gil was just the man to give it to her.

"I bet your brain could use a break, too." He stroked lightly up the tender skin of her arm, inside of the sleeve of her T-shirt, and was rewarded by her shiver. "It's time to stop playing with each other, Carmelita. Come down here and let me make you stop thinking for a while."

Carma drew in a quick breath, already so intensely aware of Gil that just the husky rasp of his voice was almost painful. The blankets rustled as he shifted onto his side and drew her in toward him, his arm hard and persuasive around her hips.

"Please?" It was as close to begging as she could imagine from this hard, proud man. This was more than lust. In the face of what could be a life-changing revelation, he needed contact. Connection. His fingers burrowed under the hem of her T-shirt, lifting it so his mouth could find the bare curve of her waist. "I want to taste all of you. Starting here."

His words were hot against her skin, and her thighs clenched. His arm curled around her shoulders, tipping her back and turning her as he pressed openmouthed kisses along her ribs, working his way up to nuzzle between her breasts, making a deep sound of approval when he found them free of the bra she'd stuffed in her bag after her shower. He turned his head to kiss the swell of first one, then the other, the tickle of his hair as arousing as the glide of his tongue. She had to grab his arm to steady herself, only to be undone even more by the silk-over-steel flex of his biceps under her hand.

"I… *Oh!*" Whatever she'd meant to say ended in a gasp as he found her bare thigh. Long, slow strokes from the almost painfully sensitive skin on the inside of her knee to the cuff of her shorts. First one leg. Then the other. Then back. So excruciatingly slow that her teeth clenched against a moan of frustration.

Higher. Oh, God, just a little higher.

Driven beyond patience, she pulled away.

"Don't—" he began to protest, then gave a low laugh when she whipped her shirt over her head and shoved her shorts and underwear off. "—let me stop you," he finished.

"Now yours," she said, kneeling on the side of the bed. "I don't want to hurt you."

He laughed again. "That almost sounds like a threat."

"You don't want to find out."

"I dunno. I like a challenge." But he gingerly stripped off his shorts.

He wasn't wearing underwear.

Then he pulled her down onto the bed and they were pressed skin to skin, their mouths and bodies fusing, hot and hungry. She let her hands roam, reveling in his intensely male textures. There was no softness in him, only raw power, sharp angles, and the rasp of newly grown stubble as he dragged his teeth along the curve of her shoulder.

She had expected this first time—the release of months of pent-up desire—to be a wild ride to the razor edge of sanity. But she'd forgotten that this was a man who prided himself on attention to detail. And multitasking. Oh, dear

God, he was good at that. Her body arched as his mouth and hands simultaneously inflicted intense pleasure.

Her nails dug into his shoulders and she had a vague thought that she should be doing more, but he didn't leave her space to figure out what. He rolled her underneath him and she whimpered, drawing an answering groan as she rocked against him, driving them both farther into the madness.

"My purse..." she gasped, flailing one hand toward the floor.

"Got my own." His weight pinned her down when he reached into the cupboard above their heads. Plastic crinkled and tore as he ripped the condom wrapper with his teeth. He slid down, teeth and tongue finding and torturing her nipples until she hissed from the need that screamed to be filled.

When he moved up again, he hooked her left knee with his hand, bending it and pushing it wide. "Keep that right there."

So she didn't bump his bruised hip, she realized hazily, as he caught her right ankle and pulled it up around his waist, leaving her fully exposed to the fingers that slid inside her as his thumb stroked, sending pulses of sensation rocketing through her, carrying her up, and up, until she was on the verge of coming undone. His fingers pulled out and he drove into her, so hard and full that the shock of it broke her into a thousand brilliant pieces that flashed behind her eyes as he took her again and again, every thrust a new, emphatic possession.

Tightening her leg, she drew him deeper, crazed by the desire to own him, if only for those few moments when he lost his grip on everything else. In that instant she tightened around him and held on as he shuddered in her arms, grinding nearly unintelligible words between his teeth. For several minutes they sprawled, chests heaving and muscles limp, unable to speak.

Then she gave a breathless laugh.

"What's so funny?"

She turned her head to find his mouth and press a kiss at one corner. "You even swear during sex."

She felt the wicked curl of his lips. "Only when it's fucking awesome."

Chapter 21

By Monday night, Gil was so wired he was practically levitating. Every outlet for his stress had been blocked since Saturday night, when Carma had gotten dressed and gone back to her own bed after what he'd figured was just the warm-up round. She'd insisted that his hip had had enough, even if he hadn't.

Then he'd surprised himself by dozing off almost immediately.

But the next morning Tori had refused to let him drive the tow truck and Carma had taken the wheel of the rental car, over his protests that she didn't have her new license yet.

"I am a very law-abiding driver. And this isn't the powwow van," she added cryptically.

Gil had no choice but to twiddle his damn thumbs in the sleeper, where he could stretch out and take the pressure off his sore hip. And think.

God, he wanted to stop thinking.

The standard Monday chaos had given him some relief. Then he'd run over to the hospital in Dumas for the follow-up MRI, and once it was done, he couldn't shake the knowledge that the specialists in Boston were studying the results, deliberating his future.

He'd come to terms with the death of his rodeo dream a long time ago. What would he do if it was suddenly resurrected?

Normally he would have gone straight to his sponsor to spew it all out, but Tamela's oldest was home for a rare visit and Gil wouldn't steal any of that precious time from her. There were others in the group he could talk to if he was experiencing a true crisis. They didn't know him the way she did, though. And until the verdict was in, he only had a list of maybes to consider.

Meanwhile, he couldn't even sweat the stress out in the weight room. His right shoulder was feeling the effects of the fall, and Tori had banned even the elliptical bike pending the test results.

Carma had left after work Monday to finally visit the Brookman ranch and hadn't come back until nearly eleven. Gil knew the time exactly. He'd heard every vehicle that approached on the highway, ears tuned for the distinctive rumble of her van's retro tailpipes. Then she did come home and that was worse. Busting over there felt wrong, like he was taking advantage of her living in his apartment. He couldn't even text her some stupid GIF in hopes of getting an invitation, since she hadn't got her new phone yet.

Besides, it would be too damn easy to spill his guts and invite her into spaces where no one other than Tamela was allowed. Not even Miz Iris. He was aware it wasn't entirely healthy, but it worked for him. This was no time to go messing with success.

So he pulled up the Heartland Foods contract and tried to focus on the mind-numbing legal speak, designed to lull him into overlooking clauses that could bite Sanchez Trucking on the butt somewhere down the road. But every time he blinked, his head filled with Carma, and how good it would feel just to be touching her. The way she could siphon off his tension like a ground line drained excess static electricity from a tanker truck, preventing combustion of pent-up fuel vapors.

And then he'd have to offer to return the favor, and that felt too much like assuming that her proximity meant unlimited access to her body.

He really should've thought of that before offering her the apartment.

With a peevish sigh, he swiped back to the top of the page and started rereading all the bullshit he'd inadvertently skimmed. Maybe he could bore himself into oblivion.

When he finally walked into Panhandle Orthopedics on Tuesday afternoon, his stomach was a churning mess of hope and dread—and he still hadn't decided which answer about his future would potentially do the most damage.

The receptionist greeted him with an unsugared version of the smile she used on most patients. Life hadn't left Beth with an oversupply of sweetness, so she didn't waste it on Gil. "I'll let the aide know you're here."

"I'm supposed to see Tori."

The smile sharpened. "We have to document everything for your file, so unless you want Tori to take pictures of your bruises..."

No damn way. He scowled at Beth.

She held up both hands. "Hey, I offered to sacrifice my virgin eyeballs..."

"Virgin, my ass."

"That would be the body part in question. Prepare to drop those jeans, buckaroo."

Half an hour later he buttoned his jeans, reflecting that now he and Carma had both had their bare butts photographed for posterity. As he took a seat on the padded treatment table, there was a knock at the door. "I'm decent," he yelled.

"That's debatable." Tori came in, pushed the door shut, and leaned against it, her ever-present tablet in hand.

Tension curled Gil's toes. "What's the verdict?"

"Thumbs up." Her smile reflected his relief. "Everyone agrees that the MRI and X-rays look great. The docs are thrilled that their work stood up to the impact. I'll do a full evaluation of the soft tissue, but once the bruising and stiffness have resolved, you have their blessing to return to full activity."

His heart broke into a gallop. "How full?"

"My question exactly." Her expression shifted into neutral. "Your pelvis is, if anything, stronger than normal because of the buttressing they did with the bone grafts. As far as the hip…there's no definitive data regarding participation in contact sports after a total arthroplasty, but there are a lot of cowboys who've gone back to roping and steer wrestling without any problem. I found one bull rider who has competed successfully post-replacement, although he was in his early twenties. In every case where a fully healed prosthesis failed, it was under circumstances that most likely would have caused a fracture or dislocation in a normal individual."

"So my risk of wrecking my hip is about the same as any other bareback rider?"

She inclined her head. "Everything else being equal… probably."

"*Probably?*" he echoed. "That's the best you can give me?"

"*I'm* not giving you anything. This is a call I can't make."

He frowned. "Why? You know me better than any of them."

"Exactly. I'm too close." She paused, lining up her words. "Delon has hit pretty much every goal a cowboy could have. Where his career is concerned, he could walk away tomorrow with no regrets...except one." She raised her head and met Gil's gaze. "It was supposed to be the Sanchez brothers, kicking ass and taking names together. I can't trust myself to be objective when I know how much this could mean to him."

Gil had to look down at his hands and swallow hard. He'd ruined that dream for both of them. On a personal level, he'd been lucky enough to get a second chance with his brother. But against him, in the arena? When they'd last gone head to head, Gil had had the advantage in age and experience. Delon was only nineteen years old and still finding his groove when Gil crashed. Now he was the best in the world.

And it wasn't just Delon. The current bunch of cowboys were insanely talented. The horses were twice as rank. Gil might never have had what it took to compete at this new level.

Tori was studying her tablet, brows creased. "I am amazed at how well you're bouncing back from this injury. You're moving almost normally, and the bruising is much less than I expected."

Geezus. Was she actually looking at those pictures? Gil blurted, "Carma did something Saturday night. A sort of massage."

"Sort of?" Tori's gaze snapped to his face, thank God.

"With peppermint and...well, it's hard to explain." He considered mentioning Carma's story about the eagle and the rock, but it felt like spilling a very personal secret. "She doesn't like to go into detail. I don't want to push her."

Tori frowned, but nodded. "It could be a tribal ritual. According to Hank, there are a lot of healers in the White Elk family, and from the stories he heard, it sounds as if quite a few of them would probably be INFJs—if you believe in that stuff."

"You don't?" Gil asked, surprised.

"Myers-Briggs isn't based in solid science, even though some people treat it like gospel. Personally, I'm more intrigued by the theory that hyper-empathy is an electromagnetic phenomenon."

"Which means?"

"They could be tuning in to brain waves and absorbing the energy emitted by the earth, the atmosphere, the sun…"

"And using it to heal?"

Tori flattened her brows. "It's a big jump from sensing energy to being able to manipulate it."

"You don't think it's possible?"

"I think there are a lot of things science can't explain… yet." She lifted the tablet. "I'll consider anything that shows positive results, as long as there's no risk of harm. I'd like to see what she could do with some of our patients."

"That's why you wanted to give her the personal tour."

She nodded.

Carma must be thrilled by the invitation, since she'd admitted that getting inside the Patterson clinic was the reason she'd come to Texas.

And if they liked what they saw, Gil would have some stranger parked outside his office again. The thought was even less appealing than usual, and he feared it was the prospect of Carma's absence that bothered him most.

"If I did swipe her, I'd give you Beth," Tori said.

Gil blinked. "*Give* me? Does she get any say?"

"Sure, but she'll jump at the chance to get out of Amarillo. Her first ex-husband's new wife is stalking her, sure she's trying to steal him back." Tori rolled her eyes. "As if she'd want him. Suffice to say, Beth is ready for a change, and she's seen enough of you to know exactly what she's getting into."

Gil massaged the bridge of his nose between thumb and forefinger. "That's great, but can we deal with one thing at a time?"

"Sorry. Got a little sidetracked." Tori folded her arms over the tablet. "Here's what I can say. Riding again is physically possible. Your age is obviously a consideration, but you are in excellent condition. Since you train with Delon, your workouts are specifically designed to build a better bareback rider—speed, core strength, flexibility. Plus your body hasn't had near the wear and tear of someone who has been competing for the last fifteen years."

But he also hadn't ridden a real live bronc in all that time. "I don't know if I remember how to put on a pair of chaps."

"I hear your form looks pretty good on the spur board." She smirked at his double take. "Delon isn't that oblivious...and you aren't that sneaky."

Hell. That's exactly what Tamela had said when Gil claimed his brother and friends didn't know he had a drug problem. And here he was, having a real discussion about jumping back into his first and most powerful addiction.

"I wish I could give you more definitive answers," Tori said.

"Me too." Then he shook his head. "You can give me the odds, but I'm the only one who can decide if it's worth the risk."

And whether he could survive if he gambled everything he'd fought so hard for...and lost.

Chapter 22

Carma had agreed to work on Tuesday, since Gil had to be gone. She made an excuse to hang around after her shift and watch Analise soothe and scold, coax and command, an unlikely den mother to drivers more than twice her age, but Gil didn't come directly home from his appointment with Tori.

He hadn't texted. He hadn't called. Did that mean bad news? Good? That he didn't want to talk about it either way?

She'd expected him to say *something* Saturday night, when they were curled together in the cozy confines of the truck sleeper. People always spilled their guts to Carma. It had made her a master of ducking down grocery-store aisles before certain folks cornered her. But not Gil. He'd made it clear he intended to let his fingers do the talking... and walking.

What was she gonna do, say no to earth-shattering orgasm number two?

But now it was almost three days later and he still hadn't said a word. When Analise caught Carma checking the clock for the umpteenth time, she shook her head. "It's Tuesday. Gil's got his weekly meeting in Dumas. He never misses unless he's out of town, and he usually goes out for coffee with his sponsor afterward."

The fist of worry inside Carma loosened. Gil wasn't inexplicably late. He just hadn't chosen to share his schedule with her. Or any other vital information. Why should he? One night in a truck sleeper hadn't changed their just-here-for-the-sex status. Gil was playing by the rules they'd laid out in black and white. It wasn't his fault that Carma kept slipping into fantasies of something more.

Her visit to the Brookman ranch had not helped. Bing and her big, handsome Johnny. Hank and his precious Grace. Who wouldn't envy that kind of happiness? But she couldn't let all that bliss cloud her judgment where Gil was concerned.

Analise tapped a blob of green on the weather radar monitor. "Go take a walk before that rain hits. You need some fresh air."

"Do you tell everyone what to do?" Carma asked, amused.

"Yes." Analise crossed her legs and dangled one white Ked, impressively forceful for a woman in ponytails, pedal pushers, and a red gingham blouse. "It's easier to just go along. Ask anyone."

So Carma went, one eye on the gathering clouds as she hiked the quarter mile to the edge of town, then up and down random streets, her first real foray into Earnest. It looked and felt like it could've been plucked whole from anywhere on the Montana plains, complete with the blatantly curious stares from car windows and front yards. A few nodded or lifted a hand in greeting, but the gestures felt more like *So you're the one we heard about* than a welcome.

By the time a gust of wind and dust chased her up the stairs to the apartment, the constant surveillance had left her more irritable than when she'd left.

The drum of rain on the metal roof only made the place feel more claustrophobic, so she grabbed a bottle of water and a towel and headed down to the weight room, where she sweated out three miles on the elliptical bike. The squall had passed when she stepped outside to gulp cool, damp air, but it was only the opening act of a series of storms. Thankfully, there were no tornado watches or warnings, though.

A quick peek showed nothing but wet concrete in front of Gil's garage, where the Charger normally would be parked. Damn. Still not home.

The next line of thunderheads mustered on the western horizon, their billowing tops lit pink and gold by the setting sun. Drawn by the sight, Carma cut back up through the apartment, dragging the couch cushions and a fleece blanket onto the outside landing to enjoy the view. Very occasionally a vehicle passed, the engine a swelling then fading counterpoint to the ever-present cicadas and the repetitive *ooh-OOH-ooh-ooh-ooh* of the mourning doves—another familiar note from the Montana prairie.

As the sky darkened, she willed her mind to open, releasing her thoughts to be whisked away by the restless breeze. Despite her best efforts, Gil remained firmly lodged in her head. The suspense alone was driving her crazy. What had he learned today? Could he ride again? *Would* he?

She refused to break her self-imposed ban on interfering to ask...dammit.

Footsteps crunched on the gravel, launching her heart into her throat. There shouldn't be anyone here but Analise. Carma rocked into a crouch, ready to make a break for the apartment door, then sagged in relief as Gil stepped around the front corner of the shop.

"You're back. I didn't see your car."

"It was pouring when I got home, so I parked in the garage. I hope I didn't scare you."

"A little. Analise said you usually don't get home until late on Tuesdays."

"My sponsor is out of town, so I left right after the meeting." He paused at the foot of the stairs, the angles of his face accentuated by the harsh glare of the security light, the guitar slung across his back somehow adding to the hint of danger clinging to him. "It shouldn't matter tonight, but did Max show you the tornado shelter?"

"Yes." The foreman had given her a grand tour of the concrete bunker built into the floor of the shop, big enough to squeeze in ten people, stocked with a two-way radio, first aid kit, flashlights, bottled water, and snacks. Gil's doing, of course, situated for easy access if he and Quint had to dash over from their house.

Gil set a hand on the railing. "Can I come up?"

"Sure." While he climbed the stairs, she rearranged the cushions to make space for him. "Have a seat."

He shifted his guitar around to the front and settled beside her, the silver glow of the security lights emphasizing the lines of muscle bared by the short sleeves of his T-shirt. The breeze freshened and chilled, raising goosebumps on his skin.

Carma offered one end of her blanket. "I should warn you, though, I haven't showered since I worked out."

"No problem. I live with a junior-high boy." Gil wrinkled his nose as he scooted close, bringing his heat and his woodsy scent along as he pulled the blanket across his shoulders. "I do not remember my feet smelling that bad, no matter what Violet says."

"It's probably like how other people's farts stink worse," she blurted, disoriented by his sudden invasion of every one of her senses.

He laughed. "And I thought *I* was romantic."

"I, uh…" Her breath caught as his leg shifted against hers, denim caressing the bare skin below her shorts. "I didn't realize romance was part of the package."

He strummed a chord as thunder rumbled and lightning flickered inside the towering clouds. "A balcony, a guitar, a light show. What more could you want?"

Answers—but apparently they were still not talking about his future. And despite the joking, he was strung as tight as his guitar.

And then it struck her. Holy crap. The doctors must have said yes. Otherwise, why would he still be wound up? It was all she could do not to demand that he tell her everything. How could he not tell her *anything*?

Then she felt his sigh, a profound ripple of relief that traveled through every point of contact between their bodies, as if he'd been holding on by a thread for days and now, with her, he could finally let go. Answers could wait. He needed a break, so she would give it to him.

He tipped his head back to gaze at the stars that glittered in the deep velvet sky ahead of the storm. "Do you know their stories?"

"The stars?"

He nodded, his fingers playing randomly over the strings. "The Navajo have legends about the sun, the moon, the constellations. I remember my mother telling us about that little cluster…" His gaze raked across the sky. "I don't see it."

"If you mean Pleiades, it disappears from spring until fall, which is why it's part of so many ancient religions. It marked the beginning and end of the growing season before there were calendars." Even before then, when there were no religions. No rules for communing with the stars. Uncle Tony said she was a throwback to when people were in direct contact with nature, no go-between required. He thought it was pure and special.

Carma had learned that *special* wasn't always meant as a compliment.

"What do the Blackfeet call it?" Gil asked.

"Something I can't pronounce. And there's a legend about how they're starving orphans rescued by the Sun. Or maybe Morning Star."

He cocked his head. "You don't know?"

"Our branch of the family are what my uncle Tony calls powwow Indians. We show up for the dancing and major things like naming ceremonies, but we don't practice the religion on a daily basis." She shrugged, enjoying the slide of her shoulder against his. "It's the Blackfeet equivalent of going to church for Christmas, Easter, weddings, and funerals—which we also do. We're half-assed Methodists, too."

His brows creased. "You told me a story the other night."

"That was mine." One she had shared with only a few people outside her immediate family. It had seemed natural and necessary, though, a way of reciprocating for how he'd trusted his body to her. Before he could demand an explanation she said, "So now you owe me."

"A story...or a massage?"

"A song. Preferably one of your own."

He thought for a moment, then settled the guitar more squarely in his lap, his gaze still fixed on the sky as he began to pick out a melody. The notes were light, dancing on the breeze and drifting up and away into the darkness. She rested her cheek against the soft cotton and hard muscle of his shoulder, the better to feel the vibration of the strings. After a minute he angled a look at her, and she realized she'd started to hum along.

"Don't stop," he whispered, as if afraid to break the spell.

So she followed his lead from note to note, star to star, all across the sky. The clouds pressed closer and the song shifted, from low notes that resonated with the thunder to sharp, sudden crescendos of lightning. For a mesmerizing stretch of time they were all one—Carma, Gil, the music, and the churning sky.

Then a gust of wind tore across the lot, chased by a clap of thunder. Gil flattened his palm over the strings. "Time to go inside."

"Do we have to?" she protested, unwilling to be dragged back to earth.

"Metal landing, metal shop, lightning." He unhitched the strap and set the guitar aside. Then he turned, cradled her face between his hands, and kissed her.

It could have been their first kiss. Nothing that had come before had prepared her for this—tenderness and longing, gratitude and a plea. *Touch me. Feel me. Know me.* For the space of that kiss there were no walls. Only a man who'd been locked away for too long, desperate for contact. She gave it to him, opening up and letting him reach into the spaces where she stored the sunshine and moonlight she gathered to carry her through the coldest, darkest nights.

Lightning flashed again, only a few beats ahead of the thunder. When he pulled back, his eyes reflected her wonder. *What was that?*

Another gust of wind pummeled the shop and tore the blanket off her shoulders. Gil blinked, visibly struggling to resurface, then climbed to his feet, scooping up the guitar with one hand and holding the other out to her.

She let him pull her up and almost into his arms. She felt as if she should say something profound, but she couldn't form the words to describe what had just happened between them.

And he wasn't ready to hear it, so she held out a hand to catch one of the first, fat drops and offered it to him with a suggestive smile.

"In that case, it seems like a perfect night for a rain check."

Chapter 23

Gil probably should have stayed for a late supper with a few of the others after the meeting, but he wasn't in the mood for stale cigarettes and even staler regrets. He craved cherries and almond, and that indefinable something about Carma that made him feel cleaner, as if she chased the darkness out of him the way she'd seemed to draw the bruises out through his skin.

He'd come looking for a moment's peace, and he'd found that and more, until a single kiss had turned him inside out.

The apartment was cool and dim and still bare. The only visible marks Carma had made were a pair of flip-flops kicked off beside the front door, a scatter of clothes across the bed, and a jean jacket tossed over the back of a chair. She moved silently, dropping the blankets and cushions on the couch as she passed, as if unnecessary words might break the spell they'd woven together.

She left the bathroom door open and the light off, the outlines of her body blurred in the diffuse glow from the living room lamp as she pulled the tank top over her head and let it drop. Once again, she stripped without a hint of self-consciousness, then turned to adjust the taps in the shower while he did the same. Together they stepped under the spray, this time with his back braced against the wall.

Wordlessly, she wound her arms around his neck, flesh sliding against slick, wet flesh as she took his mouth in kiss after kiss. Long, deep, drowning kisses that refused to be rushed.

That mouth. God, that mouth. The taste of her was as potent as whiskey sliding over his tongue, simultaneously heating his blood and smoothing his ragged edges. The kisses went on and on and on, until he lost track of where one ended and the next began. Only then did she pull away to scoop the bar of soap from the dish, rubbing circles of lather over his chest, his shoulders, his stomach, and finally…

"Holy fuck," he rasped as her hand closed around him. She gave a low laugh when he banged his head against the shower wall, and he swore again as she worked the lather over him, until every red blood cell in his body seemed to have rushed to that immediate area.

Then another curse as she let go and stepped out of the stall. The shower hit him full on, sluicing away the soap, a thousand stinging fingers on his aroused flesh. Directly above them thunder boomed and lightning flashed. He felt their power vibrate clear to his bones, as if the song they'd created had bound him to the elements. Steam billowed around him and Carma materialized from the cloud, a vision of mist and dreams he'd called down from the sky.

But she was very, *very* real.

As his greedy hands reached for her, she pressed the condom into his palm, then turned and lifted her arms up and over her head, her back to his chest, to link her fingers behind his neck.

Utterly exposed, a sacrifice to whatever pleasure he chose to take.

The trust implicit in that gesture was more staggering than the sight of her amazing body, wet and glistening. He fumbled the condom into place, then gave himself the luxury of running his palms over her, shaping every curve, memorizing every texture. Then it was too much. He grasped her hips and centered her. They moaned in unison when his cock slid between her thighs, and she rocked her hips to work herself against the hard length. Geezus. *Geezus.* He had to get inside her.

And then he was, echoing her gasp as he drove deep. For a moment he held her there, savoring the clench of her body around his, teeth gritted against the urge to run wild. When he had himself under some semblance of control, he began to move in long, hard strokes, punctuated by low, almost feral sounds from deep in her throat. He pushed them both to the edge, holding them there for as long as physically possible, until he couldn't keep his grip any longer and had to let them both tumble over.

When his mind began to clear, he reached up, circled her wrists, and drew her arms down, wrapping them around her along with his own. And then he just held on while the storm outside continued to rage—echoing the thunder of his heart.

When the water started to cool, Gil peeled both of them off the shower wall and handed Carma a towel. She twisted her hair up in it, then grabbed a second to wrap around her body, glad the roar of the rain on the metal roof eliminated a silence that she might otherwise have been tempted to fill. In the close confines of the almost-dark bathroom, it felt as if they were suspended inside the storm, cut off from reality. She didn't want to break the spell.

Gil seemed to agree, drying off and pulling on silky black boxer briefs without speaking. God, that body. Even the scars were beautiful in their own way, a mottled testimony to his strength.

She gave the towel on her head another squeeze, then unwound it and reached for her hairbrush.

Gil caught her hand. "Can I?"

"Um, sure." Odd, that she felt more vulnerable now than when she'd put her body at his mercy. He could hurt her so easily, even if he was trying not to. And there was something so intimate about standing in front of the mirror, seeing that pucker of concentration between his brows as he lifted a section of hair and gingerly stroked the brush through it, so much gentler than she was with herself.

Suddenly, it was too much. She had to create some space between them, even if it was only with words. "Is this a thing with you?" she asked.

"Not until now." His fingers separated another section with infinite care. "There are no Sanchez girls."

And he didn't even consider that a boy might have long hair and braids. It occurred to Carma that until now, she hadn't known anyone who was Native in blood and appearance but who'd never lived on a reservation. If she sometimes felt disconnected from what was supposed to be her culture, what must it be like for Gil?

He smoothed the last tangles away. "Where's the dryer?"

"In the bedroom."

He set the brush down, took her shoulders, and steered her out of the bathroom. She balked when he tried to sit her on the side of the bed. "If you're gonna tuck me in, let me get my jammies on, 'kay?"

"Sorry. I lapsed into dad mode there for a second."

She found her sleep shirt on the floor at the end of

the bed and was pulling it over her head when he plucked something from the nightstand. Crap. Maybe he wouldn't remember...

"It's the rock from the story." Blue fire glittered in his hand, and an instant later understanding sparked in his eyes. "*Your* story."

"Um, yeah." It was too late to grab the stone and hide it under her pillow, so she found clean underwear and waited for the inevitable.

It came with more amazement than disbelief. "It's real?"

"Yep. They're called geodes. They come from..." She trailed off when he narrowed his eyes at her attempt to evade the real question. Sighing, she said, "Yes."

He turned the hollow, crystal-lined stone so it caught the light, his mind working through all the implications. "It was given to you in a vision."

During a vision. By a vision. She'd never decided how to put it. "Yes."

"And your brother carries the other half?"

She nodded.

He ran his thumb along the jagged edge of the crystals. "You said you were an INFJ."

"Actually, Analise said it. I just didn't disagree."

He frowned, his tone on the verge of accusing. "So the thing you did to my hip and back Saturday night..."

She sighed and sank onto the side of the bed. "When my mother hurt her back, the pain meds and muscle relaxers made her sick, so we were trying whatever else we could find. One of my aunts gave us the peppermint tea, and while I was rubbing it on, I realized I could feel hot spots, and if I touched her just so, I could release the pressure and ease the pain." She held out her hands, palm up. "I don't know how it works, or why it does wonders for some people and absolutely nothing for others."

"And the songs?"

"I started making them up when I was three years old. They're just my brain taking what I hear and feel and turning it into a song like you do with your guitar."

His face registered surprise, as if he'd never thought of his music that way. "I'm not tuning in to nature or whatever."

"Are you sure? What you played tonight..." She rolled her shoulders restlessly. "I can't *make* a new song. They only come to me when I'm not trying, just...letting go."

Again he looked startled, and she knew it must be the same for him. Bing had told her that he'd learned to play the guitar when he was laid up after his wreck. Music therapy—songwriting in particular—had proven itself to be a valuable way for addicts to process their emotions. Had Gil known that, or was his music a beautiful accident?

Either way, she was sure he had no idea how much of himself he'd put in his song.

"Do your songs have lyrics?"

He shook his head. "Only a few, and they suck."

"I guess some things aren't meant to be put into words."

"Hmm." He went back to turning the geode between his fingers, his mood shifting into something almost angry.

"What?" she asked.

"If I'd had something like this"—he set the stone down with a sharp click—"it wouldn't have mattered. The pills were never just about the pain for me."

She blinked. "You think what I do could have helped you not get addicted?"

"It wouldn't have hurt." His mouth twisted into a mockery of a smile. "Hah. Punny guy."

Carma stared at him, stunned. She'd expected skepticism at best. Outright disbelief was more likely. This level of acceptance was so unexpected she found herself voicing the arguments that had been used against her. "It could be a mental trick. A kind of hypnosis where I just make you think you feel better."

Gil shrugged. "If I have less pain, what's the difference?"

"I might not be fixing anything. Even that..." She gestured at the stone in his hand. "To me, the vision was real. Someone else might say I hiked until I was so exhausted that I laid down and fell asleep beside a lake, had one helluva dream, and found a pretty rock when I woke up."

Except geodes weren't found in her part of the northern Rockies, so where did it come from? Unless another hiker had dropped it, a souvenir from one of the gift shops. Carma had been so unnerved by the experience, she'd grasped at every possible explanation. Who was she to have a vision? She didn't pray to the right entities, or participate in the right ceremonies. And when she'd tried to become the kind of person who should have been chosen, she'd felt as if she was only playing the part.

Amazingly it was her brother, with his engineer's love of all that could be calculated and measured, who'd put it in perspective.

"Science can't even explain what consciousness is," he'd pointed out. "What we perceive as reality is a series of electrical impulses, based on input from sensors that may or may not be relaying accurate information. No two people see, hear, or feel anything the same way. We already know you pick up wavelengths that most of us don't." Then he'd mussed her hair, flashing one of his increasingly rare grins. "Maybe you've got tinfoil in your head and you're receiving signals from extraterrestrials."

She'd shoved him away, poking out her tongue, but his words had stuck. And despite his devotion to logic, he never left the country without his half of the geode.

Gil's frown was back. "Aren't visions sort of… expected?"

"Among who? The mythical, magical Indians?" She snorted her impatience. "We're not elves or fairies, with glitter in our DNA. My dad gets so pissed when some idiot on a movie set admires his spiritual connection with the horses, as if he was born being able to talk to animals instead of busting his ass to be the best trainer in the business."

His mouth twisted. "And I'm no better, despite everything my mother tried to teach me."

"Stop." She tugged on his arm. "That was me being snarky when you're just trying to understand."

Gil sat down, bare knee touching hers, his skin the denser shade of brown thanks to her scattering of white ancestors, one a fur trader whose Blackfeet wife had proved invaluable as a mediator when doing business with her notoriously hostile tribe. On one hand, she was a strong, smart woman who had improved circumstances for her people, putting guns and other trade goods in their hands.

But her children were also the first on the family record to be baptized Methodist, given Christian names, and taught to speak English as their primary language, setting a precedent that had been carried down from generation to generation, leaving massive chunks of their Blackfeet heritage discarded along the way.

"Listen," she said. "There's no such thing as *the* Native way. Or even *the* Blackfeet way. I assume it's the same with the Navajo. Ask four people, you'll get four opinions on how to do it right, or who even deserves to try." She laid a hand on Gil's ridiculously hard thigh. "There's always gonna be someone who thinks you're too Native for their taste, and others who say you aren't enough. It's a no-win."

"Speaking from experience?"

She shrugged. "The word Pretendian gets thrown around a lot, even among ourselves."

"And at you?" His brows spiked in surprise.

"Make yourself visible, you make yourself a target. For some it's a sort of elitist thing—all about being the right amount and kind of Indian, as defined by them of course. Others benefit from keeping the club as small as possible." She turned her back on him, changing the subject before it completely killed her very nice buzz. "You'd better get to work with that blow-dryer before I decide to make you warm me up some other way. I don't trust an ancient diaper stuffed in a vent to keep us from embarrassing Analise."

He laughed. "I don't think that's possible. And it would serve her right."

He switched on the dryer and Carma relaxed into the gentle stroke of his hands, letting the warm stream of air blow away the negativity. For this moment they could just be, and forget about the rest.

Chapter 24

Gil kept waiting for Carma to pepper him with questions about his appointment with Tori, but they didn't come.

Maybe it was a trick. Bing said silence was a vacuum—it sucked the truth out of her patients. Two school counselors had tried it on Gil, plus that one cop. He hadn't felt an overwhelming urge to confess that yes, he had given the Earnest Pioneer statue a pair of acorn squash balls and a zucchini dick.

Damn fine artwork, if you asked Gil.

If Carma was playing him, she was really good at it. The music, the sex, her own confessions: it was all tailor-made to beat down his resistance. Or she was simply reading him, mirroring his emotions, and giving him what he needed the way the Internet article said. How could either of them really know?

Which was bullshit, and he knew it. The sex had been incredible. Intense. Mind-blowing. But that kiss on the landing had struck a chord so deep his heart was still quivering. It had done the same to Carma. He'd seen the impact in her eyes. They could leave it unspoken but it couldn't be unfelt.

That single kiss had turned every one of their ground rules into a joke—and neither of them was laughing.

But he wasn't freaking out, either. Didn't have an overwhelming urge to make a run for it. His only compulsion was to sit and run his fingers through Carma's hair. Maybe it was that weird thing he'd seen on the internet.

He'd rolled his eyes when, in one of his desperate quests for sleep, he'd stumbled across online videos of women brushing their hair that claimed to be the cure for insomnia. Now he wondered if he should have paid more attention. It was pretty damn hypnotic.

Before he'd consciously decided to speak, his voice was saying, "Do you have any idea how many times I've thought, *If I could have one more chance...*"

She had been still before. Now she went utterly motionless, as if she had stopped the beating of her heart. After a moment, her answer whispered out. "Thousands, I imagine."

"At least." Like releasing a safety valve, thoughts spilled out through the tiny opening he'd allowed. "Now I have that chance, and I don't know if I can take it."

She didn't comment, just turned her head slightly to signal that she was listening.

"Assuming I could find the time—and that's a huge assumption—what if I got hurt again? Not just my hip. Anything. If I broke an arm and had to have surgery, it could trigger a relapse."

She nodded.

"I know, I could have an appendix attack tomorrow and be right in the same boat. But the odds are definitely higher if I was riding." He gathered a fistful of her hair, lifting the damp ends off her back and into the stream of warm air. "I've barely made time to spend with Quint, but I can find a way to take off rodeoing? How's that gonna make him feel? I mean, yeah, I would take him with me, but what if he'd rather be at basketball camp than watching his old man get his ass kicked by a bunch of rookies?"

"Are you worried you're too old?" Carma asked.

"Delon is two years younger than me, and he's sick

to death of people asking when he's gonna retire," he grumbled.

"So you're worried people will *think* you're too old."

"No!" Then he scowled. "Some. I don't want to be one of those pathetic has-beens who don't know when to quit."

She nodded again, giving him zero feedback.

"Tori says I'm in better shape than most twenty-year-olds."

Carma reached back to squeeze his butt. "I can testify to that, although it has been a while since I've had my hands on a twenty-something."

She'd better not be thinking about doing it again. And yeah, that was possessive as hell, but he'd have to worry about it later. Compartmentalize and conquer, that was him.

"And there's still this place." He tapped one foot on the floor. "I couldn't do anything without more help. You know how much luck I've had with hiring, and Analise is already working overtime."

Even as they spoke. She'd come in to cover while he went to Amarillo, and he'd promised to take over for her when he got back. But he had also told her not to expect him before ten, so technically he had another hour. "I could ask Dad to take on more of the stuff that's not contracts or dispatch. And I could turn over the inventory and maintenance oversight to Max."

"Could you?" Carma twisted around, eyebrows peaked.

Honestly? He had given it a lot of thought since Quint had moved in. It wasn't that he didn't trust Max, but Gil busted ass—his own, the mechanics', and the drivers'—to maintain an excellent safety rating, which had an impact on everything from insurance premiums to attracting new clients. Max might be too laid-back to keep everyone toeing the line.

"I can try."

"Sure." She sounded skeptical. Because she doubted Max's ability to lay down the law, or Gil's to cede any significant control?

He gave her a nudge and she faced forward again. He knew she'd noticed that he'd skipped over the most obvious source of extra labor. "I'm not gonna make Delon cut back his rodeo schedule."

"Why not?"

"He isn't gonna be able to compete at this level forever. I don't want him to waste any of the time he's got left."

"Shouldn't that be his decision?"

"It's not that simple." He leaned down to yank the dryer cord out of the socket. "Where I'm concerned, he has a bad case of survivor's guilt. He'd say yes because he'd think it was payback for all the years he went on rodeoing when I couldn't."

"And for the business you built for him to come home to?" she asked.

"I didn't do that for him. And it's not like he didn't contribute." Gil wrapped the cord tightly around the dryer. "His success has helped put Sanchez Trucking on the map."

Carma laced her fingers together in her lap and bit down on her bottom lip, visibly restraining herself.

"Go ahead," Gil said. "I want to hear what you think."

She held out for another few seconds, then shook her head. "I don't think Delon will thank you for making more sacrifices on his behalf."

"I told you, I haven't given up anything for him."

Her eyes narrowed and her jaw clenched, but her voice was neutral. "If that's how you see it."

"It is."

She drew a deep breath. "Okay. So you pawn off what you can on your dad and Max. Maybe take another shot at hiring someone who can cover dispatch at least part time. What else?"

That was the tricky part, and that kiss out on the landing had made it ten times more complicated. He set the dryer on the nightstand before turning back to face Carma. The rain had stopped and the sudden silence made his ears ring. Her fingers curled into her palms as she read his intent before he could put it into words. All the chaos inside him was reflected in her eyes. They weren't ready for this, but like the thunderstorm, it had hit them anyway.

"I would need you to stay," he said.

She sat very still again, absorbing the impact.

"I know it's sudden. But this..." He spread his hands, indicating the two of them. "It's gonna take a while to sort out."

Her mouth opened, but for a long moment she only stared at him. Finally she said, "You realize what you're asking?"

"Yes." And it made his heart knock and sputter like an engine with a bad spark plug. This was a total violation of their no-strings rule. A monster step over Gil's personal lines.

She didn't throw herself into his arms. Not that he'd expected her to, but a little unbridled enthusiasm would have made him feel less like a bad decision she was telling herself she shouldn't make. He should be thrilled that she was also leery. Her obvious misgivings made it easier for him to establish a whole new set of ground rules, this time with an eye toward damage control so that if it did end, it wouldn't have to be in a ball of fire.

Her mouth curled ever so slightly. "So…you're gonna go for it."

"Yeah. I guess I am."

The smile grew, climbing into her eyes. "And you think I should go on this wild-ass ride with you."

"Yeah. I do."

She gave a slow, disbelieving shake of her head, as if she couldn't believe what was happening. "I guess it wouldn't be the craziest stunt I've ever pulled."

"Have you ever jumped off a cliff?"

"Only a short one, but I *was* on a horse."

He had to laugh. Geezus. Only this woman could top damn near every bone-headed stunt he'd ever pulled.

He leaned in and kissed her forehead. "Thanks."

"I didn't do anything but listen," she insisted.

"That was enough." He kissed her again, then reluctantly stood. "I'll see you in the morning. I'd better go take over for Analise."

And let them both have some time to possibly come to their senses.

When the back door shut behind him, Carma flopped onto the bed, exhausted. It had taken every molecule of self-control to keep her lips zipped when that know-it-all part of her brain was screaming opinions on exactly what Gil should do. Her only slip had been when they were talking about Delon, and Gil had refused to listen to her so it didn't matter.

And as delicious as it was to have him lounging around in nothing but his underwear, Carma needed some distance to process what had just happened.

She also needed to touch a familiar base. She yanked on jeans and a sweatshirt, grabbed keys and the cheap cell phone he'd told her to keep until hers was replaced, and escaped out the front door and across rain-scrubbed gravel to her van.

The interior smelled of sun-warmed vinyl, dust, and the whiff of burnt sweetgrass that had earned her a search by the K-9 unit in Tucson after she'd been stopped for supposedly not using her turn signal—but more likely for driving while being brown-skinned. The carpeted walls and plush velvet ceiling closed around her, everything soft and unapologetically out of date, a piece of home on wheels.

She collapsed onto the bed and rubbed her cheek into the scratchiness of the wool Hudson Bay blanket that she used as a bedspread. She missed this van, with all its textures and its checkered past, a family legend in its own right.

The apartment had zero personality, unless she counted what wafted up through the floor vents. She and Gil had packed so much into the past six days—sweet hell, had she really been in Earnest less than a week?—that she hadn't given her accommodations much thought. Lying in the van, though, she knew she couldn't stay in that apartment.

She craved solitude, and a place with grass, and trees, and stars that weren't drowned by security lights. Bing would let her park out at the ranch, but that came with an obligation to socialize, and too many eyeballs that would be winking if Gil stopped by for a visit.

The Canadian River was nearby. And a lake. She vaguely recalled a sign pointing to a recreation area on the drive from Amarillo. There must be a campground where she could park in the short term.

In the long term…

She groaned out loud. Long term? After less than a week? Rolling onto her back, she dug her fingers into her blanket, breathed in the scents from her world, and slowly settled back to earth. What was she *doing*?

She'd promised to help make the therapy program a reality. More to the point, she'd promised to consider herself first the next time she got involved with a man. Her needs, her responsibilities, her motivations, her *future*. But Gil asked her to stay and she immediately said yes. No questions. No qualifications. She hadn't even asked *For how long?*

A month? A year? Until he won a few rodeos and found a shiny new blond of his own?

Oh, stop it! Of all the issues she and Gil had to deal with, that was the least of her worries. Maybe she should start with how he was a recovering addict, and she was a serial enabler who had a crappy track record with men. Well, mostly one man, but still…

Carma sighed. The hell of it was, Tori was right. Carma had caught Gil at a weak moment. He was struggling to find his footing with Quint, and Sanchez Trucking was at one of those tipping points where growth was outpacing their work force, even fully staffed. Gil's life had been in a state of forced flux before Carma stumbled in.

He wouldn't be the first man to jump into a relationship to solve his problems. She wanted to shake off Tori's words, but it was a truth that had to be faced.

And that was just Gil. From Carma's standpoint, there was a *lot* to consider. How did she feel about living in this town? Hell, this state? She had never considered moving away from home indefinitely. What about Sanchez Trucking? Could she work with Gil, side by side, day after day? If she couldn't, what would she do?

And how could they even ask, let alone answer, any of those questions when Gil could be on the verge of turning it all upside down? There was no sense figuring out how she fit into this life if he made a successful comeback and ended up living a completely different one.

Oh hell. Admit it. You were in it for the long haul the minute he said he needed you.

God, she was such a sucker.

She reached over to the stereo, tuned it to a classic country station, then gazed at the constellation of raindrops on the nearest bubble window. But for once, looking to the heavens wasn't the answer. What she needed was a good grounding.

She palmed the cell phone while she did the usual time zone calculation, minus an hour now that she was in Texas. Nine forty-five here was seven fifteen in the morning in Afghanistan. She could pay for the international call when Gil got the phone bill.

As always, reaching around the world seemed impossible, and her heart tripped in relief and affection when a gruff, infinitely precious voice answered. "Carma? I almost didn't pick up, but Mom said you got a different phone."

"Yeah. Mine got stolen."

She settled herself more comfortably on the bed and prepared to tell her brother the whole story—minus a few key parts. They *did not* discuss their sex lives, and Eddie was too sensible to believe anyone could fall in love practically overnight. But even if all they talked about was the lousy weather for calving back home, Eddie would help center her.

And Lord knew where Gil was involved, she was in constant danger of losing her balance.

Chapter 25

Gil had suffered every form of insomnia known to man, but it had been a long, *long* time since he was too excited to sleep.

Declaring his intentions out loud had been the mental equivalent of swinging open a gate. All the thoughts he'd tried to keep penned up stampeded through his head. Who should he tell next? And how? Phone calls seemed like a mediocre way to share news this big. He wanted to see faces, savor the shock and awe.

He'd have to start with Quint…unless he gathered everyone up and told them at once. Delon would be home Sunday. So would Steve and Miz Iris. It would mean sitting on this bombshell for days, but it would be worth it. And the delay would also force him to give the bruise on his ass plenty of time to heal.

In the meantime, he would sneak in as much time as he could on the spur board, and he could study video of current competition, which had always been one of his favorite ways to improve his own riding. He sure as hell wasn't making any progress on the Heartland Foods contract. If he wanted to rodeo, they couldn't sign it anyway. There was no way they could do a decent job of it if Gil cut back his hours. Delon would be rightfully pissed after all the work he'd put in, but he'd understand.

Closing his laptop, Gil grabbed his tablet, popped in his earbuds, and stretched out on the bed. Five minutes and a credit card number later, he had access to the video archives of all ten rounds of the previous year's National Finals Rodeo. He started with the first bareback ride of the first night and worked his way through, pausing and rewinding to analyze every detail. To be the best, you studied the best.

That kid from Manitoba was tall, but he hardly ever got whipped out of shape. What was he doing with his free arm to keep his upper body so controlled? On the flip side, that other poor bastard had gotten slammed into the dirt three nights in a row. Why was he getting jacked up over his rigging at around the four-second mark every time? Gil also made reams of notes on the horses. Usually they had a pattern to the way they bucked, and having an idea what to expect could give a cowboy the edge.

Plus a lot of the same stock would be bucking at the Diamond Cowboy.

Yes, he would be insane to try to go from zero to ninety-point rides in less than two months. That's what it would take to have a shot at the Diamond Cowboy title, and in his heyday Gil had only broken the ninety-point barrier twice. What made him think he could do it now?

Better training, a persistent voice whispered in his head. The program Tori had designed and constantly tweaked for Delon was light years beyond the workouts they used to do. *Better horses*. All he had to do was pull up highlights from ten years ago to see how much the horses had improved—more jump, more kick, more chances for a cowboy to score points.

Or get thrashed.

He'd be smarter to ease into this, but how could he ignore the Diamond Cowboy when it was right in his front yard? Where else could he go to face that level of competition, with that much at stake? The monster summer and fall rodeos like Cheyenne and Pendleton—wins that were career highlights for any cowboy—only accepted contestants who were currently in the top forty or fifty in the world standings, which counted him out.

Even a berth at the Texas Circuit finals would be a serious stretch with the season halfway over. He'd have to hit every rodeo left on the schedule and win consistently to catch up, and that was too much time away from the shop.

The Diamond Cowboy was the only chance he'd have at something big until next year. Gil had never competed without a championship in his sights. He didn't want to start now.

Plus it would be a good measure of where he stood. If his game wasn't up to snuff, he could pack his gear away and say he'd given it a shot. And it wasn't like he'd be jumping straight into the main event. He had to get through the qualifier first.

He was deep into the fifth round when his bedroom door swung open. He slapped the tablet facedown onto the bed.

"What are you doing?" Quint blinked groggily at him. "It's four in the morning and you still have your clothes on."

Gil swiped a guilty hand down the front of his T-shirt. "I got caught up in…stuff. Why are you up?"

"I had to piss. I saw your light on." Quint frowned, and Gil felt like he was the delinquent kid. *Busted.* "Turn that thing off and try to get some sleep."

"Yes, sir."

Quint made a growly noise and stumbled off toward his bedroom. Gil was sorely tempted to pick up where he'd been interrupted, but now that he'd stopped to blink, he realized his eyes were gritty and throbbing from staring at the screen. Plus Quint might come back to check on him. Sighing, he set the tablet aside, stripped down to his underwear, and crawled in bed.

An hour and a half later he eased into the weight room, not wanting to wake Carma while he rummaged through the storage bins under the workbench. Where were his old chaps? Oh, right. Delon had also taken those when he'd confiscated the pictures and stuff that he was afraid Gil would destroy. *Good job, little brother*. But since Gil had no idea where they were stashed, he would have to wait until after his big announcement to find out if what he'd called the Flamethrowers still fit.

He'd also need a glove and a rigging, and those couldn't go straight from the store to the arena. It took hours to get them just right, treating the glove with benzoin to add stiffness, adjusting the handhold by sanding here and gluing in pieces of leather there until the fit was perfect. But Gil could skip a few steps by borrowing one of Delon's backup gloves and riggings and adjusting it to fit him. And with some help from Steve Jacobs—

His cell phone vibrated. Duty calling. He checked the number, sighed, then shoved the bins back under the bench and headed to the office to deal with the first crisis of the day.

At seven Carma strolled in. She'd pulled her hair back into a sterling-silver barrette and was wearing a deep-pink, fluttery sundress. She looked so delicious Gil had to have a taste.

When he eased out of the kiss, she smiled. "Good morning to you, too."

He looped his arms loosely around her waist, enjoying the thrum of his blood. "How'd you sleep?"

"Better than you," she said, studying him critically. The eye drops apparently hadn't erased all the signs of his video binge.

"I'm fine. No, scratch that. I'm great." He grinned, feeling ridiculously cheerful. "I have to run over to the house—I forgot my tablet. Ignore any messages for me that don't start with *I'm upside down in a ditch and on fire.*"

"I can do that."

He kissed her again, quick and light, then headed back to his house. Outside, the birds were clearing their throats in the damp, sweet predawn air. It reminded him of waking in his mother's hogan and tiptoeing out to find her sitting on a blanket, greeting the sunrise. He didn't understand a word of the traditional Navajo morning prayer, but he'd loved to listen anyway, enchanted by the rise and fall of her voice.

Another reason, perhaps, that he'd fallen so easily under Carma's spell. Then he shook his head. No, he shouldn't say that, even as a half-assed Navajo. Witches were considered a real and present danger that walked among the Diné. Carma might be something other than so-called normal, but she was definitely not evil.

She was…unique. Fascinating. Every conversation with her forced him to rethink how he viewed the world. He couldn't imagine ever getting tired of talking to her. This was why he envied his brother and all his happily paired-off friends. Companionship. The simple pleasure of being known and appreciated. If a marriage could be like this—a partnership between two people who could talk and laugh, have each other's backs and call each other's bullshit…

His heart stuttered. *Marriage?* Where the hell did that come from?

Sure, he'd like to have that kind of life, but he'd accepted that he wasn't a likely candidate. An addict. A workaholic. A self-absorbed bastard at the best of times. Honestly, he didn't even know what he was asking Carma. *Hang out with me, baby?* She had plans. Places to go, people to help. A life and a home that weren't in Texas.

What could he offer her in exchange for all of that?

He paused halfway between house and shop as the sky brightened with the imminent arrival of the sun. As he watched, a pinpoint of light appeared, then spread along the horizon. His mother had told him it was the opening through which prayers could pass to the spirit world...or something like that. He did remember that the morning prayer was meant to clear his head and make him fully present in the coming day, so he stood, and breathed, and did his best to empty his mind. When he could no longer look directly into the sun, he closed his eyes and tilted his face toward the sky, uttering a silent plea.

I know I haven't earned any favors, but for the sake of everyone else I could hurt, if I'm taking a wrong turn, could you give me some kind of sign?

He listened for a full minute. There was no answer except the chatter of birds and the rattle of a Jake brake as a Sanchez truck came home to roost. Gil continued toward his house, impatient to get on with his day.

And his suddenly wide-open life.

Chapter 26

The night in the van and touching base with Eddie had done wonders for Carma's equilibrium, but seeing Gil this morning had set her off-tilt again, and not just from the rush of desire. He looked like sleep-deprived hell, which made his uncharacteristic cheerfulness even more jarring. Of course he was beyond excited about the prospect of riding again. She was excited for him.

So what was it in his smile that made danger signs flash in her head?

She was so preoccupied that when the door opened, she didn't immediately recognize the rangy, ginger-and-gray haired man who smiled as if he was the one welcoming her.

"Hello, Carma." Instead of offering a hand, he hooked his thumbs in his pockets and rocked onto his heels. "I'm Merle Sanchez."

Well, duh. She should have known him from the framed photos of Merle accepting half a dozen *Business of the Year* plaques from the Earnest Chamber of Commerce. How many times had she studied that face and marveled at the total lack of resemblance to either of his sons?

"I wasn't expecting you," she blurted, then almost laughed at how many ways it was true. She had been sure she would see or feel something of Gil in him. A blander version of the same flavor, maybe, mild chili sauce versus Tabasco. Merle wasn't even in the pepper family.

"The fish weren't biting so I came back a few days early," he said.

Nothing changed in his expression or his posture, no nervous twitches or shifty eyes, but with sudden, painful clarity Carma knew exactly what was on his mind.

Damn it to hell.

When Gil came back with his tablet and saw the worry lines bracketing Carma's mouth, apprehension ran a sharp fingernail down his spine. "What's wrong?"

"Your dad is here."

Gil shot a look toward the main office door, now closed. "Is he meeting with someone?"

"No."

A drawer rattled in one of the steel filing cabinets. "Why is he back so soon?"

"He said the fishing wasn't any good." But there were shadows in Carma's eyes that made Gil think of wildfire smoke dimming the sun. Something was in the air, and she could smell it.

Before he had time to brace himself, the door popped open and his dad stood there, holding a cardboard box. "Gil! It's been a while since I beat you to the office."

"I just ran over to the house for a few minutes."

"That's what Carma said," Merle said, a little too hale and hearty. "She's really on the ball. I figured I'd have a pile to wade through when I got back, but there's hardly a thing on my desk."

"I was going to talk to you about that..." Gil began, but his dad kept rolling, intent on having his say.

"It's about time y'all found someone who can keep up with you. I'm as obsolete as that ugly old coffeepot in the break room. It's about time you put both of us out to pasture."

No. No, no, no! Not now...

Merle gestured at the reception area while keeping his grip on the box. "Since you've got all this under control, I went ahead and said yes to a fishing trip with a couple of the boys from the lake. Three weeks up on the boundary waters in Ontario to celebrate my official retirement."

The numbness started in Gil's scalp and spread downward, so he could barely make his lips move. "When are you leaving?"

"Got my plane ticket for Friday. I figured I'd spend the rest of the week packing up my house. You might as well rent it to one of the drivers, since I'll be spending most of my time at the lake."

Gil lost the feeling in his arms. "You're moving out?"

"Not much sense keeping up two places." He hefted the box. "And I cleared out the desk in here. You can take over the big office instead of being cooped up in that closet."

Gil could no longer tell if his heart was beating. The nerves had gone dead in his chest, and all he could think was that it was typical Merle, having no clue that the main office would have to be completely rewired for the dispatch system. Which only proved his point about being out of the loop. Hell, if he'd made this announcement last Wednesday, Gil barely would've blinked.

But that was last week. Before Huntsville. Before Gil had thrown himself open to all the possibilities.

Carma made a quiet, protesting noise. "Wouldn't it be better to wait until school is out and I've had more than a few days on the job?"

Yes. The kids were cut loose on the last day of May, a

date marked in glistening red on Gil's mental calendar. Krista and the girls were coming home on the first of June to stay most of the month, and Gil had promised to have Quint at the Oklahoma City airport to meet them.

And possibly decide not to come back to Earnest?

Today that nagging worry was displaced by a hopeful bound of Gil's heart. The Diamond Cowboy was on Memorial Day weekend. If Merle could just hang around until...

"Can't," Merle said. "It's a limited-time offer, at a private cabin. I only got invited because one of the guys who usually goes with Jimmy had to cancel for some family thing."

Gil was aware that Carma was giving him a *Say something* stare, but he refused to look at her.

"Sounds too good to pass up," he said.

"That's what I thought." Merle smiled heartily. "I guess I'll go on now. Anything I didn't get to is on my desk."

"Fine." Gil would take care of it, the way he'd been taking care of every damn thing.

Merle started out, then paused at the door. "Oh, yeah. I almost forgot. The bigwig from Heartland Foods called wanting to talk to you about their contract. I told him you were working on it, but he could consider it as good as signed. Wouldn't want to let a big one slip off the line, right?"

And with that final kick in the nuts, he waltzed out the door.

"Gil!" Carma burst out. "Why didn't you tell him?"

Even his blink happened in slow motion. "I tried doing it your way. I looked into the sky and asked for a sign that I was making the right choice." The sound that came out of him was nothing like a laugh. "Guess that'll teach me."

"Gil..."

He had just enough sensation left in his body to do a stiff-kneed zombie walk to his office. He'd pulled the door halfway shut behind him when he stopped, turned, and said, "Pass the word—if anyone tries to take that coffeepot, I'll break their fucking arm."

Then he sat down and stared blindly at his computer monitor while phones rang, notifications beeped, emails piled up, and his brief, shining dream faded to black.

Normally Carma would have followed him into his office and demanded to know what he meant about getting a sign and why he hadn't stuck up for himself, but after that comment about the coffeepot she decided it was better to give him some space. And after no more than ten minutes he'd started answering his phone and messages, alternately cursing and cajoling.

Business as usual.

But she'd *felt* the blow land when Merle announced he was leaving. Practically heard the pops as all the plans that had been bubbling inside Gil had burst. Finally, she couldn't take it anymore. Gathering up the morning's mail, she went over, tapped lightly, and pushed the door open.

Gil was slouched in his chair, one foot slung up on the desk, phone in hand...smiling. "Absolutely. I'll be handpicking a dozen of our best drivers and assigning them exclusively to Heartland Foods. I'd like to bring them down to your facility for an orientation session before the distribution center opens. The more we know about your overall operation, the better we can anticipate your needs."

Without glancing at Carma, he held a hand out for the mail. She ignored it, clutching the envelopes in disbelief while Gil buttered up his newest client with that easygoing charm he could whip out on demand. The anger and disappointment from a mere hour ago had been bundled up and tucked away where even she couldn't see them.

Out of sight, out of mind. And so, so wrong.

The instant he hung up, she burst out, "What are you doing?"

"My job." He folded his arms, a warning glint in those dark eyes. "This *is* what I do, Carma. Hold it together. Make adjustments. Maintain."

"But what about—"

He shook off her objection. "Like I said, I asked for a little spiritual guidance and the answer was crystal clear. We've got too much in the works for me to go off on some wild hair."

"But your dad—"

"I'll write up a retirement announcement to send out to all the drivers by email, but I think we should go old school with the clients. I'll forward it to you to print out. We must have some company stationery around here somewhere."

"Bottom left drawer of my desk."

"Great." Once again he held out a rock-steady hand for the mail.

Carma was trembling when she passed it over. *Why?* she wanted to scream. *Why does everyone else get to do what they want, while you stay here and* maintain? *You should let them help you. Demand your turn.*

You should, you should, you should—her old, tired mantra, that had only ever made things worse.

Gil flipped quickly through the envelopes and handed two back to her. "Dad has always dealt with everyone who hits us up for donations or advertising. Just look back and see what we did last year for things like Little League and the junior rodeo association, and use your own judgment for anything else. We're always willing to support a good cause…within reason."

"I… Okay." She might have said more, but his phone buzzed.

"That's Delon. I texted him the news before word got back to him some other way. You never know around this place." He turned away as he said into the phone, "Hey. Yeah. It's a pain in the ass, but it's not like we haven't been expecting—"

The rest was lost when she shut the door.

She sank into her chair, hands clenched, and listened to the rise and fall of his voice through the crappy tissue-paper wall. His tone was clear—annoyed but reassuring. No need for Delon to rush home. Gil would take care of it. Gil would take care of everything…except himself.

Don't interfere. Do not *interfere.*

But she couldn't sit there and do nothing while Gil let Fate sucker punch him again. He obviously wouldn't listen to her, but there must be someone else who could talk him out of playing the martyr…

His sponsor? Carma didn't even have a name, let alone a number, and she knew nothing about the person. Would they understand what Gil was giving up?

But there was someone she did know, who was the next best thing to a sponsor. She started by texting Bing. When she got the cell number she needed—and refused to explain why she was asking—she fired off a second text.

This is Carma. Gil needs help. Can we talk?

The reply didn't come back until almost noon, but finally her borrowed phone pinged.

Meet me at the Smoke Shack in half an hour.

When it was time, she yelled through the wall that she was going out to lunch. She got a "Fine!" in response. She ran upstairs to grab the ugly purse and her keys and was parked outside the weathered wooden building that housed the barbecue joint when a battered old Chevy pickup pulled in beside her.

Hank jumped out and strode to where she was sitting with the driver's door open to take advantage of the breeze that stirred the muggy, post-rain air. "Sorry I took so long. I didn't have my phone at the arena."

"That's okay."

It was great, in fact. In two sentences he'd confirmed what she'd already suspected. Hank was willing to drop everything for Gil's sake, the way Gil had done for him. Maybe he could make Gil see reason. Maybe not. But it was worth a try.

He sure as hell wasn't listening to Carma.

Chapter 27

After the paralysis wore off, Gil had functioned almost as if he hadn't been gutted like one of his dad's fish. The trucks were still rolling. He'd nailed down the Heartland Foods deal after ironing out the issues he'd redlined in the contract. He'd talked to Delon and managed to sound no worse than irritated. When Analise had arrived at four on Tuesday afternoon, he'd called Max and the mechanics into the office to tell them that Merle had officially retired.

And he'd avoided Carma as much as a man could when she was working fifteen feet away. With everyone else he could pretend his dad's desertion was nothing but a speed bump. Carma knew better, and he had to maintain the facade.

Once he'd had a chance to go somewhere and kick and scream out his rage, he would explain to her why it had already been a lost cause.

He couldn't have left Merle in charge, even in the short term. Their dad really was obsolete, and Gil had made him that way—constantly updating, automating, renegotiating, until the business bore no resemblance to the way Merle had always done it. But worse—downright fucking scary—was the fact that once Gil had declared he wanted to ride again, he'd been sucked in so fast and so deep that he'd been ready to throw away the biggest contract in Sanchez Trucking history.

Thank God his dad had shown up today.

So no, he hadn't attempted to stop Merle. What he had

done was blast out of the office before Carma could try to pin him down again, and drop Quint off to stay with Tori and Beni while he went to an evening meeting, then on to a coffee shop with his sponsor for a slow-motion replay of the past week.

When he was done, Tamela sighed. "Gotta love the demon addiction. It'll use the wins against you as easy as the losses. New job, new relationship…anything that makes you stick your neck out a little. *Wham!*" She chopped her hand down on the table like a guillotine. "It sounds like this woman could be good for you, though."

He laced his fingers around his lukewarm cup. After zero sleep followed by the day he'd had, it was like drinking acid. "But am I good for her? She's fresh out of a long-term, codependent relationship. An addict seems like the worst choice she could make."

"I think that depends on the individual. I'm not ready to write myself off just yet, and I've been telling you for years that you shouldn't either. Especially when you may have finally found *the One.*"

He hunched his shoulders and ducked his chin. Geezus. All the things he'd confessed to this woman over the past twelve years, and admitting that he might be falling in love made him blush like a gawky tween.

She reached across the table to squeeze his arm. "It could work if you communicate and stay honest."

"I don't have any choice with Carma," he muttered. "She literally sees right through me. But how do I know this isn't another one of my runaways?"

"Give it time. The rush will wear off, and you'll be able to see what's left." She tapped the back of his hand with one beautifully manicured nail. He should ask her where she got them done and pass it along to Bing. "There will be other rodeos."

Of course. But like always, he'd wanted to go as fast as possible, aiming for the highest high, his addiction setting him up for one more massive fall. He stared down into his coffee as if he'd find the answer written in the iridescent film on top. Why not? He'd asked the sky for guidance, and he'd gotten a sorely needed slap in the face in response.

"You *can* make a comeback," Tamela insisted. "Just don't try to do it by yourself. You have to be absolutely straight with your brother and your son, so they know the danger signs. Then sit down together and make a plan. They deserve a say in something that's going to affect them, and they can keep you from getting carried away."

He frowned. "I can't expect them to keep me in line."

"No, but they can hold you accountable, and I have never seen you go back on your word to either of them." She smiled ruefully. "Besides, it's a lot harder to make bad decisions when you're listening to voices you can trust."

"Unlike my own?"

"Hey, it happens to all of us. As long as we keep coming to a meeting and each other, we're gonna be okay."

All things considered, he should be damned happy with okay. But for a few glorious hours he'd remembered what it was like to want more, and right now *okay* sounded about as appetizing as cold coffee.

Carma breathed a sigh of relief when Gil's headlights flashed across the windows of the van. She watched the Charger glide across the lot and disappear behind the shop, then rolled away from the smoked-glass window and onto her back, wrapping her arms around her stomach. The ibuprofen she'd taken earlier hadn't eased the dull headache that pulsed behind her eyes, fed by stress, fatigue, and a queasy mixture of anticipation and dread.

She'd expected Hank to go straight to Sanchez Trucking and try to talk to Gil. Instead, he'd declared he had to get a second opinion. Assuming he meant Bing, she'd waited to hear from her cousin, but there'd been total silence from that quarter. Who had Hank talked to? Miz Iris, maybe. Or, God forbid, Delon. Carma already knew how Gil would feel about that.

Her mouth twisted. At least she didn't have to worry about being fired. No matter how furious, Gil would put the business ahead of his personal problems. He might even make a point of being polite.

It would be awful.

Almost as bad as lying here waiting for the ball to drop. She rolled onto her stomach, aware in every nerve ending that Gil was *right over there*. And he'd sent Quint to stay overnight with Beni. Carma ached with wanting the heat and the hard certainty of Gil's body against her. Inside her. Taking them both to a place where thinking was impossible.

Depending on what Hank did, tonight could be her last chance.

Before she could change her mind, she sat up, shoved her feet into flip-flops, and grabbed the ugly purse. The curtains on the front windows of Gil's house were open, and as she approached she could see him in the kitchen. She paused to watch, her heart thrumming at the way his dark-gray T-shirt clung to shoulders that slumped with exhaustion.

God. He looked so alone.

There was an endless, excruciating silence after her knock. Then the door swung open and he was there, dark and a little forbidding with the light at his back.

"Carma." It was a sigh of resignation. He raked a hand through hair that had already been roughed up. "I'm sorry. I just spent two hours pouring my guts out to my sponsor. I can't talk any more tonight."

"Good." She stepped inside, wrapped her arms around his neck, and kissed him.

After a moment's surprise, his hands came to her waist, pushing up under the hoodie and T-shirt to find bare skin. She shivered at his touch, cool from the milk jug and glass. Without breaking contact, he pivoted them both, shut the door, and walked her down the hall.

A swan-necked lamp threw a dense pool of light onto a small desk in the corner of his bedroom. He took the purse from her hand and tossed it onto the nightstand. His eyes glittered, black and intent, as he peeled off her hoodie, then her T-shirt, then his own, leaving them both naked from the waist up. His gaze followed his hands as they settled at her waist, thumbs tracing dual lines of fire up her stomach until he cupped her breasts. Her head fell back on a moan as he palmed their weight, his hair tickling along her throat as he bent to taste.

They didn't speak. Only sighs, moans, a catch of the breath or a purr of gratification. They fell into a slow, liquid rhythm, riding each wave of desire, in no rush to reach the crest. When they did tumble over, it was a long slide into a pool of molten pleasure.

Carma mumbled in protest as he pulled away to dispose of the condom and turn out the light. Then he was back, tucking her into the hard curve of his body and tugging the comforter over them.

And finally, they slept.

Gil could get used to waking up next to Carma. Not just in the morning, but at midnight, at 3:00 a.m., and again as the sky was turning silver-blue at dawn. Instead of kicking off the blankets and abandoning hope of sleep, he'd burrowed into her warmth and her sweet cherry-almond scent and let the soft rise and fall of her breath lull him back to slumberland.

But now he did have to get up.

As he eased up to sit on the edge of the mattress, she stirred, sighed, and blinked her eyes open. That irresistible mouth curved into a drowsy smile. "Hey."

"Hey yourself." He leaned over to kiss her forehead, trying to keep his morning breath to himself. "It's still early."

"Mmm." She sighed again as he stroked the hair away from her face. Then she pushed up onto one elbow. The comforter slid down, revealing a lot of satiny bronze skin, and it was all Gil could do not to say the hell with it and dive back in.

"You are not making it easier for me to get to work," he said.

She laughed, low and raspy, but tucked the comforter around her chest as she sat up. "How 'bout if I kill the mood by saying we need to talk?"

"That did the trick." He reached for his gym shorts, literally girding his loins. "Should I be caffeinated for this?"

"Not that big a deal. I just wanted to tell you… I'm moving out."

Gil's heart crashed against his rib cage. Shit. She was leaving already. He'd been weaving pretty fantasies, and she'd only popped over for a good-bye fuck. "When?"

"As soon as possible. I gotta be honest, I really hate that apartment." She swung her legs over the other side of the bed, baring the length of her back and the lush curve of one hip. "Is there an RV park around here?"

"An RV park," Gil echoed, not comprehending. "In Earnest?"

"I take that as a no. It's not far to the campgrounds at Lake Meredith. I can only stay at each one for two weeks, but…" Her smile flickered uncertainly. "Well, we'll have to see."

Gil kept staring at her with what he was sure was an idiotic expression while his internal organs settled back into their assigned places. She wasn't leaving, only relocating.

To some campground full of strangers. Nope. Not on his watch. "There might be something else. Let me think about it."

"Thanks." Her smile gained strength. "And really, I didn't mean to insult your apartment."

"No offense taken. You just caught me by surprise." And so had the intensity of his reaction. Had he said he might be falling in love? Hah. That truck had definitely left the yard.

Patience. He breathed himself down to something approximating calm. As long as she was staying, they had time, especially if he wasn't wasting any trying to resuscitate old dreams. He could concentrate on Carma and Quint and ramping up for the Heartland Foods workload.

By then some of the shine should have worn off his relationship with Carma. Without that glare in his eyes, he'd be able to see both more clearly.

Then she stood up and dropped the comforter, and he went blind again.

By the time Analise reported for work at four, Gil had pretty much come to terms with his new plan, and the occasional torpedo blast of disappointment barely rocked his boat. Forget the Diamond Cowboy. The first week of June would be a great time to take a couple of days off, just him and Carma. Drive over to southern Colorado and New Mexico to explore the canyonlands. They could swing south to visit his mother, maybe head into the backcountry where most of her family lived. It would be so much easier with Carma along as a buffer.

In the meantime, Gil had plenty of good stuff to focus on. Making breakfast with Carma as the sun came up, laughing when they bumped hips because he'd never had a woman in his kitchen, her disgust that he spent so much time in the office that he didn't have a coffeepot of his own.

He would take care of that too.

There was Quint's track meet in Bluegrass on Thursday, where Hank would be hanging around because Grace was the athletic trainer there. He and Gil could debate how these kids compared to back when they were each in their glory days and be smug about how no one had come close to breaking Cole's records in the shot put and discus.

Hank would make puppy-dog eyes at Grace, and Gil would think twice about giving him grief about it now that there was a chance he was looking at Carma the same way.

Afterward Gil would take Quint out for victory ice cream, and for an hour or so he might feel like he was getting this dad thing right. And then he'd come home and tell Carma all about it while they watched the sun set.

Which reminded him—he still had to come up with a better place for her to park than some public campground half an hour away. All she needed was a level spot with grass, trees, a restroom and showers close by…

Analise opened the door but didn't step into the dispatch office to take over. "Your presence is requested, oh supreme ruler."

Hell. What now? If this was Max on a rampage about another truck cab that looked like a feral hog had been living in it, Gil was gonna make good on his threat to start deducting extra cleaning costs from the drivers' pay. He tossed his Bluetooth earpiece onto the desk, stomped out into the reception area…and stopped dead.

"Delon?" Gil blinked, but his brother was still standing there, arms folded, jaw tight. Alarm squeezed hot fingers around his lungs. It had to be horrible news if Delon felt the need to deliver it in person. "What's wrong? Is somebody…"

He flashed back to that devastating night, Steve Jacobs on their doorstep, his eyes dull with shock as he told them Xander and his parents were gone.

"Nothing like that." Gil turned toward the voice and found Hank, his eyes sharp and hard. And why would Grace be here with him, on a weekday?

In the opposite corner, Carma sat stiffly in the chair she'd pushed as far from the center of the room as possible.

Her gaze met Gil's for an instant, then dropped to the hands clasped in her lap.

Guilty. Fuck. What had she done?

Gil mimicked Delon's posture, lounging against the nearest filing cabinet to steady himself. "So what is this? An intervention? You're about a dozen years too late."

"Not really. You've still got plenty of bad habits. Like thinking you get to make all the decisions without consulting anyone." Delon's words were strung dangerously tight. "And thanks for putting my wife in a position where she had to keep secrets from me. Really appreciate that, big bro."

Muscles bunched in Delon's thick, powerful arms, and it occurred to Gil that the arena wasn't the only place where he couldn't take his little brother anymore. They had never been the kind of kids who pounded on each other, but there was always a first time.

"I was planning to tell you *after* you got back from California," he said. "Which—correct me if I'm wrong—is where you're supposed to be."

Delon stabbed a finger at him. "This is my fucking company, too, and you don't get to shove me out the door so you can keep playing the martyr."

Bam! Direct hit. Gil covered the sting with a careless shrug. "Fine. You can clean out Dad's desk."

Delon swore, several of Gil's favorite, most descriptive alternatives for the word *jerk*, not even caring that there were women in the room. Oh yeah. He was seriously pissed.

"You could have told *me*." Hank's voice was raw steel. "All the time you spent dogging my ass, insisting I had to pull my head out and get on with my life, but when you need to talk about what it's like to get a second chance and wonder if you deserve it, you don't trust me enough to say a goddamn word."

Shit. He hadn't even considered talking to Hank. Gil angled his chin, gave his best arrogant asshole smirk, and lied through his teeth. "I never questioned whether I deserve it. I just haven't decided whether it's worth the hassle."

"By which you mean letting anyone do anything around here without you looking over their shoulder." Analise's eye roll was truly impressive under inch-long fake lashes. "If it was possible, you'd have computer chips implanted in our brains so you could log in and check our status just like the drivers."

Gil flipped the attitude right back at her. "No one wants to see inside your head."

"Especially you," she shot back with a barbed smile. "It's a dangerous place for people who doubt my powers."

Gil ignored her to raise his eyebrows at Grace. "What's your beef?"

She gave him a stone-cold stare that reminded him this was a woman who, despite standing five foot nothing and looking barely older than the students, kept three hundred athletes and their coaches in line. "I did used to work here part time. I can pitch in with the basic stuff once school is out. And Hank can take some loads when you start moving drivers over to Heartland Foods."

Gil curled his mouth into a lethal weapon. "I appreciate the offer, but if I'm gonna go off rodeoing, what I really need is a weekend dispatcher. When do you want to start training?"

"I..." Grace began, and Gil laughed. Yeah. That's what

he figured. Grace had her own rodeo schedule lined out, and she wasn't about to give it up for his benefit. But to his surprise, she didn't back down. "Obviously, I'm no help to you there, but I have this brother. You know, Jeremiah? The one who's majoring in business and looking for a summer and weekend job for at least the next two years? He might even stick around after graduation if you were in the market for someone whose head could be even harder than yours."

The acid comeback fizzled on Gil's tongue. He'd sat next to Jeremiah during New Year's dinner at Miz Iris's. The kid was smart, with Grace's take-no-shit attitude and a lot of shrewd questions about the trucking business. Besides, they had to hire another dispatcher no matter what. Gil and Analise were already stretched too far.

He nodded. "Have him call me."

Grace cocked her head as if she hadn't heard him right. "Um, okay. I will."

"Great." He clapped his hands together and rubbed them. "If you've all had your say..."

"Not even close." Delon pushed open the door to the main office and stepped aside to usher a familiar figure through.

Gil blinked. Then blinked again. "Mom?"

Chapter 28

If Carma sat very, very still, maybe Gil would forget she was there until she had a chance to slip out the back door.

And run.

Gil leaned an elbow on top of a filing cabinet and speared his fingers through his hair. "I have no clue what's happening here."

"Thank Tori," Delon said. "She pointed out that Dad was perfectly happy with his three original rigs until Mom came along. Next thing you know, they were running around fifteen trucks. Then she left and nothing changed until you decided you were gonna build a damn dynasty."

Gil stared at his mother. "You built it up?"

Rochelle Yazzie stared straight back at him, an older, feminine version of Gil, right down to the just-try-to-fuck-with-me attitude.

"You don't think you got all that from your father?" She waved a hand that took him in from head to foot, and Carma almost smiled. Everything about both Gil and Delon that was missing from Merle was wrapped up in their mother, tight as braided rawhide. "When I had to leave, I hired Mrs. Nordquist to ride herd on him, and the bookkeepers downtown to keep track of the financials. I reviewed all the contracts clear up until you took over. And for a while after."

"Shit." Hank bumped himself on the forehead. "That's why you never divorced him."

"I worked my tail off to make this place a going concern. I wasn't gonna sell it or let him fritter it away." She made a fist and pressed it to her breastbone. "And we are divorced where it counts."

Meaning back home, among her people.

"Why are you here?" Gil asked abruptly.

She lifted her chin, defiant. "I have ten years' experience with the road department, managing twice as much equipment and three times as many employees as you have here. Plus you need drivers and I have a list of prospects who've graduated from the CDL program at the college in Shiprock."

"How many of these people are related to you?" Delon asked.

Her mouth quirked. "That depends on how you define 'related.' But I wouldn't consider hiring them if they weren't reliable."

"We only have three tractors that aren't already running full time," Gil argued, his edges sharpening with every word. "We need owner-operators."

Rochelle didn't give an inch. "A few of my people would be interested in buying their own rigs if they had guaranteed work. I've already looked into financing with the Navajo Nation loan program and the VA, and Hank's sister has some other good options for minorities through her small-business programs."

Wow. They had covered a lot of bases in the time since Carma had talked to Hank. Or, more likely, Rochelle had been planning this for a while, on the assumption that Merle would bow out sooner rather than later.

"Dad and I have been looking at used tractors, in case we got the contract." Unlike his brother, Delon was getting more enthusiastic. "We can afford three, maybe four, if we find older models that need some work and have Max and the crew whip them into shape."

Analise tossed in her two cents. "All the Heartland loads will be drop and hooks, so you'll have extra trailers."

Drop and hook? Oh, right. When the client preloaded trailers and all the driver had to do was drop off their empty one and hook onto the next.

None of which was making Gil any happier. Carma could practically see a red line creeping up from his chest, into the corded muscles of his neck, toward his eyebrows. She did not want to be in the vicinity when his pressure gauge topped out.

Damn this puny little office, and damn her curiosity for overriding her survival instincts. A good Blackfeet knew better than to let herself get cornered.

Everyone jumped when Gil slammed the flat of his hand against the filing cabinet. "Fine! Y'all apparently have all the answers, so I'm gonna run over to Dumas and pick up those seals for the Jacobs truck. Tell Quint to order supper from the café. I might not be back right away."

Code for *I have had more than I can take, and I'm going to a meeting.* Or to talk to his sponsor. Anywhere but here.

And anyone but Carma.

He'd confided in her, and in return she'd brought all this down on his head—although Carma had predicted Delon's reaction almost to the word.

She doubted that was gonna get her off the hook.

~

When Gil walked into his house that night, Quint was holed up in his bedroom, the patio door was open, and his mother was sitting in one of the chairs, staring out at the prairie beyond the chain-link fence.

Well, shit. Tamela had told him not to put off clearing the air. Oh yeah, and *Be nice. Your mother is trying to help.* She'd said pretty much the same thing about Carma, which was where Gil had planned to start. Typical of this damn day that he didn't get to choose.

He puffed out a sigh at the wary look in his mother's dark eyes. "What, did you draw the short straw and get stuck being the one trying to make me see reason?"

"I volunteered. It's about time I showed up for the hard stuff."

No comment. "As sons go, I've kinda been an asshole."

"As mothers go, I haven't been a real prize, either." She closed her hands around the armrests, finger by finger. "I could tell you what a pitiful soul I was, so sure nobody understood how hard it was for me."

He slid into the chair set at an angle to hers. "And I could whine about having to be my brother's keeper…but we all know how much I liked bossing him around."

"From the day he was born." Her shoulders moved restlessly. "Merle wasn't a terrible father."

"There are a lot worse. And Steve and Miz Iris were always there for us. We were lucky that way."

"That wasn't just luck. When I had to leave, I asked them to look after the two of you until I came back." She sighed heavily. "I didn't think it would take me quite this long."

A smile tugged at his mouth. "Well, Miz Iris took you at your word. She's still fussing over us."

"They are good people."

"Yes, they are."

They fell quiet, listening to the usual chorus of cicadas

and various other night things. In the cluster of trees beyond the fence an owl hooted, and Gil saw his mother's lips move in a silent prayer. What was it she'd told him about owls? He couldn't remember if they were considered a curse or a blessing. There was so much he'd willfully refused to learn, as if that would teach her a lesson. What exactly, he didn't know.

"Why didn't you come to see me when you were going through the program?" she asked.

Hell. It had been so long, he'd thought he'd dodged this bullet. "The rules say to be willing to make amends... *except* when it might be hurtful to you or the other person. You think you're to blame for my addiction, and I couldn't say that you were completely wrong, so why put us both through all that? We'll never know either way. Maybe it would have been different if you were here. Maybe I was just programmed that way." He hitched a shoulder. "Look at Bing's grandson. She's an addiction counselor and he died of an overdose, even though she'd done everything she could to help him."

A thought that scared the living hell out of Gil. What if Quint was genetically doomed to repeat his father's mistakes?

"I should have done better," she said.

"You didn't have a lot of choices."

"And I made the worst of them." She shook her head. "You were barely more than babies, but I was so angry that you chose this place and these people instead of your own mother. As if you'd done it on purpose, to hurt me."

Guilt slid like a knife between Gil's ribs. Another reason he'd avoided this conversation. The wounds went both ways.

"I did, you know," he admitted. "From as far back as I can remember, I knew that old man didn't approve of me, so I was bound and determined to piss him off any way I could." He smiled grimly. "From what I can remember, I'm a slightly paler version of him, so he only had himself to blame."

She laughed, then sighed. "But you and Delon blamed me."

"We were kids." He took a breath, then said, "And it's not easy to come back to a man who didn't miss you."

Her shoulders snapped back. "You knew?"

"I figured it out while I was talking to the counselor in rehab." He fingered a frayed spot on the knee of his jeans, worrying it into a hole. "I was telling her about you and Dad, and it just hit me. I didn't remember him ever being sad. Not the way you were. He was perfectly fine without you, except for the laundry. He hated doing laundry."

"And he was terrible at it."

"That's why none of us wear anything white. Single dad hack."

"Smart." She bowed her head. "It wasn't only him. I fell pretty hard at the start. My first grown-up romance! But if I hadn't gotten pregnant, I would've been gone in under six months. I was so homesick, I seriously considered going home and raising you by myself."

Gil tried to imagine the person he would be if she had. A life without Delon. Without rodeo and the friends it had brought him. Without Quint. His breath stuck in his chest, then wobbled out. "I'm glad you didn't."

"Me too." She turned her head and the light from Quint's window glistened in her damp eyes. "I am so grateful to Tori for insisting that Delon include me in their wedding, and invite me to visit whenever I wanted. And to you for following their lead. All my beautiful boys. I missed so much, but I wouldn't fix a single mistake if it meant not having any one of you."

"Same here." But they were being honest, so he had to ask. "How long are you staying?"

"This time?" she asked, completing his thought. "As long as you need me. I can't turn back time, but I would like to do whatever I can to help you from now on."

He cleared a rapidly swelling lump from his throat. "You know, I'd have to be a total hypocrite to keep holding a grudge now."

"How's that?"

"I get to have my son with me because his mother made pretty much the exact same choice you did—one part of her family for another. Krista can't have both. Neither could you."

She nodded slowly. "I hadn't thought about it that way."

"Well, there you go." And they were both ready to dial back the intensity, so he said, "I guess we'd better figure out where you're going to live."

She manufactured a frown. "Don't even try to stick me in that dismal little apartment."

"What is so wrong with that place?" he demanded, baffled.

"Only a man would have to ask."

He sighed mightily and reached out a hand. She tentatively laid hers in it.

"You know, I worry about Krista being so far away," he said, gazing up at the sky. "I think a boy always needs his mother...even when he tries his damnedest not to."

The tears that had been shimmering in her eyes spilled over. He squeezed her hand, and together they watched the narrow sliver of a new moon climb into the sky.

Chapter 29

Ten minutes after Rochelle's car pulled out of the front gates and turned toward downtown and the lone five-room motel, a knock on the sliding door of the van sent Carma's pulse into overdrive. She took a steadying breath and called out, "*Entrez!*"

The door rolled back and Gil frowned at it, then her. "You should lock this."

"I do before I go to sleep." She clutched the book she'd been trying to read against her palpitating heart. "Between the fence, the lights, and the security cameras, I figured there wouldn't be anyone wandering around the yard."

He hooked a hand on the sill above the door, his face too shadowed to read. "I tried the apartment first, then saw a light on in here. Are you hiding?"

"Should I be?" There was too much going on inside of him to sort out, but he wasn't radiating fury, so that was better than she'd expected.

"If you have to ask…" His gaze traveled around the interior. "This thing is like a time machine."

"It's Uncle Tony's baby." She cocked her head. "You seem awfully calm."

"I've had time to cool down." He rolled his shoulders, trying to shed the remaining tension.

"There were a lot of people poking their fingers into your pie today. I don't imagine that sat too well."

His mouth twisted. "That's what Tamela said, too."

Jealousy flared, singeing a corner of her heart. Gil had spent the evening with another woman? "Tamela?"

"My sponsor."

Oh. She'd assumed it was a man. Opposite-sex sponsorships weren't against the rules, but they did have the potential for added complications. "Is that who you were with last night, too?"

"Yes." Reading the doubt in her voice, he gave a slight shake of his head. "There is not and has never been anything romantic between us. All else aside, that would be doubling up on a bad bet."

Carma frowned. "Is that how you think of yourself?"

"It's what I know. Any relationship I'm in is a threesome. You, me, and my addiction. Staying clean takes time and energy away from everyone else in my life. How's that sound for a happily-ever-after?"

"Like you're trying to scare me off. Have you forgotten where I come from? I know about drunks and addicts."

His eyebrows spiked. "Do you? Is Jayden an alcoholic? Your brother? Anybody you've lived with, had to rely on, day in and day out?"

"No. But..."

"Then you don't really know. And it shows."

Her mouth dropped open. "Because I asked someone you helped to return the favor?"

"Because you didn't ask me if I needed help in the first place. You assumed you knew best and tried to push me in the direction you thought I should go."

"You *told* me you wanted to ride again." She slapped her book down on the bed. "Then your dad comes up with some fishing trip and you just...quit."

He sat, using the doorframe as a backrest and tilting his

face into the soft yellow light, which somehow made his angles sharper. "Do I seem like someone who lets people take advantage of him?"

"I… It depends. In general, or in the office?"

"Either. And the answer is no. It's only taking advantage if I'm not willing. I let Delon dump his extra work on me because I want him out there kicking ass and drumming up more business. I've let my dad gradually dawdle off into the sunset because he didn't move fast enough for me. There's always something in it for me, and if I'd felt used, I would have stopped. Resentment and self-pity are poison. Believe me, they came close to killing me more than once."

"But you've earned some payback," she insisted. "You could have at least asked your dad if he was willing to help."

"I intended to. I made all kinds of plans. Hell, I was running with it so hard I could barely breathe. You know. You felt it."

She nodded reluctantly. There had been something frantic about him that morning.

He combed the shag carpet with his fingers, then studied the tracks they left. "You think falling off the wagon just means getting stoned or hitting the bottle, but addiction can come at me from any direction, and everything about the Diamond Cowboy makes it lick its chops."

"The *what*?" She gaped at him. "That was your comeback plan?"

"Of course. Big money, major adrenaline, short prep time. The perfect excuse to drop everything else and throw myself into it, balls to the wall." His laugh was like rock grinding glass. "The list of shit I could put off or not do at all was getting longer by the minute. If Dad hadn't tripped me up, I would've run us right off the road. I even had a whole spiel worked out for the guy at Heartland Foods about how we'd analyzed our current resources and the availability of new drivers and concluded that we weren't in a position to provide an acceptable level of service at this time."

Carma gulped. "You were gonna decline that contract. Without consulting anyone else?"

Dear God. Delon would have dismembered him.

"Yep. And it seemed totally logical. That's how my particular brand of addiction works its evil magic. It takes a reasonable idea and pushes it farther and faster until it turns into a train wreck."

"But..." She shook her head, struggling to fit that image into what she'd witnessed. "You're such a control freak."

"Sober Gil has no choice." He gave her another of those bitter smiles. "Steve Jacobs had a horse like me once. As long as he kept it on a really tight rein, they were safe. But if he gave it a tiny bit of slack, it'd stampede through brush and fences and into washouts—just running blind."

Carma knew those horses. Her dad always said the most dangerous animal was one that didn't care if it hurt itself. She never would have put Gil in that category, though.

But she only knew sober Gil.

"That's the risk you're taking," he said. "I can't promise I won't lose my grip. And I can't be with someone who tries to take the reins."

The declaration struck with the quiet *thwppt!* of an arrow to the heart. "So that counts me out."

"I can't blame you for what I didn't explain. Now that you know..."

Her pride bristled at the implication. "What? I'm on probation? Meddle once more and we're done? If that's the case, I'm gonna need a better definition of what's off-limits. Am I allowed to encourage you in any way, or is that too dangerous?"

"That isn't what I meant." He ran a weary hand over his eyes, shadows settling in the hollows of his face. "But yes, we do need clear boundaries. I have a great support system with my sponsor and the group in Dumas, so I've never had to lean on the people close to me—and I don't want to start. This works. I'm not gonna screw with it."

There was a finality in his voice that left no room for negotiation. But he had talked to her. Once. When Tamela wasn't available. A weight settled behind her breastbone. "And you expect me to be content with whatever parts of yourself you choose to share, whenever it suits you."

"I don't expect anyone to be satisfied with what I have to offer." He dragged a thumbnail down the front of his jeans. "That's why I've avoided this kind of relationship. But we're past that point, so I have to hope this is better than nothing, because that's what I am if I'm not sober." He paused, then sighed. "I can't even swear that what I feel for you is real, and not another sneak attack."

A second arrow skewered her gut. "You think this is a…crush?"

"I don't know what to believe. It happened so fast, and the more I have of you, the more I want." He lifted his hand, then let it fall. "I can't trust any kind of irresistible urge."

Her spine stiffened, one vertebra at a time. "You're putting me in the same class as a bottle of rotgut whiskey."

"More like hundred-dollar tequila. I'm not sure if you're more dangerous when you're smoothing me out, or when you're setting me on fire. But I won't let myself make any promises until I'm sure. I owe that to both of us."

"And I'm supposed to hang around until you figure it out."

He picked at the carpet, eyes downcast. "If you think it's worth the trouble."

If you think I'm *worth it.* That silent plea, etched into the stark lines of his face, was all that kept her from heaving the book at his head. All around him, hands were snatching at those reins he'd been gripping for so long. Meanwhile, Carma was in the process of rearranging her own boundaries, without a map. It was a lousy time for either of them to fall into a new relationship.

But like he'd said, it was too late to turn back now.

That didn't mean she had to let him dictate all the rules, though, so she said, "I have to think about it."

"That's fair." He stood, surveyed the interior of the van, and took note of her pajamas. "You actually hate the apartment so much you'd rather sleep in the parking lot?"

"I prefer my own bed. And since my new phone is finally ready and I got my new debit card in the mail today, I'm going out after work tomorrow to scout campgrounds."

His frown made an immediate return. "I don't like the idea of you staying somewhere alone."

"What do you think I've been doing ever since I left Montana?"

He shook her off. "Give me a day or two. I'll find something better."

A place he chose, that met his standards. She was on the verge of telling him what to do with his orders when she realized this wasn't just Gil being arrogant. At a time when change was threatening every part of his life, he needed to maintain some control. Carma could give him at least that much, considering she had brought the clamoring horde to his door.

"Fine. I'll wait until the weekend."

"Thank you." He stood for a moment, as if he couldn't figure out how to leave—or didn't want to. Then he gave the side of the van a gentle slap. "Sleep tight. I'll see you in the morning."

Before Carma could answer, he slid the door shut with a decisive *thunk*. A few seconds later he cupped his hands against the bubble window beside her head. "Lock the doors!"

She doubted he could see her through the smoked plexiglass, but she waved a stiff middle finger at him anyway. Then she grabbed the cheap cell phone and called Bing. "I need to vent."

Bing snorted. "What did Gil do?"

"He told me this might be something serious."

"Whoa. What?"

"Or I could be just another weeklong binge."

"Ouch."

"Yeah." Carma thumped her head against the carpeted wall of the van. "How did this happen? I came to town to check out the Patterson clinic and maybe get a little action on the side, and now I'm all twisted up in this…this… *thing*! With a man who just informed me that he's afraid I'm the female equivalent of someone slipping him a mickey."

Bing laughed, a surprised *Hah!*

Carma bared her teeth at the phone. "I'm glad you're enjoying this."

"If I recall correctly, you said, 'I want to know exactly where I stand.'"

"If you make fun of me, I swear to God I will tell Johnny about the time you beat up Sara Dubois for flirting with your boyfriend."

Bing made a noise that was the equivalent of an eye

roll. "That was thirty years ago, and she also told everyone I was screwing around on him with one of the summer guys at the East Glacier Lodge. She needed her ass kicked. But as I was saying..."

"Yeah, yeah. Honesty. No games." Carma scooted off the bed and crouch-walked to the front of the van to punch down the door locks. Which she would have done even if Gil hadn't told her to. "And what about the therapy program? I promised to get it up and running."

"Your job is development. You don't have to stay and run the place. Besides, Grandma wanted you to get to know Gil better."

Carma's eyes went squinty. "And you would know that how?"

"Well..." Bing's voice held a suspicious hint of amusement. "We may have talked about it once or twice, after she heard about the two of you hooking up at the Stockman's. I told her all about Gil, and how much I admired what he did for Hank. She thought he sounded like a good man. I agreed."

Carma had to grab one of the red velvet captain's chairs for balance. "You never said anything about him to me."

"I didn't want to interfere," Bing said loftily.

Carma blew a ripe raspberry into the phone.

"And I've been a little distracted with my own love life," Bing admitted with a laugh.

"That's more like it." Carma let go of the chair and plopped onto her butt. "What now?"

"Do as they say and take it one day at a time. It comes down to figuring out what you need to be healthy and happy and whether he's willing—or able—to give it to you."

"Is that all?" Carma said, heavy on the sarcasm.

Bing's voice softened in sympathy. "And if it doesn't work out..."

It was going to hurt. A lot. Carma nudged the feather hanging from the rearview mirror. It twirled and swayed like it had all the way from Montana to Texas. Uncle Tony had had that feather blessed by the elders to protect and guide him on his journeys. Was this where it had been leading her, with a little help from Grandma White Elk? She watched it slowly come to a stop, the tip curved away from the open gate that led onto the highway...and toward Gil's house.

Hell.

"I'm such a glutton for punishment," she said.

"Aren't we all? Keep me updated."

Carma glanced at the dashboard clock she should've checked before she dialed. It read five minutes after eleven. "You may want to take that back before this is over."

The next morning she was filling her coffee mug when Gil appeared in the door of the break room, looking lean, hard, and lethal if consumed in large doses.

"Yes," she said, stirring in an extra dollop of cream.

He eyed her warily. "To what?"

"Proceeding...with caution." She added sugar, stirred again, and sipped. Ahh. Forget orange juice, this was sunshine in a cup. "But it goes both ways. No promises until we're both sure."

He frowned. "How will we know if we can't tell each other?"

She smiled, arching her brows.

"Oh." His frown morphed into a scowl. "That's fine for you, but how will *I* know?"

"I guess you'll just have to trust me."

She toasted him with her coffee, then squeezed past and gave in to the temptation to flounce down the hall in her killer turquoise sundress.

Chapter 30

Carma had barely started checking her email when Gil poked his head out of his office, a hand clamped over his phone. "I'm stuck on this call. Could you run over and make sure Quint is awake?"

"Sure." Not that she felt it was necessary, but Gil had confessed on the drive to Huntsville that he was afraid he'd cursed his son with the demon insomnia and it was the cause of his tardies. Carma suspected otherwise. She didn't think Quint did many things by mistake.

When she let herself in the front door, she wasn't surprised to find him sitting at the table eating toaster waffles with fresh strawberries and a glass of juice on the side. He smiled politely. "Good morning."

"Good morning." She closed only the screen door, allowing a soft morning breeze to follow her in.

Gil's house was all about comfort and family. The couch and chairs were made for sprawling, the walls and refrigerator scattered with photos of Quint from adorable infant, to a gap-toothed spelling-bee grin, to a recent basketball jump shot. A skateboard leaned in one corner, and the shelves of the entertainment center held the latest, greatest video gaming console and a tilted stack of plastic game cases. A pair of running shoes had been kicked off beside an end table that was cluttered with an *Overdrive* magazine, junk mail, and the current week's *Earnest Gazette*.

Like the office, there was no trace of Gil's life from before he was Quint's father.

"Your dad asked me to be sure you hadn't slept in. Since you're up, I'll just..." She started to turn back to the door.

"Analise says you're some kind of psychic."

Aw, hell. She turned back. "I have a knack for reading people."

"Yeah?" He propped his elbow on the table and let his fork dangle over his plate. "Is that how you got so close to my dad?"

"That's between him and me."

He nodded, as if accepting her terms. "What about me? Do you tell him what I'm thinking?"

"He hasn't asked." She took petty pleasure from the involuntary flare of his pupils when he realized she hadn't said she couldn't read his thoughts. She should have stopped there, but once again she couldn't resist. "I wouldn't mind knowing, though—why did you make yourself ineligible for the meet last week?"

Quint stared at her for a full count of five. Then he said, "I didn't want to show Sam up in front of the home crowd. We're gonna be playing sports together for the next four years. They're a lot more likely to be winning teams if he doesn't hate me."

"Wow. You're a big-picture kind of guy." She sat at the end of the table, at right angles to Quint so they weren't eyeball to eyeball. "It would have been easier to just let him win the runoff."

"No, it wouldn't."

She had to laugh. "Also very competitive. What happens this week when you are the anchor?"

"Not much. We're going up against Bluegrass and Dumas and a couple of other big schools. They're gonna blow us off the track."

"Ah. And Sam won't feel so bad when you're the one eating their dust at the finish line."

"Yep."

Carma leaned back, laced her fingers together on the table, and gave him a long, frank stare. He was basically a good kid. And she should just shut up now and leave, but her gut said this scheming would blow up in his face at some point, and Gil was so consumed with worry about his parenting skills that he couldn't see it.

"That's some pretty high-level manipulation," she said. "I'm surprised you give a damn about Sam's feelings after what he said about your dad."

"It was true." Then his eyes narrowed as he scented the trap. "I never told anyone. Do you really know, or are you guessing?"

"Why keep it a secret unless it was something bound to upset your dad?" And yes, he got points for protecting Gil from...whatever.

Quint watched her for another beat, then shrugged. "Sam said he didn't know why I thought I was such hot shit when everybody knows I'm the reason my dad can't ride anymore." When she sucked in a shocked breath, he allowed himself a sneer. "What, you didn't know? He wrecked his motorcycle the night my mom told him she was pregnant."

"And...they told you this?" The flat declaration had shredded her heart. What must it have done to this child?

"I would've found out eventually." His smile was a mirror image of Gil at his most scathing. "Better to hear it from them than some jerk at school. And I'll get my payback when I take the starting quarterback position from Sam this fall."

Which was undoubtedly true with Quint's talent, brains, and every advantage his mother could give him. But his approach felt so…underhanded. Definitely not something he'd picked up from his dad. Gil tackled everything head-on. Was this the way things were done in his mother's family, or at his fancy private school? Either way, parts of Quint's education were sadly lacking.

Carma tried appealing to his logic. "I grew up in a small town, and I can tell you for a fact that this kind of crap will eventually circle around and kick you in the ass. It always does."

"Well, since you're the expert, what do you suggest I do?" he asked, all brittle condescension.

"Have you considered looking Sam in the eye and calling him on his bullshit?"

Quint's lip curled. "Sure. That oughta smooth things over."

"Maybe not, but at least it would be honest, and in the long run that'll earn you more respect." She hesitated, then added, "From your dad too."

"Nice. You're playing the Dad card and calling *me* manipulative?" Quint shoved away from the table and grabbed his backpack. "Thanks for the totally unsolicited advice. I'll take it under advisement."

When the door slammed behind him, Carma dropped her face into her hands. *Unsolicited advice,* and not even a full twelve hours after Gil had told her not to go meddling in his life without an invitation.

She dragged reluctant feet back to the office. Somehow, she had to tell Gil that she'd been dishing out *unsolicited advice* again, without spilling any of the secrets Quint had shared. Or mentioning that she feared the kid had the breeding and training to be a sneaky little bastard if left to his own devices.

She hadn't even made it all the way to her desk when the door to Gil's office flew open, making her slosh newly poured coffee down the front of her favorite white shirt. "What the *hell* did you say to Quint?"

Uh-oh. Carma grabbed a tissue and dabbed at her chest. "Is there a problem?"

"Oh, nothing major." Gil braced one fist on the doorframe and the other on his hip. "The principal just called to inform me that Quint walked up and punched Sam Carruthers in the gut. *Before* they set foot on school property, thank God. Otherwise they'd both be suspended."

Oh hell. And also *Go, Quint.* Fighting might not solve anything, but what Sam had said was downright cruel. Carma wouldn't have minded punching him herself.

Which might be the Blackfeet in her talking. As a tribe, they'd never been known for turning the other cheek.

"You were worried that he doesn't express himself. I just suggested he should be more open." She smiled weakly. "I guess Sam knows exactly how he feels now."

Gil hissed and slammed the door.

Behind her, there was a stifled laugh. Carma spun around to find Rochelle standing in the door of the main office. Great. No one had told Carma that she'd be in today.

The older woman made a *Come into my office* gesture. "I have a few questions, if you don't mind."

Like she had a choice. Carma got up, marched past, and sat down, feeling like she'd been called in by the principal. Rochelle shut the door before strolling around to settle into Merle's deluxe leather executive chair, looking right at home. She rested her elbows on the desk, laced her fingers together and rested her chin on them, eyes sparkling.

"Tell me everything."

Barely over a month in his custody and Gil's formerly upstanding son had a split lip, skinned knuckles, torn jeans...and a pretty sweet right uppercut according to Hank's buddy Korby, who'd been one of the teachers that dragged Quint and Sam apart. Gil caught himself wishing he'd been there to see it and scowled. Winning was not the point, as the principal had been happy to explain at great length. Gil had also received a summons from the guidance counselor and a recommendation from the school nurse to update Quint's tetanus vaccination.

Through the paper-thin wall Gil could hear Carma put someone on hold and pick up the incoming call, her voice calm and friendly, as if there wasn't a shitstorm raging across town. One she'd helped stir up, dammit. Well, fine. She could haul Quint to the clinic in Dumas for his shot and go meet with the counselor about the kid's "violent tendencies."

He'd considered dragging Quint's butt out of class to inspect the damage and read him the riot act, but decided it was better to let the kid stew all day. The waiting had always been sheer torture for Gil when he knew he'd gotten on the wrong side of Miz Iris or Steve. So he stayed put, annoyed to realize putting it off was nearly as brutal for the parent.

His mother's obvious amusement was not helping.

He was walking Rochelle through the reporting options

in the management program when he heard Analise say, "I hope the other guy looks worse."

"His left eye is almost swelled shut," Quint said.

As Gil turned to see the scraped knees below Quint's track shorts and the bandage around his knuckles, Carma crossed one leg over the other and folded her arms, fixing Quint with a hard stare. "I would like to state, for the record, that I did not tell you to go punch anyone."

"I don't remember asking you to tell him what he *should* be doing," Gil said, throwing her own confession back at her.

She flushed. "I know. I shouldn't have butted in—"

Gil braced his feet and crossed his own arms, refusing to relent. Yeah, he was a jerk, but this was his kid, and he *would* be in control of this situation.

"I started it," Quint blurted.

Carma blinked at him. "That doesn't mean I had to finish it."

"And by *it* you mean..." Gil prompted.

Quint and Carma exchanged a glance—something like *Please don't tell* and *I won't if you won*'t on both sides.

"She called me on my attitude," Quint said.

Attitude? Gil's arms fell limp at his sides. Jesus Christ. That was the one thing he'd figured they'd gotten right. Quint was polite to the point of pain.

Quint made a face. "It's there. She's just the first person who's been able to see it. Other than Gwen, 'cuz she's just like me."

Gil transferred his disbelief to Carma, but she pressed her lips together and angled her chin away, done talking. Whatever answers he wanted, he would have to pry out of Quint. Gil stifled a sigh.

But Quint went on without prompting. "I've been

working on Mom since clear back last fall. I started complaining more about the racist bullshit at my school, and from parents at our games. And a couple of times I rode my bike in parts of our neighborhood where I knew they'd call security because one of *those people* was casing their house."

"*What?*" Gil's blood turned to slush, frozen by icy rage.

Quint's offhand shrug was not reassuring. "I always had Gwennie hanging close enough to jump in if they needed a pretty white girl to swear I wasn't there to murder them in their driveways. And we avoided the ones that are rabid enough to pull a gun."

A *gun*? Krista had neighbors who would consider taking a shot at a boy on a bike? "You're a kid, for Christ's sake! And you live there."

Another shrug. "They just see black hair and a brown face."

A face like his dad's. Holy fucking hell. And why hadn't Krista told him about any of this? "Why would you purposely scare your mother half to death?"

"If I made it seem like the city was a bad place for me, she wouldn't feel like it was her fault that I wanted to move here." He hesitated, then almost apologetically said, "I wanted to live with you."

The shock must've literally staggered Gil because his mother braced a hand between his shoulder blades as if to steady him. Maybe herself too. Had she dreamed of him or Delon declaring that they'd decided they preferred to be with her?

There was something wise and fatherly Gil should say now, but damned if he knew what it was, so he blurted, "Since when?"

"I always liked hanging around the shop, and with Beni on the ranch." Quint's shoulders crept up. "Then a couple of years ago we all went to Amarillo to watch Uncle Delon at the rodeo, and rode on some midway rides, and we stopped at the Lone Steer for supper. The whole time nobody looked at us weird or asked if I was a foreign exchange student. It was so cool to just be one of the family."

A lump the size of a baseball swelled in Gil's throat, negating his ability to say anything, right or wrong.

"Why did you wait so long?" Analise asked, sounding a little choked up herself.

"It was hard for Dad to take time away from work to look after me when I was younger. I planned to tell Mom that I wanted to come here for senior high, then Douglas got offered the position in Namibia and I had the perfect excuse." Quint ducked his chin. "I should have asked you myself, though, instead of making Mom do it. I was just..." He drew in a breath, then let it out in a rush of words. "I was afraid to see how you reacted, in case you didn't want me."

"Didn't *want* you?" The question exploded out of Gil. "What the fuck made you think that?"

"Language," his mother murmured behind him.

Gil batted a *shush* hand at her, his gaze pinned to Quint.

The boy turned a shade of red somewhere between embarrassed and pleased. "I didn't want to be in the way."

"Oh, for Christ's sake. You're my son." Gil walked over, grabbed him by the shoulders, and looked him in the eye. "Yeah, I was shocked when your mom told me you wanted to live with me. After all the years of fighting for every hour with you that I could get, I couldn't believe she'd hand you over. And I was scared shitless that I'd screw it up."

Quint started to smile, then winced when it reopened the split in his lip. "I'm usually pretty low maintenance."

"Are you?" Gil tried to look below the surface to whatever Carma had seen. "Or is this the real Quint coming out?"

"Nah. I just needed to make a statement." He shot another glance at Carma. "There's some things you don't say about a Sanchez."

And Gil could tell that was as much detail as he was gonna get. He made a monumental effort to level his system, giving Quint's shoulders a squeeze and letting him go. "Well, at least we've got everything out in the open."

"Not quite," Rochelle said. When they all stared at her, she held up a piece of the company letterhead. "You need to tell him about the logo."

"What about it?" Quint asked.

Gil frowned at his mother. "It's not like it's a secret. Everybody knows."

"We do?" Analise said.

Quint's forehead puckered. "Knows what?"

"I told you. On your fifth birthday." Gil sighed, realizing his mistake. "When all you could think about was the brand-new Lego set back at the house. Of course you don't remember. Come here."

He waved at Quint to follow him into the shop. Everyone but Rochelle exchanged puzzled looks as they followed, and Max and the mechanics joined the parade. As Gil marched out the front door and turned to stand with hands on hips, head tipped back, Beni came zipping through the gate and braked his bike hard, throwing up gravel and dust.

"What's going on?" he asked.

"We seem to be having a moment," Analise said.

They all gazed up at where *Sanchez Trucking* was painted in two-foot-tall letters, circling the life-sized silhouette of a bucking horse blowing straight in the air, the cowboy's shoulders flung back, chaps flying and spurs reaching for the sky.

Gil threw up both hands. "Behold. Seventh round of the National Finals, ninety two points—the best ride I ever made."

"Whoa," Beni breathed. "That's you?"

"It is. I made that logo to celebrate Quint's birthday, which was also my second anniversary of getting sober."

"But...why aren't there any other pictures of you?" Quint asked, actually looking dazed.

"When I got home from the hospital after my wreck, I got drunk and smashed a few things." Gil made a pained face. "Delon and your grandpa packed up everything else and hid it. But I do have this one."

He pulled out his wallet and extracted a photo. They all leaned it to see a photo of Gil and Quint posed manfully in front of the freshly painted sign—one adorably young and the other, well, younger. Gil had never been baby-faced.

"Oh!" Quint unzipped a side pocket on his backpack, dug out his wallet, and removed a tattered copy of the same picture. He turned it over to show lines of blue blurs. "There was something written on the back, but right after you gave it to me, Gwennie spilled milk on it. What did it say?"

Gil's hand was unsteady as he took the photo. He started to speak, paused, cleared his throat, and began again. "Sometimes Delon would get upset because we didn't belong anywhere. We didn't look like our dad, and we weren't like our mom. I used to tell him..."

He turned over his photo to show words that were faded but clearly legible, and read them aloud. "*We are the Sanchez boys. We make our own place.*"

He slung an arm around Quint's shoulders and the other around his mother's waist, anchoring himself against a groundswell of pride and love. Beni dropped his bike and joined them. Gil cleared his throat. "Now you're all here, so it's truer than ever."

Carma could hardly breathe at the sight of them, standing tall and proud on ground where they had staked an unquestionable claim. Four faces, so striking and so much alike, each an integral piece of what that logo represented. Gil hadn't hidden from anything. He'd taken the proudest moment of his career and stamped it on everything he'd accomplished since.

Past, present, and future, all wrapped up in one incredible man.

As she watched Quint's arm creep around his dad's waist, pressure swelled inside Carma's chest, squeezing out every emotion that had come before. Dear God. She'd thought that weak-ass muddle of desire and frustration she'd felt for Jayden was love, but it had never had the power to make her sun shine brighter, her sky sing, and the earth beneath her feet tremble.

Or to break her heart into a million jagged pieces.

"There's something else we haven't told you boys," Gil

said. “When that fall in Huntsville didn’t bust me up, the doctors released me to do anything I want.”

There was a long, confused pause. Then Beni said, “Wait a minute. *Anything?*”

“Yeah.” Gil drew a deep breath. “I can ride again. And I’m gonna enter the Diamond Cowboy.”

And then all hell broke loose.

Chapter 31

When Gil showed up at her van that night, Carma didn't even bother with hello. "What happened to 'the Diamond Cowboy is the road straight to hell'?" she demanded.

He shrugged, not even a little sorry. "Tamela pointed out—again—that the rodeo isn't the problem. It's me trying to do it alone."

Of course. It was fine when Tamela encouraged him to chase his dream, but Carma...

Had already screwed up twice, even if both situations had turned out pretty well. The look on Gil's face when Quint confessed he'd wanted to live with his dad...God. She fisted a hand against the ache that flared under her heart.

"But why the Diamond Cowboy? Why not ease into it?"

"That's not really my style." When she bared her teeth at him, he threw out both hands to ward her off. "That's how I've always been. If I'm gonna compete, I want something big to go after."

"And you're not worried about getting carried away?"

"Yes. And no. That's the beauty of the Diamond Cowboy. It's one and done. I go, I give it my best shot, and call it good."

Carma shook her head, confused. "That's it? One big rodeo, then you quit?"

"I had a long talk with Delon, and we agreed that riding bareback horses isn't like golf. You don't just play a few rounds now and then. It's like—I don't know—boxing, I guess. You have to do it on a regular enough basis for your body to stay accustomed to the beating. But I still want one more shot—so this is it."

"And you think you can do that. Just walk away?"

He leaned against the frame of the open door and stuffed his hands in the pockets of his jacket, the chilly breeze ruffling his hair. "At least this time it'll be under my own terms. And it's a pipe dream anyway. What are the chances that I'm gonna bust out of a fifteen-year retirement and kick everybody's ass?"

Knowing Gil? Probably pretty damn good. Carma shivered as the wind gusted through the open door. A cold front had slid down from the southern Rockies, and what had been a blustery fifty-degree day had lost another ten degrees since sunset.

Shivering, she said, "Come in before we both freeze."

He did, sliding the door shut behind him, then stood hunched over, uncertain whether to join her on the bed or sit in the passenger's seat that was swiveled to face the rear. Should she keep him at a distance, where he wouldn't muddle her brain? But his forbidden-forest scent was already making her senses hum. Five feet of shag carpet wouldn't save her.

She scooted over to make room on the bed. With the door shut, the propane heater quickly banished the chill. What was left evaporated when Gil settled beside her, close but not touching. She had to give him points for not assuming that her invitation was all-inclusive, and for angling his legs so his shoes weren't on the bedspread. Did she have Rochelle or Miz Iris to thank for both?

The radio was playing, a rambling, poetic song by Reckless Kelly about a weather-beaten soul, and when Gil leaned back and closed his eyes, the lyrics could have been written about him.

The silence stretched, until Carma finally said, "So you're really doing this."

"Yes, I am."

"Well. Congratulations. That's great."

"Thanks." *But.* She didn't have to be any kind of mind reader to know what that pucker between his brows meant. "I'd appreciate it if you'd come to me from now on, instead of confronting Quint."

"I guess that depends on where things stand with you and me."

He opened his eyes, and what she saw in them made her heart turn over. "I'm still in. What about you?"

"I'm...yes." So far in she would need that tow truck of his to haul her out. Her insides melted with relief, but she had to get through the rest of this conversation before she followed suit. "If there's going to be an us, Quint and I have to figure out how to deal with each other."

Gil bristled. "That doesn't include keeping secrets from me."

"Yes, it does...if he chooses to tell me something he doesn't want to share with you."

His expression darkened. "Even if it's potentially harmful?"

"That question had better be coming from your inner control freak," she snapped, letting him see that he'd offended and, yes, hurt her. "If you don't trust me to tell you if he's in any kind of danger, we're wasting our time."

"I didn't mean it that way."

She raised her brows. He held her stare for a couple of beats, then huffed out a breath. "It's not that I don't trust you specifically. I'm just not good with blind faith in general."

"You're gonna have to learn. Or would you rather he didn't talk to anyone?"

Gil's jaw worked, a visible battle between his concern for his son and the need to have his finger on every pulse. "You'd tell me if it was serious?"

"You have to ask?"

His shoulders rose and fell on a beleaguered sigh. "No."

Inside, Carma did a fist pump. Chalk up one not-so-small victory. "So...when does this big comeback start?"

He tried, and failed, not to grin. "It already has. I worked out on the spur board right before I came here. I barely even noticed the bruise on my hip."

By which she assumed the pain was less than being stabbed with flaming daggers. "What about actual bucking horses?"

"We're aiming for sometime next week. Delon flew to California tonight and will be back Saturday. Steve and Miz Iris will be home late on Sunday. We're all gonna sit down Monday and work out a game plan."

And where do I fit in? But instead, she said, "I assume Tuesday night practice is out, since that's when you get together with Tamela."

She'd tried to sound totally neutral...and failed. He angled her an impatient glance. "I meant it when I said there's nothing sexual between us."

"It's not that." Honestly, Carma couldn't imagine Gil cheating. Not physically. Emotionally, though, every word and thought he gave to the other woman felt like a betrayal—and Carma would have to either get over it or get out. A sponsor was no different than a therapist—the whole point was being able to tell them the things you couldn't say to anyone else. But…

"Then what?" he asked.

How could she explain without sounding jealous or insecure? "I assume the two of you have discussed me, and I'm not sure how to feel about that."

"You talk to Bing about me."

She shook her head. "That's different."

"How?"

I'm not deliberately shutting you out of whole chunks of my life. But if she pushed too hard, he'd bolt those doors and throw away the key.

Patience, she reminded herself. One day at a time. She'd convinced him to trust her with Quint. Eventually, she'd break through to him too.

"You and Bing are friends," she hedged. "I've never met Tamela. It's weird, knowing a stranger is hearing every detail of our relationship."

His mouth curled wickedly. "Not *every* detail."

Even though she knew he was deflecting, heat oozed through her like warm, sweet caramel. The conversation wasn't leading anywhere constructive, and it wouldn't take a minute to get him out of those clothes and into her bed.

While Quint waited back at their house. She sighed. "I suppose you need to get home."

"Yeah. Sorry."

She gave him a quick kiss. "Don't forget, next Wednesday is when I'm going down to the Patterson ranch with Tori."

"Damn." He frowned for a moment, then shrugged. "I guess we're waiting until Thursday then. You have to be there when I climb on that first horse."

He'd do that for her? After waiting an eternity for this, he was willing to put it off another day just so she could be with him?

She kissed him again, harder, and he returned the favor.

They were both flushed when he broke it off. He picked up her hand and folded it between his. "What do you suppose the chances are that we're going to screw this up?"

"Close to a hundred percent." She snaked an arm around his waist and nuzzled inside the vee of his jacket, where his scent was so condensed she almost lost her train of thought. "My trick riding coach used to say, 'You knew when you signed on that you *would* fall and it *would* hurt. Do you want it bad enough to dust yourself off and try again?'"

He caught her chin and tipped her head back so he could look directly into her eyes. "I do."

Her heart stuttered at what sounded perilously close to a vow. This man knew failure, he knew pain, and he had refused to let either stop him. If he decided what they had was real and worth the inevitable stumbles, nothing would stop him from having it.

And if he decided it wasn't, there would be nothing she could do to change his mind.

On Saturday morning, Carma wandered into the office in search of coffee and found both Gil and Rochelle at work. Gil followed her into the break room, backed her up against the wall, and gave her a slow, leisurely kiss.

When he lifted his head, she blinked at him with a lust-hazed smile. "What happened to rule number one?"

"There's a weekend and holiday exception." He

demonstrated again, leaving her limp and flushed. "Also, I brought you something."

He steered her into his office and presented her with a pair of top-of-the-line noise-canceling headphones. "I've scared off half a dozen receptionists all by myself. I can't imagine what it's like in stereo."

Carma rolled her eyes toward the closed door of the main office, which might as well be made of cardboard for all the sound buffer it provided. "She does realize we all know she's swearing, even if it's in Navajo?"

He grinned. "You gotta admit, it sounds pretty badass."

And like her son, Rochelle wasn't pretending. She was one tough lady. At least she and Gil weren't swearing at each other.

Rochelle flung the door open, coffee cup in hand, pausing when she saw Carma. "Do you work Saturdays?"

"No, she does not," Gil said. "And I'm leaving for a while. I have something to show Carma."

"Fine. I've got plenty to keep myself occupied." If she wondered exactly what kind of thing that might be, she didn't let on.

"Bring your keys," he told Carma, and herded her out the front door to the powwow van, which was looking especially glorious since Max had had his detailer hand wash and wax every inch, bringing the beadwork trim out in vivid color. Gil walked around and climbed into the passenger's seat, gesturing at Carma to get behind the wheel. "Drive around back to that gate on the other side of my house."

She did. The gate was open, and beyond it a strip of grass had been mowed to reveal a faint set of old tire ruts that led to the trio of live oaks that stood in the otherwise open prairie. Inside the shady triangle formed by the trees, the grass had been cut to form a good-sized parking area, with a tan portable toilet tucked between two of the massive trunks and a generator set beside it.

"Welcome to the grand opening of the Earnest RV park," Gil said with a wide sweep of his arm. "All the amenities, plus it's within walking distance of downtown… and Sanchez Trucking."

Carma stepped out and turned in a slow circle. The branches of the oaks hung low, screening the shop and the highway from view. In the other direction there was nothing but prairie in sight. She could have been miles away instead of barely outside the gate. "Who owns this?"

"We do. Our lot is part of a twenty-acre parcel."

And he'd chosen to put his house inside the fence, surrounded by gravel and chain link? Honestly, sometimes it was like he was actively avoiding nature. Carma tilted her head back to admire the shimmy of dark-green leaves against a deep-blue sky, then down to watch the breeze play through the bunches of native grass beyond where it had been clipped almost down to the dirt. "Why did you mow it?"

"Snakes."

Oh. Right.

He paced to the most likely place to park the van, the breeze ruffling his hair and enthusiasm warming his eyes, a sight that stole her breath. "It faces east. I know that's important to my mother. You can use the shower in the apartment, and it'll be easier to spend time together than if you're clear down at the lake."

As usual, he'd thought of everything. And if Gil was riveting when he was cool and arrogant, this hint of boyish eagerness made him irresistible. He had put so much thought and effort into this, taking everything she could want into account.

She threw her arms out and spun two more circles before stopping to beam at him. "It's great. And if you're not in a big rush to get back to the office..."

He arched his brows in mock disapproval. "Are you trying to lure me into your van?"

"You betcha."

He grinned, and another piece of her heart crumbled. "I thought you'd never ask."

Chapter 32

On Monday, the atmosphere inside the Sanchez Trucking shop crackled across Carma's nerves like heat lightning. Gil had called Steve and Iris over the weekend, and they'd agreed on Thursday evening for Gil's first practice session. Suddenly, what had been nothing but talk became concrete. Gil had been vacillating wildly between anticipation and doubt ever since.

For her part, Carma was very much aware that Gil had never taken a woman to Miz Iris's house. His fast and furious affair with Quint's mother had not included dinner with what was, in every way that mattered, his family. Their approval meant more to him than either of his own parents' opinions.

No pressure there.

And they had his brother underfoot too. Delon had already planned to spend most of April at home, only taking off for a weekend here and there to hit some bigger rodeos. With Gil's announcement, he'd extended his hiatus until after the Diamond Cowboy.

"My arm and my knee can use the rest," he told Gil. "You can use the coaching. And I want to be here in case you and Mom decide to reorganize the entire business when I'm not looking."

Gil couldn't argue with any of those points—not that he didn't try—but Delon was no easier to budge than when he was on the back of a bucking horse. On the upside, with her younger son at the next desk buttering up existing or potential clients, Rochelle had to mutter her curses under her breath.

At just before noon, it was only Carma and Rochelle in the office. Gil, Delon, Hank, and Steve Jacobs were all meeting for lunch at the café to start plotting Gil's comeback. Quint and Beni were walking over from school to join them.

Lucky waitresses, Carma thought. That was a lot of very fine male scenery in one place.

At the sound of a fresh batch of curses, Carma slumped in her chair and closed her eyes. If they intended to expand the staff, they really should consider adding office space, too. And soundproofing. Maybe they could move Delon and Rochelle upstairs into the apartment. Or better, Carma, although it might seem a little odd to have the receptionist hiding from the public...and everyone else.

Six weeks until the Diamond Cowboy. With a lot of determination and a nonstop playlist of Uncle Tony's flute music collection in her headphones, she could hold on that long. Once it was over, though, she'd have to tell Gil she couldn't do this anymore, the same way she'd had to leave her job at the middle school in Browning, and a movie set where the director kept everyone so riled up with his tantrums that Carma had had her one and only anxiety attack.

Her head jerked up at the sound of a knock. A woman stood in the open shop door—short, slender, around sixty, with dark-brown hair professionally colored and highlighted and her nerves nearly as starched as her blouse.

"Can I..." Carma began, then the question died as recognition dawned and her stomach did a backflip. "Oh. Hello."

Iris Jacobs smiled, clutching a soft-sided cooler to her midsection. "Hello...Carmelita, is it?"

"Carma to most."

"It's a lovely name either way." Her gaze skittered around the office.

Carma eyed the cooler. "Gil and Delon went out for lunch."

"I know." Of course she did. They were meeting her husband. She looked past Carma and her smile widened, but her fingers tightened on the cooler. "Hello, Rochelle. I wanted to stop by and welcome you back."

"Thank you." Gil's mother stood with one hand wrapped around the knob on the office door. Like Iris, her smile was a little tense, dark eyes watchful.

Iris made an awkward gesture with the cooler. "I brought lunch. Just chicken, potato salad, and rolls. And some of the oatmeal cookies the boys like. I don't bake much these days with Steve's cholesterol and my blood sugar, but this is a special occasion so…" She trailed off and made an impatient face. "Sorry. I'm babbling."

"I should just go…" Carma started to rise.

Iris shook her head. "Stay. I'd like a chance to get to know you."

"Then let me take that." Carma circled the desk to pry the cooler out of her hands.

Iris drew a fortifying breath and fixed her gaze on Rochelle. "I've always felt like I owe you an apology for monopolizing your boys. I should have encouraged them to spend more time with you. I told myself that I kept quiet because I didn't want them to think I didn't like having them around, but the truth is, every time they left I was afraid they wouldn't come back, and it would have broken my heart to lose them."

Rochelle inclined her head. "I knew when I asked you

to take care of them for me that they would be like your own. I counted on it." Her eyes dropped, her shoulders rounding. "I just didn't understand that they would feel the same about you and Steve."

"And I didn't keep my promise to keep them safe. After we lost Cole's parents and brother, we were such a mess." Iris swiped at her damp cheek. "I didn't realize how far Gil had slipped away until we almost lost him, too."

Rochelle crossed the space between them in a few swift strides and gripped Iris's shoulders. "You did the best you could in horrible circumstances—dealing with your own grief, your husband's, your daughters', Cole. It's Gil's nature to seal himself off." She made a derisive noise. "God knows, he gets it from both sides. But he's made an amazing man of himself…and you can take the credit for that."

With a choked sob, Iris drew the taller woman into a tight hug. "He has your strength. That's what got him through."

They embraced for a long moment, then drew back, hands falling to their sides as they lapsed into awkward silence. Carma fought through the tornado of emotion that swirled around the room and inside her, gripping the edge of the desk for balance. She forced a bright, reassuring note into her voice and hefted the cooler. "I'd say we all deserve a cookie. *Before* those two sugar fiends come back and snarf them all."

Tears were scrubbed away as the older women laughed and nodded, then settled in to enjoy their lunch. Whew. That turned out better than she'd hoped. Carma had just bitten into a mouthwatering drumstick when Miz Iris turned to her with a bright smile.

"So, Carma. I've been dying to meet you. Tori said

you're interested in equine-based therapy, and Beni said you've been in the movies. Tell us all about yourself. What brought you to Texas?"

Hell. She was facing not one, but two of Gil's mothers. And there was no way she could tell these women anything less than the whole truth.

She set down her chicken and started at the beginning. "Gil and I met in Montana, when I was performing at a benefit, and we kept in touch off and on..."

She left out the juicier parts, but she was sure they could fill in the blanks. Rochelle nodded approvingly as she told the story of the eagle vision. Miz Iris gave Carma a hug as she left.

And whispered, "Good luck, honey" in her ear. Which was sweet...but also a little worrisome coming from someone who knew and loved Gil better than anybody.

Patterson Ranch—south of Amarillo

Carma was in awe from the moment Tori turned down the driveway of the Patterson ranch. Everything was gorgeous. White rail fences, stone pillars, pristine graveled paths. Below the barns, rows of cabins for staff and guests circled a small man-made lake. But inside the paddocks she was as likely to find a sway-backed, gray-muzzled rescue horse as one of the famously elegant and athletic Patterson-bred Quarter Horses.

"This is one of the last three-year-olds we'll enter in the reining futurities." Tori tugged the brim of her cap down against the wind that buffeted them as they admired a stunning palomino. "I got my dad hooked on team roping, and he's been gradually shifting the breeding program toward rodeo horses."

She pointed to a foursome of downy sorrel foals with white strips or stars on their foreheads and hindquarters already packed with muscle. "Those are all out of the sire of a two-time heading horse of the year and a mare that won over a hundred grand at the National Finals a couple years back."

It took Carma a beat to figure out how that was possible. "Embryo transfers?"

"Yes. Those are recipient mares. The mother's owner gets pick of the litter."

"So basically like when we took my dad's good cowdog over and bred her to the neighbor's border collie."

Tori grinned. "Just on a slightly larger budget."

Like the entire Patterson ranch. Everything—from the individual blades of grass to the gleaming equipment in the physical therapy clinic—was the highest quality available. Tori introduced Carma to the therapists, the aide, and a man with muscular dystrophy who was undergoing his initial evaluation. They paused on the viewing platform reserved for friends and family and watched half a dozen riders, some being led by staff, others independently putting horses through assigned exercises.

"Unfortunately my dad got called to Houston on business," Tori said, leading the way down a set of stairs to ground level. "But you'll get to meet him next time you come."

"There's going to be a next time?"

Tori smiled. "Let's go meet some more of our patients. We promised them a special show today."

Which was why she'd insisted that Carma bring her ropes.

As they stepped through the gate, a wail rose from the corner of the arena. A boy was huddled against the fence, arms clasped over his head, while a woman tried to soothe him and a staffer stood holding a horse and looking helpless. Even from a distance, Carma was rocked by his suffocating anxiety.

Tori called softly, "Is Marshall having a rough day?"

"It's the wind. The noise scares him, and once something sets him off..." The woman gave them a frazzled, apologetic grimace. "I shouldn't have brought him today, but he got so upset when I suggested that we stay home. I was hoping that seeing the horses would distract him."

Carma's heart squeezed in sympathy, for child and mother. They couldn't win. Even inside the building the wind was a low, almost visceral moan, felt more than heard. She took a few careful steps closer. "Does he like things that spin?"

"Usually." His mother cast a doubtful eye as Carma dropped all but the shortest of her ropes.

"Let's give it a try," Carma said. "If it bothers him, I'll stop."

She made a dinner plate-sized loop and began to spin it vertically in front of her, like a shield. Marshall's gaze darted toward her, then away, back and away, each time lingering a little longer until finally it became fixed on the rope. Very softly, she began to hum what she called the Chinook song, inspired by the warm but powerful winds that rolled over the mountains and onto the plains, bringing a rapid, welcome end to bitter cold snaps.

When she felt a subtle easing in the boy's tension, she

took a few more steps, so they were a dozen yards apart. Then she let the loop begin to move in slow, graceful arcs, rising and falling with her voice like a bird gliding on the wind currents. Marshall's eyes remained locked on the rope. Gradually the rigid muscles of his arms softened.

Carma's own arms were beginning to burn, but she switched from one hand to another to keep going. There. She felt a tiny flicker of light through the churning darkness inside the boy. She repeated that part of the song and felt it again. "Can you sing with me?" she asked, repeating the melody once, twice, three times, along with the exact motion of the rope.

On the fourth, he made a low, monotone noise. She smiled and nodded. "Yes. Like that."

His gaze and his voice followed her, the darkness fading slightly with each repetition. She kept going until her muscles quivered from the exertion and she had to let the rope drift to the ground.

"Don' stop!" he protested, the words guttural and slightly slurred.

"I'm too tired." She lifted her arms and let them fall limp. "But we can keep singing."

He eyed the crumpled rope as if he hoped it might float up on its own. Carma felt the pressure inside him begin to rise, but right on cue, the horse snuffled and blew as if to say, "What about me?" drawing Marshall's attention. They gazed at each other for a long, soulful moment.

Then the boy turned hopeful eyes on Carma. "Can I ride and sing?"

"I bet your horse would like that," she said. "What's his name?"

When she turned to take the lead rope, she realized

everyone in the arena had gathered in a ragged circle to watch and listen. They all mimed applause, silent to avoid startling the boy. Carma gave a slight bow. Her chest burned and her head spun as if she'd hiked straight up a mountain into the thin, sweet air at the edge of the sky, but a special kind of joy bubbled in her veins that only came from knowing she had touched another soul and eased its pain.

Innumerable laps around the arena later, Marshall began to droop, and didn't protest when his mother called a halt. She flashed Carma a grateful smile as he slid off the horse and into her arms.

"Thank you. That was..." She pressed her quivering lips together.

Carma's eyes went hot in response. "I'm glad I could help."

The boy was still humming his toneless version of the song. His mother squeezed his shoulders. "I don't suppose you have a CD we can buy?"

"Afraid not, but I can record it for you."

"Done." One of the staffers waved a phone. "I already emailed it to you, for the trip home."

Wow. These people were on the ball.

When mother and son were gone, Carma sank down to sit in the dirt, folding her arms across bent knees and resting her forehead on them. Behind closed eyelids, her thoughts blurred into an exhausted haze.

"Is there anything I can get you?" Tori spoke in the subdued voice of a person used to dealing with patients who were at their physical and psychological limits.

"Give me a few minutes," Carma managed. "Then a Coke and some air."

Tori gave her all three, sitting silently beside her until

Carma dragged in a deep breath and raised her head. Immediately, a staffer hustled over with a cold Coke and a Dr Pepper for Tori. As the sugar hit her system, Carma's muscles began to lose the rubbery feeling, and when she'd drained the can, she grabbed the fence rail to haul herself to her feet.

Tori followed suit. "Are you up for a ride?"

Carma couldn't think of anything she wanted more.

Outside, another staffer waited, holding a blood bay mare with black mane and tail and a flashy chestnut with four white socks, both saddled. The girl handed Carma the reins to the bay. As she swung aboard, she wondered how many tens of thousands of dollars worth of horseflesh was being so casually offered for her use. They'd even adjusted the stirrups to the perfect length.

Tori led the way to a path that cut between two of the paddocks, toward the wide open space beyond. The mare moved to follow and Carma pushed everything out of her mind except the horse flowing beneath her, smooth as water over the packed red earth. The revitalizing warmth of the sun soaked into her skin, and the purifying wind whipped through her hair.

When their horses stepped onto native prairie, Tori kicked into an easy lope. The scents of earth and grass rose up from beneath their hooves. Carma inhaled again and again, each breath cycle pushing out some of the darkness she had absorbed, then dragging in light to fill the space. They crested a long, low hill, skirted a brush-choked ravine, and crossed a wide flat before Tori slowed. The horses dropped into a ground-eating walk, a testament to hours spent riding these pastures.

"I assume that's why you never finished your degree in

counseling," Tori said without preamble. "If it takes that much out of you..."

"Not always." But often enough that she couldn't make a career of seeing patient after patient. "It's more what I take from them. With someone like Gil, I'm only redirecting their energy away from the pain. With others it's like drawing out the poison."

Tori nodded thoughtfully. "Does it get easier? If you saw Marshall again, for example."

"The few I've worked with more than once seem to respond quicker once we've established a connection. I don't have to break through to them every time."

In the near distance, sleek black cows raised their heads to eye the passing riders, and dozing calves jerked awake and clambered to their feet. Finally, Tori said, "If you're willing to give it a try, we'd love you to join us. We would be sure not to burn you out."

It was exactly what she'd hoped for, with the unexpected bonus of Tori's quiet respect. She didn't question Carma's talents, only appreciated the results. "I have Tuesdays off."

Tori stopped her horse and nudged the gelding around to face Carma. "I meant full time, once the Diamond Cowboy is done."

"But...you've only seen me work with one patient."

"It was pretty damn impressive. Plus there was Gil. And we need people who don't lose their heads if a horse gets spooked or acts up. I'd say you passed that test with flying colors that night with the snake."

When Carma opened her mouth, Tori held up a hand to forestall any other argument. "We'd give you all the time and help you need to get the program back home up and running, plus we have some used equipment we'll donate regardless. And unless you'd rather stay in your van, you could stay in one of the cabins whenever you wanted."

"I… Wow."

Tori kept pushing. "I've already got a replacement lined up for you at Sanchez Trucking, so you don't need to worry on that count."

Carma's jaw dropped. "Does Gil know?"

"Yes. I told him I wanted to bring you down here, and that my receptionist at the clinic was looking to make a change if I decided to steal you."

Damn. Gil had said Tori could be relentless, but Carma had only seen hints of it until now. And she definitely hadn't come here expecting Tori to throw open doors that could change the entire course of her life. To make her feel so valued. She pressed her palm to a heart that was suddenly racing. She could work in this incredible place, with people who believed in her abilities, and patients who desperately needed what she could give.

An hour and a half from Earnest. And half a country away from what would always be home.

Carma puffed out a breath, brought back to earth with a painful thud. "I have to think about it."

"Because of Gil."

"Partly."

"You know we're not going to fire you if things don't work out with the two of you, right? And we're far enough away that you wouldn't be bumping into him."

"That's not the problem." Carma twisted the reins between her fingers. "If I'm down here, and he's up there—I'm afraid that we won't break up, but not really be together either. You know what I mean?"

"Unfortunately, yes." Tori's mouth twisted at one corner. "The distance is just about perfect for him to pop down here whenever he's in the mood."

"But far enough to get so hung up in our day-to-day lives that we don't give our relationship the time and attention it deserves." Carma screwed up her face. "And I have a feeling it's going to take a *lot* of energy for the two of us to get it right."

"He is Gil."

"And I am me. I don't exactly have a stellar track record of my own."

Tori reined her horse around to continue on their way. "I have seriously considered suing the Beatles for letting me grow up believing that all you need is love. How come nobody wants to admit that it's more like happily-if-you-work-your-ass-off-at-it-ever-after?"

"Because if you put it that way no one would bother to try?" Carma suggested.

"I guess you have to lure 'em in somehow," Tori admitted grudgingly, then grinned. "And it is *so* worth it."

They crested the next hill and the wind grabbed Carma's braid. She caught the end before it slapped her in the face. From where Tori paused, they could see nothing in any direction but an endless stretch of land and sky. Carma wanted to climb off her horse, sprawl on her back in the grass, and just stare up at the streamers of filmy white clouds.

"We could help you," Tori said. "If we thought you were letting him take advantage, me and Shawnee and Bing and the rest of the girls could slap some sense into you whenever you needed it."

Carma huffed a surprised laugh. "Gee, thanks—I think. But he's family to you. I wouldn't want to cause trouble."

"*Pfft!* If there's one thing we all don't mind, it's butting heads with Gil." She paused for effect, then added, "And it goes both ways, so if we thought you weren't treating him right..."

Carma gave a choked laugh. Far above, a shrill cry pierced the gusty air. Tori squinted into the intense blue of the sky until she located the bird. "That's odd. We hardly ever see eagles around here in the summer."

A sense of knowing filled Carma as she looked up and watched the dark shape ride the air currents, swooping and circling directly overhead. Watching them.

Watching over her.

She closed her eyes and listened to the rustle of the grass and the whistling of the wind, until the music began to well up inside her to the tune of a thousand tiny voices singing out a welcome.

She opened her eyes. "Tell your receptionist to go ahead and give her notice. I'll be ready to start the second week of June."

Tori's brows climbed above the rims of her sunglasses as she looked first at Carma, then up at the eagle, then nodded. "Okay."

"Okay."

And it would be, somehow, as long as the land and the sky told her it was so.

Chapter 33

Jacobs Ranch—six weeks before the Diamond Cowboy Classic

It was surreal, standing on the back of the chutes at the Jacobs arena, strapping on a pair of chaps instead of watching all the other cowboys get ready. As Gil fastened the last buckle, Delon raised his eyebrows.

"Where'd those come from?"

"The pawn shop in Dumas."

Delon frowned. "I gave you back all your stuff."

And while Carma was at the Patterson ranch, Gil had spent the previous evening going through the boxes with Quint, telling the stories behind old pictures, taking grief for how scrawny he'd been at Quint's age.

But when they'd pulled out the chaps—black with shimmering gold and metallic red fringe—Quint had picked them up with a sort of reverence. On impulse, Gil had said, "You can have them. In case you ever want..."

"But you need chaps," Quint had said hastily.

Gil ran a hand over the battle-scarred leather. "I think I've outgrown these. But they'd fit you."

It was as close as he'd come to asking his son if he was interested in riding broncs. Quint hadn't taken the bait, but later, when he'd claimed he was tired and going to bed, Gil could've sworn he'd gone into his room and tried them on.

Maybe there was one positive tradition Gil could share with Quint. For now, though...

He straightened and adjusted the new chaps more squarely on his hips. They were the opposite of the Flamethrowers, plain tanned leather with no fancy conchos or tooled designs. "I'm trying to keep a low profile, remember?"

Delon gave him a long look, then nodded. Low-key. Low-risk. That was the plan they'd made, step by reasonable step. No one did controlled and sensible better than Delon. He also understood why Gil couldn't bring combustible pieces of his past into this future.

Beyond the fence, Miz Iris, Tori, Rochelle, and Carma sat in lawn chairs, sipping sweet tea like old friends. Carma had been subdued all day, and even now she seemed removed from the conversation. Gil had worried that her day at the Patterson clinic hadn't gone well, but when he'd asked, she'd said it was good, just a little overwhelming. Then Grace's brother, Jeremiah, had arrived for his interview, and Gil hadn't had another chance to talk to her.

But every time he looked over to where she was sitting, her gaze was fixed on him.

The evening was balmy and still, as pretty as the Panhandle could offer in April, but Gil was sweating under his leather vest. Beni and Quint were ready to open the gate. Out in the arena, Hank and Steve were mounted on pickup horses to fetch Gil at the end of the ride. Three horses were loaded in the chutes, all old campaigners that were barely a step up from climbing on a merry-go-round.

And still his heart thwacked against his ribs as he lowered himself onto Topper's broad back. Was he really doing this? Yes, he was. This time, the scents of dirt and rosin were real. Instead of the wooden spur board, there was hard, warm horseflesh between his thighs as he worked his glove into the rigging. His pulse wanted to race, and his breath along with it.

Calm. Steady.

He'd expected to fumble, but after all those fantasy rides in the back room, every movement felt routine. Check his bind, slide up on the rigging, cock his free arm back. Nod his head.

The gate swung open, and Gil's heels snapped up to plant in the gelding's neck as he braced for the yank of the first jump. It was more like a long tug. Gil dragged his feet up to the rigging, snapped them forward again—and waited another endless moment for Topper to finish the next jump, like a slow-motion replay.

Miz Iris finally blew the eight-second whistle and Topper leveled into a smooth lope, knowing his job was done. The pickup men closed in, and Gil pried his hand out of the rigging to throw an arm around Hank's waist and drop to his feet, not even winded.

Steve reined up beside him with a broad smile. "That wasn't even a good warm-up. Give us a few minutes, and we'll bring up some horses that'll give you a little more of a challenge."

God yes. His body was primed for a real battle. He started to agree, but Delon cut him off.

"Not tonight. The plan is to start out easy and see if you get sore. We're sticking to it."

Exactly as Gil had sworn...dammit. *Keep me reined in.* Left to himself, he'd have told Steve to run in the rankest bastard he had. Instead, he gave a resigned nod. "These will do for tonight."

But when he stripped off his vest after the third ride, still vibrating with unused adrenaline, he felt like kicking something. Possibly his brother, who was enjoying his frustration way too much. Delon was smart enough to clear out, the boys close on his heels, though Beni muttered, "*I* coulda rode that last one," as he passed.

Hell, any kid could've owned that horse. He hadn't kicked high enough to scatter his own shit. Gil hoisted his butt onto the platform behind the chutes, legs dangling as he yanked out the tails of his shirt, popped open the buttons, and shoved the sleeve off his right arm to pick at the waste of good athletic tape on his elbow. Nothing he'd climbed on tonight was gonna do any damage.

Which was the point, dammit. He had no pain. And, he realized with a jolt, he hadn't had a single doubt, no niggle of fear about reinjuring his hip, conscious or subconscious. Technically he'd made excellent rides, patient and precise, another on their list of goals. His all-out style might have thrilled the fans, but too often his loss of control had cost him. If he wanted to compete with Delon and the like, he had to eliminate every flaw.

And in two days he'd be back to take on some broncs with a little more firepower...if he didn't explode before then.

"Lookin' good, cowboy."

He glanced over to see Carma stepping through the gate from the arena, her hair and skin set aglow by the lowering sun, her eyes greedy as they skimmed over him. Answering heat flared instantly, deep and hard.

That mouth of hers curved into a smile that set his blood on full boil. "I'm impressed," she said.

"Even when I'm riding a bunch of rocking horses?"

One eyebrow rose. "Were you? I must've been distracted."

She stepped between his knees, her gaze bold and

hungry as her hands slid up his thighs. God. He was so on edge her touch was like fire even through his chaps. She ran her palms along his bare torso, up his sides, over his chest, leaning in to scrape her teeth along the side of his neck.

He shuddered, groaning, and took her mouth in a kiss that shot straight past any preliminaries. His hands dove under the hem of her lacy, half-transparent shirt. They had to stop. Someone might…

He tried to turn his head, but she caught his chin. "They're gone to have apple pie and ice cream. I told them not to wait for us."

Only the roof of the house was visible over the barn. No one could see down here, especially behind the chutes. And they all had more sense than to come looking.

Gil's hands closed on her hips, dragging her against him as he nuzzled kisses into the sweet silk of her hair, every ion of pent-up energy translating into mind-melting desire. He made one last-ditch attempt at sanity. "You know what they'll think if we take too long to show up."

"Well, then…" She reached into the ugly purse she'd slung over her shoulder and pulled out a condom, dangling it in front of his nose like a ticket to heaven. "We'd better make it quick."

Carma fell asleep on the ten-minute drive back to town, and the sun hadn't even set.

"Wow," Quint whispered from the back seat. "Tori was right."

Gil shot her a concerned glance as he eased into the driveway and put the car in park. "About what?"

"Miz Iris said Carma seemed tired, and Tori said it got pretty intense yesterday with one of their patients, and she guessed it might take a day or two for Carma to recharge. That they'd have to be careful not to let her get too drained." Quint's eyes met his in the rearview mirror, that pucker between his brows. "Is Carma leaving us to go to work for them?"

Not that she'd told Gil. All he'd gotten was a text, a few minutes after he'd heard her van rumble into the trees out back.

Home safe. See you in the morning.

No goofy GIF. And no invitation to come on out and kiss her good night. He'd assumed the long day had worn her out, but he'd had no idea a treatment could do this to her.

Did *he* do this to her?

She'd never seemed drained after the times they were together, but maybe he just hadn't noticed. He could be pretty damn oblivious. And it might be a matter of degrees.

He stroked her cheek, and her lashes fluttered open, then shut again as she burrowed into his palm. "Mmm. Sorry. Long day."

And there would be many more to come. They were only getting started. The coming weeks would be a madhouse at Sanchez Trucking, and Gil knew from experience that he would get more demanding and even less patient as the Diamond Cowboy got closer.

But he had to be careful with Carma. Less…consuming. He'd been using her like a USB port he could plug into whenever he needed to offload excess pressure. She would never tell him it was too much because Carma was a born giver.

And Gil was born to take more than his share. Now that he knew better, though, there was no excuse. He'd have to find other outlets for his stress.

She turned her head and pressed a warm, sleepy kiss into his palm. If there hadn't been a console between them—and a teenage boy watching—Gil would have gathered her close and let her sleep on his shoulder.

He ran a thumb along her eyebrow instead. "Wake up, darlin'. We need to get you to bed."

He ignored the stifled snort as Quint climbed out of the back seat. "Go ahead. I'll see you"—Quint flashed a knowing grin—"later."

Which left Gil no choice but to drive Carma over to her van, tuck her in, and go directly home. Damn wiseass kid.

Carma woke up Friday morning feeling energized and clearheaded, her batteries finally recharged. She hummed along with the birds as she got dressed, her body twinging pleasantly from those hot, frantic minutes behind the chutes, and a little glow around her heart as she touched the spot where Gil had kissed her forehead as he tucked the blankets up to her chin.

Spurring a bronc, teeth clenched and muscles straining, he was a glorious sight. But those random, unexpected moments of tenderness were what completely undid her.

As she strolled past his house on the way to the office, the front door popped open and Quint stuck his head out.

Carma paused, one hand on the world's most ironic white picket fence. "Good morning."

"Mornin'." Quint shuffled onto the front step, barefoot and rumpled in a wrinkled T-shirt and jeans, as if he'd jerked on clothes in his rush to catch her. "Are you feeling better?"

Damn. Tori must have told them why she'd been so zoned out most of the previous day, with the notable exception of that quickie behind the chutes—testimony to the fact that the sight of Gil Sanchez in chaps was enough to raise the dead.

Carma held her smile. "I'm great. How about you?"

"Good." He smoothed a hand over his mussed hair in a very un-Quint-like gesture. "Are you going to work for the Pattersons?" he blurted. "I asked Dad and he didn't answer, so I figured that meant yes."

Or that he didn't know, since Carma hadn't quite got around to telling him. No secrets in this crowd, though. "Eventually," she said.

Quint shoved his hands in the pockets of his jeans. "Because of me?"

"Um...what?"

"Are you leaving because I got you in trouble with my dad when I punched Sam?"

Oh. *Oh!* "No! Not at all. He wasn't even mad at me." Much. She wrapped her hands around two of the white pickets. "I came here hoping to work with the Pattersons. On-the-job training, I guess you'd say, for the program my family is starting back home. Sanchez Trucking was sort of a detour."

"You were never planning to stay?"

"Not indefinitely. I was clear on that from the start."

Quint's eyes narrowed. "What about you and Dad?"

“We didn’t expect things between us to get, well, complicated. Especially not so fast.” Carma shifted under his increasingly critical stare. “And I hadn’t planned on accepting a full-time position with the Patterson clinic.”

Quint’s shoulders loosened a fraction. “So you’re just leaving this job, not us.”

Us? Did he realize what he’d…

Quint grinned, and Carma heaved an internal sigh. Silly girl. Of course Quint knew what he was saying. Didn’t he always?

“I’m staying in Texas,” she said, a whole new glow warming her heart. *Us.* This incredibly particular child wanted her to be a part of them. “But I’m not making any guarantees about me and your dad, except that we are trying not to screw it up.”

He nodded, looking absurdly wise for a kid with bedhead. “He can be kinda difficult. Let me know if you need any advice.”

“I’ll do that,” she said, just as solemnly. “I bought myself a firepit Wednesday. How would you feel about roasting hot dogs and marshmallows tonight? Or is that for kids?”

“Hey, I’m a kid.”

“In what universe?”

He smiled, pleased. “We’ll see you tonight.”

Quint disappeared back into the house, and Carma hummed all the rest of the way to the office.

Chapter 34

Three weeks after his first practice session, Gil stood on the back of those same chutes, contemplating the spot where he and Carma had used his chaps as a cushion against the prickly grass. They hadn't fooled anyone—including Beni and Quint—but even Hank's smirk couldn't stand up to Carma's total lack of embarrassment.

What? her dancing eyes asked. *You've never gotten jumped behind the bucking chutes?*

Gil had caught Miz Iris eyeing them, then shooting a grin at Steve that made his ears turn red, which made Gil have to wonder…

His mind shied away from the details, but those two had seen a lot of arenas and a lot of bucking chutes in almost forty years on the rodeo trail together.

Tonight, though, the air was charged with a different sort of energy. They'd been following the damn plan to the letter, which meant he'd been on more than twenty horses, handpicked by Steve and Delon to give him a little more of a challenge each time he nodded his head. Faster, more elevation, more drop of their head and shoulders as they came down, increasing the yank on his arm. Gil had matched them jump for jump, his confidence growing with each ride.

Now they were cranking up the power. There would be no margin for error tonight. These five-year-olds were the rising stars of Jacobs Livestock, brought home for some R&R after the winter rodeos so they'd be fresh and strong for the big summer run. They could carry a cowboy to the pay window if he made a good ride. But one mistake, one twist of the shoulders or slip of a spur, and they would hammer you.

The one he straddled now was Blue Anchor, a roan mare whose front end was as heavy as her namesake, each jump threatening to jack your shoulders forward and slam your face into her neck. And if you made it past those first two or three seconds…

Delon slapped Gil on the back. "Remember, she's gonna want to throw some swoops at you."

"I'll be ready." He gritted his teeth and said, "Let 'er out."

Every tendon and ligament in his arm sang when she ejected from the chute, but he got his heels in her neck and was braced for the impact when her front feet drove into the ground. His gut clenched, fighting to hold his upper body tight as she launched again. He dragged his spurs up to the rigging, and barely snapped them back down to her shoulders before the next sledgehammer blow of hooves on dirt. Reach, drag, reach, drag…

And then her head disappeared.

He reached for her neck and found nothing but air, his foot swinging over her neck as she dropped her nose, ducked back to the left, and launched him ass over heels. Before he had time to react, his shoulder and the side of his head plowed into the dirt, rattling every bone and tooth. He'd forgotten the blunt trauma of slamming into the ground.

And the total fucking insult of getting bucked off.

Fury exploded in his chest, chasing the aftershocks from his body, but the stars were still dancing in front of his eyes as he lunged to his feet. He stomped toward the bucking chutes where the others stood, eyeing him with varying levels of concern.

"I thought you said you were ready for the swoop," Delon said, smirking.

Gil bent, grabbed a dirt clod, and flung it at his brother's fat head.

There was no wild sex that night. Or the night after. Or the next Thursday, when Gil staggered into his room shortly after five—which Quint suggested might be a record—and sprawled facedown on his bed. "Geezus. I forgot I could hurt in this many places."

"You'll get used to it," Carma predicted, settling an ice pack onto his right shoulder.

She didn't say *over it*. Bareback riders were like running backs in football. They took a pounding even on the good days. But once he worked through the worst of the initial soreness, it would settle back to a weird sort of normal, like Carma's aches and pains back in her trick riding days. Quint walked in and handed Carma another ice pack for Gil's elbow.

"Are you gonna be able to help out at the meet next week, or should I tell Coach you're too busy?" He sounded vaguely hopeful.

"I'll be there."

"I can help, too," Carma offered. "We're all coming to watch you anyway."

"Cool. Maybe you can keep Dad from starting another riot." Quint's departure was followed shortly by the sound of rummaging in the refrigerator and a muffled "We're out of milk again."

This was what their lives had become. Gil spent his days at the office, brainstorming—and bickering—with Delon and their mother. His evenings at the arena or in the gym, all the Sanchez men together—sweating, scheming, giving each other a raft of shit. Wednesdays Carma got up at five to get to the Patterson ranch in time for the first patients, spending the night to be sure she didn't doze off on the road after the long day—in her van, not one of the cabins—and driving home early on Thursday.

And occasionally Gil found time to wander over to Carma's van, after they got home from Quint's track meet, or after Gil got back from his Tuesday night coffee date with Tamela, or after he and Delon finished another rodeo video marathon.

After. After. After.

It had become Carma's mantra. *After the Diamond Cowboy is over...*

And when Gil did show up, he was still only half there, his mind occupied with thoughts he rarely shared. There were nights he was so wired he could light up a Times Square billboard, but when she asked if he wanted a massage for the headache she saw throbbing behind his eyes, or offered to share one of the Native star legends from the book she'd bought after he'd asked her, or to sing him a sunset song while he just lay back and relaxed, he nearly always said he was fine.

Nearly. But the exceptions were enough to keep her believing.

The rest of the time...he deflected by making love to her. And it was wonderful—sweet and slow, explosively fast, anywhere in between—he gave her the kind of pleasure a woman dreamed of. But he never gave her any of the thousand pieces he doled out to others.

Tamela got the lion's share of Gil's confessions including—Carma assumed—how he felt about her. She was way beyond the point where she could trust her own readings where their relationship was concerned. As for the rest…

Delon got all the planning and analyzing and wondering whether Gil would be ready in time for the Diamond Cowboy, or if he was delusional for even trying at this late stage. Rochelle got most of his concerns related to the business. Quint got to be in the thick of things with his dad and Beni and Delon every minute that he wasn't at school or track. And now the college term had ended, Jeremiah got most of Gil's attention at work as he tried to put into words and notes all the hundred and one things he did at Sanchez Trucking.

And Carma? She got great sex…and funny GIFs that doubled as their only real communication more days than not.

Three more weeks…

She sat beside him on the bed, and he mumbled his gratitude into the bedspread as she stroked the stiff muscles of his neck, a simple massage. The other kind of touch, where she felt as if she could reach inside and connect with him, required a combined focus and pooling of energy, and he seemed determined not to ask that of her. She supposed he considered this pain a rite of passage, his price of admittance back into the club. Carma understood.

Carma always understood, even when she didn't want to.

He hummed his appreciation as she kneaded the

wire-tight muscles of his back. "If you want a piece of me tonight, you're gonna have to roll me over and take it yourself."

She laughed, making a concerted effort to stop brooding. He'd warned her it wasn't going to be a joyride, and she'd jumped on this runaway train anyway. She could hardly complain now.

She adjusted one of the ice packs. "You've got almost two hours to chill before we meet everyone at the Lone Steer."

For what would be their first actual date. And a slab of the prime rib everyone bragged about, promising Carma it was the best she'd ever eat. As if she wasn't from Montana, for crying out loud.

What was that saying? *You can always tell a Texan…*

Gil groaned. "Is that tonight?"

Carma stiffened, already knowing what he was going to say. "You can't make it," she said.

"I screwed up." He rolled over, wincing when he tilted his head to meet her gaze. "I told Jeremiah he could have the night off, so he went to Canyon to see his girlfriend."

"But Analise has to leave at six to pick Cruz up at the airport." A twenty-four-hour layover between his last rodeo in Florida and the next one in Oregon.

"I know. I completely forgot about Bing's birthday dinner, and I just…" Gil squeezed his head between his hands. "I couldn't take any more questions. Jeremiah is gonna be great, but right now, he's wearing me out."

Carma got it. She did. Gil's attention was being pulled in so many different directions, it was amazing that he didn't lose track more often.

"It's okay," she said stiffly. "I understand."

"Carma…"

"No, really." She squared her shoulders and sucked in the bottom lip that wanted to pout. "I'll have plenty of company, and you can have a little alone time. Just you and a couple dozen drivers."

"I am really sorry." He grabbed her hand and squeezed it. "I promise, I'll make it up to you..."

Yeah. Sure. When the Diamond Cowboy was over.

But that evening as she pasted on a smile and explained to yet another person why Gil couldn't make it to dinner, Carma couldn't help feeling a powerful sense of déjà vu. How many times had she sat beside an empty chair and told friends or family or nosy strangers how Jayden's practice session had run late, or he'd stayed in Billings a couple extra days to try out a new horse, or he was too tired from driving through the night after a rodeo north of Edmonton.

All valid excuses. All priorities that had meant more to him than Carma.

Now here she was again. And how would she know if she crossed the line from being patient and understanding to a starry-eyed fool who believed that all would magically become right at the stroke of midnight on the last Saturday in May?

Gil sure as hell wasn't going to tell her—unless there was a GIF for that. Right on cue, her phone buzzed with an incoming text. It was not a GIF.

Slow night. Waiting for a call, then locking up. See you in forty-five, max.

He was coming. For her. Carma hugged the phone and mentally took back every doubt she'd had.

Chapter 35

It was the first time in years—since they'd hired their twentieth driver, to be exact—that Gil had even considered leaving the dispatch office untended on a weeknight. Their fleet was rolling like greased steel, though, and the customers were silent as happy little clams. When he'd arrived, Analise was painting her toenails something called *Suck Me Scarlet.*

"That's all there is," she said, tossing him a note.

D-H Ted called. Has a deal in the works to expand Express Auto Rental into Colorado, Utah, and Nevada. Wants to talk numbers with THE MAN.

When Gil reached for his phone, Analise shook a finger at him. "He's on a Very Important Conference Call until seven. He'll call you when he's done."

Gil hadn't heard a peep from anyone else since. He should just go—deal with Ted in the morning—but in addition to being a classic dickhead, Ted was a fickle bastard. If Gil didn't stroke his ego sufficiently, he might take his new business elsewhere, and there were paychecks to consider, especially now that they'd hired Jeremiah and another mechanic, not to mention the king's ransom he would be paying Beth when she took over as receptionist.

Thank you, Analise, for making sure the woman didn't underestimate her worth. This was the trouble with hiring known entities. Sometimes they knew too damn much about how bad Gil needed them.

He stretched, groaning as several vertebrae and both elbows cracked, and checked the time again. Seven fourteen, a.k.a. three minutes after the last time he'd looked.

Call, dammit. If Gil got out of the office by seven thirty, he would be at the Lone Steer before everyone finished their salads.

He drummed his fingers on the desk, wishing he'd remembered his guitar. There was that new meditation program Bing had given him. It would be good practice for competition, forcing himself to relax and focus when he felt more like decapitating Ted dolls.

He also had a knot behind his left shoulder blade that would feel a lot better if he wasn't slouched in a chair. Maybe later he could ask Carma to work her magic on it.

Thank God for Carma. He wasn't half the wreck he would've been without her. Carma's van had become his oasis, the one place he could go where no one was asking him anything.

With Carma he could shut his brain down and just exist.

And do his damnedest not to fry her circuits when he was on overload. He'd been trying hard to decompress before he showed up at her campsite: workouts, progressive relaxation, picking a few songs on his guitar, and his latest hobby, packing various parts of his body in ice. Either this shit had hurt a lot less when he was twenty, or he'd been half-buzzed a lot more than he remembered.

It was also a lot more exhausting, but he hadn't been trying to run a trucking company and raise a kid back then. There weren't so many people asking him questions that he felt like his brain was being turned inside out and pecked by crows on a daily basis—so that he forgot something like Bing's birthday. He *never* forgot that kind of thing, and doing it now did not bode well. If he wore himself too thin, his willpower might be the first thing to give.

All the better reason to close up shop and go have a meal that didn't come in a takeout bag.

He went out and got the sweater Carma left hanging on her chair for the days when she wore sleeveless sundresses and his mother was having hot flashes. Gil loved sundress days.

Hell, he loved any time he stepped out of his office and saw Carma. He'd caught himself finding excuses to leave his desk just for the sheer pleasure of watching her glance up and smile as if he was the best thing she'd seen all day. He'd even started playing the old game he used to with the pills. *How long can I stand to wait until the next one?*

So far this week his best had been an hour and half. How the hell would he manage when she went to work at the Patterson ranch full time, and he had to go cold turkey?

Maybe he could talk her into texting him selfies every hour on the hour.

He shoved the CD into the disk tray on his computer, turned up the volume, lowered his aching bones onto the floor and stretched out on his back. When he rolled up the sweater to use as a pillow, Carma's scent surrounded him.

Three more weeks. Then he'd have to learn how to share. Her time. Her energy. Even her smiles. And selfish bastard that he was, instead of solutions, all he could come up with were excuses to keep her right where he could see and smell and taste her whenever he wanted.

But Carma shouldn't be locked in a dingy little office.

At the clinic she could put all her gifts to use, surrounded by horses and people who needed her particular brand of magic. Helping. Healing. Spreading her warmth.

And ending her days on a horse, surrounded by miles of open prairie.

She was a creature of the wind and sky, and only a complete jackass would try to ground her. He should be thankful she was only going a hundred miles and not clear back to Montana. Besides, if the clinic could capture her spirit and keep her in Texas, Gil would have more of a chance at holding onto her heart.

He glared at the stubbornly silent phone he'd left lying on the desk. He could start by showing up for dinner. Or dessert, at this rate. But at least she'd know he was trying.

Over the high-end speakers, a soothing voice murmured instructions. *Breathe in, the deepest breath you've taken all day. Breathe out, releasing your worries. Let go of the stress. Feel the tension leaving your shoulders, your neck, and your face.*

He closed his eyes and batted away his persistent, whirring thoughts like moths under a porch light, putting all his focus into relaxing, muscle by muscle. Just a few minutes…

"Dad?"

Gil jolted awake, heart pounding, body cold and aching. *What? Where…*

"Dad!" Quint stood in the door, his face pinched with worry. "Are you okay? Did you pass out?"

Gil pushed up onto one elbow, groggily scrubbing at his eyes. "You're supposed to be at the Lone Steer."

"Duh. We waited so long everyone else left. I even talked Carma into dancing with me once, but you still didn't show up. I texted twice. Carma said you probably got hung up on your call."

Son of a bitch. Ted. Gil grabbed his phone. Nine twenty. No missed calls. The bastard had stood him up. And since the phone hadn't woken him…

He'd left Carma sitting alone. Embarrassed her. Made her feel stupid for trusting him. This was not the man he'd made of himself. He did not blow off any kind of a date for any reason. But tonight he'd let Carma down twice over.

Gil hung his head and swore.

Quint sighed. "You can say that again."

Gil did, as the guilt and the craving hit him like a one-two punch straight to the gut. He clenched his hands around his head, fingers digging into his skull as if he could strangle that damn whisper.

You know what would really take the edge off…

He punched up speed dial on his phone, intending to call Tamela. He could send Quint out to explain to Carma. But he didn't want a voice over the phone. He wanted a warm touch, and he needed to apologize. Find some way to erase the hurt he'd inflicted. Let her curse him if that's what it took.

But first he had to get himself there, despite the nearly irresistible urge to go the opposite direction.

He held out a hand to Quint. "I need a little help here. I'm not sure I can get up by myself."

Let Quint assume he was just talking about his stiff muscles.

They walked side by side to the house. In the driveway, Gil stopped, trying not to even look at the Charger, his potential chariot to hell. "I'm going to talk to Carma," he told Quint. "Call your grandmother and have her come and stay with you."

"I'm fine..." Quint began, before something in Gil's expression stopped him. A flicker of unease crossed Quint's face. "Anything else?"

Gil looked down at hands that were trembling with the effort to maintain control. "Tell her to keep an eye on the car keys." He glanced around the lot—there was the tow truck, three semi tractors, plus the service pickups. "*All* the keys."

Then he forced his feet to take him away from all those wheels and toward Carma.

Carma didn't bother getting undressed, just stretched out on the woven wool rug she'd spread on the ground beside the van and stared up into the trees while she waited for Gil to show up bearing an armload of apologies and excuses. She knew the drill. Some emergency had popped up with some driver, or he'd remembered he had some paperwork that had to be done by morning and he'd lost track of time, or the call he'd been waiting for had taken way longer than he'd expected.

I'm sorry, but this is my job. If I want to win, I have to put in the time.

Oh, wait, that was Jayden—but the basic idea was the same. And it would leave Carma feeling petty and unreasonable for expecting Gil to slack off on her account.

Fitting, that lying on her temporary patio made her feel like a sacrifice in waiting—circled in citronella candles to ward off the mosquitoes, with the cushy pad from a lounger for comfort.

Dramatic much? No one had forced her to come here.

No one was forcing her to stay. And the gullible part of her was still hoping Gil would be different. That both his reasons and his apology would make it all right.

She didn't turn her head when she heard the soft pad of footsteps coming up the trail they'd beaten from his door to hers, just watched in her peripheral vision as he lowered himself stiffly onto the rug. He didn't say anything for five of her deliberately calm breaths. Then he huffed a sigh. "I should've just come to the party and let Ted talk to the answering machine like everybody else."

"Dickhead Ted?" Carma guessed.

"Yeah. He's dangling a bunch of new business and seeing how high he can make me jump."

Of course it would be someone important, the better to make Carma feel guilty for not getting over herself.

Gil hunched his shoulders, gaze fixed on the fingers that worried a snag in the carpet. "And then he didn't call, so I didn't wake up—"

Carma swiveled her head to stare at him. "You fell *asleep?*"

Gil? Who could barely manage two consecutive hours of shut-eye in his pricey adjustable bed with his white-noise machine playing? But he did have that not-quite-there look, as if he'd been woken in the middle of the night.

He found a new spot on the rug to torture, still not making eye contact. "I'm sorry. It was stupid. I should've set an alarm or something."

"You didn't even hear Quint's texts."

"I know. I can't believe it either." How exhausted did he have to be to doze off in his office, and not hear the phone that Analise swore was wired directly into his brain? He spread his arms with a derisive smile. "Behold, my natural gift for taking any mistake and fucking it up beyond repair."

No excuses. No explanations. Just pure self-flagellation. With his defenses leveled by fatigue, she could all but taste the wretched burn in the back of his throat. Gil didn't make empty promises. And the failure to keep the ones he'd made was eating him up.

He was already beating the ever-lovin' crap out of himself. He didn't need her piling on.

She rolled onto her side to face him, pillowing her head on one bent arm. "Why didn't you tell me you were so tired? I would've sent you home to get some rest last night."

"I think you just answered your own question," he said, with a pale imitation of his usual smirk.

She rolled her eyes. God forbid he admit that he wasn't superhuman, capable of conquering the world on coffee and sheer determination. "Not that I haven't appreciated the, um, services rendered, but to be totally honest, I'm wearing a little thin myself. I wouldn't mind less Olympic-level sex and more just lying here vegetating together."

"I'm sorry." His expression went a shade darker. "I didn't mean—"

"Gil. Relax." She laid a hand on his arm, imagining a beam of sunlight passing between them. The calm of a mountain lake mirroring the sky. The muscles under her fingers slackened, then tensed again as he pulled away.

"You shouldn't waste that on me."

Excuse me? Carma had been upset and hurt earlier in the evening. Now she was downright pissed. She jabbed her finger into his biceps. "First off, Gil Sanchez, don't you dare call yourself a waste of energy. And secondly, I am a renewable resource."

His jaw worked. "But you can be drained."

"In extreme situations. Or if I don't give myself time and space to recharge." She angled her head, but he was still avoiding her gaze. "You are not sucking the life out of me. And as someone recently told me, you don't get to decide what I need without asking first."

"Great. On top of everything else, I'm making up my own double standards as we go." He raked a hand through his hair. "But you *were* wiped out after that first visit to the Patterson clinic."

Was that why he'd been keeping her at a distance? "Again, extreme circumstance. Which you would know, if you'd asked."

"If I hadn't been too wrapped up in myself, you mean." He breathed out a weary curse. "Anything else I need to apologize for, while I'm at it?"

Carma thought of the list of gripes she'd compiled at the Lone Steer. Then she looked at the slump of his shoulders, and felt the sheer physical and mental exhaustion smothering him like a dense black cloud.

She squeezed his arm gently. "At the rate you've been pushing yourself, you were bound to crash. And yes, I was unhappy with you, but I'll get over it if you tell me what I can do to help."

Anyone but Carma might've missed the hesitation before he said, "That's plenty."

"Bullshit. Tell me what you really need."

He shook his head. "You're already doing enough."

"Gil." She put an edge in her voice. "Do you really want me to tell Analise that you call her new look Marilyn Monroe meets Marilyn Manson?"

"God no. She'll come in dripping fake blood just to show me how much worse it could be."

"Then tell me what you need."

"I can't ask..." He raised a hand to ward off her hiss of frustration. "Fine. When you're gone, it's a dog pound in there—everybody yapping and whining and growling at each other."

She scrunched her face. "Worse than when I am there?"

"Last week Mom and Delon and I got so loud during one of our *discussions* that Max threatened to turn the hose on us."

Carma blinked. "Max is scared to death of your mother."

"You see what I mean."

She nodded, her stomach settling to somewhere in the vicinity of her belly button. Her entire week revolved around Wednesdays. Whenever the chaos in the Sanchez office got overwhelming, she put on her headphones, closed her eyes, and imagined herself at the Patterson ranch, helping one of the amputees rig up a system for saddling a horse one-handed. Or loping across the prairie without another human in sight—or sound.

"Forget it," Gil said abruptly. "The clinic is the whole reason you came down here."

Not the *whole* reason. Carma suspected that even if her grandmother hadn't given her a shove, she'd have manufactured a reason to come visit Bing—and Gil. No matter which direction she'd wandered since that night, her internal compass had been pointed toward Earnest, Texas.

And she'd known from the moment she laid eyes on him that Gil wasn't an easy man. That he'd only get more volatile and less accessible in these weeks leading up to the Diamond Cowboy. How much pressure he would put on himself. Just showing up wasn't enough for Gil. He was in it to win it, one big chance to leave his mark.

Three more weeks. Then the Diamond Cowboy

would be over and Gil's dream along with it, one way or another.

"Okay," she said. "You've got me five days a week, until Beth takes over."

The wave of relief that washed through him and on to her was worth the balled-up disappointment in her gut.

"One more thing," he said.

She braced herself. What more could he want?

"Can I stay for a while?" He finally lifted his gaze, and she nearly jerked her hand away from what she saw there. A bottomless, hopeless void—one he'd managed to hide from her and most everyone else. "If I leave here now, I'm not sure I won't keep going until I get to the bar and tell them to give me a double of whatever will kick me the hardest."

Her heart knocked unsteadily as the demon that lived inside of him sneered at her. *Did you really think it would be that easy to take him away from me?*

Yes, she had, she realized with a sick jolt. Despite all she knew and all his warnings, deep down she had let herself believe that Gil had conquered his addiction, unable to imagine anything holding up against his raw determination.

This was what he'd tried to tell her. What he shared with Tamela that no one but another addict could ever truly understand. But tonight he had come to Carma instead, and the significance of that choice stole her breath.

"I'm right here, as long as you need me," she said, barely managing a whisper.

He melted into her with a profound sigh, wrapping an arm around her waist and burrowing his cheek against her chest, a position so unlike his natural state of dominance that it took her a moment to react. Her hand hovered, uncertain, like he was one of her mom's barn cats who'd sidle close, then bolt if she reached for them. But Gil sighed again as her fingers settled on his back and began to move, slow and reassuring. His breath played warm across the inner curve of her breast, and Carma was suddenly, intensely aware of the beat of her own heart, the air moving in and out of her lungs.

He was still for so long she thought he might have fallen asleep again. Then he asked, "Did Quint really make you dance with him?"

"Yes. Beni too." She ran her fingers through his hair, smoothing where he'd raked it into spikes. "Great pair of wingmen you've got there."

She felt him smile through the thin cotton of her sundress. "True Sanchez boys."

They drifted into silence, the night filled with chirrups, hoots, and off in the distance, the eerie wail of coyotes.

Softly, she began to hum along.

Chapter 36

Earnest, Texas—two weeks before the Diamond Cowboy Classic

The day after Bing's birthday party, Carma left Gil once again holed up with his mother and Delon, debating how they could absorb the increased business from Express Auto while still in the process of expanding to accommodate the Heartland Foods loads.

Debate being a polite way of putting it. There was intense disagreement over what other clients might have to be weeded out, and which drivers had the skill and attention to detail required for hauling cars, apparently one of the trickier types of loads.

Carma had made her escape at five o'clock on the dot.

The temperature had climbed into the mideighties, too hot to go for a walk for another couple of hours, but she was too restless to sit. She cranked up some Linkin Park on the van's stereo and dug one of her ropes, idly twirling it in the shade of the huge trees around the van.

"Would you teach me?"

She spun around to find Quint watching her, hands in pockets. Other than the night of the weenie and marshmallow roast, he hadn't come near her campsite. Whatever he wanted now, it wasn't just roping lessons. "Sure. There's another rope right there next to the van."

He picked it up and, to her surprise, deftly built a loop. When he saw Carma watching, he said, "Tori taught me how to rope the dummy. And Shawnee showed me a couple of things."

"Did she now?" Carma propped her hands on her hips. "Let's see what you've got."

He demonstrated a basic twirl and a wobbly ocean wave, with the rope wrapping around his arm halfway through the second circle. "I haven't practiced much," he muttered as he untangled it.

"Have you ever tried roping cattle?" she asked, remembering his interest in Tori's team-roping video.

"Not real steers." He made a new loop and gave the ocean wave another try. "A couple of times at Tori's place they pulled the practice dummy around while I roped it off her horse, but we were barely even trotting."

Carma paused in the middle of adjusting her own loop. "I got the impression you weren't crazy about horses."

"They're fine, if they're super calm and I know I can trust them. I like Cadillac and Fudge. And Shawnee's got a cool horse named Roy."

And what did they all have in common, other than being extremely well broke? *Duh.* Carma couldn't believe it had taken her this long to get a clue. "You want to be a roper."

Quint's rope tangled around his arm again. "Someday."

"Why not now?"

He took great pains to straighten out the rope. Carma waited while he adjusted the loop to some precise, predetermined size. Then he let his hands fall to his sides without taking a swing. "How was Dad when you saw him last night?"

Frightening. She didn't have say it. She saw it in Quint's eyes. "What happened before he came over here?" she countered.

"Nothing. Not really. I mean, he was really upset about falling asleep and all, and he told me to call Grandma and have her come stay with me." This was the point when Quint usually would have rolled his eyes or made a face to let her know that he knew why his dad might not be sure when he'd get home. Quint didn't do either of those things. "He said to tell her to guard all the keys."

"Um...keys?" Like, lock him out of the house?

"To the car and the trucks and everything. So he couldn't go to the bar."

Carma did a double take. "He told you that?"

"Not the part about the bar, but why else?" Quint fiddled with the hondo on the rope. "Grandma and I kept watch to be sure he didn't try walking instead."

It was only a quarter of a mile, max. Carma sometimes walked down to the Kwicky Mart or the Smoke Shack just to get out of the office at lunch, and the Corral Bar was just across the street. "He stayed here," she said.

In the van, eventually, but they'd slept in their clothes, on top of the blankets. She hadn't suggested otherwise, getting the distinct sense that Gil felt naked enough just coming to her in that state. He'd left her at dawn with a kiss on the forehead and a whispered "Thank you."

And today in the office, he'd seemed like his normal self, which said volumes about how good he was at hiding his struggles. So good that he'd fooled Carma into thinking his addiction was just the reason he didn't drink, the butt of his caustic jokes.

She suspected it was the same for Quint, and he must be even more shaken than she was. This was his *father*.

"Anyway," Quint said, "Grandma and I talked about how everything is changing in the office and everybody's stressed, but it's the worst for Dad because he's the one they all go to when they have a question. So we talked to Uncle Delon, and he was gonna talk to Max and Analise and Jeremiah, and everybody's gonna try real hard to take some of the load off of him so he doesn't get so..."

"Tired," Carma supplied.

Quint smiled faintly. "Yeah. And we figured you should know what's going on, too."

"Good call." Her own smile wobbled. She'd spent the whole day scheming how to make Gil's life easier, and they already had it covered. She didn't even have to worry about butting in. "We'll take care of him."

"Thanks. Just don't tell him, okay?"

She was feeling way too close to tears, and that was someplace neither she nor Quint wanted to go, so she deliberately went off on a tangent. "About the team roping, you mean? 'Cuz I could swear I saw you working out on the spur board with them the other day."

Quint was suddenly fascinated by the hondo on his rope. "Uncle Delon insisted. He thinks I might want to be a bareback rider."

"Where did he get that idea?"

He sighed. "I sorta accidentally gave my dad the wrong idea."

"I see." Carma folded her arms and leaned back against the side of the van. "How does a person sorta accidentally do that?"

Quint huffed impatiently. "We were looking at his old pictures and stuff, and his chaps were there, and they're just really cool, you know? He wore them at the *National Finals.* The biggest rodeo in the world. And I don't have anything else of his, the way Beni has his dad's old Finals jackets and stuff. I was checking them out, and Dad asked if I wanted them."

Ah. Now it made sense. "And he assumed you were fascinated because you wanted to follow in his spur tracks."

"Yeah."

Carma took the time to really look at him. See what she could feel. "Are you scared to ride bucking horses?"

"What sane person wouldn't be?" he shot back. "I've seen how sore Dad is, and he's only been bucked off that one time. They joke about how bareback riding hurts even when you make a great ride. What's supposed to be fun about that?" Quint eyed her suspiciously. "You aren't gonna tell him, are you?"

"Nope. Are you?"

"Not until after the Diamond Cowboy." He stubbed at a weed with his toe. "He probably won't be very happy."

Typical roughstock rider. But Carma couldn't help teasing Quint a little. "You could try riding a couple of those easy horses. You might be so terrible they'll write you off after the first few tries."

"Fat chance." He gave a gloomy snort. "I'm good at everything."

"There's that Sanchez humility." She picked up her loop and started it spinning. "Let's see if we can teach you how to do a butterfly before it gets dark, Ace."

For the next hour, they spun ropes and talked about the highlights and lowlights of Carma's career as a performer. She made Quint laugh with a story about singeing off the ends of her hair when she'd tried twirling a flaming loop. He made her choke on her own spit with the dry observation about fire-resistant fringes.

And yes, by the time they finished, he could do a near-perfect butterfly.

~

"This may be the first time in my life I've been sweaty at a track meet." Carma swiped an arm across her glistening forehead. "At our regional finals it's always about fifty degrees with the wind howling off the mountains. Sometimes there's a chance of snow."

And Gil wouldn't be admiring how that white tank top clung to every curve and set off the bronze glow of her skin. There was a lot to be said for warmer climates.

Everyone was staring at her, and it wasn't entirely due to the fit of her khaki shorts. The regional track meet was her official Earnest debut as GIL SANCHEZ'S GIRLFRIEND. All caps, in neon orange, even though it was mostly being whispered between bent heads and muttered behind hands. She was an outsider, she was Native, and she was the first woman they'd seen him with since high school. The two of them couldn't have caused a bigger buzz if he'd driven one of his trucks onto the field while she danced on the hood.

Gil was not ashamed to admit he was enjoying it. *Look all you want, assholes. She's mine.*

He should have been disturbed by the hot surge of possessiveness. Instead he savored the burn. That night beside her van, when she'd forgiven his sins and rescued him from the devil temptation, something fundamental had shifted inside him. He had sunk close enough to smell the muck that coated rock bottom, and because he'd reached out to Carma instead of turning away, he'd been able to haul himself back to the surface.

And he'd felt a hundred pounds lighter ever since. Even the pressure at the office had dialed down, and he wasn't sure if it was because everyone was finally settling into the new routines or he was just handling it better.

He peeled his gaze off Carma and called the next high jumper. Over in the bleachers, Bing, Miz Iris, and Rochelle had set up camp, complete with fans, wide-brimmed hats, and coolers of food and cold drinks. Beni and his buddies were lounging just far enough away to be cool, but close enough for frequent snack raids.

They had plenty to watch, as Quint hustled from the long jump to the hundred-meter dash, back to the triple jump, then to the starting line for the two-hundred-meter hurdles. He flew around the track and through the air with such ease and grace that it made Gil's heart twist in envy. He'd been that boy once—all wiry muscle, distilled energy, and cocksure grins.

He wouldn't go back for all the beer in Texas. He'd barely survived the first time through, and besides, look at what he might have missed if he changed the tiniest thing. One fewer mistake and he could've ended up somewhere else entirely. No Quint. No Carma.

He just had to figure out how to hold it together this time.

As they picked up either end of the downed high-jump bar, he grinned at her across the thick foam landing pad. "If the school had known we were bringing you, they could've sold tickets."

"And I didn't even have to take off my clothes this time." Shocked giggles erupted from a trio of Earnest girls who were strolling past. Carma rolled her eyes behind big movie-star sunglasses, lowering her voice. "Give it an hour, and half the town will be debating whether Carma is a stripper name."

He laughed and called the next high jumper.

Cheers erupted from the triple-jump area, and Gil glanced over to see Sam Carruthers accepting high fives as he brushed sand from his legs. The fight had obviously served to break the ice for Quint. The eighth-grade boys appeared to be equally divided between the pro-Sam camp and the pro-Quint crew, with a few either brave or oblivious souls who tried to be both.

Sam and Quint kept a careful distance from each other until the last event of the day. The 1,600-meter relay was the race that had started their feud. One lap around the track for each boy, with Quint running the cherished anchor leg. With Quint's added speed, Earnest's team had done well at the last few out-of-town meets, and today they finally had a legitimate chance to beat archrival Sunburst.

But what in God's name was the coach thinking, switching Sam to the third leg? Sure, he might match up better against that Sunburst runner, but it meant he had to hand off the baton to Quint. The exchange was all about timing, coordination, and communication...between two boys who didn't speak to each other.

Of course when Gil asked, Quint said it was fine.

As the teams took their positions, Gil steered Carma to a prime viewing spot near the finish line and beside the exchange zone. Sunburst and Earnest had drawn lanes three and four, side by side and in the middle of the track, ideal for the expected head-to-head battle. As the first runners stepped into the starting blocks, a hush settled over the crowd.

Bang!

The gun fired and the runners burst out of the blocks, pushed by a roar from the crowd. When they rounded the second turn and came down the straightaway, Earnest was fifteen yards off the pace.

Gil clamped tense arms over his chest as they watched the runners pass the batons without mishap. "We're good. They led with their second-fastest guy, so we expected to lose some ground."

Carma nodded, her attention glued to the action.

The rest of the teams fell back, but the margin between Sunburst and Earnest remained steady throughout the second lap. Then the baton slapped into Sam's hand and away he flew, closing the gap stride by stride as the two runners raced down the back straightaway, while coaches and fans screamed themselves hoarse. They rounded the far turn, and both boys grimaced in agony as they fought through the last hundred yards.

"Stay loose," Gil muttered, remembering all too well how his hamstrings had felt as if they were tied in knots at that point. "He's just gotta give Quint the stick with less than three seconds to make up."

Carma grabbed his arm, her fingers digging into his biceps, her lips moving in a silent plea.

In front of them, Quint stood waiting in the exchange zone, cocked like a pistol. The Sunburst runner arrived first, with Sam a dozen strides behind. As the baton passed to the Sunburst anchor, Sam yelled, "Go!"

Gil cursed under his breath. "Too soon!"

Quint went, but his head start was too much for Sam's flagging legs. Realizing the error, he slowed just as Sam gave a desperate lunge, thrusting the baton forward. There was a collective gasp as Sam's leading foot caught Quint's heel and they both staggered. Sam pitched forward, the baton bouncing off Quint's elbow and clattering onto the track as Sam fell, skidding on the rough, rubberized surface.

The entire Earnest contingent groaned in unison.

Quint stumbled to a stop and dropped his hands to his thighs as the remaining teams raced past and the Sunburst runner circled the track uncontested. Blood tricked down the back of his ankle from a pair of gouges left by Sam's spikes.

Son of a bitch. Gil took a furious step toward his son, but Carma held him back. "Wait."

Slowly, Quint straightened, then turned toward where Sam sat on the track, angry red scrapes marking both bent knees and one of the elbows he rested on them, head hanging. Quint walked up to him and extended a hand.

"Sorry," he said. "I took off too fast."

Sam angled his head back, squinting suspiciously. "My legs were shot. I should've got closer before I told you to go."

"So we both screwed up." Quint wiggled his fingers, and after a beat, Sam took hold and let Quint pull him up. They stepped off the track and watched with identical expressions of disgust as the Sunburst runner cruised through the tape, throwing his arms up in triumph.

"Shit," Sam said. "That was our last shot at them."

"This year." Quint scowled at the celebrating mob of Sunburst athletes, then extended his fist. "But we've got all of high school to get even, and that's the last time we *let* them beat us."

Sam's eyes narrowed, his jaw squared, and he bumped his fist with Quint's. "Bet yer ass."

They strode off shoulder to shoulder, refusing to limp or swipe at the blood trickling from their wounds. Gil let out a long, pent-up breath.

Carma pressed a quick kiss on his cheek. "That's some kid you're raising."

He gave a strangled laugh. "Hey, I'm the daddy-come-lately. I don't get to take the credit."

Carma gazed around, catching the approving nods among the parents and fans.

"Sure you do," she said, and dragged him over to raid Miz Iris's cooler for cold drinks and cookies while Quint accepted back slaps and condolences from both his fan club and Sam's.

Gil looped his arm over her shoulders and squeezed, sure she could feel the pride that threatened to bust his chest wide open. That was his son, and dammit, he must've done something right along the way.

And maybe—just maybe—Gil was more like the man Carma saw in him than he'd let himself believe.

Chapter 37

Earnest, Texas—one day before the Diamond Cowboy Classic

Once again, Carma sprawled alone on her patio, brooding up at the pulsing twinkle of the planet Venus. In the old story, a young woman gazed at what the Blackfeet called Morning Star and declared that she wanted to marry him because he was the brightest of all. Hearing her vow, he took human form and came down to earth to claim her as his bride and take her up to the Sky world to live with him forever.

In Carma's experience, a man might be brought down to earth, but once she lifted him up again he floated away, glittering out of her reach.

And yes, that was her damned insecurity talking, but it had an annoying habit of making valid points.

Things had been better since the night Gil had all but collapsed. At least he let her really touch him now. But tomorrow he would step back onto the rodeo stage. It had already started. Carma had fielded the calls herself, after the list of contestants had been posted on the website last week and a few eagle eyes had spotted his name. *Is that* the *Gil Sanchez? Delon's brother? Isn't he too, um… well, you know?*

Her answers had been abrupt. Yes. Yes. And no, whether they were referring to his age or his physical condition. If they were a member of the media, she'd emailed them the press release Delon had insisted they put together.

Gil shrugged off the potential stir he was going to cause. Nobody was interested in his ancient history.

Delon knew better. He was the reigning world champion, and Gil was the tragic could-have-been, a talent possibly even bigger than his brother. The story would be irresistible to the promoters of an event that billed itself as the David versus Goliath of rodeo.

If Gil did make a splash—well, any man or woman could get swept up in the rush of attention and lose track of who they were leaving behind. God knew Carma could personally testify to that.

In the dense branches above her, an unseen owl hooted and another answered. The cicadas whirred incessantly. And softly, a guitar joined the nightly serenade. She turned her head and found Gil leaning against the trunk of the nearest tree.

He stepped out of the shadows, and her pulse took an uneven bound. Lord, he was something to look at, as chiseled as the jagged peaks of her mountains—something else she could never quite possess but still yearned for in a deep, indefinable way. She rolled to sit cross-legged so she could admire every cocksure inch of him, right down to the classic, toed-out bareback rider's gait.

"You've got your cowboy swagger back," she said.

He stopped at the edge of the blanket. "Nothing makes you strut like winning third at a podunk open rodeo where you're the only one old enough to shave."

She shrugged. "You got more out of that horse than most would."

The previous weekend they'd slipped a few hours up the road into Colorado, where Gil wasn't likely to be recognized on sight, and he'd entered as Gilbert

Yazzie—borrowing his mother's name and hometown. One competition to work out some jitters before the big day.

Even on a belly-kicking nag he'd looked amazing. So strong. And so fast. The young punks had snapped to attention, while Carma's heart—and a few other key body parts—had quivered at the sight of him sauntering back to the chutes, hat pulled low and shoulders thrown back.

He sat down facing her now, also cross-legged, and settled the guitar in his lap. It was the first time he'd brought it along since the night of the thunderstorm. "What do you want?"

"Excuse me?"

He hefted the guitar. "Anything you want to hear. I'm taking requests."

Her heart fluttered. She'd never been serenaded. And she'd never heard Gil sing, but judging by Quint's solo at the spring choir concert, she was probably in for a treat.

Honestly, the Sanchez boys really were good at everything.

"Um, what about 'Wild Horses'?" she asked, then cringed. The Rolling Stones classic sounded romantic, but was actually about a relationship that never quite worked. Once, when it came on the pickup radio during one of their fights, Carma had told Jayden it was the story of their lives.

Or maybe just hers.

Gil's forehead scrunched. "It's been a while, but I think I can remember all the lyrics."

Then he started to sing, and she just melted. His voice was slightly rough, like velvet stroked against the grain. When he reached the chorus, the combination of the music, the moonlight, and the way he sang about wild horses not being able to drag him away was so achingly poignant that she couldn't stand it. She toppled onto her back, the music washing over and through her as she watched the moon climb higher.

When he ended the song with a flourish, her breath shuddered out. How many women had he slain with his music?

"Do you do anything but private concerts?"

"Just the odd party or wedding reception. I play with a trio of guys from Amarillo." He shifted, straightening the leg nearest her to get more comfortable. "You meet lots of musicians in recovery."

"Is that why you haven't taken a shot at fame and fortune? Too many bad influences?"

"Music has never been about performing for me."

"Says the preacher to the choir. Plus I hated all the downtime. Sitting around in strange towns with nothing to do between performances."

"Yeah. That got me in a lot of trouble." He adjusted a string on the guitar. "What else do you want to hear?"

"Sing me a rodeo song."

He thought for a moment, then began to strum. She laughed when she recognized "He Rides the Wild Horses." Instead of waiting for her next request, he went on from there, working his way through a medley of Chris LeDoux tunes—"This Cowboy's Hat," "Copenhagen," and a kick-ass rendition of "Little Long-Haired Outlaw."

Then the music and his voice turned as soft as the moonlight, and he dismantled her with the first line of "Just Look at You, Girl."

Had Bing told him how much she loved that song about the woman with starlight in her hair? Or—her heart did a little swoon—did he just think it suited her?

The last notes faded into a silence so loaded that Carma was afraid to breathe. God, those lyrics. And the way he'd sung them, like they came straight out of his soul. Did she mean everything to him? Would he do anything to have her stay forever? It was so easy to believe when he looked at her that way.

"Carma." Her name was a sigh. A plea. A prayer. He cleared his throat. "Before things get too crazy, I just wanted to say..."

She tensed, heart thudding in anticipation as he reached out to cradle her hand between both of his. *Yes? Yes, please?*

He kissed her fingers, then pressed them to his cheek. "Thank you. Quint, my mom, all the insanity in the office—I don't know how I would have handled any of it without you."

Oh. *Oh.* He was grateful. Intensely appreciative. That was...so not what she wanted to hear. "You're welcome," she whispered, not trusting her voice.

He opened his mouth as if he wanted to say more, then kissed her fingers again before settling her hand back on the blanket.

"I, um, have something for you, too." Her fingers tightened around the stone, the broken edges digging into her skin. She'd had it in her possession since the day she'd found it. But there was a niggle in her gut that insisted this needed to be done. She held out her hand, palm flat, so the candlelight was reflected a thousand times over in the geode's crystals. "Carry it in your gear bag this weekend."

Gil started to reach out, then pulled his hand back. "Are you sure? I mean, it was given to you, specifically."

"And now I'm lending it to you." She fluttered her

fingers in the air, going heavy on the drama. "The voices have spoken. I must follow their command."

Gil laughed, then gingerly picked up the stone and cupped it in his hand. "Thank you. I'll take very good care of it."

"And vice versa."

He tucked it in his pocket with a grin, then strummed a chord on the guitar. "Listen close, I'm playing your song."

Five bars in she growled and kicked him in the thigh. He laughed, not missing a beat of Willie and Waylon's "Good-Hearted Woman." And she had to pretend every word wasn't a blow as he sang her the ballad of a woman who kept hanging on to a man who could never give her the love she deserved.

Chapter 38

Amarillo, Texas—Diamond Cowboy qualifying event

Gil walked into the coliseum at a few minutes before nine in the morning. He couldn't remember ever climbing on a bucking horse before noon, but for everyone except the five golden invitees, the Diamond Cowboy was a marathon.

Today forty-two bareback riders, forty-eight saddle bronc riders, and fifty-six bull riders would nod their heads, with the top ten in each event riding again in the evening. From there, the four with the highest combined scores would advance to Saturday's semifinals, to compete against the winners from the three other qualifying events that had already been held across the country—a total of sixteen battling it out for the golden spot in the finale.

The odds of Gil being one of them were so long he didn't waste time or energy worrying about anything but the first horse he had to ride.

There was no fanfare. This was down and dirty, no-frills competition, intended only to weed out the field. Most of the butts that were in the seats belonged to friends and family of the contestants. At least a dozen had come just to watch Gil, commandeering prime seats to the left of the bucking chutes, a few rows up from the rail, close enough for him to see every face. The same section where Sanchez Trucking bought a block of tickets every year for friends and employees.

And they'd left Jeremiah alone at Sanchez Trucking.

He'd be fine. Everyone had agreed Jeremiah could handle it for one day. Gil was not so sure, but what was he gonna do? He couldn't tell his mother to stay at work, and he was counting on Delon's support and expert assistance.

And he sure as hell wasn't doing this without Carma—who'd showed up this morning despite Gil's dumb-ass stunt the night before.

"You are such a moron," he muttered as he waded through the mob behind the chutes.

"I assume you're talking to yourself," Delon said over his shoulder, running interference as if he was Gil's bodyguard. "Having second thoughts?"

"About riding? No."

About Carma? He'd second-guessed himself all night after he'd left her. It had been the perfect place, the perfect setup—music, candlelight, stars—to finally tell her.

I love you. I want you to stay forever.

But the timing had been all wrong. He couldn't say something that huge, then turn around and deliberately shut it all out so he could focus on riding. They'd waited this long. He could hold off another couple of days.

Patience, he kept telling himself. Carma had agreed to proceed with caution. And she'd said he'd have to trust her to let him know when she was sure of both of them. Didn't that mean he was supposed to wait until she gave him some kind of sign?

But then he'd gone and sung that song—schmaltzy and romantic and way too on the nose. The look on her face—well, hell, it was obvious she was wondering what he meant by it, but he couldn't just blurt it out.

So he'd thanked her instead, like he was presenting her

with a fucking Employee of the Month plaque. Geezus. He was *such* a moron.

He dropped his bag in the last unoccupied space against the wall and kicked it.

"Hey!" Delon punched him on the arm. "Respect the gear, dipshit."

"Sorry."

Yep. One sorry bastard. And he'd doubled down by making a joke with that Willie and Waylon song. "Good-Hearted Woman," for Christ's sake. The anthem to women who wasted their lives on worthless men, and he'd dedicated it to Carma, who'd stood by one for way too long. Of course she'd taken it as the kind of sarcastic assholeness Gil was famous for.

No damn wonder she'd suddenly declared it was getting late and they both needed to rest up for his big day.

By the time he'd realized how deeply he'd insulted her, it had been too late. What could he say? *Sorry I reminded you that your ex is a dipshit?* Yeah, that would make it all better.

He had texted her a GIF of a cartoon cat with a guitar, yowling on a fence, with Sorry for the torture. Did I do any permanent damage?

Then he'd crossed his fingers that she'd read the apology between the lines. Ten interminable minutes later, she'd texted back a classic Star Trek GIF of Captain Kirk clamping his hands over his ears and staggering in pain, and I think I'll recover...eventually.

So...they were good?

There'd been no chance to ask this morning, in the chaos of getting everyone loaded in the Charger by seven thirty while simultaneously firing off last-minute instructions to Jeremiah.

"Hey." Delon gave him another nudge. "You're

supposed to be savoring every minute of this, remember? What's up your ass?"

"My head."

Delon snorted. "How's that different than usual?"

"Generally when I insult someone it's on purpose."

"Who…" Delon gave a low whistle. "Carma? What did you do?"

Gil braced his forearms flat against the wall, hands fisted, and resisted the urge to bang his head. "It's too stupid to explain. Suffice it to say, I'm amazed she showed up this morning."

Delon leaned one shoulder against the wall beside Gil. "Is this something you can grovel your way out of?"

"What I did last night? Probably."

"Is there more?"

"What do you think?" Gil thumped one fist against the concrete. "I was trying to be straight with her."

"So you said…"

"That as an addict, I have to question whether anything that happens this fast is real. And considering she's on the rebound, she probably should, too."

Delon rolled his eyes. "Geezus. Were you *trying* to run her off?"

"It's the truth."

"Or classic emotional distancing."

Sometimes he wished his brother hadn't started going to Al-Anon meetings. Delon was a lot easier to bluff back when he was clueless. Gil shot him a glare. "I know myself better than that."

"Uh-huh. Gil Sanchez, confirmed bastard. Don't even bother with him, sweetheart. Too bad you finally met a woman who can see through that load of crap."

Behind them, hooves clattered and gates banged as horses were loaded in the chutes. "You really think it's a good time to get into this?" Gil asked.

"You brought it up." Delon hitched his free shoulder. "And you're in the second section, so you've got at least an hour and a half to stew. Seems like as good a way as any to keep you from overthinking."

"By counting all the ways I suck as a...whatever." He could not bring himself to say the word *boyfriend*.

"Something wrong?" a familiar voice rumbled. Steve Jacobs towered over most of the crowd, flanked by his son-in-law, Joe, and Melanie's husband, Wyatt Darrington. The two younger men looked all wrong in jeans and boots instead of the soccer shorts and cleats that had been their uniforms as professional bullfighters.

"It's just cold feet," Delon said.

Joe's eyebrows rose. "About the horse, or the woman?"

"Her name is Carma," Gil said tightly.

Wyatt and Joe exchanged a telling glance. "Yeah. We heard," Joe said.

"Don't even think it," Gil warned.

"What?" Joe spread innocent hands. "Wyatt was just saying how we knew she'd catch up with you one of these days."

Wyatt rolled his eyes. "If you want to blame me, you have to come up with something more original."

"Iris sure does like her," Steve said. "And the two of you seem to get along fine."

Delon nodded. "That's the problem. He's freaking out because he's ass over teakettle for her after less than two months."

Joe shrugged. "Seems about right. Violet had me

hooked in two weeks. And doofus there..." He jabbed a thumb at Wyatt. "He was halfway gone the first time he talked to Melanie on the phone."

Wyatt smiled. "She finished me off by the end of their wedding reception. What about you, Steve?"

"Ah, well..." He rubbed the back of his neck. "I took Iris home with me after our third date, and she never really lived at the dorm after that. Every time her parents called, her roommate said she was at the library." When they all stared at him, he scowled. "It was the eighties, not nineteen-fifty."

Huh. Gil had to make a serious mental adjustment, picturing the two of them rocking out to Bon Jovi and Guns N' Roses instead of waltzing to Bob Wills. He eyed Steve and said, "Just swear you never had a mullet."

Steve made a noise that wasn't quite denial. Geezus. Really?

"I win, by the way." Delon raised his hand. "Tori had me dead to rights in about three hours."

"Had...as in literally," Joe deadpanned. "On a barstool."

A detail Tori had blurted out to Shawnee, of all people. Like that wasn't going to haunt them all forever.

Delon grinned, until Gil pointed out, "It took you six years to seal the deal."

"Which I mention every time Melanie hassles me about our five," Wyatt said.

"Makes me look like a genius," Joe declared. "It only took me two months."

Wyatt shot him a look of patent disgust. "For Violet to finally lock you in a small, windowless room until you broke down and begged for mercy."

"That too." Joe raised questioning eyebrows at Steve.

"I proposed on our one-month anniversary. With roses and candlelight and the whole works." They stared at him again, and his thick white brows drew into an irritated vee. "Hey, *I* knew how to romance my girl, unlike you bunch of lunkheads."

Joe did a *point taken* shrug and turned to Gil. "So there you go. When the right one comes along, you gotta follow your gut."

"Right now my gut says that it wants doughnuts and coffee." Gil made a point of searching the crowd around them, sending a few eavesdroppers shying away. "Anybody else want to comment on my love life first? Beni must be around here somewhere."

"He's up in the stands sulking. The stock contractors only got two passes each. I had to flip Violet for this." Joe flicked his badge.

"What are you doing here?" Delon asked Wyatt.

Gil blinked. Damn. Delon was right. Wyatt and Melanie lived in Oregon. Now that he'd retired from fighting bulls, he had no reason to be in Texas, let alone behind the chutes.

"They came to see the Gil Sanchez show. And he waltzed right by the security gal while she was gawking at that pretty face," Joe grumbled.

Wyatt flashed the smile and brilliant-blue eyes that had opened a thousand doors. "Only long enough to tell you Melanie says to kick ass. Now I'm out of here."

"Good," Gil said, glancing around. A dozen cowboys had edged close, ears perked. "I was attracting enough attention before you legends of rodeo decided to gather 'round for a man chat."

"Joe and I came with intel on the horse you drew," Steve

said. "They say if she has a good trip you can be eighty or better, but she's young so you gotta help her out. If you don't really set your feet and pick her up, she'll want to move out down the arena."

"Now that's the kind of advice I can use." Gil slapped Delon's chest with the back of his hand. "Clear a path, Bruiser. I need to find a concession stand and someplace to watch the first section."

And try to control the adrenaline that wanted to flood his system. *Not yet.* He was here. Not a fantasy. Not playing pretend. Soon enough, he would be nodding his head. Eight seconds after that, it might all be over.

He *would* savor it while he was here. And he wouldn't be riding alone. Gil crouched to reach into an inside pocket of his bag and run his fingers over what he thought of as Carma's sky stone.

If she trusted him with something that precious, her heart couldn't be too far behind.

Right?

Chapter 39

The wait was killing her. Fifteen bareback riders, fifteen saddle bronc riders, and fifteen bull riders had to compete before they reloaded the chutes for Gil's section.

An eternity.

Carma wasn't alone. Everyone around her was tense—Rochelle, the Jacobs sisters, Miz Iris, Melanie. Only Tori and Bing were absent, both unable to take the day off from work.

But if all went well, they would get to watch Gil ride in the evening short round.

One ride at a time, as Gil and Delon had said about a thousand times over the past few weeks.

Needing something to do with herself, Carma had offered to cuddle Lily's two-month-old baby. The alternative was to help ride herd on the notoriously rambunctious Ruby. Violet had finally pawned her off on Beni and Quint, collapsing into a seat beside Melanie while the boys played tag with the toddler in an empty section of the bleachers.

The background music died, and the announcer's voice boomed out over the arena. "Welcome, contestants and fans, to this final qualifying event for the third annual Diamond Cowboy! Hope you've all got your tickets for tomorrow because it's a sold-out show, but if not you can tune in..."

As he gave his spiel for the television coverage, the ambient energy level in the building shot up and set Carma's pulse thudding so loud she was surprised it didn't wake the baby. For the next few minutes, before the first chute gate opened, every glittering dream in the building was alive. As the day went on, some of those dreams would grow even brighter, but the majority would dim. Only this moment was filled with pure hope, untainted by disappointment.

A single rider carried the American flag into the arena for a recorded version of the national anthem. And then, without pomp or ceremony, the pickup men took their places and the competition began. Carma pushed everything from her mind but the action. Worries and discussions could wait.

Today was for chasing dreams.

The moment that Gil stepped up onto the back of the chute was so hyper-real that it felt like a movie—every sight, every sound, every sensation amplified by surround sound and in 3-D. He was ready—chaps buckled, vest zipped, glove laced—and he would never be ready. He'd waited too long, imagined this too many times. It was impossible to absorb.

"Gil Sanchez, you're next!" the chute boss barked.

He dragged air into his lungs. The clock had ticked down to zero. It was time.

"It's so weird, seeing him dressed like that," Melanie said.

Plain blue denim shirt, plain brown chaps—and he still made Carma's heart stutter.

"He's trying to be low profile," Quint said.

"Gil?" Melanie snort-laughed. "That's gotta be a first."

And impossible. Gil Sanchez was born to be noticed. As he lowered himself into the chute, Carma clenched her hands so tight, her knuckles cracked. Violet was keeping a list of the scores on her tablet, ranked from high to low. Miz Iris and Rochelle were doing it old school, writing the scores on paper day sheets—a bittersweet reminder of all the times Carma had watched her grandmother do the same. Currently an eighty-two point ride by an NFR veteran led the pack, and a high school standout was hanging onto the all-important tenth spot with a seventy-six.

Carma tried to swallow, but her mouth was bone-dry as she watched Gil go through his final routine—check the rigging was cinched tight, work his hand into the rawhide handhold, flip the bottoms of his chaps back over his thighs to leave his feet clear as he clenched his knees against the horse's shoulders, then tip his shoulders and free arm back.

There was an interminable pause as the horse leaned into the back side of the chute, until Joe Cassidy caught a fistful of mane to pull her head around. The instant her weight shifted, Gil nodded.

With her first move out of the chute, his legs snapped straight, his heels planted solidly in the hollow where neck met shoulder. The mare responded by dropping her head and kicking high. For the next two, three, four jumps she barely moved from that spot as Gil seemed to lift her straight in the air, his spurs rolling clear back to his rigging. At six seconds, though, the horse's head started to come up.

"Come on," Violet muttered. "Don't weaken, dammit."

Gil didn't, but the horse did, with less hang time on each jump. The eight-second buzzer sounded and Carma let out her breath in a ragged *whoosh.* The pickup men moved in, and Gil grabbed onto one of them to pull free of the horse and swing to the ground.

His fan club cheered and whistled, and he raised both hands in appreciation, but Violet slapped the tablet onto her thigh, hissing out a disgruntled breath.

"What do you think?" Melanie asked.

"Of Gil? He's a freak of nature. I swear, he looks better than when he was twenty." But Violet shook her head. "It depends on how many points they take away from the horse."

And with the mare's performance counting for up to fifty of the possible hundred points, the way she'd tailed off at the end could be costly. Had those opening jumps and Gil's effort been strong enough to put him in contention?

He walked slowly toward the chutes, bending to unbuckle the leg straps of his chaps, his expression hidden by the brim of his hat. He'd done all he could do. Now it was up to the judges. On the back of the chute, Delon and Joe stood side by side, hands clenched on the top rail as they waited. Carma's nails bit into her palms for the twenty-second eternity it took to calculate the score.

"Eighty points!" the announcer declared, to a burst of applause. "That'll move Gil Sanchez into a tie for fourth and fifth place. With only a dozen cowboys left to ride, there's a good chance you'll be seeing him again this evening, folks."

Around Carma, cheers broke out while she gulped for air. Beni and Quint pounded each other's backs. Gil's strides lengthened as his chin came up, but Carma saw the telltale loosening in his shoulders.

Relief. He'd shown them all he wasn't just a quirky side note to the real story...and anyone who hadn't been paying attention before definitely was now.

Chapter 40

Gil was swarmed before he got out the arena gate. A barrage of hands slapped his shoulders, the sting a welcome reassurance that yes, this was real, not another fever dream.

The breath he'd barely caught went out of him in an *Oof!* as Delon caught him in a bear hug. "Goddamn! God*damn!* That was sweet, bro!"

Joe and Steve pushed through the mob to add a few more thumps and congratulations, and Gil rode the wave of triumph clear back to where he'd left his gear bag. Exhilaration sang in his veins, more intoxicating than any booze on earth.

"Dad! *Dad!*" Quint came thundering down the bleacher stairs to lean dangerously far over the railing above Gil's head. "That was awesome!"

Gil clasped the hand he thrust down, a new, even more potent high jolting through him at the sight of his son's face, lit with pride. Even if he washed out in tonight's short round, Quint had seen him doing the thing he loved most, and doing it well.

He tipped back his hat and swiped an arm across his damp forehead, leaving a streak of sweat and dust on his sleeve.

He looked past the boys, hoping Carma had followed them down for a congratulatory…something. She and Lily were huddled over a tablet—watching a replay of his ride?—while Violet leaned in, pointing and gesturing.

Beni caught the direction of his gaze. "Mom's got the

contestant list and stock draw. They're trying to figure out who's left to ride that might have a chance to beat you."

"You won't get bumped out of the top ten," Quint said with conviction.

"Nah, he's safe," Beni agreed. "But there's a few big guns left, and since they combine this score with tonight's to decide who makes the top four..."

Gil couldn't afford to spot those veterans too many points. But it was out of his control, so he'd let everyone else speculate and calculate. He needed a drink—of water—something solid to eat, and Carma.

When he opened his gear bag to stow his gear, his phone was buzzing. There were a dozen texts. He ignored all of them and sent Carma a GIF of a relieved SpongeBob wiping sweat from his brow.

Whew!

She sent back a meme of the Rock doing his famous eyebrow thing.

Too easy, man.

He laughed, then shrugged out of his vest, peeled off his chaps, and packed both into his bag before heading to the stripping chute to fetch his rigging. Not a quick trip, with someone stopping him every few feet to shake his hand. Half of them were complete strangers.

He finally grabbed his rigging, looked to where Carma had been sitting, and saw only his mother, Miz Iris, and a baby stroller. He shoved through the crowd to where Beni and Quint had settled in by the railing.

"Where'd everybody go?" he asked.

"Carma hasn't had Tex-Mex since she got here, so they dragged her off to that place downtown," Beni said.

"They *left*?" So much for that ten-minute kiss he'd planned to lay on her.

"They said they're getting bleacher butt from sitting here so long," Quint said. "And Grandma's gonna text them the scores during the next section, so…"

Something in the glance that passed between the boys set Gil's *uh-oh* radar humming. He eyed the empty chairs, doing a mental tally. The Jacobs crew had driven to Amarillo in pickups hauling trailers loaded with bucking horses, and Gil assumed the others had ridden along with them. Which meant their only transportation would be…

"They took the Charger." The barely restrained violence in his voice made the boys cringe. Sweet hell. That crew, turned loose in his car. He had a blood-chilling vision of Melanie smoking his tires on Polk Street. Or God forbid, Lily. She could barely see over the dashboard. "How'd they get the keys?"

"Um…Dad got them out of your gear bag," Beni said, then hurried to add, "Melanie made him do it."

"Who's driving?"

"Carma," Quint said. "They figured you probably wouldn't throttle her."

Gil drew a deep, careful breath. She'd driven that van clear across the country with not so much as a scratch. Surely his car was safe in her hands. In a strange city. In the busiest part of the day.

He breathed until he was sure he could sound calm. "As long as she doesn't let any of those other maniacs touch the wheel."

"Whoa." Beni made wide eyes at his cousin. "You weren't kidding."

Quint smirked. "Told you."

"What?" Gil demanded.

"You didn't even…" Beni flung up both hands to mimic an exploding head. "You must be in love."

Oh, for Christ's sake. Now these two? Gil pinned his nephew with his best death glare. "That is none of your business."

Beni grinned. "See? Denial…the first sign."

Gil sighed and bent to tuck his rigging and glove safely away and touch his fingers to Carma's sky stone, his pulse thrumming. He'd done it.

One down. One more chance to ride.

In the meantime, it looked like he would be spending some quality time with the boys.

Three hours later, Gil wasn't feeling quite so magnanimous. His car and Carma still weren't back, but she had texted that they were stopping by to visit Tori at the clinic and meet Beth.

Leaving Gil with nothing to do but try not to think.

No damn wonder rodeo life had made him a problem drinker. The waiting was torture, and the guys in the last section had shown no mercy. He'd had to watch his score get knocked down the leaderboard three times, by eighty-six-, eighty-five-, and eighty-four-point rides.

That was a lot of ground for Gil to make up in the two-ride aggregate.

Unable to sit, he paced the length of the mezzanine, deserted in the break before the evening's competition.

Delon and Wyatt had wandered over to one of the other fairgrounds arenas to watch the qualifying rounds for the team ropers—Delon so he could report the results back to Tori, and Wyatt because Melanie had turned him into a bona fide twine twirler. Miz Iris and Rochelle had taken Lily's baby and strolled to yet another arena to watch the barrel racers.

Steve, Joe, and the boys were busy sorting horses. Through the open garage doors behind the chutes, Gil could hear the shouts and clanging steel gates as crews loaded the afternoon's stock onto trucks and trailers, making space for fresh horses and bulls. Tonight's broncs were all the kind cowboys loved to get on—lots of jump and kick, not too much power, and no dirty tricks. Ride 'em right and you'd be in the mideighties every time.

But the user-friendly horses meant Gil couldn't count on any of the top cowboys getting thrown off, or even making a big mistake. A pair of eighty-five scores was a hundred and seventy points on two head. Gil would have to be ninety on his next ride to match it, ninety-one to win. Plus there were three cowboys with eighty-two points in the opening round. If they scored—

Stop! Geezus. He mashed his candy-bar wrapper into a tight ball and slammed it into a trash can. There was no strategizing to be done—only Gil, the horse that was drawn for him, and eight seconds of maximum effort. But he couldn't try too hard or get too wild. He had to find that perfect balance, ride the very crest of the adrenaline wave without tipping over the edge.

And not psych himself out before he climbed over the back of the chute.

His skin prickled with millions of supercharged molecules zinging around like pinballs, pummeling his nerve endings. His muscles twitched, craving action. Back in the bad old days, this was when he would've tossed back a couple of drinks to take the edge off. Or coaxed Krista into blowing off some steam with him. Now here he was with no booze and no woman.

He had to get out of this building. Away from the combined aromas of buttered popcorn, arena dirt, and the burning desire to win. He crossed the front lobby and paused at the main entrance doors. *Hello.* There was the Charger, just pulling into the far end of the parking lot reserved for contestants.

Gil smiled and stepped outside to lean in the shade of the portico, where he could watch and wait. And maybe talk her into sneaking off for a little pregame warm-up.

~

When she spotted Gil lying in wait, Carma seriously considered just staying in the car. She could leave the air-conditioner running, tip the seat back, and sleep off their massive lunch, not to mention the round of celebratory margaritas.

But it would probably be better to hand over the keys to Gil in front of witnesses.

She popped another piece of peppermint gum into her mouth to cover all trace of her sins, then stepped out, squinting into the brilliant sunlight. Hooves clopped on pavement as ropers and barrel racers made their way across the parking lot from the various arenas.

Carma barely noticed, her gaze locked on the lean, dark male lounging by the coliseum doors, projecting menace from fifty yards away.

"Carma?"

Her head jerked around, and her stomach felt as if it did the same before dropping to her rhinestone flip-flops. "Jayden."

As Carma stared at him, frozen in place, Melanie and Violet moved to the front of the car, assuming identical postures—arms crossed, feet planted, eyes narrowed. Lily joined them, a belligerent Smurf beside a pair of Amazons.

"I...um..." *Need to get my shit together.* She made a concerted effort to gather herself. "I didn't know you were going to be here."

Jayden's gaze flicked to the car, then back to her. "I guess you've been too busy to notice I was entered."

"Um, yeah. Sorry." *For what?* She wasn't in charge of him anymore.

His horse shuffled impatiently, and he laid a hand on its neck. "I'd like to talk to you, if you have a few minutes."

"I don't know..."

"Please." For once, there was no pout. No whine. Just a quiet request. "I don't want to leave things ugly, after everything."

"Don't go unless you want to." Lily eyed Jayden up and down. "If he won't back off, we can take him."

Carma was sure they could—but so could she. Except...

She glanced toward where Gil had straightened, looking as if he might come storming across the lot. "This isn't the best time," she told Jayden.

"I'm leaving as soon as we pack up, headed north."

"Tough luck today?" Melanie asked, with zero sympathy.

"Yeah." Jayden shrugged, surprisingly unperturbed.

"We drew a runner and ended up one place out of the top fifteen."

A year ago he would've been kicking trailer fenders and ranting about his shitty luck. And he wasn't happy now, but he was dealing with the disappointment.

He gave Carma a coaxing smile. "Just a few minutes? For the sake of old friends?"

Hell. How could she say no? And it would be good for everyone—Gil included—if she put this behind her, once and for all. She gave her three musketeers a helpless look. "Would you explain to Gil?"

"Sure." Violet jerked her chin. "Go on. Do what you need to do."

"Thank you."

Lily gave Jayden one last warning glare, then grinned at Carma. "Don't worry. We can take Gil, too."

The three women set off to intercept him while Carma fell into step beside Jayden, winding through the maze of pickups and trailers to one with Montana plates. A twinge of homesickness caught her at the sight of the prefix on the license number.

38. Glacier County. Home.

"You look great," he said.

"Thanks. So do you."

Better than he had in a long time. His shoulders were more defined, his waist trimmer, like he'd been working out and eating healthier. Yet another bone of contention between them, with Carma constantly nagging him about his family history of high blood pressure and heart disease.

No wonder she'd driven him nuts.

"So...I guess it's going pretty good down here," Jayden

said, tipping his head toward where the Charger was parked.

"I like it. The people are friendly."

"Yeah, I noticed," he said dryly.

She laughed. "If they're on your side."

"And I'm the enemy?"

"Not...exactly."

He stopped beside the trailer, haltered the horse, then turned to face her, his eyes shadowed by more than the brim of his black hat. "I know I screwed up, Carma. Too many times to count. When I saw you with *him* down in Huntsville...I guess that was the kick in the head I needed. I wish it wasn't too late."

He was sincere. Sad. Resigned. Habit years in the making made her want to go to him. Do or say whatever it took to make it better.

She held her ground. "It wasn't all you."

"I know." There was no accusation in his voice, just resignation. His smile held the memory of all the mistakes, all the near-misses, and all the good times, too. "I miss you."

Her throat knotted and tears welled, but there was nothing left to say. She almost laughed at the irony of it all. This Jayden and this Carma might've actually had a chance.

But she wouldn't be this woman if it wasn't for Gil, and from the first time she'd kissed him it had been too late to go back.

Jayden nodded, as if she'd said it out loud. "I hope it works out. After everything we put each other through, you deserve to be happy."

"But?" Because it was impossible not to hear.

"Everyone is talking about him." Jayden fidgeted with the bridle he still held. "After that ride he made this morning—you know it's not gonna end here, like he keeps saying. And if he keeps going, I just wonder where that's gonna leave you."

"The same place you did?" she snapped.

He inclined his head, barely flinching at the slap. "I'm not saying you aren't good enough for anybody, but the Sanchez boys run in pretty fancy company."

Hearing Jayden say it—*the Sanchez boys*—made her fists bunch. Those were Gil's words. His pride and joy. Jayden didn't get to put his grubby fingerprints all over them.

But he wasn't wrong.

It was a truth Carma had put off facing, while she clung to the promise of *After the Diamond Cowboy*...

It wasn't all going to get easier. Especially not now, when Gil had proven he could still compete. The better he did here, the more likely that he would keep going on down the rodeo road.

And leave Carma in the dust?

She shook her head, as much for herself as for Jayden. "I'm not discussing this with you."

"That's fair." He reached out and touched her chin, a gesture so familiar it made time spin backward for a dizzying instant. "But if you ever do need to talk or whatever, you know where to find me."

She shook her head again. "We've used up all our chances."

His hand dropped. Then he nodded. "Take care of yourself, Carma."

"You too."

And for the last time, she turned and walked away from him.

Chapter 41

Gil didn't mean to pounce the instant he saw Carma, but she stepped onto the mezzanine just as he strode out of the men's restroom and he nearly mowed her down.

He caught her arms and they ended up face-to-face, chest to chest. "Hey," he said.

"Hey." She went still under his hands, eyes wary. "Great ride."

"Thanks. It felt good."

"I'll bet. Do you know what horse you have tonight?"

He shook his head. "They're not posting the draw until an hour before the rodeo."

"So pretty soon."

"Yeah."

"Well…fingers crossed that you get a good one."

"Thanks." Geezus. He could have this conversation with one of those damn reporters. Talk, talk, talk and never say a thing. He loosened his grip so he could get a better look at her. She didn't look shell-shocked like she had when Jayden showed up in Huntsville. "Everything okay?"

"Yeah. The restaurant was awesome, and your friends are amazing."

They'd said the same. Carma had their unanimous stamp of approval, and that was good, even though it meant Gil had spent the afternoon rattling around at loose ends. "I think you can consider yourself accepted by the Earnest Ladies Club."

"When do I get my password and secret decoder ring?" The sparkle in her eyes did wonders for his mood.

"You have to ask them. Boys aren't allowed." According to Tori, when they called an official meeting, boys couldn't even be mentioned under penalty of a shot of tequila. And speaking of unwanted men…

"I saw Jayden." *Saw you go off with him, like good old buddies. And didn't chase you down and strangle him with his own rope.* He barely gritted his teeth when he asked, "Everything okay?"

She nodded, getting that skittish look again, as if expecting him to come unglued. "It was something I needed to do. Closure and all that."

"No loose strings." He gave himself the pleasure of imagining Jayden dangling off a cliff, and Carma cutting the rope.

She ran her hands over his biceps, the corner of her mouth twitching as if she could read his homicidal thoughts. "He's hightailing it out of town as we speak."

"That's good," Gil said, both statement and question.

"That's very good." She angled an impish look under her lashes. "I would say I was sorry about taking your car, but I'm really, really not."

"Yeah?" He banished Jayden from his thoughts and ran his hand up to the base of her neck, loving the feel of her hair flowing over his knuckles. Her even-silkier skin bared by another of those soft, flouncy sundresses that he could get underneath in about thirty seconds flat. "You like things that go fast, pretty girl?"

Her return smile was equally wicked as she walked her fingertips up to his shoulders. "Obviously."

Just as they started to lean into the kiss Gil had been

starving for all day, Delon came blasting down the mezzanine with Quint and Beni on his heels, all grinning like loons.

"Ho-lee shit! You got the best damn horse in the whole pen!"

Gil scowled. *Dammit! Can't they see I'm busy here?*

"Dad!" Quint shoved at his arm. "Did you hear what we said?"

"Yeah." And then to Carma, as they dragged him away, "Later."

She gave him a smile that made his heart flop like a beached fish. "Ride hard, cowboy."

An hour later, Gil was geared up and ready for a date with a horse called Angel Wings.

"She's just like her name," Delon said. "Pure heaven."

As the national anthem played once more, everything inside Gil coalesced into a certainty as crystal clear as gazing into the sky stone. It was all coming together. His family. Carma. The luck of the draw.

This was his night.

He stood on the back of the chutes, eerily calm, until it was his turn. The silver-gray mare seemed to absorb and reflect his mood, as relaxed as a saddle horse when he settled onto her back and worked his hand into the rigging.

Until he nodded his head and she took flight, the equine epitome of power and grace. With each high, floating jump, it felt as if they might brush the rafters. His chaps beat like wings as they flew in perfect unison, the roar of the much-larger evening crowd rushing past his ears.

Exhilaration flooded him, and he was so absorbed in the sheer joy of the moment that the shrill of the whistle came almost as a shock.

It was over already?

When his feet hit the ground, he pivoted to watch the mare canter around the arena, head high, mane and tail rippling—and tipped his hat to her. Hot damn, what a horse.

Then the bubble burst and the rest of the world came blasting in.

"Eighty-nine points!" the announcer bellowed. "That is the high-marked ride of the entire day! Ladies and gentlemen, Gil Sanchez came to make a statement, and all the other bareback riders had better be listening."

He leaned on the fence to catch his breath and drink it all in. The smiles, the cheers, the sheer exhilaration. Rather than dying down, the applause rose as his ride was replayed in slow motion on the giant video screen. Unfucking-believable. That was really him up there.

And it was a thing of beauty.

Now all he had to do was wait and see if it was enough.

Carma felt as if she'd ridden that horse right with Gil, jump for jump, breath for ragged breath. If she'd had any doubt that this was what he was meant to do, that eight seconds of pure brilliance had erased it—and she wasn't selfish enough to wish otherwise. For now, it was enough to be carried along on the wave of awe and adrenaline he'd generated.

Gil had every person in the arena rooting for him.

But the real suspense came after he was done,

multiplied by the tension rippling off the dozen people around her. And it was bad enough to have to sit through each ride once, without Violet's preview of each rider, and each horse, and the chances that they might beat Gil. The high school champion bobbled, the pressure obviously getting the better of him. The next two matched their first round scores of eighty-two, falling well short of Gil's total on two head of 169. The next ride had them all digging fingernails into palms.

"Eighty-five! That gives the cowboy 167 on two, and puts him in second place."

Air leaked out of Carma's lungs. Four to go. Gil only had to beat one of them to advance.

The Californian who went next wasn't about to let it be him. The judges awarded him a well-deserved eighty-six, dropping Gil to second. The next cowboy matched it, moving his name to the top of the leaderboard and Gil to third. Two more to go. Quint had his elbows on his knees and his face in his hands. He peeked through his fingers as the next chute gate cracked, then flung himself back in his seat when the whistle sounded.

"Shit. That's another one."

Carma nodded dumbly as the score was posted and Gil dropped to fourth place. A single cowboy left to ride, and he was a former world champion and perennial contender.

"He can be eighty-four in his sleep," Violet said gloomily.

And that was all he needed to leave Gil in the infamous crying hole, one place out. They all watched, resigned to the inevitable, as horse and cowboy launched from the chute, jump after flashy jump, with the cowboy in perfect position.

Then the horse stumbled. Just a buckling of knees as its front feet hit the ground, but enough to bounce the cowboy's shoulders forward, dropping his spurs almost to the belly. The horse gave a hop and skip, then recovered, but the rider took a few beats to catch up.

A critical handful of wasted seconds.

"You...are...shitting me," Melanie breathed, as the pickup man set him on the ground.

Chin ducked, the cowboy shook his head, knowing what everyone in the arena had already guessed.

"Tough luck for the former champ," the announcer intoned. "That'll be a seventy-nine, five points short of what he needed. So here are the four who'll be back tomorrow!"

He directed their attention to the results posted on the massive video screen. And there it was, in blaring white letters on a red background, so bright Carma could barely stand to look at it.

4th—Gil Sanchez

Their section of the stands exploded, screaming and hugging. Before she realized what was happening, Carma was being herded onto the mezzanine and around to the stairway that led to the ground level, Beni and Quint blazing a trail, Violet and Wyatt at her back. They didn't even pause at the security entrance, blowing past the startled guard. Each of the semifinalists was surrounded by a cluster of well-wishers, but by far the majority of the stock contractors, cowboys, and crew had mobbed Gil—a solid wall of bodies.

Beni and Quint dove into the scrum, but Violet, Wyatt, and Carma held back.

"It'll clear out in a minute," Wyatt predicted. "They have to get ready for the saddle bronc riding."

As he spoke, men began peeling off the edges to hustle back to their duties or prepare for their own rides. Soon Carma could see Gil, sweaty and euphoric, with Delon standing beside him looking as flushed and proud as if he'd made the ride himself. Quint threw his arms around his dad, all teenage cool forgotten as they exchanged a back-thumping hug. Beni shoved his cousin aside and followed suit.

"Let's go," Violet said.

Wyatt gestured Carma to precede him. As she stepped forward, Gil spotted her. Their gazes met for a brief instant. Then a woman laid a hand on his arm. Blond. Beautiful. Smiling at him with a microphone in her hand and an extra sparkle in her eyes. Gil turned to smile at her.

Oh God. It was starting already.

Someone tapped Carma's shoulder. The security guard, apologetic but firm, said, "I'm sorry, ma'am, but you shouldn't be in here."

Wyatt started to plead her case, but Carma waved him off. "No. She's right."

This was Gil's moment. His triumph. Whatever part of it he wanted to share with her, they could do it later. Assuming there was anything left to share.

No, dammit. She would not let Jayden's doubts creep into her head. Or her own. She would have faith. Gil had trusted her with Jayden. She had to trust him now.

As she climbed the stairs, the last of the exhilaration faded, and just like that, she was done, going flat as a punctured tire. It was all she could do to drag herself back to her seat. The barrage of questions about what Gil said and where he went and "Seriously, they wouldn't let you talk to him?" felt like a physical assault.

Too many days and weeks of anticipation, too many hours spent restlessly kicking at the sheets the night before—excited, anxious, wasting energy and sleep fretting about a couple of stupid songs. Plus the music, and the lights, and the rodeo announcer yammering on and on mostly to hear his own voice…

Then Bing was nudging someone out of the seat beside Carma, and Tori was saying, "Would you all hush and let me pay attention to the team roping?" and Carma realized she must have hit the wall in a big way for both of them to see it.

She gripped her phone in both hands, peering into the crowd behind the chutes for a glimpse of Gil, barely aware of the other events proceeding in the arena. Any minute now she'd see his triumphant smile. He'd wave, call to whoop it up, send her a GIF full of fireworks.

Any. Minute. Now.

Gil had grossly underestimated the shitstorm he was about to unleash…and the number of reporters who gave a damn about some has-been from Earnest squeaking into the Diamond Cowboy finale.

He'd escaped the TV reporter only to have some guy with an *Event Personnel* badge herd him toward the area roped off for media. Gil barely had a chance to take off his chaps and vest and hand them over to Delon before he was planted in front of a mob armed with recorders and questions.

How does it feel to be riding again? Were you intimidated by the level of the competition? Do you have any pain?

Incredible. Yes. And, "Right now, I feel bulletproof."

They kept at it, question after question about what had made him decide to try a comeback, how he'd prepared, what did he think his chances were in tomorrow's finale, until the voices and faces blurred together.

Gil might've just said *Enough!* and walked away, but Delon had had their logo slapped on everything Gil planned to wear and warned him that he was representing Sanchez Trucking and he'd better not make them look bad.

No swearing, no sarcasm, no rudeness. Or as Delon had put it, "Don't be yourself."

Gil was doing okay until a sweet-faced girl who looked about Quint's age flashed him a dimpled smile and said, "I understand that you're recovering from an addiction to pain medication. How did that play into your decision to return to a sport where injuries are considered inevitable?"

Everyone froze, as if she'd hit a pause button. Gil's mind went blank. He opened his mouth, but he had no idea what would've come out if Delon hadn't jumped in to cut him off.

"My brother's struggles with substance abuse are not a secret, but as we are all aware, the opiate crisis is a serious issue. This isn't the time or place to have the kind of discussion it deserves." His politeness made it even more of a reprimand, and the reporter's face flushed as the others followed Delon's lead, shooting her disapproving frowns.

One of them called out, "What's it like having your brother back in competition, Delon?"

"A dream come true," he said without hesitation.

"Are you still going to feel that way if the two of you end up riding off for the ring?" another asked.

"Absolutely, but with the cowboys who are entered here and the caliber of the stock, we both need to bear down and have Lady Luck on our side to get to the finals."

Then he deftly guided them into a discussion of the horses he'd most like to draw and which cowboys he considered the biggest threat...other than the two of them, of course—*wink, wink, laugh*. Then the winners of the steer wrestling and team roping were ushered in, and Gil and Delon made a beeline for a side door, into a hallway accessible only to staff. His ears rang in the sudden silence.

"Sorry," Delon said. "I got back as soon as I could, but about a hundred people tried to stop me."

Gil slumped against the wall, feeling like he'd been drained by a pack of vampires. "Whatever happened to pretending cowboys don't do drugs?"

Back in his day there had been a strict, if unofficial, *don't ask, don't tell* policy. Nobody wanted to hear that the guy who'd crushed it over the Fourth of July had made eleven rodeos in seven days courtesy of a steady supply of uppers.

"We hit the mainstream media." Delon's easygoing humor had evaporated. "We used to only talk to local papers promoting their rodeo, or writers from western magazines. They have a vested interest in preserving the noble cowboy image. This bunch was everything from bloggers to national sports outlets, and there's always one who's trying to prove they're a serious journalist."

"Thanks for covering my ass. I didn't even think..."

Delon shrugged. "You're not married to a Patterson. They try to blindside me with questions about whether my father-in-law is considering going back into politics since his party has gone off the rails."

"What do you tell them?"

"That they'd have to ask him. The answer is no, by the way. He's done his time." Delon heaved a pained sigh. "His daughter, on the other hand..."

"*Tori?*"

"Yeah. She's so disgusted by all the bullshit her patients go through with our healthcare system, she's about ready to go fix it herself."

Gil did a full-body shudder. "Geezus. With the Patterson name and all their connections behind her, she'd be a shoo-in even if she wasn't a human bulldozer."

And from a purely cynical standpoint, having a Native husband with a Hispanic name would not hurt when it came to attracting certain demographics. Hell, the Patterson political machine could probably even make Gil's addiction work for them.

My family has personally experienced the impact of the opiate crisis.

Delon scrubbed a hand over his face. "If she sets her mind to it, I'm gonna end up sleeping in the fucking White House."

"Be sure you're wearing a Sanchez Trucking shirt when you do the Easter egg roll," Gil deadpanned.

Delon gave him a look that should've blistered the paint on the wall behind his head. Gil ignored it and reached into his pocket, only to find it empty.

"I was gonna bring your phone, but it was down to one percent battery and the calls and texts were rolling in non-stop. They ran mine down too." Delon slouched against the other wall, tipped his head back, and gave a stunned laugh. "Eighty-nine goddamn points. You are unbelievable, you know that?"

"Thanks." For once Delon actually meant it as a compliment. Gil pushed away from the wall. "I'm going to talk to Carma."

"Good luck with that. I'm not throwing my body in front of the mob if you go strolling into the stands." Delon pushed the door open a crack, cocking his head as he listened to the announcer. "I don't think you have time anyway. They're almost done with the saddle bronc riding. By the time we sneak around to the sports medicine room to cut your tape off and grab a bottle of water, they'll want you lined up for the introduction of the finalists."

Damn. *Damn.* Delon was right, but that didn't make it any less frustrating.

And it only got worse. Everyone they met wanted to shake Gil's hand and hear his story. After the spotlight introduction of all the finalists there were photos, more interviews, and a review of the next day's schedule from an event official, with dire warnings for anyone who didn't comply. Geezus. They'd barely get home before they had to turn around and come back for an 11:00 a.m. press conference. That meant leaving Earnest no later than nine thirty, to be safe, then cooling their heels for three hours until the rodeo started.

Gil couldn't imagine there was a reporter left who hadn't already talked to him, but attendance was not optional.

When he finally broke free, Gil was craving a tall, ice-cold Coke and an armful of sweet, soft woman, not in that order. He ached from the physical effort of the rides and the need to feel Carma's warmth. To wrap her up so tight and close she could absorb the triumph coursing through him. Hold her hand on the drive home and squeeze it every time he was hit by one of those aftershocks of awe and disbelief.

He'd done it. From over a hundred cowboys who'd entered the four qualifying events on a hope and a prayer, he was one of the sixteen who'd survived. No matter what happened tomorrow, that was one hell of an accomplishment.

And he wanted more. Now that he'd proven he had a shot, he wanted it all.

The seats were empty except for janitors sweeping up spilled popcorn and empty beer cups when he blew past and into the lobby—and found only his mother and Quint waiting.

She gave him an awkward half-hug. "Great ride."

"Thanks."

"Everybody else took off," Quint said.

Not surprising. It had been one hellaciously long day. Gil glanced around, frowning. "Where's Carma?"

His mother didn't quite look him in the eye. "She, um, left with Bing and Johnny, right after the tie-down roping."

"She *what?*" Gil looked around again, sure Rochelle must be kidding. Carma couldn't just leave. He'd been waiting for hours to see her. And yeah, maybe he should've fought his way through the crowd to go see her. Borrowed a phone to call her…except he didn't have her number memorized. Still, he probably should have done something.

But she hadn't bothered to call or text that she was taking off with the girls—*and* his car. He'd even stood back and let her go off with Jayden and trusted her when she said that whole thing was over and done.

And now she'd just gone off and *left*.

"It wasn't her idea," Quint said. "After the excitement passed, she did that thing where she sort of wilts, and Bing insisted on taking her home. She said Carma needed her strength for tomorrow, and you'd understand 'cuz you know how Carma gets sometimes."

Drained. Fuck. It had been a brutal day—mentally and physically—and it would have taken a toll on her. The nerves. The suspense. That marathon first round followed by tonight's performance, with an entire coliseum flooded with overwrought emotions. And goddamn Jayden popping up like a noxious weed. Naturally Carma had redlined.

None of those things made Gil feel a damn bit better.

"Fine. Let's go," he said.

But her absence had taken the shine off his mood. They shuffled outside, the cumulative fatigue hitting Gil hard as he stepped into the still-balmy night air.

"I can't believe you did it," Quint said, with an insulting amount of disbelief. "Uncle Delon and Uncle Steve kept saying you could, but I thought they were just trying to build your confidence."

"Gee, thanks."

Quint shrugged. "You gotta admit, it was a long shot."

Past the moon and to the stars. Gil felt as if he'd been launched into hyperspace, where this man had never gone before. Tomorrow he could go even higher.

Chapter 42

When they were in the pickup and headed back to Earnest, Bing turned in her seat to check on Carma. "How bad, on a scale of one to *I never want to speak to another human again?*"

"Six. Maybe seven. I've been worse." Carma tipped her head back, her exhaustion battling with the desire to be with Gil. "I shouldn't have left."

"Gil saw how you were after that first trip to the Patterson ranch. He'll understand. And you don't want to be so wiped out that you can't function tomorrow."

Bing was right. Dammit. And it wasn't like Gil was dying to see Carma. He hadn't so much as stuck his head out and waved, even after the initial chaos had died down.

"How was Jayden?" Bing asked.

"Better than usual. It's really done this time."

"Good to hear." Bing reached back and squeezed her hand. "Probably not what you needed on top of everything else, though. Gil took it okay?"

"Seemed to."

Other than not even trying to see her after his ride. She kept telling herself that he'd had a thousand people trying to talk to him, but it felt like payback. *You want to ignore me all afternoon…*

Which was better than if he'd completely forgotten her. At least if he was mad it meant he gave a damn. She closed her eyes as they rolled through the outskirts of Amarillo, the bright lights of an endless procession of gas stations and fast-food restaurants and used car lots adding to her sensory overload.

She'd done this to herself. When Gil had asked her to give up her Wednesdays and the after-work rides at the Patterson ranch, she'd vowed to find some other way to decompress. Long walks. Meditation. A ride along the river at the Brookman ranch when she could fit it in.

But two evenings a week she went with Gil to practice. On the others, Quint showed up for more trick-roping lessons, or Rochelle invited them to supper at the house she'd taken over from Merle, or Carma was invited to a girls' night at Analise's apartment in Dumas. She'd enjoyed all of it—and she'd known it was too much. Never a good sign when she almost burst into tears because she couldn't find her favorite gel pen to write her weekly letter to her brother.

Eddie said emails weren't the same as getting an actual envelope to rip open.

The uncertainty of her relationship with Gil had only compounded the problem. In the past few days she'd started to dread the moment when the Diamond Cowboy was over. Would Gil finally tell her how she was pretty sure he felt about her? Or would he be so caught up in the thrill of riding again that he'd decide it wasn't the time to make any kind of commitment?

If tonight was any indication, she might want to brace herself for a rapid retreat on his part.

Stop. Everything felt hopeless when she let herself get this tapped out. After a good night's sleep...

The next thing she knew, Bing's hand was on her shoulder. "Honey, you're home."

Carma yawned her thanks for the ride and stumbled

into the van, where she crawled onto the bed and crashed again without getting undressed.

But now her sleep was filled with fractured sounds and images. Faces loomed out of nowhere—Lily, Violet, Miz Iris, total strangers—all of them demanding to know where Gil was. *Why hasn't he called? He didn't even send a text?* The questions hammered at her along with the announcer's voice, and the chorus of one of those irritating country-pop songs they'd played too many times. *Shake it yourself, asshole.*

Then she was in Jayden's pickup, and he was driving back to Montana and they were arguing about Gil, and Texas, and how Carma had to come back home where she belonged. She wanted out, had to get back to the rodeo, but Jayden wouldn't stop and let her out. And then he did, in downtown Denver, and there were scary men staring at her, following her as she stumbled blindly down street after street looking for a cab, a bus, anything.

She had to get back. The rodeo was starting and Gil was about to ride and he would be furious if he found out she'd missed it because of Jayden. Then somehow she was running through the Denver airport, checking gate after gate for a flight to Amarillo, but they kept saying no, not this one, and telling her to get on the train but it was always going in the wrong direction, and she was so tired her legs kept buckling and she set her purse down for just a second and it was gone. Stolen. No phone, no money...

She fought her way out of the anxiety dream, her pulse pounding in her ears. Rolling onto her back, she pressed both fists to her chest and fumbled for her purse, just to be sure. It was there, phone tucked in the side pocket. No texts. No missed calls. 3:19 a.m.

Carma stripped off her dress, pulled on her sleep shirt, and found an audiobook on her phone, an old favorite with a mellow narrator. The soothing voice and well-worn story drew her mind away from its endless loop of chatter, but the sky was turning pearl gray in the east when she finally slept soundly.

She woke up at eight, tired and still unsettled by that frantic dream. *Coffee. Sugar. Ibuprofen.* And a little fresh air wouldn't hurt. She could walk the long way around to the front gate and sneak into the office for her caffeine fix. Max would be the only one in this morning, doing his usual Saturday morning inspection of the shop to be sure the mechanics had left everything ship-shape.

A dry, gritty wind buffeted her as she walked, her body feeling as if she was overdue for maintenance and running low on oil. When she shuffled into the break room, she nearly wept at the scent of strong, fresh coffee. *Bless you, Max.* A loud bang made her jump, sloshing creamer onto the floor. Gil stomped through the door, hair raked into spikes, wearing his standard T-shirt, jeans, running shoes, and scowl—so exactly like every other morning that for an instant she wondered if she'd imagined the past twenty-four hours.

"What are you doing here?" she blurted.

He frowned. "Where else would I be?"

"Uh…resting? Focusing?"

"If I get any more focused, I'm gonna burn a hole in my skull." He flipped open the top on a fresh box of doughnuts and growled when he saw *Way to go, Boss Man!* in Max's blocky scribble inside the lid. "Analise broadcast the rodeo results to all the drivers, and they told half the clients, and it was on the radio this morning. Everyone in the Panhandle seems to think they need to personally congratulate me."

"Assholes," Carma said. God. He was so wired, the electricity danced across her already-raw nerves.

"Tell me how you feel after you've listened to them for an hour." He glared balefully at the doughnuts before snatching one dipped in chocolate and peanuts. "There's a whole shitload of messages. I had to mute my cell phone and send the landlines to voicemail so I could wade through my inbox to find the stuff that's actually business-related."

That was the real problem. They were knocking holes in his walls, slopping together parts of his life he kept neatly divided. And wait a minute. He expected her to check the messages on a Saturday morning, when she'd only come for the coffee?

She plunked a couple of sugar cubes into her coffee and stirred, wincing when the spoon clanked against the mug. As always, the suffocating fatigue had coalesced into prickles underneath her skin, making her hypersensitive to every touch and sound. And person.

For the first time, he actually looked at her...and frowned. "Geezus. Mom and Quint were right. You do look fried."

Her mouth dropped open, but she had no words. *That* was how he greeted her this morning? *Wow, you look like shit.*

He blinked as if he suddenly heard himself and plowed his fingers through his hair. "Sorry. I'm just really...well, you know."

"Sorry? Yeah, I noticed." She grabbed the last chocolate doughnut even though she would rather have had maple, then headed toward her desk out of pure habit.

He came after her. “I didn’t mean that the way it sounded.”

“Yes, you did.” She fired a glare at his office door. “Just go make your computer stop doing that.”

He hesitated, then muttered a curse and disappeared into his lair. The pinging stopped. The swearing didn’t. Carma slapped her headphones on, picked up the phone, and started writing down messages.

After all, that was their deal—first and foremost, Carma answered his damn phone.

Obviously, Gil wasn’t the only one on edge this morning. He had crashed when he got home last night…only to snap awake three hours later, certain that all of it—from Huntsville to the practice sessions to Amarillo—was just another dream. Scratch that. It was a nightmare, so vivid that he’d hauled himself out of bed to dig his grubby shirt and jeans from the hamper, going limp with relief at the very real dust and sweat and scent of horses.

And if Quint had woken up and found him sniffing his dirty laundry, he’d think Gil was back on drugs.

Getting back to sleep had been impossible. After the rides he’d made, the prospect of hitting the road was hammering at him. He could buy his pro card today, enter up all through July and August…

No. He’d promised that this was a one-shot deal. Trying to juggle just this rodeo along with everything else had almost pushed him over the edge.

But once the others are all settled into their jobs…

No! For once, he would listen to his younger self and

live like tomorrow might be his last day in an arena. But that left him with only Carma to think about, and that wasn't any more restful. If she wasn't supposedly worn out, he would have gone knocking on her van at about 4:00 a.m., when the agitation drove him out of his bed.

He'd watched two episodes of one of those wilderness survival reality shows instead, wondering how long any of them would last in Carma's mountains without a cameraman constantly on hand to toss them a sandwich. The grizzlies would probably get them all, he'd decided…and the sandwiches, too.

But he hadn't expected Carma to be the real bear this morning.

Half an hour after she stole the last chocolate doughnut—and he knew damn well maple was her favorite—she marched into Gil's office and dumped a mountain of pink *While You Were Out* slips on his keyboard. "There are a few dozen more jerks who wanted to congratulate you." She handed him two sticky notes. "I saved the voicemail from your dad saying he wishes he could be there today, but he didn't want to make it awkward for your mom, so he'd be watching on TV and cheering you on. And those are both from owner-operators who are looking for regular loads."

Gil had wondered if Merle would show up. From the time they were kids, he'd been in the stands for the big stuff whenever he wasn't on the road. But for once, it was better that he wasn't—and knew it. Maybe he wasn't as oblivious as they all thought. Gil stuck the other notes to his monitor to deal with on Monday, then grabbed a fistful of messages and started flipping through them. "Who the hell *are* all these people? I don't even recognize half the names."

"Guess that's what happens when you go getting all famous." She started out the door. "If there's nothing else, I actually only came to grab coffee."

Gil checked the time as he followed her into the reception area. "We'd both better get out of here. It doesn't look like you've even showered, and we have to leave in half an hour."

She whipped around to face him. "Excuse me?"

"I have to be in Amarillo at eleven," he said, then remembered she hadn't been with them when they'd discussed this morning's departure time. "Oh right. I guess you missed that since you went home early, but it's been on Delon's schedule all along. Mandatory press conference for the finalists."

She narrowed her eyes at his impatient tone. "I remember the press conference. I don't recall being invited."

"*Invited?*" Why wouldn't she think she was welcome—hell, wanted—to come along?

"You know, where you ask a person if they would like to attend a particular function?" She folded her arms and set her jaw. "Contrary to what you seem to think, I am not your spare tire."

"My…what?" he asked, dumbfounded.

"That thing you assume will be in the car wherever you go. The one you don't even think about until you need it? When's the last time you actually invited me to go someplace, instead of just informing me of your schedule and assuming I'd be in the car?"

What the *fuck?* She'd insisted she wanted to be included in every part of his life, and now she was busting his balls for not sending her an engraved invitation every time they left the damn trucking yard? Gil mirrored her posture, cinching his arms over his chest. "If this is about last night...then yes, I probably screwed up. I could have waded through that sea of reporters to lay a kiss on you and thrill the fans. But since you didn't bother to tell me that you were taking off with *my car* and leaving me cooling my heels for three hours, I figured radio silence was standard operating procedure."

She gave a contemptuous snort. "There were plenty of other people who could've given you a ride wherever you wanted to go. And considering how hard we've all been busting our asses to make this happen for you, I thought I'd earned a little time off."

"From work?" He thumped his chest. "Or from me?"

Her eyes glinted dangerously. "Right this minute? I'd take—"

"Time out!" Quint barked from the hallway, making an emphatic T with his hands. "Geezus. I could hear you clear back in the weight room."

Carma stuck out her chin. "Because this place is built out of Popsicle sticks and tissue paper. I can't sneeze without one of the mechanics yelling 'Bless you'!"

"If you hate it here so bad, why didn't you just quit?" Gil demanded, guilt digging a fetid claw into his gut and stirring up his temper even more. "I didn't want you to give up your Wednesdays off, but you *insisted* on doing more."

"You needed me!" she all but yelled.

"I didn't ask you to run yourself ragged for my benefit. I would have managed!"

"But you weren't," Quint said, quiet enough to shut them both up. "That night of Bing's party, you were..." He shook his head, unwilling to put it into words, and his mouth went tight. "It wasn't Carma's idea. Grandma told everyone to come to her or Uncle Delon or Analise with their questions instead of bothering you. Max hired the new mechanic himself, without running all the applications by you. And I—"

Quint cut off abruptly.

"You what?" Gil glared at first one, then the other. "What else has been going on behind my back?"

Quint shoved his hands into the pockets of his jeans and hunched his shoulders. "Nothing. Forget about it."

Gil took a step closer. "I don't think so. I'm damn tired of being left in the dark. What did you do?"

"Nothing," Carma repeated. "Because it might upset you to find out that there's a Sanchez boy who doesn't want to be a bareback rider. So he hung around here pretending to be interested instead of going to roping practice with Tori and Beni."

"Roping?" Gil echoed, incredulous. "Like…steers?"

"Yes," Quint muttered, sounding like an actual sullen teenager.

Team roping. *His* son. It was all well and good for Beni, who was already on his way to outgrowing any of the roughstock events. But Quint? He had the build. The athletic ability. He could do anything…and he wanted to take up the rodeo equivalent of bowling?

"You have got to be—"

Before Gil could finish the sentence, Carma's cell phone rang. Visibly relieved to have something else to focus all her pent-up energy on, she pulled it out of the back pocket of her faded denim shorts and frowned at the screen. "Hey, Bing. What's—"

Then her face went pale and she grabbed the edge of the desk for support. "Eddie," she whispered.

Chapter 43

"He's alive," Bing said, her voice firm. "And he's in one piece. Is there someone with you?"

"Yes." Carma sagged with relief, vaguely aware of Gil and Quint grabbing her by the arms and guiding her into a chair. "How bad is it?"

"They aren't absolutely sure. Your parents got the call from one of his friends, not through the official channels, and the soldier didn't know many details. A mortar round landed on the base, just outside the canteen. At least one person was killed and several injured. It sounds as if Eddie was far enough away that he was thrown clear. The guy who called said it looked like he was talking to the medics, and it didn't look like he was bleeding other than some small cuts. They loaded everyone on a plane to the military hospital in Germany, and no one would tell him anything except that Eddie's injuries didn't appear to be life-threatening."

Oh God. Oh, thank God. Carma's hands were shaking so bad she could hardly hold the phone. Gil took it from her. "What do you want us to do?" he asked Bing.

"Bring her to me."

They put her in the back seat of the Charger, and Quint held her hand the whole way out to the Brookman ranch. The scenery was a blur, her mind flooded with possibilities that varied from bad to worse. If she'd let him, Gil probably would have carried her into the house, but she forced her rubbery legs to walk from the car to Bing's couch while Johnny hovered nearby, silent and helpless. The landline rang and Bing snatched it from the cradle, holding it so both she and Carma could hear.

"He's gonna be fine," Carma's mother said, her voice breaking on a sob. "A concussion, broken ribs, and superficial burns."

"Did you talk to him?" Carma choked out.

"No. They've got him under sedation for now. What he saw… It was bad."

Carma couldn't let those images into her head. Eddie was safe. That's all she could think about. She collapsed onto the sofa, only half listening as her mother went on about Tony finding them a direct flight out of Calgary to JFK, and then on to Germany.

She closed her eyes as Bing hung up and relayed the information to Gil and Quint, and heard them both heave massive sighs of relief. Hands closed around Carma's where they'd fallen limp in her lap, and Gil dropped to his knees in front of her. Something hard pressed into her palm, and she looked down to see him curling her fingers around the geode, his face stark.

"I shouldn't have let you give me this. It was supposed to protect your brother."

"And it did," Bing said. "The shell missed him. Others weren't so lucky."

Carma closed her eyes. So close. She had come so very close to losing Eddie. And right now, some other family was hearing the worst possible news instead. Gil pressed the stone between their hands. "Just hold on, darlin'. I'll be right here."

Here? But it was Saturday. Diamond Cowboy day. He

must already be late for that press conference. "You have to go," she said.

"No, I don't. You need me."

She shook her head. "I'm with Bing."

Gil pulled himself up and onto the couch next to her. "There must be something I can do to help."

"Not unless you can magically transport me from here to Germany." The sheer distance was crushing; the many, many steps it would take to get from here to there overwhelming. Carma was usually galvanized by a crisis. Why couldn't she pull herself together now, when Eddie needed her to be strong? Had she given so much of herself to Gil that she didn't have anything left for the other people she loved?

"Please," she whispered, holding onto her composure by a thread. If Gil stayed, she'd have to think about the fight they'd been having, and whether Quint was mad at her for telling his dad about wanting to rope, and...everything. She'd have to admit that she'd picked a fight with Gil on one of the most important days of his life because he'd been focused on what he had to do instead of worrying about making her feel special, and what kind of person did that make her?

She pulled her hands free of his. "If you miss the rodeo, I'll feel guilty, and I don't think I can stand to feel one more thing right now."

"But I should be here," he insisted.

No, he shouldn't. She was about three seconds away from screaming, or crying, or both, and she did not want him and Quint to witness her meltdown. What they'd already seen this morning was bad enough. All Gil had asked of her was one more day, and she couldn't even give him that. She was too damn selfish to be a rodeo wife—and it was probably good that he'd seen it for himself.

So just this once why couldn't he be like Jayden, and run away when she looked remotely like she might require emotional support?

"I should get online and find you a flight," he said.

No! He had to go before she gave in and attached herself to him like a leech. She scraped up some grit to put in her voice. "You should listen, instead of telling me what I need."

He stiffened. "I am not—"

"Yeah. You are," Bing drawled. "And she should know. She's been doing it to other people all her life."

For some bizarre reason, the snarky comment made Carma want to laugh. Hysteria, probably.

But even through the chaos of her own emotions, she felt Gil's hurt and desperation. There was a problem, and he couldn't fix it, and that must be driving him crazy. "I can't just leave you like this," he said.

"Yes, you can. And you should." Carma sounded surprisingly firm. She forced herself to square her shoulders. "I told you…I've got Bing. And Eddie isn't in immediate danger. I'll be fine."

He waffled for another endless minute. Finally, he kissed Carma on the forehead. "All right. If you're sure that's what you need. Call if you change your mind, or…anything."

Bless him for stopping short of saying, *If Eddie gets worse.*

"I promise," she said, just to get rid of him.

"Me too," Bing said. "Now go. Give 'em hell. We're rooting for you."

He kissed Carma again. Then he stood and stalked out the door. Quint paused to give Carma an awkward pat on the shoulder before he followed. The engine revved and the tires on the Charger squealed as they hit the highway. Either he was in a hurry, or he was not happy about being told to go away. Carma would have to decide later. Right now…

She folded in half, pressing her face into her hands. Bing wrapped an arm around her shoulders and they let the tears fall.

~

Gil's first inclination was to slam the gas pedal of the Charger to the floorboard, but he'd tried that the last time a woman had blown him off in her time of need and look how that turned out. Besides, he had Quint with him.

The silence inside the car stretched as taut as Gil's nerves, so he felt the snap when Quint broke it.

"There really wasn't anything you could do," he said.

Gil gripped the steering wheel so hard his knuckles cracked. "That's not the point."

Quint nodded and fell silent again.

A few miles farther down the road, Gil said, "I guess I'm just not someone people lean on…or confide in."

After a few beats, Quint said, "You mean me."

Gil jerked a shoulder. Wasn't it obvious? When the chips were down, he was the last one any of them turned to.

"It's not your fault," Quint said. "I'm like this with everybody."

"Except Carma?"

"She's different. You can't help but tell her stuff."

Yeah. Gil knew exactly what he meant. Like the way he'd been on the verge of telling her he loved her, and forget the stupid rodeo, he'd drive her to fucking Germany if he could. But she didn't need him. She had Bing. Her family. Anyone but Gil.

"It's fine," he said. "I would've just ended up being the worst thing that happened to another woman."

Quint let a couple of miles pass before he answered. "That's not what Mom says."

Gil's head snapped around. "You asked her?"

Quint did an elaborately casual shrug. "I wanted to know why it didn't work out with the two of you."

Of course he did. The same as Gil and Delon had struggled to understand why their parents couldn't be like Steve and Miz Iris. "I had a serious drinking problem," he said, restating the obvious.

"I know." Quint fiddled with his seat belt. "Mom said if there were any way to go back that wouldn't mean not having Gwennie and Liz, she would, for your sake and for mine. She said her biggest regret is that she was spoiled and stupid, and she never gave you a chance to show her the man you turned out to be."

All of the sudden the road went blurry, and Gil had to stop the car. He pulled onto the shoulder, put the Charger in park, and blinked hard a few times. He'd always thought… He'd assumed… "She actually said that?"

Quint rolled his eyes. "Nah. I just made it up because you were starting to get carried away with the pity party."

"Brat." Gil swatted him on the arm.

Quint shrugged. "Runs in the family."

Along with the tendency to fall back on sarcasm when things got too sentimental. They sat for a while, gazing out at absolutely nothing on the flat plain. Then Gil sighed. "Team roping, huh?"

"Yeah."

"Well, I suppose it could be worse. It'll just take me a while to figure out how."

Quint huffed out a laugh. "A kid my age won twenty-three grand at a roping last week in Guthrie, Oklahoma."

Gil blinked. "No shit?"

"No shit. Find me a bareback rider who can top that."

At fourteen? Not likely. Gil ran a few mental calculations. Huh. This might be a little easier to swallow than he'd thought.

"You know she's crazy about you, right?" Quint asked.

Gil's heart did a weird skitter. "Carma?"

"Duh." Quint drenched the word with an impressive amount of mockery. "That's why she made you leave. She could no more let you miss this rodeo on her account than she could sprout wings and fly. She's almost as bad as you, taking care of everybody else first."

For the second time, Gil was rocked back in his seat. *That's* how Quint saw him? "I'm just bossy," he argued out of reflex. "The control freak, remember?"

"Yeah. Whatever." Kid-speak for *You are also full of shit.*

An insult that had never given Gil the warm fuzzies until now. He rubbed his chest, full to bursting with so many emotions—pride, love, nerves, worry about Carma and her brother, *everything* about Carma—that he felt like an over-inflated tire. "I can't stand not doing anything to help her."

"Except go kick ass the way she told you to," Quint suggested.

He could try. Gil dragged his mind back to the Diamond Cowboy, checking the clock. He was definitely not going to make the press conference. He smiled grimly. At least something good had come out of all this. Calling up Delon's number on the hands-free system, he pulled back on to the road and drove back to the shop while he explained the situation. After a quick stop to change into rodeo attire and grab more coffee, they were on the road again.

Halfway to Amarillo, a thought struck him. "If you're not interested in riding, why did you want my old chaps?"

"They're cool. *The Flamethrowers.*" Quint ducked his head. "And you're wearing them in the picture Mom gave me of the two of you right after you won San Antonio. Having them just makes it seem more…real."

Hell. Why hadn't he ever shared stories about back when he was riding, or the good times with Krista? At least Gil had some happy memories of his parents together. Quint had nothing but hostile politeness and tense cease-fires.

Gil could do better than that. He and Quint both could. And they needed to quit wasting time, because today had been a vivid reminder that tomorrow wasn't guaranteed. Hell, in four very short years Quint would be graduating from high school and off to who knew where. They'd already missed too much.

Gil propped his wrist on the top of the steering wheel and rolled some of the tension out of his shoulders. "I'll make you a deal. Every day I'll tell you a story about me, if you'll tell me one about you."

"Like what?" Quint asked, ever suspicious.

"Anything you want. What happened at school. Something dumb you did that I never heard about." He raised an eyebrow. "The girl who was following you around at the track meet."

Quint made a classic *Ew!* face. "You have to go first."

"Okay." Gil considered his options. "Did your mom tell you how we met?"

"One of her sorority sisters at Oklahoma State was a barrel racer. Mom went with her to a college rodeo and you walked up and told her she was too gorgeous to be wandering around alone, so it'd be best if you stuck close and protected her from all those raunchy cowboys."

Gil shook his head. God, he'd been full of himself. And so had she. The devil gave him a nudge. "Did she tell you about our second date?"

"No."

Gil smiled with only a touch of evil pleasure. Hey, the kid should know what a badass his mother had been. "We were at a dance after the rodeo. Your mom went to the bathroom, and while she was gone, another girl plopped herself down on my knee, just joking around. Krista came back, gave her one look, and said, 'You've got two seconds to get your ass off his lap or I'm gonna rip your face off. And next time there is no warning.'"

Quint goggled at him. "*Mom* said that?"

"Oh yeah. And she meant it." Gil tossed him a grin. "Where do you think you got the 'punch first, talk later' attitude?"

Quint laughed in disbelief, then said, "Did she tell you about the time I decided to play buried pirate treasure with Grandad's silver-dollar collection?"

"No! Geezus. He must've had a coronary."

"Oh man. And then I hid the map, and they spent *days* going over the grounds with a metal detector..."

They filled the rest of the drive with talking, laughing, and slowly, finally getting to know each other. Carma would be very proud of them.

As he parked at the coliseum and hitched his gear bag over his shoulder, Gil made a silent vow. He would do his damnedest to keep making her proud. If Carma wanted him to ride, he would spur his guts out. But the second he was done, he was going straight back to her, wherever she might be by then.

And no one—not even Carma—was going to stop him.

Chapter 44

The crying jag turned out to be exactly what Carma needed. When she was drained dry, she toppled over on the couch and slept. At one point, she was vaguely aware of Johnny tiptoeing in for lunch, then she went under again. Her own stomach was hollow when she finally surfaced to the smell of fresh coffee.

She shoved her hair out of her face and blinked groggily at Bing, working on her laptop at the island that separated kitchen and living room.

"Better?" Bing asked.

Carma took stock. The dull ache behind her eyes was nothing caffeine and a couple of ibuprofen wouldn't cure. More important, the suffocating knot behind her sternum had loosened. Her fear for Eddie was still there, but she felt capable of managing whatever came next. The coffee lured her off the couch and into the kitchen to pour a mug, adding extra cream and sugar for sustenance. "Anything new from Mom?"

"Just that they were almost to Calgary. Their flight boards at five thirty." Bing tapped her screen with one glossy fingernail. "If we drive you to Dallas, you can hop a flight to Atlanta at nine tonight. You'd be in Germany by late tomorrow afternoon."

A little more than twenty-four hours and she could be with her brother. Hold his hand. Flood him with every iota of positive energy she could summon.

She cradled her mug between her hands, finally

letting herself acknowledge the horror she'd heard in her mother's voice. "His injuries aren't the worst part, are they?"

Bing rested her hands on the keyboard. "One of the men he's served with for years was blown to bits right in front of him."

Carma's heart convulsed. Oh God. Poor Eddie. "Then he's not okay."

"I don't imagine he ever really will be again. The mental trauma—combined with a concussion—is why they're keeping him heavily sedated until your mother and Tony get there."

Carma nodded slowly. "He's going to need me."

"He's going to need a lot. For a long time."

And she couldn't phone in that kind of help. She would have to go home.

"You're already plotting your escape, aren't you?" Bing asked.

"My...what?"

Bing laced her fingers together, getting that annoying, know-it-all look in her eyes. "I've been watching you manufacture excuses to run away ever since you realized this wasn't just some fling."

"They're not excuses!" Carma shot back. "You said I had to figure out what I want and whether he's willing to give it. Well, I want more than he has to spare, and he doesn't need an anchor."

"Oh, for God's sake." Bing heaved a bottomless sigh. "I have never seen two people so determined to tell everyone else what they need. But that's a whole lot less scary than asking for what you want, right?"

Carma bristled. "I am not scared."

"Hah! I can see your boots shaking from clear over here—and you're not even wearing any."

Carma felt her face going mulish but couldn't make it stop. "It doesn't matter. I have to be with Eddie and you said it yourself—it's going to be a long recovery. I can't expect Gil to wait around for me."

"Actually, I think you can. Or you could bring Eddie to Texas."

"What?" Carma gaped at her. "I can't drag him down here."

"Why not? Bring him to the Patterson ranch. There's no better place on the planet for what he'll be going through."

"But..."

But. Bing was absolutely right. Tori's new mental health program was specifically geared to treat PTSD and other trauma-related conditions. There were horses. Cows. Space. And yes, Carma, who would be stupid not to encourage Eddie to take advantage of everything that place could offer.

But...

She cradled her mug between her hands, head bowed. "Gil and I were having a fight when you called."

"About what?"

"I don't know. We were just..."

"Cranky?" Bing suggested. "Tired? Feeling a tad insecure? *Scared?*"

"Yes!" Carma threw up one hand in surrender. "Fine! I was all those things, and I took it out on him."

Bing's mouth curled. "I wasn't talking about you."

"Gil?" Carma made a *pah!* noise. "He's on top of the world. What's he got to be insecure about?"

"Maybe because he's also scared, and nervous, and the

woman he loves won't let him get close enough to see that she loves him, too."

"Hey! I'm not the one drawing all the lines."

"And crossing every single one of them," Bing pointed out.

"Sort of. Maybe." Carma scowled as her precious arguments crumbled around her, replaced by a frantic fluttering behind her breastbone. "I don't know for sure that he loves me."

"Are you trying to be dense, or is this some kind of denial?" Bing countered, with a pointed look at the spot where Gil had been sitting on the couch. Right next to the coffee table where the geode sparkled in a shaft of midday sun.

Carma's last line of defense came crashing down. He'd given the stone back in case it might help Eddie. And he would've stayed. All the work, all the pain, all the anticipation, all the thrill of last night and potential triumph of today—Gil would've given it up to be with her. What kind of man would do that?

The best kind. A man who was strong, and stubborn, and occasionally aggravating. Who would set aside his dream without a second thought if someone he cared about needed him.

"He loves me," she marveled, sounding like a sappy TV movie.

"Duh." Bing did a remarkable impression of Quint at his most sarcastic and turned her laptop so Carma could see the screen. "And now that that's settled...if you want to catch that flight in Dallas we've gotta leave in about forty-five minutes."

Flying straight to Eddie. Who would also have their

mother. And their mother would have Tony. The hospital would have a whole platoon of mental health professionals with way too much experience in treating soldiers like Eddie. If Carma was one hundred percent honest with herself, there wasn't anything she could offer her brother in the next few days that he wouldn't get from someone else.

Her love was a given, and she could send that clear around the world without leaving Texas.

She walked into the living room, picked up the geode, and turned it so the crystals sparked blue fire. It had kept the eagle's promise. Eddie had been spared. Now someone else she loved was preparing to go into a different kind of battle. Was she going to sit back and let him do it without all the support and protection she could give him?

"Gil isn't gonna quit when this rodeo is over," she said.

"It would be a massive waste if he did," Bing said. "And I can't imagine his family letting him."

Carma smiled a little, picturing that *conversation*. Max had better keep his water hose ready to douse the flames. "It won't be easy, trying to squeeze a relationship in with everything else we've both got going on."

"No, it will not. And you two will find all the ways to make it more difficult."

Carma shot her a scathing look. "Gee, thanks for the vote of confidence."

"Just remember to use your words. Communication is a beautiful thing."

"You say that like it's simple." But Carma's smile took over her whole face. "If we're gonna get ourselves looking presentable and in Amarillo by rodeo time, we'd better get a move on."

Bing grinned back. "Clean towels are in the hall closet, and Johnny will have the pickup running."

Delon would make an excellent campaign manager if Tori did decide to go into politics. Or was that a press agent? Whoever made sure the reporters left you the hell alone when talking to them could be dangerous for both parties.

Gil didn't know exactly what word Delon had passed around, but it had worked. When Gil slung his bag down behind the chutes at the coliseum, even the other cowboys gave him plenty of space.

He went through his preride routine on autopilot—gearing up, stretching, prepping his glove and rigging. Each time his mind wandered to Carma, he dragged it back. If he was going to do her proud, he had to focus. Plus there was a double rank bucking horse waiting for him in chute number six, and if Gil didn't get his head together Carma might be visiting him in a hospital, too. He'd almost laughed when he saw the name of the horse he'd drawn. Blue Anchor—the mare that had body-slammed him out at the Jacobs arena.

And would again if he wasn't primed and ready for that swoop.

The other cowboys didn't have it any easier. This was what they called the eliminator pen—the toughest bucking horses the contractors owned. The chances of hitting the dirt were high for everyone, but they couldn't safety up and just get to the whistle. Only one cowboy out of the sixteen qualifiers got to face off for the title. If Gil wanted to be that man, he'd have to open up and take his chances.

When the horses were loaded, Gil draped his rigging over his arm and stepped onto the back of the chutes. From there he had a clear view of the seating contingent. They were all present and accounted for. Analise and Tori were sitting with Beth, who already fit right in even though she didn't start until Monday. Hank and Grace had rushed back from a rodeo in Lubbock. All the mechanics were there, and a few drivers, along with various spouses and kids. Rochelle was between Miz Iris and Violet.

But three seats beside the aisle had been left glaringly empty. No Carma, no Bing, and no Johnny.

A hand clapped Gil's shoulder, hard enough to rattle his teeth. "You ready?" Delon asked.

Gil nodded, once again making the effort to clear his head of everything except this moment, this horse, this ride. He took the frustration and worry and channeled it into the hard, low thud of his pulse as he strapped his rigging on Blue Anchor. The mare cocked her head to eye him with a combination of challenge and contempt. *Hope you brought more game this time, round ass.*

Ten minutes to go. The music swelled and a public address announcement urged everyone to take their seats before the lights were dimmed for the opening ceremonies. Delon gave him one last slap on the back, then went to line up for the introduction of the world champions, who would stride onto an elevated walkway lined with nozzles that spewed fog to catch the colored spotlights. Then a stirring patriotic video and the national anthem would draw the audience's attention away from the crew that swarmed the arena to haul the stage out.

Five minutes. Four. Three. Gil couldn't tear his gaze away from those empty seats.

Two minutes. One. The coliseum went dark, and laser-generated fireworks burst across the arena floor while spotlights played over the audience. One of them caught a woman standing at the head of the stairs, and Gil's heart stalled.

Carma. In a short, cream-colored dress, hair falling free around her bare shoulders, pausing with one hand on the rail—and that damn ugly purse slung over her shoulder. She met his gaze across the space and noise and commotion and smiled. A wide, no-holds-barred smile that hit him harder than any shot of whiskey. Then she extended her hand, palm up, and he saw the blue sparkle of the sky stone.

Gil grabbed the top rail of the chute and sank into a crouch, his knees suddenly weak.

Another, larger hand settled on his shoulder. "You okay?" Steve asked.

Gil laughed. Okay? Try drunk on relief, riding the high only Carma could give him. She was here, for him, despite everything. She might as well have had them plaster the message up on the jumbo screen in neon letters.

Carmelita White Fox loves Gil Sanchez.

He dipped his chin and touched his hat brim, a gesture of everlasting gratitude to whatever higher power had dragged him out of his truck and into the Stockman's Bar that night in Babb. No matter what happened now, he had already won.

He straightened, braced his feet, and planted his hands on his hips. "Bring it on."

"Impressive timing," Violet said, as Carma waited for Bing and Johnny to scoot in ahead of her before she took the aisle seat. "Whoever's running that spotlight deserves a big tip."

"Pure luck," Carma said.

"And a killer dress," Melanie added. "The spotlight guys love a great pair of legs."

Those legs were still trembling from the sprint across the parking lot to get inside in time for the opening ceremonies. Carma's hair wasn't even completely dry from her shower, and she'd had to do her makeup on the drive down. But she'd made it.

Violet nodded toward where Gil was crouched on the back of the chutes. "Is he praying or cussing a blue streak? It's hard to tell through all the smoke and lights."

And with Gil in general.

Carma had braced herself for a barrage of questions and concern, but there was only Miz Iris leaning over to put one gentle hand on Carma's shoulder and the other on Bing's and give a gentle squeeze, obviously the designated giver of support and sympathy. Carma's throat tightened. Bless them and their grapevine. There was no need to pester Carma with all the questions Bing had no doubt already answered. These were amazing people her cousin had fallen in with.

And Carma too.

She stared at the crown of Gil's hat and wondered what was going on under there. He had seen her, there was no doubt about it. Was that good, or had she completely blown his concentration?

Carma reached into her purse and closed her fingers around the geode. *Win or lose, just let him be safe.*

Steve Jacobs leaned down to slap Gil on the shoulder.

He nodded and straightened, chin up, chest out. As the lights came up and the smoke cleared, his gaze zeroed in to meet Carma's, and for a long moment they could have been the only two people in the coliseum.

Then he smiled, a wicked promise that whatever happened next was gonna be worth watching.

"The competition will start with our qualifiers, all fighting for that number one spot," the announcer explained to the audience. "Then the five invitees will duke it out to see who goes head to head with the challenger for the diamonds. First up, a hot young Idaho cowboy..."

That was the last thing Gil heard. When he stepped over the back of the chute, his mind went still and deadly calm, like a sniper zeroing in on his target. The noise, the nerves, the doubts—they all faded as he worked his glove into the rigging and tested his bind. The only voice he heard was Steve's, deep and low, as he and Joe checked the flank strap and helped Gil place his rigging in the perfect position and cinch it tight. The only thing he saw was the curve of the mare's shoulder below her wild mop of black mane.

That was the target. If he planted his heels right there on every jump there was no way she could get out from under him.

He was barely aware of the clangs and cheers and whistles that accompanied the rides before him. He didn't watch. He didn't listen to the scores. They didn't matter. Only him and this horse. Then Delon's hand was on his back, Steve stood ready to pull the flank strap, and Joe was at the mare's head, keeping her square in the chute as Gil gritted his teeth and nodded his head.

The gate opened, and she launched.

Drive, drive, drive… Gil slammed his feet down, fighting the power that tried to yank his arm straight and smack his head off her ass. From the first jump, it was a slugfest. She punched, he countered, so dialed in that he felt the bow of her spine as she began to swoop left. He was ready, his free arm jerking hard to keep him centered, his shoulders back. But as the seconds ticked down his control began to slip, and his hips slid a precious inch away from the rigging, then two. *Come on, come on…*

Just as the whistle blew, the mare yanked him to the end of his arm, flipping him down and over her head to slam him onto his back. He rolled with the impact and came to his knees, gaze shooting from one judge to the next, looking for a telltale yellow disqualification flag on the dirt.

There were none.

The roar of the crowd crashed down on him as he staggered to his feet and slumped against the fence, sucking air. Up on the big screen, the gate swung open again in slow motion. Geezus. It looked almost worse than it had felt. Those last few ticks of the clock were definitely going to cost him.

"Eighty-five points!" the announcer intoned. "That'll put Gil Sanchez in first place for the moment, but we've got six more top cowboys and rank horses yet to go."

And that was it. Game over. That score wouldn't hold up through the next six rides. Gil drew a breath and got his bearings. As luck would have it, he'd ended up almost directly below where the Sanchez fan club was seated.

Back at the chutes, the television reporter was waiting, microphone ready, to broadcast his opinion of the beating he'd just endured. He was supposed to make a few comments on his ride, then go stand on a platform where the television and in-house cameras could catch his reaction when someone inevitably knocked him off the top of the leaderboard.

Screw that. He had one more promise to keep. He jerked the lace of his glove loose with his teeth, unwound it, and stuffed it into the waist strap of his chaps. Then he grabbed the top rail of the fence, hoisted himself over and headed straight for Carma.

"What are you doing?" she hissed, as he latched onto her hands and hauled her out of her seat.

"Making absolutely damn sure you know how happy I am to see you," he said, grinning like he'd won all the diamonds, and then some.

After the barest hesitation, she sighed and said, "I should've known you'd make a spectacle of this."

And she kissed him, long and hard, while cheers, laughter, and catcalls rained down around them, and somewhere nearby he heard Quint groan, "Aw, geez. On TV?"

Chapter 45

When they finally came up for air, Gil laced his fingers through hers and tugged her up the stairs.

"Where are we going?" Carma protested, not exactly dragging her feet. "You're supposed to be down there doing…stuff."

"They'll get over it." They reached the mezzanine and he glanced both directions and cut right, towing her past startled spectators, then left down a short service hallway between two concession stands. When they reached the end, he spun her around and planted a hand on either side of her shoulders, bracketing her in place. He was wearing that purple shirt she loved and he smelled of sweat and rosin, leather and horse, so potent it sent her head spinning.

"We need to talk," he said.

Her breath was coming in short puffs from a combination of exertion and lust. "This might not be the best time—"

"I've wasted too much already." Then he abruptly pushed to arm's length to study her face. "Your brother. Anything new?"

"He's at the hospital. Mom and Tony are on their way."

"And you're here." There was a note of awe in his voice, followed immediately by concern. "Did you have trouble getting a flight? Do you need, um, money or something? Those last-minute ticket prices are legal extortion."

A tad insecure. Damn, Bing. Did she always have to be right? Now that he had time to think, he was already wondering if she'd only come because she didn't have a better option.

Carma held up the pink camo rhinestone purse. “Do you see this?”

“Uh…yeah.”

She waved a hand to indicate her dress, her makeup, her absolute favorite lace-up sandals. “Do you see this?”

His eyes went liquid and hot. “Oh yeah. Everybody in the building saw that.”

“And do you honestly think a woman would go to this much trouble to look good, then carry a purse this damn ugly if she wasn’t trying to make a statement?”

That startled a laugh out of him. “I guess not. But I didn’t realize—”

“No, wait. I just want to say that earlier, when I sent you away, you shouldn’t have felt…” She trailed off, hearing herself, and slapped a hand to her forehead. “Oh my God. I’m doing it again. We can’t even have a big romantic moment without me trying to dictate what you should feel.” She flapped her fingers at him. “Go ahead. You start.”

His mouth quirked. “So this is you telling me exactly how I should stop letting you decide what I should do.”

She groaned. “I am pathetic. Do you know yesterday was the first conversation I ever had with Jayden that I didn’t say the words, ‘You should’?” When his eyebrows shot up, she groaned again. “Right. Mentioning the ex. Also not recommended for big romantic moments.”

“Let me try.” He nuzzled into her hair, kissing the side of her neck and making her shiver. “I *should* have made a U-turn way back in November and drove straight back to Montana, because I never stopped thinking about you. Or I *should* have texted you an invitation to come south for the winter and promised to keep you very, *very* warm. At the very least, I *should* have told you the first time we showered together that I would be honored to be your spare tire, just tell me where you want to go." He leaned back to angle her a dangerously boyish smile. "How am I doing?"

"Um…not bad," she stammered, fighting for the air he'd knocked clean out of her. "I think you *should* keep practicing, though."

"Nope. Your turn."

She tried to reassemble the brain cells he had so thoroughly scrambled. "Oh. Okay. I *should* have left you a note when I left last night that said *I am so incredibly proud of you, and we are still on for* Later, *just stop by my van when you get home.*"

"Dammit!" He smacked the heel of his hand against the wall. "I knew I should have come knocking."

"Well, see, that's the kind of thing that happens when we don't communicate. We end up tired and cranky and unsatisfied, when we should have been celebrating." She gentled her smile, reaching up to cup his face. "We are both way too good at protecting ourselves by putting other people first."

"Because if you take all the responsibility, they can't let you down?" He narrowed his eyes. "Are you sure you haven't been talking to Tamela behind my back?"

"Believe me, I know my limits, and that is one I would not test." She slid her palm down to the side of his neck. "We wouldn't have to do things behind your back if you'd just ask for help."

"Sure. And while I'm at it, I'll just come to work naked."

She smiled. "It's not *that* hard."

"Asking for help?"

"Coming to work naked." She shrugged. "Been there, done that. Have the movie credits to prove it."

He tipped his head back, laughing in amazement. "God, you are something, Carmelita. Am I ever gonna stop finding new things to love about you?"

It was almost incomprehensible, the way this tough, self-contained man tossed that word around so easily. He would never fail to surprise her, either. And they would probably never stop getting crossways of each other.

"So, rule number one," she said. "Tell each other what we really want. And rule number two: No assuming we know what's best for each other."

He sighed, resting his forehead against hers. "So basically change our entire molecular structure."

"I'll rearrange your electrons if you'll rearrange mine," she offered.

He grinned. "Now *that's* a date. How about I start here?"

She hummed her pleasure, then cringed when she saw the crowd clustered at the end of the hall, straining to hear over the noise from the arena, and watching with avid interest as he nipped at the bare curve of her shoulder.

"Um, Gil, maybe we should wait..."

Quint shoved his way through, face flushed. "Dad! You need to get out here."

Gil waved him away with an impatient hand. "We're busy. Tell them *No comment.*"

"Dad!" Quint planted his fists on his hips. "They need you in the arena."

Gil half turned, scowling. "Why? Was there some dumb-ass question they forgot to ask yesterday?"

"You have to get on another horse."

Gil's jaw dropped. "I... What?"

Quint enunciated each word separately. "You won. You're in the finals."

"I can't be. That ride was ugly."

"And everybody else's was uglier."

His eyes went wide. "Are you fu—"

Carma slapped a hand over his mouth to cut off the curse. "Definitely not the place."

"Holy shit. I won. I have to go." Gil grabbed her wrist and, tucking her behind him so he could break trail, hustled out of the hallway. The onlookers peeled away to clear a path, applauding and shouting encouragement. As they reached the mezzanine, a roar shook the coliseum, almost drowning out the announcer.

"What a ride! The reigning world champ just showed you why he's the man with the gold buckle. And rodeo fans, you know what that means." He paused for dramatic effect. "It's gonna be Sanchez versus Sanchez for all the diamonds."

Gil stopped and spun around. "Do you have the sky stone handy?"

"Sure. In my purse." She fished it out and gave it to him.

"Thanks." He dropped a quick kiss on her mouth. "I'm gonna need all the help I can get."

The coliseum went silent as once again the lights dimmed and a spotlight snapped on, creating a bright circle in front of the bucking chutes. Inside, the behind-the-chutes announcer stood with her microphone at the ready beside one of the judges, who held a silver bowl with two chips that would determine which horse they would ride. The rodeo announcer tuned his voice to mimic the opening of a prize fight.

"Buckle your seat belts, folks, and prepare yourselves for the final showdown in our first event, the bareback riding! Representing the challengers, former pro rodeo rookie of the year and the comeback story of this year's Diamond Cowboy event, from Earnest, Texas...Gil Sanchez!"

Gil stepped nearly to the center of the circle, hands on hips, gaze hard.

"And representing our invitees, also from Earnest, Texas, three-time and reigning world champion Delon Sanchez!"

He stepped into the ring from the opposite side, meeting Gil in the middle with barely enough space between them for the judge to hold up the bowl. "As the rider with the highest score in the previous round, Delon Sanchez will choose first and ride last."

Delon held Gil's gaze as he plucked a chip from the bowl. Gil followed suit. Neither of them broke eye contact or looked at what they'd drawn.

The judge stepped back. The arena announcer stepped forward, her smile bright.

"This is quite a moment for both of you." She tipped the microphone toward Gil. "When you decided to enter the Diamond Cowboy, did you ever dream it would come down to this?"

"Yes."

She waited. He didn't elaborate. She turned to Delon, obviously expecting to be rescued. If anything, his expression was even stonier than Gil's.

Her smile wavered. "Regardless of who comes out on top, the ring will be going home with a Sanchez. It must be such a thrill to see Gil back in competition."

"It is," Delon said. "I've been waiting a long time to show him who's the top dog now."

Gil sliced him a kiss-my-ass smile. "Give it your best shot, little brother."

"Bet on it."

Rather than retreating, they stepped forward, deliberately bumping shoulders as they passed in the center of the spotlight.

Gil said, "I get Steve."

"I've got Joe," Delon shot back, like duelists picking their seconds.

Abandoned, the arena announcer gave a nervous laugh. "Well, there you have it. These boys are serious. Let's send it back up to the announcer's booth for a few words about the horses they'll be taking on."

"Thank you, Stephanie! We're sticking to the family theme, with a mother-and-son duo from Smith Brothers Rodeo, and there's not a nickel's worth of difference between them. They're just gonna bust outta the chute and throw on the power. If the cowboy gets tapped off, it'll be spectacular, but if they have one bobble, they'll be eating dirt. Like the song says, folks, with these broncs, it's 'Ninety or Nothin.'"

Geezus, the mare was big, her back wide as a truck and nearly level with the top rail of the chute.

Gil flexed his riding arm, testing the tape he'd cut off and replaced to be sure he had all the support he could get. His spirit was more than willing, but he wasn't so sure about his flesh. The cumulative effects of three rides quivered in his muscles and twinged in his tendons.

Eight seconds. He only had to muster up enough strength for eight more ticks of the clock. He could go a helluva lot longer than that on pure stubbornness and pride, and the sheer joy of knowing that even if he got drilled into the ground one jump out of the chute, Carma would be there to kiss it better.

Again, the hype and hoopla faded to the background when he straddled the mare. She was as calm as if they were headed out on a Sunday trail ride, but he wasn't fooled. When the gate cracked, she'd go off like a cannon. Two chutes down, Delon stood waiting, arms folded, jaw set.

Gil had no doubt his brother wished him the best of luck. And then Delon intended to kick his ass.

"You got this," Steve said.

Gil nodded, slid up on his rigging, and called for the gate.

This horse wasn't a cowboy's dream like Angel Wings, but she wasn't a back-alley brawler like Blue Anchor either. When the force of the first jump hit Gil, every fiber from his fingers to his shoulder sang in protest, but his heels were solidly planted over the break of her shoulders. She didn't pull any tricks. Just threw on the muscle and dared him to take what she dished out.

Push. Push. Push. Keep it tight. Keep it snappy.

He managed to stay just ahead of the mare, getting his spurs into her neck as her feet hit the ground, dragging them up to his rigging as she launched into the next jump. She grunted with effort as she bucked in a big circle in front of the chutes, giving the judges a front-row seat to pick out every flair and flaw. Time stretched as Gil fought to hold his form as the mare's rump slammed into his shoulders.

And then it was over. The whistle blew. The pickup man set him down right where he'd started and he braced a hand on the chute gate, his legs going rubbery as the adrenaline abruptly ran out. He barely had the energy to tip his hat when his eighty-eight score was announced.

He'd given 'em hell. More than he'd thought he had in him. If this was the movies, he'd be holding the cash, the diamonds, and the girl when the credits rolled.

But Delon hadn't read that script.

From the first jump out of the chute, the difference was clear. His body was tighter, his feet snappier, his confidence a force unto itself. Gil had matched the mare. Delon owned her son. When the whistle blew and his feet hit the ground, he didn't even break stride, just pumped a fist in the air and accepted the well-deserved ovation as he sauntered back to the chutes, the outcome certain before the ninety-three-point score was tallied.

Gil forced some starch back into his legs and met his brother halfway. They paused a beat, then flung their arms around each other and pounded one another on the back.

"Helluva try," Delon said.

"Helluva ride."

"Maybe next year," Delon said.

Gil shook his head. "That wasn't the plan."

"Screw the plan. I've been waiting my whole life to hit the road with my big brother. You owe me, asshole."

"You think so?" Gil thumbed his hat back and saluted their fan club, still on their feet and whooping it up after the rest of the crowd had subsided. Miz Iris threw out her arms in a long-distance hug. Carma blew him a kiss. Rochelle clapped slowly, her expression thoughtful as she watched her sons.

Gil nodded toward her. "If you want to drag me outta the office, you'll have to get permission from our mother."

Delon snorted. "I'm her baby. She can't say no to me. I can get you to enough rodeos this summer and fall to be in the top fifty, so you're eligible to enter next year's big winter rodeos."

"Sounds like you've got it all penciled out."

"Nineteen different ways. I started the minute I heard you were sound enough to ride again."

Gil shook his head. And he thought he was the only one who got carried away. They turned in unison to stroll toward the exit gate.

Delon ignored the event personnel who were waving at him to hurry. "Everything good with you and Carma?"

"Until I fuck it up again."

Delon laughed. "So next week?"

"If not sooner." He glanced at where the dignitaries were lined up, waiting to present Delon with the huge cardboard check and glittering ring, and sighed. "You can't wait to wave that thing under my nose."

"At least once a day," Delon agreed, then gave a jerk of his chin toward where they'd left their gear bags. "Pack your shit. You've got a plane to catch."

"What?"

"You're going with Carma, dumb ass."

To Germany? Gil looked down at his vest, chaps, and boots. He had the clothes on his back and a thousand and one things to do at the office. He couldn't just drop everything...could he?

He glanced up at where Carma sat, then back at Delon. "I hear you've all been picking up my slack at the office."

"We'd be doing a lot more if we didn't have to tiptoe

around some hardheaded bastard who thinks he's the only one who knows shit." Delon pushed him in Carma's direction. "Go away. Tori's got your passport, and we've got the rest covered for as long as Carma needs you."

"Fine. I will."

"Good." Delon gave Gil one last shove and went to collect his loot.

"Never bet against the champ." Tori plucked a twenty-dollar bill out of Carma's hand. "Now, you're probably gonna want to get a move on. Our jet is fueled up and waiting at the airport."

Carma gaped at her. "Your...what?"

"Jet. You know..." Tori made airplane wings. "If you leave now, you'll probably beat your mother to the hospital."

Carma blinked at her. "That will cost a fortune."

"What good is money if you can't use it to help your friends?" Tori said with a shrug. "Besides, we'll make you earn it once you start working full—"

Carma threw both arms around her and squeezed, her voice hitching. "Thank you so much."

"Sure. No problem." Tori endured the embrace for about ten seconds, then started to squirm. "Um, really not a hugger here."

Carma laughed through a blur of tears as she let go and turned to Bing. "I guess you're driving me to the airport after all."

"I think he'll have something to say about that," Bing said, pointing over her shoulder.

Gil was striding along the mezzanine toward them,

impossible to miss in his purple shirt with his gear bag slung over his shoulder. He barely acknowledged the fans who called out congratulations, his gaze locked on Carma.

And just like that, she *knew*. That gut-deep certainty she'd felt when she saw the way Johnny looked at Bing, or when her dad reached over to give her mom's hand a squeeze just because.

This one was meant to be hers. Forever and always. Carma met him at the top of the stairs and he caught her hand.

"Mind if I tag along?" he asked.

She blinked. "To Germany?"

He flashed one of those trademark sardonic grins. "Why not? I've heard stories about the bedroom on this jet. There's a club I think we need to join."

Carma leaned into his arms, her head spinning. Somehow, this had become her life. Friends who would—and could—literally go above and beyond to get her to Eddie.

A man who would drop everything to be with her.

And making love suspended between the clouds and the stars.

Epilogue

Almost one year later at the Parsons arena near Browning, Montana

The evening was warm for spring, and the breeze drifting through the open doors of the new indoor arena was soft with the promise of summer, despite the snow still gleaming on the peaks outside. Inside, one end of the dirt had been packed hard for the night's festivities. As Gil leaned against a post at the edge of the makeshift dance floor, he was caught in a powerful wave of déjà vu.

Where would he be right now if he hadn't gone into the Stockman's Bar that night? Not here. And not this unbelievably happy.

He probably wouldn't have a whole new family to get to know either. Sanchez Trucking had hired several of Rochelle's relatives to help keep up with all the new business, and three of the cousins had moved to Earnest, two of them with their wives and kids. A person could say they were reverse colonizing the Panhandle, and Gil took great pleasure in imagining Earnest students being taught by the newly hired Mrs. Yazzie.

Those kids were gonna get a whole new perspective on American history.

The band wrapped up a song, and Eddie stepped onto the temporary wooden stage. Carma and Bing fretted about how he needed to gain back more weight, but Eddie was less haggard than he'd been almost a year ago. Those first weeks back from Afghanistan he'd struggled to leave his cabin at the Patterson ranch.

Gil and Eddie shared a mutual obsession with technology and how to make things work better. Plus they both loved Carma...and knew a thing or two about nightmares. But it was Eddie and Quint who'd truly bonded. Quint who'd stayed in the cabin with him, playing cards or watching TV late into the night. And Quint who'd lured him to the arena to rope steers with Tori's dad and whoever else was passing through.

Gil and Carma had rented a cottage in a small town almost dead center between Earnest and the Patterson ranch. The thing was tiny and possibly even uglier than Delon and Tori's, but the backyard was surrounded by trees and a high wooden fence, which allowed Carma to stretch out under the sky in whatever state of dress—or undress—she preferred.

Gil couldn't imagine anything better than rolling in late from a big win at the rodeo in Las Cruces, New Mexico, to find Carma basking in the moonlight, unless it was the two of them naked under the stars together.

And when spring had begun to chase the white from the mountain peaks and scatter wildflowers across the Montana prairie, Eddie had decided he was ready to come home and manage the program his family had built for him.

The lead singer relinquished the microphone, and Eddie cleared his throat. "Thank you for coming to the official opening of the Thelma White Elk Program for Hope. Our grandmother would have been so happy to see all of you here, supporting her dream." Eddie gestured to a couple standing near the back. "We also have to thank David and Mary Parsons for giving us a home here in their arena."

"Hey! What about me?" someone called.

Eddie laughed, more freely than since Gil had met him in that hospital in Germany. "And their son Kylan Running Bird, who has volunteered to be our official farrier."

Kylan waved from the corner where he, Beni, Quint, and a few other teenagers were lounging, all of them ropers. When Beni had heard Quint's plans, he'd declared that they were gonna partner up to start a new Sanchez family tradition.

Team roping. Geezus.

Beni had also suggested that his dad and Gil consider learning, too, since they couldn't ride broncs forever. It was a lot more tempting than Gil liked to admit.

"Don't forget that the silent auction closes in half an hour," Eddie reminded everyone. Then, with a grand sweep of his arm, he announced. "And now, the moment we've all been waiting for...my lovely and talented sister, Carmelita!"

Gil was lost as soon as Carma started to dance. She looked almost exactly the same as when he'd first seen her, in black leggings, moccasins, and that clingy black dress. Tonight she'd cinched a silver and turquoise belt around her waist and left her hair loose.

He would never get tired of watching her turn a piece of rope into a living thing that danced along with her. Hell, he'd never get tired of watching Carma do anything.

Directly across the dance floor, Delon stood with both arms around Tori's waist, her head tipped back against his shoulder. He and Gil had spent the day at the rodeo grounds, teaching a free clinic for a horde of eager young cowboys—and two that were pushing thirty. In high school they'd been the ones to beat, before drugs and alcohol had derailed them. Gil's story had persuaded them to give it another shot—and they were only the latest of many who'd made a point of letting him know that he'd changed their outlook on life.

Gil Sanchez, inspiration. That took some getting used to.

Meanwhile, the Sanchez brothers had been trading spots in the top ten in standings through the first half of the year, sticking to Delon's carefully plotted schedule of only the best rodeos. And there were still nights when Gil woke up in a cold sweat, sure it was all a dream. Then Carma would shift or sigh, and he'd nestle in close and count his blessings until he fell asleep.

The music changed to something slow and sweet and Carma paused, tossed aside her rope in favor of a longer one, then held out a hand, beckoning Gil onto the floor. She didn't have to ask twice.

He closed his hands around her waist and moved with her, swaying slowly as she fed more and more rope into the loop, then lifted it up and over so it spun around the two of them.

Her eyes were warm and dark, her gaze locked on his as she said, "You know they call this the wedding ring."

"Yeah."

"And there's a special tradition, where you invite the person you love inside the ring with you."

"Really? I've never heard of..." Then it hit him, and he nearly stumbled. "Is this a proposal?"

She smiled in the way that made him feel as if he'd been created just to put that light in her eyes. "Yes?"

"Well, shit."

Carma's loop wobbled, along with her smile. "I'm sorry, I shouldn't have—"

"No! I mean, it's fine. I just had this plan..." He splayed his fingers over his breast pocket, so she could see the distinctive outline of the ring he'd tucked in there.

"Oh no." She closed her eyes. "I did it again. I jumped the gun. God, I suck at big romantic moments. Let's just pretend I never said anything, and—"

"Uh-uh. I'll give you the proposal...and raise you about a hundred thousand." He reached into that same pocket and pulled out a business card with a date scribbled. "When we get home, we have an appointment with the architect who's doing the remodel of the office."

As long as no one wanted to live in the apartment, it might as well be office space. Plus they wouldn't have to worry about Quint and Beni sneaking girls up there the way he and Delon had.

Her brows pinched together in confusion. "What's that got to do with me?"

"We're gonna go out back in the pasture, and you're gonna show him where you want to build our new house."

She took the card with the hand that wasn't still busy spinning the rope, almost flawlessly. "But...you have a house."

"Not for much longer. I'm leasing it to Analise and Cruz as a sort of wedding present. They can't live in that dinky apartment of hers forever. Besides, now that she's in charge of dispatch, she can be the one living right behind the shop. I figure our place will be done about the time you and Tori get that second clinic up and running in Dumas, and you don't have to commute anymore."

She leaned in and kissed his cheek. "Have I ever told you how much I love the way you pay attention to all the little details?"

"I believe you have." He let everything he felt blaze through his grin. "But I'm willing to let you compliment my skills again later."

"Meet you at your sleeper?"

"You betcha."

Her eyes glistened through a sheen of tears as she handed him back the card, then held up her left hand. He slid the ring into place and she laughed with pure joy, lighting up every corner of his soul. He kissed her, deep and possessive, while the rope drifted to the ground, the loop wrapping around their legs and binding them together. All around them, friends and family applauded, calling out congratulations.

And through the wide door that was thrown open to the night, Gil could have sworn he heard the stars singing.

"As a competitive cowgirl, I am all about action and speed and the kickass women who love them, and this book delivers in spades."

—*Kari Lynn Dell*

Curious to see more? Enjoy this sneak peek at the first in a high-octane cowboy romance series, where highly competitive racers find themselves torn between the glitz of the international stage and the ranches they call home.

Coming July 28, 2020

Chapter 1

Billy King—Present Day

TURNS OUT THE WORLD'S A LOT BIGGER THAN MEMPHIS.

"Billy! Billy King!" My name is like cracks of thunder on the Spanish wind, and as I cruise past the press corps, I can't quite feel the relief yet that this is it. It's over. Flashes from the cameras are too busy sparkling through my helmet's face shield, shining off my motorcycle and nearly blinding me, there's so many of them. Valencia is already a massive festival, since it's the last race of the Moto Grand Prix circuit. But in all my years racing, I've never seen the press and the fans this excited before.

I pull off victory lane and stop in the designated winner's spot, already decorated with royal blue Yaalon Moto everything. The fans are barely held back by the chest-high gate rocking under their hands and repeated chants of my name. "Billy! Billy King!"

"All right, y'all, just wait your turn," I call out to the crowd. My laugh rings with the pure, sweet adrenaline pumping thick through my veins, a testament to battling twenty guys on the racetrack for who's coming out on top. And then beating them all, one by one.

Life doesn't get much sweeter than this. Especially since tomorrow, I can finally go *home*.

Back to Memphis: the ranch and my saddle, my horse, and my ropes.

Home to Taryn: her whiskey hair and sunset eyes.

I pull off my helmet, and after a quick wave to the fans, I start to find my breath again. I don't get to keep it long.

My manager's unmistakable twang cuts cleanly through the roar of the press corps. "I knew you could make it back, Billy!"

Frank yanks me off my bike and into a suffocating hug, slapping my back so hard I actually feel it through the armadillo spine of my leathers. At least he doesn't notice my wince from the pain in an ankle that's supposed to be long healed by now.

Telling him I'm hurt will only risk my future even *more* after what I did. Not that anyone seems to care about the reason *why* I did it.

Frank's too excited to pay attention to my stumble, setting my sponsor-coated Stetson on top of my head, then gripping my shoulders. "Not just first place, Billy! First in the *world*. Didn't I always say about putting bull riders—"

"Did Taryn call? She see it?" I wave toward the press and the fans again, beaming next to my blue motorcycle. They don't need to know there's sweat pooling in my leathers, and my feet desperately miss the buttery soles of my Ariat boots.

Mostly, though, I just miss *her*.

Frank clears his throat as I tip my cowboy hat toward the cameras, making sure they capture the names of all the people I'm paid to promote. "She hasn't called yet," he mumbles.

My pulse starts racing for a whole bunch of reasons I still can't make myself face, and I turn away from the Moto Grand Prix fans, praying no one caught the look I just felt flash across my face. My only hope is to keep clinging to Plan A: *act like it didn't happen, and maybe it didn't.*

"But she *will*," Frank adds in a rush. "You know Taryn. She's probably just—"

"Busy." I shift my helmet to my other hand, wiping sweat off my face. "Busy being mad at me."

Suppose she's right. I never was nothing special.

"Horseshit," Frank says. "That woman loves you. And need I remind you, you just won first place at Valencia, Billy. Twenty-five points, and that makes you a damned Moto Grand Prix World Champion. Now be happy, would ya? 'Cause you're starting to piss me off." He gives me a half grin and takes my helmet from me, slinging an arm around my shoulders. It does nothing to comfort the guilt swirling in my stomach. "Come on, cowboy. You about ready to show 'em what a champion looks like?" He nods toward the wall of reporters waiting to ask me the same questions they always ask.

"How did it feel to win today?"

"Were you riding for anyone special back home?"

"Is it hard being an American in a European sport?"

I clear my throat and tip up my hat so their lights won't cast shadows down my too-long nose. "Yeah. I'm ready."

Frank claps my back and heads off to organize the interview lineup, and I glance toward the press spot for third place, my twenty-five-year-old little brother already hamming it up for the cameras, probably giving sound clips about his smell-proof underwear again.

Frank is right. No matter what's been happening at home, I won here, and I should be celebrating. My knee surgery from two years ago has finally stopped causing me problems, and I've worked my ass off to get back to the top of the leaderboard. And like my father always says: I should try to be more like Mason.

He never lets love get in the way, and he's as good on a bike as he is at riding bulls. Everyone says so. It's probably why he's allowed to keep his hands in both cookie jars, and mine have been firmly tied.

No more wondering if that bull's gonna spin or blow when that gate opens. No more wondering if eight seconds are gonna be my last. Now, it's two red lights keeping me caged and my wrist on the throttle setting me free.

Mason finishes his interview, immediately turning to sign a lady's chest with a marker as red as her cheeks. Until someone walking by bumps his shoulder hard enough that he stumbles, nearly knocking her over.

"Hey!" Protective instincts blare through me, and I'm three steps closer than I was a moment ago, my outstretched hand already steadying Mason by the shoulder. My eyes home in on the back of Santos Saucedo from Hotaru Racing, strutting away with a chuckle.

Mason looks at me, and neither of us has to glance at the surrounding press to know they saw that shit go down. And I'm not about to let our family name get tarnished.

"What was that, friend?" I call out to Santos, cupping my ear. "We didn't catch whatcha said."

Santos turns and rattles off something in Spanish that makes the press collectively gasp. *The nerve of that guy.*

"Oh, I'm sorry, man," I drawl, acting all guilty. Mason crosses his arms. He's three inches and a good fifteen pounds littler than me but with twice the ego and ten times the temper. "We don't speak fifth place." I flash a grin that is sure to ramp Santos's annoyance through the damn stratosphere, but he can kiss my ass. Nobody messes with my brother but me.

A thick hand settles heavy on my far shoulder. "Thanks,

y'all," Frank says behind us toward the press, "but we gotta get Billy and Mason upstairs to get their medals. The Kings'll have more time to answer questions later, I promise."

I salute a scowling Santos, letting our manager sweep us out of the parc fermé and toward the stairs to the podium. The last thing I need is for Mason to back me into another damn corner. Thanks to him, racing's about all I have left.

A familiar throb that has nothing to do with leaning my bike through pin-tight turns twists through my insides, my ankle hurting more with every step as I climb the last of the stairs. And three feet from the door that gives me back to the crowd I've spent years trying to convince to love me, I find myself desperately wishing they'd just mail me the medal they want to hang around my neck.

"Showtime, boys." Frank opens the door to a blast of sound that's my name on repeat, and since I don't get a choice, I'm first outside onto the podium.

The sun is in the wrong spot and the wind doesn't smell right, but I wave and smile a little harder at the cameras taking my picture. Even though the one person who matters probably won't ever see them.

She still isn't answering my calls.

No matter what I do, she hasn't forgiven me, and it's why I need to get my sorry ass back to Memphis. Running home's the only way I'm ever gonna get her back.

I'm already sweating in my best pearl-snap shirt despite the cool November air, hinting at the icy December we're gonna have. I pluck once more at my starched collar, pointing my battered old boots toward the barn, trying to gain some kind of confidence from being in Memphis, even if my body still thinks I'm in Spain.

My ears haven't stopped ringing from the end of season awards ceremony, my tux a wrinkled mess since I went straight from the televised stage to the Valencia airport. But I'm back under the same Osage orange trees I grew up climbing while my horse munched on the bumpy hedge apples. And when I head inside, the chatter from farm-hands is gonna be in English and not the liquid Italian of my pit crew.

None of it's making me feel better when I'm about to see her, and I know damn well all she's gonna do is yell at me, and all I want to do is kiss her and get back to how we used to be. I've only been gone a week this last time. But it was a week too long after the way she sent me off.

I touch my hat in Hargrove tradition as I cross under the homemade "Bless Your Boots" sign hanging above the barn entrance, instantly welcomed by a chorus of sniffs and snorts from the horse stalls I pass. It eases something in my chest that's been wrong since I last left home for the circuit.

Since I could kind of use it, I go ahead and stop by Gidget's stall, hooking my arms over the latched gate. "Hey, buddy." He stops fluffing his bed of straw, his ears already turned my direction before he lifts his head and stares me dead in the eye. A broad grin stretches across my face when he huffs and starts walking over, his pace extra slow and stompy, clearly irritated with how long I've been gone. At least he's willing to forgive me for it. "I know, bud. I missed you, too."

I reach out and stroke the side of his neck, wishing

everything was as simple as blazing-fast blue motorcycles and golden horses who only ask that you bring treats before you ride. But like everything else I wasn't supposed to fall in love with, Gidget isn't really mine. He's Lorelai Hargrove's, the future heiress to the Hargrove Horse Ranch.

No one except a rancher's daughter could afford an Akhal-Teke of their own. But no one really cares that I ride Gidget all the time, either. Lorelai is usually too busy training for our next race. She's Frank's original rodeo-racing experiment, and she's fast, feisty, and stubborn. Once the sponsors let her move up from Moto2 and into GP with me and Mason, we're all gonna be screwed.

"No, I didn't bring any apples," I tell Gidget when he starts nipping at my shirt and sniffing toward my jeans. "I'll bring you some later, though. Promise."

"Hey, Gidget. I didn't know your cowboy was back." James smiles on his way behind me, leading a silky chestnut mare out the other entrance to the barn. "Glad to have you home, Billy."

I return his smile on instinct, tipping my hat in the direction of his silver mustache. "Thank you, sir. Good to be back."

"Girls are working Bopper, if you're wondering. Though you might wanna take a bodyguard with you," he adds with a rumbly chuckle. "They're out for blood, those two."

I chew on my tongue, knowing better than to bite the hand that feeds my horse. James is married to Lynn, who owns Hargrove Ranch. And I've spent the last year very unsuccessfully trying to convince Lynn to sell me Gidget. She won't budge, though. Because I don't have the land to keep him on. "Yes, sir."

James is still happily making his way out of the barn and looking like he's whispering to the mare about me. I doubt it has anything to do with my record-breaking win, because whatever it is he says to the horse, he cracks himself up.

I make a face at Gidget, who's still sniffing for food in my shirt front pocket before I press a kiss to his nose. "Well, buddy, wish me luck."

Gidget snorts because we both know I'm fresh out of it. Any last bit of luck I had, I just used up in Valencia salvaging my career. But taking a risk has never stopped me before. Hell, the first time I rode a bull, I was convinced I was gonna die.

One second was all I got. It was enough, though. I woke up on a stretcher begging my father to let me have another go despite my mama's tears still running down her cheeks. That next time, I lasted for three seconds before Nova Bomb spun and sent me flying, cracking two ribs and fracturing my collarbone.

I'm always better on my second attempt—*always.* Still, Taryn says that's the worst thing about bull riders: we don't expect to stay on. It's just a game of how long we can last until the bull beats us, and they always beat us. But no bull bucking me ever hurt as much as when Taryn did it.

It's a long walk toward the training pen, set far enough in the pasture that the colts don't get distracted by the noise of the barn and the commands of the trainers. But with the wide-open sky and no trees between us, Taryn sees me coming every step of the way.

I know it, though she pretends she doesn't—she refuses to look my direction. But she's sitting a little stiffer in the saddle, the clenched muscles in her long legs stretching her jeans, and accusing me of the crimes she screamed at me from across her kitchen table.

I cast them out of my mind. I don't want to be mad, and seeing her sit a horse like that has always sent a freight train barreling straight into my chest. It's almost as good as when she wakes up slowly next to me, her silky spine long and bare as she reaches for the coffee I've already made and set on her nightstand. When I'm lucky enough to be home.

"Afternoon, ladies," I drawl to Taryn and Lorelai, taking the last few feet up to the fence of the training pen. My heart's beating straight out of my chest, a fresh brew of sweat tickling my hairline, and I can't stop thinking I should've shaved. But I couldn't get my truck here fast enough.

Lorelai tosses her wildly curly brown hair. "Taryn, I'm heading to the house. Call me later." She throws me a murderous look before leaving the way I came.

Taryn still hasn't said anything, except small corrections to the colt she's working. Round and round she goes, her hands light on the reins and the sun on her hat but not on her face. Pride laps at my heart from the dirt smeared on her shirt and mud caked up her jeans, everything about her more beautiful than I remember, and so damn *hard*. A woman who works, every day of her life. A woman who *rides*.

I can't keep the adoration out of my voice. "Hi, honey."

She gives two clicks to her colt and turns him the other way, bumping his trot to a canter and testing his different gears. It prods my smile even more, because she knows them all—on a horse, on a motorcycle. She's even taught me a few tricks that have helped me keep an edge on the racetrack, because she doesn't only train colts. She also races Superbike eight months a year, and then she comes home to Memphis and barrel races in rodeos.

I never stood a chance over whether I was gonna fall in love with her. It was always just a matter of how long she was gonna let me hang around.

"I brought you something." I pull my medal out of my back pocket and hang it on the fence post. If anyone knows what it takes to earn this, it's Taryn. And she should have this, more than me. "Hope you like it."

On her next pass, she reaches out and knocks my medal off the post, letting it fall in the dirt. "Fuck off, Billy."

Frustration simmers in my chest, and I keep watching her, remembering how sweet she was before I ruined it. When once upon a time, she loved me back.

At least she cussed at me.

She never yells at her horse when Aston Magic starts being moody, and she lives her life by the motto "Kill 'em with kindness." I've seen her bite her tongue so many times, she shouldn't have one left. But none of that restraint ever seems to apply to me, and the moment I get downgraded to the sweet-pea public persona, I'm calling in the big guns.

Two more circles, and her colt's hooves have firmly buried my medal beyond sight.

Stick to Plan A, I tell myself. *Act like it didn't happen, and maybe it didn't.*

"He's looking good," I muse mostly to myself. "He from Buddy Holly's line?"

"Goddamn it," she mutters, pulling her horse to a stop and dismounting. "You just can't leave me alone, can you?"

I risk a smile; it's been a hell of a long time since I've

had the pleasure of her riding my ass about something, and I missed it more than she'll ever know. "No, ma'am. Apparently not."

She feeds her colt a treat before leading him toward the gate. I hurry to open it for her and wait while she leads him through, my eyes stealing a quick peek at her curves in her jeans and her long blond braid swishing from under her cowgirl hat. Damn, I missed her.

I remember to latch the gate once I get my blood flowing back above my belt line, turning to find her already walking away. "Aw, come on, Taryn. I know you're mad, but—"

She whips around, and I'm struck dumb at the pain sparkling in her blue eyes like she's moments away from crying. And Taryn isn't a crier. "I'm not just mad, Billy. I'm done. And I told you that. So stop torturing me by showing up here and calling me all the time, and find a way to get it through that thick head of yours. It's *over*."

Her voice wobbles on the last word, and it's left me no kind of man. My head hangs, every endless prick of pain she's feeling cutting me a thousand times over because I caused it, and she's the only one who can make me feel better about it.

Her boots shift in the fresh dirt beneath her, but she's not walking away yet, and I risk a small step closer while she's giving me the chance. I'd bet my bike she doesn't want to be broken up any more than I do. But lines in the sand have a bad habit of shifting, and it isn't always easy to see where they land.

When Taryn shifts again, my gaze lifts to her hand fisting by her side, her other grasping desperately to the reins. One more step, and I breathe deep the call of leather and sunflowers, peach shampoo and lavender bug spray.

My eyes finally dare to meet hers, simmering sapphire and begging me for a thousand things I don't know how to give her when I can only think about the one thing I want. The one thing I shouldn't have done and all the soul-twisting reasons I'd have to do it again if faced with the same decision.

"I'm sorry," I croak out, her eyelashes fluttering closed as I run a knuckle down her cotton-soft cheek, only a breath away from kissing her. I've done it so many times, and it's not fair that the last time, I barely brushed my mouth against hers before I'd sprinted out the door. I can't let it end that way. "I'm so sorry, honey."

She shivers, a small noise that threatens to crack my heart right down the middle escaping her parted lips. Then she reaches up, barely covering my mouth with her fingertips, stopping me. "No, Billy," she whispers. "I can't do this anymore. You've already broken my heart once. I won't let you do it again."

Two tons of guilt and a sharp buck of fear lock my words in my throat, and she spins to her colt and leads him away. Back to the barn and her truck and her family's farmhouse ten miles down the road. And I know it's supposed to be hopeless, because she told me it was, but I can't help it.

Nothing in me knows how to hang it up and walk away. Not even when I've only got three months before the winter break melts into next season's testing, pulling us to the opposite ends of the earth along with it.

I *love* that woman, and I'm not giving up on day one.

"I missed you!" I call after her.

"Missed you, too." Hope sparks in my chest as she peeks over her shoulder with a look that takes everything funny out of her words but, for some reason, still gets me going. "Had you right in my sights, and the damn wind shifted."

Jesus. Maybe day two will go better.

Chapter 2

Taryn Ledell—Back Then

There wasn't anything special about Billy King. He was just another cowboy.

At first, anyway.

"Admit it," Holly was saying, nuzzling kisses onto my horse's nose while I relaxed in Aston Magic's saddle. "After winning this morning, you've completely run out of room on your trophy shelf and have taken to stuffing your barrel racing medals into your underwear drawer."

"Come on! Just a couple in my nightstand." I winked off the compliment, patting my mare's neck. We were smack-dab in the middle of traffic between the warm-up pen and outdoor arena, people coming and going from one rodeo event after the other. But I hadn't seen Holly since Fort Worth, and I'd really missed her.

It didn't help that the annual Starry Nights rodeo—where, in true Kentucky tradition, they scheduled everything backward—was the last rodeo I was able to attend before starting the long back-and-forth of the international Superbike circuit.

Holly shook her head, widening her eyes at Aston. "I know, girl. I hate her, too."

A genuine laugh from too many years of friendly competitive banter rang through my heart, Holly leaving another kiss on Aston's nose before she stepped toward me, stretching up as far as she could to hug me as I carefully leaned down from the saddle, breathing in her curly hair tickling my nose. "I love you. Been way too long."

"I know, and we all miss you so much. But we're so proud of you."

"Thanks," I mumbled, wondering if she'd still say that if she actually googled me.

It hadn't always been this bad. In the beginning, racing was a dream after the nightmare of leaving sports medicine. But under my new publicist's slimy hands, my racing image had become less about my placements and more about my photo shoots. Now, every fan in the sport knew my face, my bra size, and not a damn thing about where I stood, on or off the podium.

"Hon, I mean it," Holly said. "You may be famous over there, but to me, you'll always be the same lanky beauty queen who couldn't rope if her life depended on it."

Everything in my heart squeezed as I held Holly tighter, and I wished so much that what she said was true, that the people who knew me really were proud of me. At the very least, I was back home where the world smelled familiar: like fresh dirt, stiff hay, old ropes, and Old Spice.

Old Spice?

"Pardon me, ma'am."

I lifted my head, finding a jean-clad knee next to my face and a cowboy smiling down from a golden horse like he was waiting his turn for a hug, tall and lean in a black competition shirt, a Stetson to match, and his voice just as dark and deep as both. He was also paying no mind to the fact that traffic was now even more blocked with two horses standing side by side, and people were starting to grumble as they passed by. *Jackass.*

I looked at Holly questioningly, but her bunched-up

eyebrows said she had no clue who the guy was. He couldn't possibly have recognized me from my racing photos. No one in America gave a flip about Superbike, seemed like.

I looked back to the cowboy, telling myself to be brave. Assertive. Fearless. "Can I help you?" I asked, bleeding Southern politeness through my tone.

"Oh, Gidget wanted to come say hi. He saw your mare when you were barrel racing and thought she was real agile. Pay me no mind." He sat back in his saddle, his hands crossed on the saddle horn as he started whistling a tune that was far too relaxed to be believed while his stallion tried—and failed—to get the attention of Aston Magic, swishing his tail into hers and bumping her nose.

Okay, so definitely not a racing stalker or an immediate threat.

The knot in my stomach slowly unwound as Aston snickered, then nipped at his stallion. Served his horse right. I arched my eyebrow in the cowboy's direction, a sugary smile curling around my double entendre. "Doesn't seem like she's interested."

He kept grinning away under his black hat, the rim so wide it was almost as broad as his shoulders. "Well, Gidget's real nice, but he gets excited when he finds something he likes, and that can take some getting used to."

Holly let out a sharp laugh. "You sure we're still talking about your horse?"

I looked away to hide my snicker. *Damn, Holly.*

"Yes, ma'am, certainly." He sounded a little offended, but the slight touch of ire faded instantly from his voice. "And since I already interrupted y'all's conversation, if you don't mind me saying..."

"Go right on ahead, honey," Holly told him. "I can't wait to hear this."

I looked back to Holly, but this guy apparently had guts of steel. He was staring straight at me. "Congratulations on winning, miss. Even though I think that other girl ran it a little cleaner."

My eyes popped in disbelief, darting to Holly and back to him. "I'm sorry, *what*?"

He scratched at his jaw, rusty with dirty-blond stubble. "Tonya Ladle, I think her name was? You're real fast and all, and your quarter horse sure seems to know what she's doing. But I just thought that other girl's turns were tighter."

Holly's face flushed and deepened in color, and I sat up straighter in my saddle, my feigned indifference churning into fast-growing irritation. "*I'm* Taryn Ledell. Not Tonya Ladle. *Leh-dell.*"

His hand shot out toward me across the space between our horses, his grin bigger than ever. "And I'm Billy King. Nice to meet you."

"Oh *wow.*" Holly burst out in laughter. "Taryn, honey, since you're fine"—she tried to contain her chuckle but couldn't, making eyes at the cowboy and then at me—"I'll, uh, head on out. It was good seeing you."

She couldn't be serious. "Holly, really—"

"Really." She winked, already backing up into the crowd and disappearing within the camouflage of Wrangler jeans and pressed shirts, waving over her shoulder. "Congratulations again!"

I looked at the reason my friend just bailed on me, and Mr. Wearing Too Much Old Spice was still grinning from his saddle and reaching toward me over the lariat he had strapped to it. Heat flooded a bunch of parts of me that shouldn't have been affected by just a damn smile, and I mentally refused to shake his hand.

Why in the hell were the most annoying cowboys always the cutest? Especially with lopsided smiles and teeth that were pearly white but just a little bit crooked because he wasn't made to suffer the corrective braces I was.

My gaze drifted as far from his easy country grin as I could stand, landing on his horse's golden mane. There was hardly anything there. And his muscles were all uphill and forward built. Not the level or even downward build of a quarter horse.

But a lariat was strapped to his saddle horn…

A whole lot of something wasn't right.

"Where'd you get this horse?" I asked, inspecting his stallion more closely while my mind raced to put the pieces together.

His arm pulled back. "Huh?"

Aston Magic was beautiful, but this guy's horse had no equal at the rodeo. And if I wasn't mistaken, not only was it the precious gold of an Akhal-Teke, but with the guy's telltale Memphis twang, it should have a brand in the shape of—

"Oh my God!" A couple walking by jumped and stared at me, but I couldn't do more than gawk in utter astonishment. It was right there, and I couldn't believe what I was seeing. "This is a Hargrove horse!"

A funny smile crept across Billy's lips. Like he was impressed and still not the slightest bit guilty. "You from Memphis? What a small, funny world it is."

"No, it's not," I snapped, way past seeing him as a

potential distraction and closer to imagining what he looked like in handcuffs. The police kind. "And he's for dressage, not for roping. Where'd you get him?"

Billy's nose scrunched up like he couldn't believe I was accusing him of doing anything wrong. Wonder how long that had been working for him? "I borrowed him."

My eyes nearly flew out of my skull. "You *borrowed* him?"

There was no way Lynn Hargrove knew about this. I didn't exactly know her, but I knew about her, and she didn't just let farmhands take her prize stallions to rodeos in Kentucky because they wanted to have some fun on the weekends. He'd probably stolen a fifty-thousand-dollar horse.

"Yes, ma'am, I borrowed him," he drawled, starting to sound a little indignant about the accusation. "And it's been real nice talking to you, but Gidget and I gotta—"

"Oh, *hell* no. You're not going anywhere. Give me that horse." I went for his reins, but he'd already sidled them out of my reach, allowing a new flow of traffic to fill up between us.

"Now, hold on just a minute—"

"Come back here!"

More people turned to stare, and I would've too if our situations were reversed. But they didn't realize the magnitude of what he had done. Especially when he was laughing at me about it. "Wish I could, honey, but I gotta go rope. I'd love if you'd come watch me, though. And it was nice meeting you."

With one touch of his finger to his hat, he was gone, trotting his "borrowed" horse toward the arena, his lasso ropes thwacking against his jeans with the motion.

No sight had ever pissed me off more.

I gave two clicks to Aston Magic, urging her to go after them. But we never caught up.

Apparently, that was the moment when the whole freaking world needed to talk to me, and there were too many people crowding and blocking us, stopping me to say congratulations, welcome back, and asking where I was riding next.

By the time I got to the outdoor arena, I couldn't find him. All I could hear was his damn name blaring through the speakers and echoing on the wind.

"All right, folks," the announcer boomed. "Next up for calf roping, we have Billy King. If that last name sounds familiar to you, it's 'cause his baby brother, Mason, took first in the bull riding showdown this morning. Them King boys are ones to watch, I tell you. Let's hear it for Billy!"

The crowd cheered like they knew him, and despite my temper sparking, I couldn't help sitting up a little higher in my saddle. Peering through teased high hair and black and tan Stetsons, I finally saw him: sitting atop that golden horse with his heels sunk in his stirrups, the sun shining off his belt buckle, and a fearless grin beaming from behind the rope he had clenched in his teeth.

I narrowed my eyes. He probably wasn't any good. And the second he was done, I was reporting him. To... somebody.

God, what was it about this guy that had pushed all my freaking buttons?

At the harsh sound of the buzzer, a calf was loose and running. But Billy's horse bolted faster and he was already there, his outstretched arm casting a lasso that found its target with ease, his stallion instantly pulling to a stop and backing up while Billy swung off his saddle.

Fine, so maybe he trained the horse for roping, too.

Faster than a wink, Billy ran up to the calf and grabbed it and flipped it—and those calves are freaking *heavy*. But it was already done, Billy whipping the rope from his mouth and twisting it around the calf's ankles, then leaping up from the ground with his hands in the air.

Damn...

The fans shot to their feet, their cheers a blast of sound that reminded me again of the Superbike circuit. I took a steadying breath and promised myself I wasn't going to worry about it. Not the coming press shoots, the pressure, or the insinuations about my greasy-handed teammate, Colton.

None of it.

"And that's how it's done, folks!" the announcer hollered. "That man is slicker than snot on a doorknob. Whoo!"

Billy flipped his hat into the air, and I slowly clapped along with everyone else. Under protest. And maybe I whistled a little, too. But only because he was...he was really something.

I should've known better than to draw attention to myself. The jackass saw me, smiling even wider as he pointed in my direction, then did one final wave, his hands blinking at the crowd instead of hitching at the wrist like he was Lane Frost reincarnate before he collected his hat and his horse.

The crowd got ready for the next calf roper, and I turned away from the arena, swearing to myself ten times over that temptation could fuck right off. I had a job, and it wasn't at rodeos anymore. After tomorrow, I'd be leaving for Australia. For the Phillip Island Grand Prix Circuit and testing ahead of our first race of the season. I had things to focus on, and I'd never see this cowboy again.

Which is exactly why I never should've walked Aston over to the arena exit, where I knew Billy would be waiting. Right then, he was still no one. Just another stranger, a name I'd be able to forget if I tried. And I needed to get Aston brushed and back in her trailer.

But temptation also knows there's a devilish part of me I can't deny—the part that did it right and got her degree, then flipped it all off to race motorcycles for a living—and she *loves* breaking the rules.

Billy started scrambling the second he saw me coming, dusting off his shirt and tucking in the back, then showing his teeth to his horse like he was asking if something was stuck in them. His horse pulled back his lips and did the same, and I couldn't help smirking a bit, they were so cute. It was also a relief: they clearly knew each other, borrowed or not.

Maybe reporting him wasn't necessary. Lynn Hargrove must have known he was here with her horse. No one from Memphis would ever risk crossing her.

"Don't embarrass me now," Billy was whispering to Gidget when Aston and I walked up to the arena exit, my temper and tongue firmly in check. When he turned toward me, he took a long time tilting his eyes up to mine, like I was miles above him. But he skipped over the parts where other men usually lingered. "Well, hi there," he drawled. His horse snorted and nosed him in the back, making Billy stumble, and it took all my experience training colts not to laugh and encourage the stallion's bad behavior. "Damn it, Gidget," Billy muttered before looking at me and resuming his smile. "Thanks for bringing me all that good luck."

Okay, so he could keep his cool. Didn't mean he was special. He was probably like the rest of the calf ropers—cocky and twitchy and only interested in listening to a woman for as long as it took to get her zipper down. "Didn't seem like you needed much. Definitely not your first rodeo."

Billy grinned, shaking his head. "No, ma'am. It's my second." He was doing just fine...until Gidget bit the back of his shirt and pulled it out from where it'd been tucked in, jerking it around before Billy got free. "Really?" he grumbled, but he never raised a hand to his stallion. He just started tucking his shirt back in. "I'm trying to talk to this lady. You can wait." He turned to me, calm as anything. "Sorry. He may look like a horse, but he's really a heifer when he's hungry."

Aston shifted beneath me like she wasn't impressed, though I was having a harder time than ever keeping a straight face. "It's all right."

But it apparently wasn't, because Gidget's nose was right back in Billy's face, blowing raspberries. I couldn't help it anymore, clasping my hand over my mouth.

Billy took a deep breath, holding up a single finger. "If you'll excuse us."

I nodded, pulling my hand away and chewing the hell out of the inside of my cheek to keep from laughing. Which was so *weird*: cocky guys in my experience were typically grabby and pushy but hardly ever funny. At least, not as funny as they thought they were. "By all means."

He took Gidget's lead and walked them a few feet away.

He kept his head close to his horse's, talking and gesturing and looking like he was cutting a deal to get him to behave. It ended with Billy pulling a treat from his back pocket and pressing a kiss to Gidget's nose while he ate it. *Aww.*

Aston huffed and shifted again as Billy led Gidget toward us, my quarter horse clearly over the advances of the Akhal-Teke and ready to be pampered after working her ass off in the arena. And as much as Billy was…intriguing, to say the least, Aston Magic came first.

"Sorry about that." Billy made a supposed-to-be-stern face at his horse. "Gonna have a long talk about our manners when we get home."

Oh, damn it, that was cute.

"It's fine." I kept my spine straight and chin high, voice kind but firm. "But I can't stay, so you may as well get to telling me what your deal is."

"Ma'am?"

I sighed—so much for sugarcoating it. I leaned down from the saddle, closer to where he was standing next to his horse. There were still plenty of people around, and I didn't want to embarrass him any more than I was about to. "Drop the Mr. Innocent act, and be straight with me. What is your goal here? Because I'm telling you right now, I'm not sleeping with you. No matter what war you're about to head off to."

Not entirely true. I hadn't decided yet whether to sleep with him. He was hot and seemed nice, and it'd been a long time since I'd had a man in my bed. And heading off to the circuit meant my chances were narrowing quickly.

Billy ducked his head so I could only see his hat as he looked away and shifted his feet. When he looked up, there was some pink in his cheeks, his hand fidgeting with his reins, and his thumb stroking the leather like a lover's lips. "Don't have an act or a goal. I was just wondering if you'd let me hang around you a bit, see if I can get you to like me some."

I took another look at everything about his size, his build, the way he held a rope, and the adrenaline still clearly drugging his veins and shining in his blue eyes. "Are you a bull rider?"

A new kind of smile tugged at the edge of his lips—the guilty kind. "Maybe?"

Damn it.

Of course, there had to be a catch. I had sworn off his kind long ago, knowing too well the faces of bull riders' wives, their girlfriends. The pain and worry the women go through. Because I used to *be* one of them.

Kind of hard not to date bull riders when you're working the medic tents at rodeos. They're the only men you meet, because they're the ones always getting hurt. I should've known better, because before I knew it, I was setting bones for men I loved. Watching them get bucked and broken and praying they would wake up. In the ambulance, in the hospital. At *all.*

Bonnie Landry had been the last straw for me and that way of life. She'd *loved* Beau Blackwell and supported his bull riding career every step of the way. But Beau wasn't as lucky as Eric, who broke his arm in two places. He wasn't as lucky as Austin, with his busted ribs and concussion. He wasn't even as lucky as Cash, who'd never walk again.

Beau Blackwell got bucked at twenty-six years old, two days before his wedding, snapped his neck and died, and Bonnie Landry wore a black dress that Sunday instead of a white one.

I stopped working rodeos after that. I broke up with Levi after that. And I promised myself that I would never forget how it felt to be so helpless over your future. Because those bull rider wives, those poor girlfriends, they watch their men volunteer for their deaths. And all so they could have eight seconds of glory when they could've had a lifetime with her.

I wasn't doing it. I'm worth more than eight seconds.

What a waste.

"Bye, Billy. Congratulations on your win." I gave two clicks to Aston Magic and turned her away, struggling to swallow my disappointment as I headed back the way I came—to the pens and my family's travel trailer and my laptop with the turn sequence for Phillip Island I was supposed to be learning.

I'd be able to forget him. If I tried.

Maybe tried *hard*.

"Hey, Taryn, hold on!"

I never should've looked back.

Billy was already up in his saddle and trotting Gidget toward me, catching up. "I don't ride bulls no more. I swear it."

I scoffed, still walking Aston toward the pens. I didn't even care to act gracious or charming or any of that fake stuff anymore. All I could think about was the scent of his cologne mixing with my fabric softener. I hadn't been laid in *months*. "Bullshit. Bull riders don't stop until they're too old or too broken to keep going." I gave him a quick once-over. "You're neither of those things."

"Well, that's kind of you to say," he said. "And I'll grant you, that's usually true. But in my case, I got a new job, and I can't do both. I'm not allowed."

I stopped Aston and looked over, my curiosity regrettably piqued. "You an elementary school teacher or something?"

He laughed, the sound pure and crystalline. No man should be allowed to laugh like that. Especially when he could throw calves like they were feather pillows. "No, ma'am. I'm a motorcycle racer."

Oh shit.

I didn't know what that meant. He wasn't on the Superbike circuit with me, but the fact that he even *mentioned* a motorcycle…

The devil was whispering all my favorite words.

I urged Aston on, resolute to keep my cool. Just because he was also from Memphis, roped like a god, was sweet to his horse, and apparently rode a motorcycle for a living didn't mean meeting him was destiny. Chances were I'd never see him again. "That right?"

"Yes, ma'am. Moto Grand Prix."

Really? *Damn*—those bikes were *fast.*

He guided his horse around a group of people stopped in the middle of the aisle. When he came up beside me, he tipped his hat a little farther back so his face wasn't as shadowed. *God,* he was cute, with one of those iron-sharp jaws that always felt really, really good in your hands.

"It's kinda like Formula 1," he said, "but with motorcycles instead of cars. And my contract with Yaalon, well, it says I can't ride bulls anymore. My brother Mason can, but he's with Blue Gator on a satellite team."

My brow furrowed. As a Superbike racer, I knew plenty about Moto Grand Prix. But the last thing he said didn't seem right to me. My contract with Munich Motor Works had all sorts of provisions, but MMW never said anything about me barrel racing when I was home. "How come?"

"How come Mason can ride bulls and I can't?"

"Yeah."

He shrugged, no stress in the movement or twitchiness to be found. "Don't know. Probably because he's better at it than I was."

Another thing that didn't sound right. Bull riders were famous for their egos. "You ever miss it?" I tested.

"Hmm, sometimes, I guess. It's a hell of a rush. But I get that from racing now, so I don't mind giving it up." He sounded totally sincere as he smiled at me and said, "Besides, I got too much to lose."

I cocked an eyebrow at him. "In all my life, I've never heard a bull rider say that."

"Well, I told you: I'm not a bull rider no more." He winked at me, and Lord, if he was telling the truth? I was in so much trouble. "And hey, since I'm not, you wanna be my date to the Mutton Bustin' tonight?"

I burst into laughter, no idea why my heart was jumping to agree and even my overly critical brain was struggling to refuse. "No?"

"Why not?" He'd still never lost his grin, drifting his horse closer until his leg bumped mine, sending a *zing* through my veins that hit me straight between my thighs. "It'll be fun, cheering on all those little kids climbing up there to ride their first sheep. And I hear after, they're gonna have a dance for the big kids. And I'm a great dancer."

"Oh, are you now?"

"Yes, ma'am."

I couldn't make myself stop smiling as I walked Aston up to her designated pen, then got down from the saddle, tying her lead and endlessly debating.

I had hard and fast rules about dating bull riders. But Billy said he wasn't a bull rider anymore. Plus, it was so sweet that instead of asking to take me out to a bar, he wanted to watch toddlers try to ride sheep. Where the families were.

I turned around, finding him down from his saddle and standing a comfortable distance back from me, absently petting the underside of his horse's jaw. "I promise to get you home at a decent time. And I won't try nothing. I just...want to dance with you. If that's okay."

His drawl was slaying all my defenses, husky and deep and rumbling beneath black cotton fabric doing its absolute *very* best to stretch across the broad expanse of his upper muscles. His arms were bigger than I'd realized, too. I bet with one solid flex of his biceps, the seams would be forced to rip apart.

How awful for that poor, innocent shirt.

Get a grip, Taryn.

"I don't...know you," I said, because I honestly couldn't think of anything else to say.

The dancing part didn't sound too bad, and it had been forever since I'd been on a real date with a guy and not just hooked up. Even longer since I'd been on a date with a *nice* guy. I wasn't sure they existed anymore, truthfully. And I was tired of being disappointed when they all turned out to be after the same thing, which *definitely* wasn't my brain. It wasn't even my damn bike.

But Billy...

He was so disarmingly kind but still confident enough to ask for what he wanted—and in that Stetson blacker than any lingerie I'd ever dared to buy.

He nodded to himself, taking a small step closer and

slipping his hat off his head. My eyes widened a bit at the shock of sunny blond hair, seeming to match so much better with the gentleness in his baby-blue eyes. "Well, I'm trying to fix that, Taryn. If you'll let me."

I don't know why I said what I did. I don't know what was wrong with me.

I knew better, and I never should've looked back.

Never.

"Pick me up at seven."

Acknowledgments

It took what felt like a million and one days to write this book and there are an equal number of people who helped me along the way, even if they didn't realize it at the time (I'm looking at you, purveyors of iced, blended coffee beverages with extra whipped cream). I thanked most of the usual suspects in the dedication, and I'm throwing out mass gratitude to the rest of you now. But in particular...

Writer and friend Megan Coakley, for being brutally open and honest about the never-ending battles of a long time recovered addict.

Writer and friend Steve Ulfelder, for sharing the challenges of making a new romantic relationship co-exist with the unique, intense bond between long time sponsors and sponsees.

My younger sister, Gina, who has dedicated much of her career to learning firsthand about the cultural and practical realities of being Native in this country, and who was my go-to resource when I didn't even know what to ask. If I didn't get it right, it's her fault. (Just kidding, sis. I quit blaming you for my goofs once you got taller than me.)

To our guide Duffy in Monument Valley, who responded to my probably insensitive questions by opening up about his personal beliefs, practices, and experiences along with invaluable information about the land, the lifestyle, and the Diné in general.

To the Lunak family, who served as a very loose model for Carmelita and her parents. And our mutual aunt

Lorraine, who hosts all those Christmas parties where I listen to Dutch tell stories about bartering for a horse with Chris Hemsworth and cussing Harrison Ford's helicopter for spooking his herd. Yes, I have been taking notes.

My mother's cousin Carmelita. I have always loved your name. I hope you're proud of the person I gave it to.

#NativeTwitter. Wow, have you schooled me. And in particular @DeadDogLake, whose posts saved me from at least one really embarrassing misstep.

To Hank, my number one rope horse, who did not actually speed up the writing process *at all* when he elevated his game last summer and dragged me along for the ride, giving me the chance to live a few of my own moth-balled rodeo dreams. But we'll give him credit for inspiration, okay?

And most of all David, Sharnai, Andrea, Amanda, Gigi, Paula, Maureen, Mary Jo, Kathleen, Suzanne, Sarah, Courtney, Leah, Stephanie, Rebecca, Dr. Harrer, Dr. Kaae, and all the awesome people in radiology, lab, and pharmacy—some of you have been there for me at the best and worst of times from clear back before my first book was published, and without you I literally wouldn't be where I am today.

Also, please note: this story and these characters represent the experiences and opinions of these specific individuals, not any one tribe. I strived to be as accurate as possible concerning real life facts and events. If I failed, please know it wasn't for lack of effort.

About the Author

Kari Lynn Dell is a ranch-raised Montana cowgirl who attended her first rodeo at two weeks old and has existed in a state of horse-induced poverty ever since. She lives on the Blackfeet Reservation in her parents' bunkhouse along with her husband, her son, and Max the Cowdog. There's a tepee on her lawn, Glacier National Park on her doorstep, and Canada within spitting distance. Visit her at karilynndell.com.

FEARLESS

These highly competitive racers are torn between the glitz of the international stage and the ranches they call home.

Billy King may be smiling under his black Stetson, but the plain truth is this cowboy-turned-racer is hurting. The moment he's free from the press circuit, Billy bolts home—resolved to heal, and ready to win Taryn's heart a second time. Hopefully, before the love of his life is gone for good.

Taryn Ledell never wanted to fall for sweet blue eyes and a deep southern drawl. As a World Superbike racer, she had plans, and none of them involved playing second fiddle to any man. But now he's back, and she's forced to make some hard choices. But broken bones and broken hearts don't heal overnight, and the cost of forgiveness can be sky high: unless Billy can prove that his heart never left the ranch...or her.

"Vivid and fearless."
—Kari Lynn Dell

A COWBOY STATE OF MIND

The good folks of Creedence, Colorado get behind Creedence Horse Rescue in a brilliant new series from Jennie Marts

Scarred and battered loner Zane Taylor has a gift with animals, particularly horses, but he's at a total loss when it comes to knowing how to handle women. Bryn Callahan has a heart for strays, but she is through trying to save damaged men. But when a chance encounter with a horse headed for slaughter brings Zane and Bryn together, they find themselves given a chance to save not just the horse, but maybe each other...

"Full of humor, heart, and hope...deliciously steamy."
—Joanne Kennedy, award-winning author, for *Wish Upon a Cowboy*

Also by Kari Lynn Dell

Texas Rodeo

Reckless in Texas
Tangled in Texas
Tougher in Texas
Fearless in Texas
Mistletoe in Texas
Relentless in Texas

Last Chance Rodeo